Perfect Fit

Also by Brenda Jackson

Perfect Timing

Perfect Fit

BRENDA JACKSON

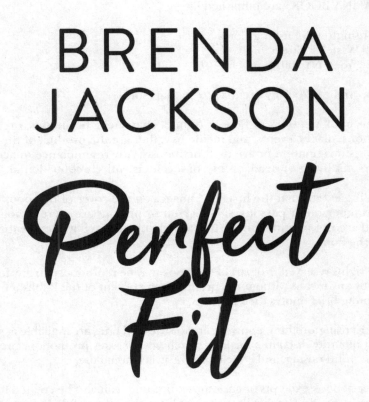

Perfect Fit

DAFINA

www.kensingtonbooks.com

DAFINA BOOKS are published by

Kensington Publishing Corp.
119 West 40th Street
New York, NY 10018

All Kensington titles, imprints, and distributed lines are available at special quantity discounts for bulk purchases for sales promotion, premiums, fund-raising, and educational or institutional use.

Special book excerpts or customized printings can also be created to fit specific needs. For details, write or phone the office of the Kensington Sales Manager: Kensington Publishing Corp., 119 West 40th Street, New York, NY 10018. Attn. Sales Department. Phone: 1-800-221-2647.

The Dafina logo is a trademark of Kensington Publishing Corp.

First Dafina Hardcover Edition: May 2003

First Trade Paperback Edition: April 2004

ISBN: 978-1-4967- 3792-2

ISBN: 978-0-7582-6773-3 (e-book)

10 9 8 7 6 5 4 3 2

Printed in the United States of America

PART ONE

It is better to trust the Lord than to put confidence in men.

—Psalms 118:8

CHAPTER ONE

Gabe
Detroit, Michigan

Gabriel Blackwell had a low tolerance level for women who constantly tripped on excess emotional baggage, and the one sitting across from him had bags packed so heavy he wondered how she was lugging them around.

After listening to her moan, weep and groan for the past hour, he'd just about had it. There were only so many burdens a mortal man could take from a woman who refused to see the light of day because her lover of the past two years had made one mistake too many.

He lifted the wineglass to his lips and took a sip as he continued to listen to her whine. Since this was their first date, she was evidently clueless that this was not the way to go about establishing a new relationship with someone. When he'd picked her up for dinner, he'd been truly impressed since she definitely was a looker who had everything in all the right places. For once he had thought his mother, who'd harassed him into going out on this blind date, had finally done something right. It didn't take long for him to change his mind and decide that instead, she'd definitely done something wrong.

En route to the restaurant when a certain song by Luther Van-
dross began playing on the car's radio, the woman had begun
crying her eyes out over what she'd tearfully described to him
as "painful memories." Evidently the pain only got worse, because she'd been sobbing ever since. Several times he had offered to take her back home, but she'd refused, saying that at
some point she had to get on with her life. And each time he'd
come close to telling her that she was exhibiting a piss-poor job
of doing so.

He knew of very few men who needed or wanted the stress of
getting involved with someone who couldn't regain control of
her emotions and let go. He'd found out the hard way three
years ago that some women actually enjoyed bemoaning a lost
cause. He had fancied himself in love with such a woman. After
they had dated exclusively for ten months, she broke things off
between them the moment her ex-lover returned to town and
decided he wanted her back. The scars from that encounter
had been slow to heal.

"I guess I'm not making a good impression tonight with it
being our first date and all, but I can't help it," the woman said,
breaking into Gabe's thoughts as she sniffed into the handkerchief he'd given to her earlier.

When he didn't say anything, she continued by saying, "I
can't believe I'm still upset over the fact that he left me. He was
nothing but a total jerk anyway." A few minutes later she added,
"But still, after what we used to mean to each other, you'd think
he would have the decency to at least return my phone calls."

Gabe lifted a brow, wondering if she really thought a jerk
would actually do something decent. Then, belatedly, what
she'd said caught his attention. "You've tried calling him?" he
asked, more in astonishment than interest. She had spent the
past hour telling him how she'd discovered the guy had
hocked her jewelry to pay his gambling debts, as well as the
fact that he'd been carrying on an illicit affair with a woman in

the office where he worked. As far as Gabe was concerned, the man had two strikes against him. She was definitely better off without him and had said so herself several times during the course of the evening. Yet in the same breath, she'd just admitted that she'd tried contacting him. Gabe determined she was a glutton for punishment and was taking obsessive love to an all-new high . . . or in his opinion, a very disgusting low.

"Yes, I've been trying to reach him for the past two days, ever since I found out about my condition," she finally answered as fresh tears appeared in her eyes.

Gabe inhaled sharply, almost choking on the wine he'd just sipped. He cleared his throat and shifted uneasily in his chair, then inquired as calmly as he could, "Your condition?"

Red, swollen, tear-soaked eyes met his gaze. She again put his handkerchief to use as she sobbingly replied, "I'm pregnant."

The next day

Joella Blackwell looked at her son and said calmly, "The situation you described doesn't sound like a major crisis to me, Gabriel."

Gabe shook his head in disbelief, clearly stunned. After a brief moment of recovery, he was almost certain he had misunderstood his mother's response, so he decided to tell her again.

"I said the woman who you talked me into taking out last night announced over dinner that she's pregnant."

And just in case his mother still didn't get it, he clarified by saying, "She's going to have a baby, and before you give me an all-accusing stare, just remember that last night was our first date and under the circumstances it was definitely our last."

Joella Blackwell raised a dark brow as she continued the task of setting the table for dinner. Christopher Chandler, Gabe's best friend and business partner, whom she considered her surrogate son, and his wife and their ten-month-old son would be coming, and she looked forward to seeing them. She was pleased that at least one of her *sons* had finally put aside his whoring ways to marry and start a family.

"I know what being pregnant means, Gabriel. All I'm saying is that at least she was honest and up front with you. So the way I see it, to decide you won't be seeing her again is acting rather hasty. I would think you could put the issue of her pregnancy behind you and move on."

Gabe leaned in the doorway that separated the kitchen from the dining room, wondering if his mother actually thought such a thing was possible. But then, he knew she really did. Everyone who knew Joella Blackwell was well aware that she had a soft, loving and forgiving heart. She was a good Christian woman who saw good in everyone and believed a positive spin could be derived from any negative situation. In this case, she was dead wrong. "You're expecting too much if you assume I'll consider asking her out again," he finally said.

Joella Blackwell shrugged. "I see no reason why you shouldn't. Being pregnant is not the end of the world. Men date pregnant women all the time."

Gabe frowned. "Yeah, and usually when they do it's because they have a vested interest, like being the father of that child. Don't you see the problems that can develop if I become involved with Keri Morton?"

"No, I don't see the problems since she's made you aware of her condition. It's not as if she's trying to pass the child off as yours. I think you're being too judgmental. Your name may be Gabriel, but you're far from being an angel yourself."

Gabe shook his head. "I happen to like children, no matter whose they are, but there's a lot more to it than the pregnancy issue. She's still hung up on her baby's father."

"She actually told you that?"

"She didn't have to. She talked about him enough over dinner for me to tell, and I refuse to get involved again with a woman carrying around excess emotional baggage. And trust me, Keri Morton is up to her ying-ying in it. I'm not interested in dating a woman with issues."

Joella Blackwell didn't say anything for the longest moment. She remembered how a few years back Gabe had fallen in love; a woman he had practically offered everything—his time, his money and most important, his heart. The day before he was going to ask her to marry him, she broke off things between them to get back together with her old boyfriend and had even had the gall to send Gabe an invitation to their wedding. Since that fateful time, he had refused to date women who he thought had personal problems they couldn't let go of. What she'd tried to get him to see was that everyone had some sort of issues. No one lived a completely carefree life.

"There's no such thing as a perfect woman, Gabriel."

Gabe met his mother's gaze. "I'm not looking for one, but any relationship I get seriously involved in again has to be un-complicated and straightforward."

Joella shook her head. "I hate to disappoint you, but there's nothing uncomplicated or straightforward about any woman. God made us unique and he gave us emotions and I do thank him for that Otherwise, this world would have ended long ago if it was left up to a man. Your gender on occasion has shown to be rather heartless. And heaven forbid if anything has to be done. Men take forever to do nothing. Women are known not to beat around the bush. And we are a nurturing breed. We're sensitive, understanding, and luckily for the male, we're also compassionate. That's the reason we can't let go of things as easily as a man. Then there are some of us who can't seem to let go at all. They're the ones in need of more personal growth and healing, along with tender, loving care. But in due time they'll learn there is life after a love that's ended."

Gabe heard everything his mother said, but still he felt women like Keri were the ones to watch out for and avoid. As far as he was concerned, the best way to handle those types of women was to put concrete and solid rules into place. And his number one rule was to not become involved with a woman who obviously sweated the small stuff and who refused to let go and move on.

"Is it wrong for me to want a woman who'll complement me in every way?" he finally asked. "A woman who I'll consider as my soul mate, my perfect fit? Until that time comes, I have no intention of getting seriously involved with anyone with issues."

"And what if you fall in love with her first?"

Gabe frowned. "Trust me, that won't happen. I may not be an angel, but neither am I a fool. I've learned from past mistakes." He then turned and walked away.

Joella watched her son leave and shook her head sadly. She wondered when it would occur to him that in addition to not being an angel or a fool, he lived in a glass house and shouldn't throw stones because it was quite obvious that *he* had issues of his own.

Late that evening Gabe entered his apartment, went straight to the kitchen, grabbed a beer out of the refrigerator and took a swig. His mother had been too busy lavishing her attention on her surrogate grandchild to remember to harass him any more that afternoon. But he wasn't crazy enough to think she was through with him. With Christopher married that meant Gabe was now the recipient of all of her attention. As soon as she could, she would try playing matchmaker again.

Walking down the hall to his bedroom, he smiled as his thoughts fell on his partner and best friend. Christopher had begun working for Gabe's father's construction company at eighteen. Omar Blackwell had taken the young, hard-working loner under his wings and become not only Christopher's boss, but a mentor and father figure. The Blackwells had offered Christopher things he'd never had before, family ties, trust, respect and complete love.

Gabe knew his parents considered Christopher their *other* son, and since the two boys were the same age, they had talked Christopher into furthering his education right along with Gabe. They both had graduated with MBAs at the top of their class. Christopher had a degree in Industrial Design, and Gabe had earned a degree in Structural Engineering. And when Omar Blackwell retired six years ago, signing ownership of the company over to Gabe and Christopher, they had taken it in a whole new direction, one that was now world known. The Regency Corporation had built numerous upscale shopping malls, industrial office parks and department stores all over the United States in the past five years. Their biggest contract to date was the Landmark Project, which involved building a multimillion-dollar ski resort near Anchorage, Alaska. Plans were to start on it by the first of the year.

The fact that a deal of that magnitude had been awarded to a company owned by two African-American men had made headlines. He and Christopher had been featured in several newspapers and magazines, and had even made the covers of *Black Enterprise* and *Ebony*, as well as being the recent recipients of *Black Enterprise*'s prestigious Minority Businessmen of the Year Award a few months ago. At the age of thirty-two, they were the youngest individuals to receive such recognition.

As Gabe began stripping off his clothes, he thought about his mother's fixation with marrying him off. It was as if she was on some sort of mission. Unfortunately, it was one he was having no part of. He had tried placating her by dating a few of the single women from her church, but since it seemed the majority of them had issues that he refused to deal with, he continued to make his work the top priority in his life.

Now that Christopher was a family man, their roles in the

company had switched. Gabe did the majority of the traveling these days as well as working most of the international deals. Christopher was the one who stayed in the office and ran things on the home front, and the few times he did travel, he took his wife, Maxi, and the baby with him.

Gabe sighed deeply. The new demands of the job had taken over his life. He didn't have time to develop any sort of serious relationship with a woman other than a brief fling, which was just fine and dandy with him. Anything else took time and energy he couldn't spare.

Stepping into the shower, he couldn't help but appreciate his on-going affair with Debbie Wells. Like him, she was a successful professional who preferred a sex-only relationship; no romance, no commitment—just raw physical contact and sexual release, which was an invigorating way to work off stress.

Over the past three years, after his disaster with Lindsey Jefferson, he'd found that a nice unencumbered, noncommitted sort of relationship with a woman was what he needed. It definitely had its advantages. There wasn't a chance you would fall in love, and neither party had expectations of anything turning serious. There was no room for jealousy or possessiveness or broken hearts. And best of all, you could walk away at any time without looking back. Debbie was great in bed, and like him, she played by the rules. He couldn't ask for more, nor did he want to. He liked things just the way they were.

He heard the doorbell the moment he'd stepped out of the shower and had begun drying off. Tucking the towel around his waist, he walked barefoot to the door. Glancing through the peephole, he smiled as he opened the door. It seemed his thoughts of Debbie had conjured her up on his doorstep.

She entered his home after placing a chaste brush of her lips across his cheek. He closed the door behind her. "How was your trip?" he asked, knowing she had been out of town on business for the past week.

"Atlanta was fun as usual," she replied, tracing a polished fingertip along his earlobe. "I know this visit is rather unexpected, but I hope you're in a position to help me out with something."

Her voice was low and seductive, and he liked that. "Something like what?" he prompted, although he had a fairly good idea. He watched her eyes grow dark and sensuous which caused a deep stirring in his body.

She leaned forward, and after reaching around him to release the towel covering his body, she moved into a position that placed a silken-clad thigh between his nude legs. It was obvious she felt his erection when her lips tilted into a smile. Her mouth was mere inches from touching his. He let his gaze linger on that mouth, thinking how well practiced it was in pleasing him.

She then grinned wryly. "I need to be screwed senseless tonight, Gabe."

He couldn't help the smile that tugged at his lips. The one thing he liked most about Debbie was her honesty, her candidness and more importantly, her hearty sexual appetite. He felt a hard throbbing that started low and deep in his groin. "That makes two of us. I need to be screwed senseless tonight myself."

Her smile widened. "Oh, yeah?"

"Hell, yeah." He lowered his head and claimed her mouth, nibbling, sucking and tasting, creating the level of intimacy they both needed and wanted. As always, her enthusiasm and hunger thrilled him and took his sexual cravings to a whole new level.

Picking her up into his arms and taking her into his bedroom, he knew that before the night was over, they would get what they both wanted.

The sun was setting low in the sky when Gabe and Christopher completed their final inspection of the job site, a small yet upscale shopping mall on the outskirts of Detroit. Everything was on target with plans for the opening by the first of October. After a brief discussion with their building foreman, they removed their hard hats and safety glasses and walked back toward their cars.

"Dinner's at six if you want to drop by," Christopher invited before opening the door to his vehicle.

Gabe shook his head. Even after a full year, it was hard seeing his best friend as a happily married family man when Christopher had always sworn to never marry. He had been the ultimate bachelor, a ladies' man, and one who strongly believed in sex-only relationships. But Maxi, a woman from Christopher's past, had reentered his life and changed all of that, which proved there were such things as miracles. Hell, Chris had even traded his Mercedes sports car in for . . . of all things . . . a minivan.

Gabe silently grinned. *A minivan.* He was ashamed for Christopher since Christopher was too happy with life to be ashamed for himself. "Thanks, Chris, but I need to get prepared for that trip to Anchorage next week. Since the Landmark deal was originally your baby, I have to make sure I'm up on everything about it."

Christopher nodded. He knew that John Landmark intended for his exclusive ski resort to be the largest in the world, as well as the most renowned. It would be nestled among miles and miles of snow-covered mountain slopes and scenic wood trails; a project that would take a year to complete, maybe longer if the weather wasn't cooperative. Landmark had handpicked a firm in Charlotte to handle the resort's marketing and advertising, and a firm from California to take care of the landscape designs. With an undertaking of this magnitude it was important that all three entities work together if the end result was to be successful. "All right, but if you change your mind, you know you're welcome."

Back in his car Gabe began his journey home. A part of him was eager to start work on the ski resort. Being awarded the contract had literally opened doors, and business was booming. Recently, he and Christopher had discussed hiring an additional building crew just to handle the new business they were acquiring.

Gabe looked forward to the two weeks he would spend in Anchorage, a city that was vastly different from Detroit. He needed to get away for a while, especially because of his mother's overzealous matchmaking schemes. She had called earlier that day, telling him about another young woman that she wanted him to meet. He had come up with an excuse why he couldn't meet the woman any time soon and had quickly ended the conversation.

His thoughts turned back to Anchorage and all the work he had to pack into the two weeks he would be there, including finding suitable temporary housing for his men. Because of the length of time many of them would be staying there, some had decided to take their families with them, an option he and Christopher had offered them. The last thing the company needed was any member of the work crew getting homesick or pining for companionship. And those who decided to leave their families behind could fly home at least four times, which included the major holidays.

Gabe planned to make time to check out the city while he was there. He'd heard that Anchorage was beautiful and the perfect place to fish, which was something he enjoyed doing. And since he would eventually be spending a lot of his time there, he may as well look for temporary housing for himself as well.

Less than twenty minutes later, Gabe had arrived home. The first thing he did was check his phone messages. He wasn't surprised to find several from his mother, but he *was* surprised to find one from Keri Morton. She had called to thank him for dinner and to let him know that she and her ex-boyfriend had decided to try and work things out for the baby's sake. Gabe shook his head as he made his way to the refrigerator for a beer. After the earful Keri had given him, he truly wished them the best.

She had been a woman on the rebound, and he had to remember that type of woman was nothing but trouble.

CHAPTER TWO

Sage
Charlotte, North Carolina

Sage Dunbar gritted her teeth against the words her boss had just spoken. Taking a deep breath, she reminded herself that Stephen Poole was invincibly arrogant, something he seemed to take pride in. She also had to remind herself that the man was extremely smart and knew the business of marketing, something she was still learning under his wing. Her role at the Denmark Group was to assist companies in developing strategies that were right for them and would ultimately maximize their profits.

She glanced at the clock on the wall and wondered if anyone else in the room was as anxious for the meeting to end as she was. The man had started off by praising them for their hard work, and then without missing a beat, he had begun criticizing them for failing to come up with a suitable proposal to present to a company he was eager to bring on board.

"So what do you think, Ms. Dunbar? Is there a possibility your department can have an acceptable proposal on my desk first thing in the morning?"

Yeah, if we spend the night here, we can. Instead of giving him those thoughts, she simply smiled and said, "Yes, that won't be a problem."

She watched him smile. He was well aware that he had handed her a challenge, and like always, come hell or high water, she would come through with flying colors. "Good. I knew I could depend on you."

She smiled back to avoid gritting her teeth again. All she could think about at the moment was him in bed tonight making out with his latest conquest, while she and her staff slaved away at the proposal he wanted on his desk first thing in the morning.

It was no secret that the majority of the women in the office thought that at fifty-five Stephen Poole was drop-dead gorgeous. It was rumored that he'd been involved in a number of office affairs since his divorce eight months ago.

Ten minutes later back in her office, Sage called her staff together for a meeting. One look at their faces after she'd made the announcement and she could tell they weren't happy that come five o'clock, they wouldn't be going home.

"Doesn't Mr. Poole think any of us have a life outside of work?" Nora Skinner pouted. Apparently she had a date tonight, and then again, it could be that she was still pretty pissed at Stephen Poole. It was rumored that Nora's bed had been the first he had found his way into after his divorce, before moving on to other viable conquests.

"Yes, Nora, I'm sure he's aware that all of us have other interests besides the Denmark Group. However, he wants us to fine-tune the proposal we gave him last week. He feels there are things it lacks. I'm sure if the four of us put our heads together, we'll be able to come up with just what those things are without spending the entire night here."

Sage glanced around the room at the others. "Do I have

everyone's cooperation? I'm aware this is short notice, but we need to start work on this right away."

When everyone nodded, she couldn't help but smile. She had to admit that she worked with a swell group. She knew Rita was a single mother, which meant she would have to make arrangements for someone else to pick up her daughter from day care. Jim was a newlywed and was probably anxious to get home to his bride, and Erica, who was married with a teenage son, would probably miss his soccer game tonight.

"Good, and I appreciate all of your hard work and dedication. And to make sure that we don't spend the night here, let's meet in Conference Room A in thirty minutes to begin work."

It was a little past nine when Sage entered the apartment she shared with her fiancé, Erol Carlson. Unerringly, after closing the door behind her, her gaze was drawn to the floor-to-ceiling windows that dominated one wall in the living room and provided a panoramic view of downtown Charlotte. One of the main reasons she and Erol had selected this particular apartment over the others in the building had been for its beautiful polished hardwood floors and the view it provided of the city from twelve floors up.

After dropping her briefcase off on the desk in her office, she made her way into the kitchen to make soup and a sandwich for her dinner. This was Erol's night to play basketball with a few of his fraternity brothers, and usually he didn't get in until late since the guys made a habit of going out for drinks afterward. She had called him from the office earlier to let him know she would be working later than usual. He had understood. As a landscape architect who owned his own company, he knew the importance of hard work and doing what had to be done to complete any job, and for that she appreciated him immensely. There had never been any arguments between them regarding the long hours she often spent at the office. Their only disagreement had been with her reluctance to make a decision about their future together.

From the time they had met and started dating in college, Erol had made it known that he wanted them to marry as soon as they finished school. But something had held her back, although she felt they shared a pretty solid relationship. So they had moved in together and had landed jobs in their chosen professions.

After three years of living together, Erol had begun complaining. So had their respective parents, who could not understand why they would not marry. As far as everyone was concerned, they were a perfect couple. Both of them had good jobs. They had been together five years—lived together in harmony for three—and had deep respect and love for each other. Erol's parents had been married over thirty years, just as long as hers, and most of her friends' parents' marriages had lasted just as long; so she didn't have any hang-ups about the institution of marriage.

Finding no reason to hold back any longer, she'd finally given in and consented to be Erol's wife. The wedding was planned for June of next year, nine months from now. Everyone was happy—Erol, both sets of parents, their friends—and now, she admitted, so was she.

At times she wondered what had made her wait so long to agree to marry him. He was everything a woman could possibly want in a man—good-looking, trustworthy, just as neat and tidy as she was—and, she thought with a smile, he was good in bed.

Sage had taken her shower, gotten into bed and was halfway asleep when she heard the apartment door open. She stretched to a more comfortable position when she heard Erol cross the room and go into the bathroom for a shower.

Moments later when he eased into bed beside her and pulled

her into his arms, she went willingly. Her heartbeat quickened, and her body automatically responded when he reached between her legs and began stroking her.

"I need you, baby," he whispered, just moments before joining their mouths in a scorching kiss.

She closed her eyes, thinking that making love to him was the best stress reliever there was. A few moments later after removing their clothes, he almost had her purring.

By the time he entered her, he'd been able to successfully block a number of things from her mind—Mr. Poole's arrogance, the long hours she had spent at the office that day and Nora's less than desirable attitude while they had worked trying to come up with a better proposal. Instead of dwelling on any of those things, she let Erol take control of her mind and body as he pleasured her in ways only he could do.

"I love you," he whispered, as he instinctively locked her legs with his and cupped her behind in his hand. He lifted her up to meet his hard, solid thrusts.

He kissed her again, taking her mouth in a possession that shook her to the core and made her body respond in pleasure so fierce it almost bordered on pain. Gasping, she let her body flow with the sensation he had built inside of her, and heat of the hottest kind washed over every part of her.

She heard him moan the same time she did as a climax tore into their bodies, forcing her to cry out his name just as loud as he was crying out hers. She felt him crush her against his body as he began pumping into her with a frenzy that made her suck in a startled breath, and she felt her body, as well as his, come again.

When finally, minutes later, she felt him slump against her, spent and just as exhausted as she was, she held him to her, wondering what had been the driving force behind their frantic lovemaking tonight. He had taken her with a force that had nearly bordered on obsession, desperation.

"I'm sorry, Sage."

She lifted her brow, but before she could ask him what he was apologizing for, she heard his soft, even breathing, letting her know that just as quickly he had fallen asleep. She shifted their positions so she would not feel crushed beneath his weight and held him in her embrace.

Her gaze dropped to his features, and she thought he looked troubled about something, even while he slept. She wondered if perhaps a business deal had gone bad. But even if that was the case, that was no reason for him to be apologizing to her, so the words he had spoken before drifting off to sleep hadn't made much sense.

Sage stroked his chest, deciding she would talk to him in the morning before she left for work. It wasn't a long time after that before she, too, closed her eyes to sleep.

"Why did you apologize to me last night, Erol?"

In the awakening dawn that was flowing through their bedroom curtains, Sage could see the surprised look on Erol's face. As was the norm, he was up early to go jogging.

He lifted a brow. "I apologized?" he asked, walking back over to the bed and sitting down on the edge of it, facing her.

"Yes," she said, staring at him, studying his features. For some reason, even after a good night's sleep he still looked beat. "After we made love and before you drifted off to sleep, you said you were sorry, but you didn't say what you were sorry about."

Erol frowned. "Are you sure you weren't dreaming about that, sweetheart?"

She shook her head as she pulled herself up and drew her knees up to her chest. "No, I'm positive that I heard what you said."

Erol shrugged as he stood. "In that case," he said, crossing the room to get his keys off the dresser, "it must have been because I thought I may have been a little too rough with you last night." He turned around and looked at her. "Was I?"

She smiled as she adjusted the bedspread around her raised knees. "No, in fact I rather enjoyed it that way. God knows I needed it. Yesterday was a bear at work."

He nodded. "I gathered as much when you called me. Did you and your staff get things finished last night?"

She inhaled deeply as she ran a hand through her hair. "I hope so. Mr. Poole has been rather picky about stuff lately. But then, I guess he has every right to be since he's worked there forever and has helped make the company into the success it is."

"Yeah, it's not easy climbing the ladder of success," Erol said, rubbing a hand over his face.

There was something in his voice that pulled at Sage, alerting her that something was bothering him. She knew that although his business was flourishing, he had yet to reach that level of success he was pleased with. Erol's dream was to be the most sought after landscape architectural firm not only in the region, but in the country as well. He'd often shared with her his dream to see his company grow nationwide. And that was one goal he planned on accomplishing.

"Are things going okay with the company, Erol?" she asked with concern.

He smiled wryly as he walked back over to the bed and pulled her into his arms. "Yeah, don't worry, babe. Things are going fine."

She hugged him back with the same fierceness that he was hugging her. "And you would tell me if they weren't, wouldn't you? You would let me know if something was bothering you?"

He slowly released her and tilted his head back to look down at her. He reached out and cupped her chin. "Yeah, babe, you would be the first to know."

* * *

Sage held her breath as she watched Mr. Poole thoroughly read the new proposal, hoping it was what he wanted. Moments later, she let out a sigh of relief when she saw him smile.

"This is excellent, Ms. Dunbar. I knew you and your staff would come through. There's no doubt in my mind that both Mr. Dell and the board will be pleased."

Sage couldn't help but beam in delight. "Thanks, sir." She then watched as he leaned back in his chair and gazed at her thoughtfully. She wondered what he was thinking.

Nervously, she shifted in her seat and crossed one leg over the other. "Is there anything else you wanted, Mr. Poole?" After asking her question, she quickly wondered if he'd considered her words as a come-on. She definitely hoped not. Since coming to work for the company two years ago, she had been nothing but professional in her dealings with him, unlike some of her coworkers who she knew had all but stamped the words *I'm available if you're interested"* on their foreheads.

"Yes, there is something else, Ms. Dunbar, and I believe you would be just the right person for the job."

She lifted a dark brow. "What job, sir?"

"To do a presentation at a meeting in Alaska."

"Alaska?"

"Yes, Anchorage, Alaska. We were awarded a contract to handle the marketing for a company that's having an exclusive ski resort built there. The owner, John Landmark, wasn't impressed with the ideas our first group put together and needs another proposal presented. He wants us to meet with the Regency Corporation, the company he's hired to build the resort, and work with them to come up with some good marketing and promotion ideas."

He leaned forward. "I believe the trip will provide us with an opportunity to evaluate several suggestions Mr. Landmark has and to come up with a few of our own. Another team from our

West Coast office is being assembled to ultimately take over the handling of this project, but right now they need us to fly out there and smooth things over with Mr. Landmark."

Sage nodded. She had heard through the grapevine that Denmark had gotten a nice contract with Landmark Industries, a company known for its upscale industrial parks and shopping malls. And if she wasn't mistaken, she recalled reading in *Black Enterprise* magazine that the construction company awarded the contract to build the resort was owned by two black men from Detroit. That in itself was impressive.

"I'd love to attend the meeting, Mr. Poole."

"Good. I've also invited Rose Woods to represent our advertising department. The meeting is next week."

Sage nodded. She liked Rose and considered her a good friend as well as a coworker. They were the only two sistahs with management positions within the company. Occasionally, they got together after work for drinks and to talk. In a company like Denmark where competition was the name of the game, it was important that they maintained a clear head, kept their feet level with the ground, stayed in constant prayer and watched each other's backs. "Thanks, sir. Is there anything else?"

"No, Ms. Dunbar, that will be all. Again I want to commend you and your staff on a job well done."

She smiled as she stood. "Thank you, Mr. Poole."

"Girl, I can't believe Stephen Poole is taking the both of us, two sistahs, with him to that meeting in Alaska. You should have seen Grace Holder's face when he announced it this morning in our weekly staff meeting. She thought that she would be the one going with him."

"Grace thought she would be going?" Sage asked after taking a large sip of iced tea. They had met after work at a soul food restaurant they frequently patronized. "Why would she think that? You have more seniority with the company."

Rose grinned. "I think mainly because the two of them have been sleeping together."

Sage leaned back in her chair, shocked. Grace had begun working for the company right out of college a little over a year ago, and Sage thought Grace had a steady boyfriend. "Grace and Mr. Poole? You got to be kidding."

"No, I'm not, although I admit he's been more discreet with her than the others, probably because of their ages, but I know for a fact something is going on. Last month I came back to the office one night after remembering I had left something. It was late, way past eleven o'clock, and I ran into them coming out of his office."

"That late at night?"

"Yes, and it was evident from the looks on their faces that they had been caught doing something. And although Grace had tried putting her clothes back on straight, it was obvious she had been out of them."

Sage's eyes widened. "But what about her boyfriend? The one who lives in D.C. and works for the government. The last I heard they were talking marriage."

"They broke up a few months ago, and she was all shook up about it. I guess with Stephen Poole's help, she's gotten over him."

Sage shook her head, shocked at the number of women in the office who were or had been involved with Mr. Poole. She couldn't help wondering what was going on with him. He was taking affairs in the workplace to a whole new level. "What is it with him?" she finally asked Rose. "Hasn't he heard of sexual harassment in the workplace?"

Rose grinned. "I guess in his estimation, it's consenting sex and not harassment. From what I've heard, he makes it under-stood that sleeping with him isn't a guarantee of any special treatment or advancement within the company. In other words, any woman sharing his bed is wasting her time if she thinks she's banging her way to the top."

Sage shook her head. "Then, why do it?"

Rose chuckled. "I guess some of them get off at the thought of sleeping with the boss. But then, Sage, you have to admit he's pretty good on the eyes for an older man, suave and sexy. Hell, he could pass for Richard Gere's twin, and that's saying a lot."

Sage did have to admit the man was good-looking, but he just didn't do anything for her and told Rose as much. But from the way Rose's eyes were sparkling, evidently he did do something for her. "But don't you think he's too old for Grace? She's only twenty-three."

"That's for Grace to decide if he's too old for her. Besides, age is nothing but a number," Rose said, grinning. "And in some situations, experience counts, trust me," she continued with a smirky grin on her face. "And to come to Mr. Poole's defense, it's not uncommon after a divorce or the end of a long-term relationship for one or both parties to start engaging in safe sexual marathons. Especially if there was a lack of sexual satisfaction in the prior relationship."

Rose leaned in closer to whisper, "While a senior in high school, I dated the same guy exclusively for a year and not once experienced an orgasm until after going off to college and sleeping with older, experienced guys. Then I was pissed to find out what I'd been missing out on." She inhaled deeply before continuing. "As far as Mr. Poole goes, I've seen his wife the few times she's come into the office, all prim and proper acting and who don't look the type to do the *nasty* for fear of getting her hair messed up. Now he's like a kid set free in a candy store. He intends to sample all the treats he's been missing during his twenty years of marriage. Pretty soon he'll develop a stomachache from overindulging and settle down with just one treat—

or in his case, one woman. And if he's as good in bed as the rumor mill claims, he won't have a problem finding a woman with a robust sexual appetite to match his own."

Sage said nothing in response to Rose's summation. She couldn't help but wonder what Rose's reaction would be if Mr. Poole were to hit on her. Had he already? Had Rose's name been added to the list of women who were enjoying whatever it was Stephen Poole was dishing out? A part of her wanted to ask but quickly decided it really wasn't any of her business. Rose was twenty-eight, two years older than she was, and could definitely take care of herself.

Besides, she had been friends with Rose long enough to know she had a thing against a committed relationship with a man. She enjoyed engaging in affairs, which was basically the very thing Mr. Poole was doing.

She had once asked Rose what the advantages of affairs versus committed relationships were. Rose had been quick to tell her it was a sure way not to get hurt by love, and for someone who'd been severely burned twice, Rose had no intentions of letting her heart rule her mind again.

When Sage got home later that evening and played back her messages, there was one from her mother asking her to call back as soon as she got in.

"Mom, you wanted something?" she asked after placing the call. For years her mother had worked as a sales clerk for one of the major department stores and had recently gotten promoted to manager of her department. Her mother was a person who embraced life to the fullest and was quick to give a helping hand to others. Sage didn't know of any other person with such a strong constitution who proved there was such a thing as superwoman. Sometimes she wondered where her mother got her energy.

"Yes, sweetheart? How was your day?"

"Busy as usual. Mr. Poole wants me to go out of town with him next week to Alaska."

"Alaska? This is rather sudden, isn't it? And how long will you be gone?"

"Yes, it's unexpected, and I'll probably be gone for at least a week."

"Well, we need to get together before you leave to start planning your wedding."

"Mom, this is September. The wedding takes place in June. By my calculations I have nine months," Sage said. She could see it coming. She had told her parents that she wanted a small wedding, but knowing her mother, her words had gone in one ear and had come out the other. There was no doubt in Sage's mind that Delores Dunbar intended to give her just the opposite of what she'd asked for. Her mother had waited a long time for her only child to finally decide to get married, and she planned to do it up in style whether she wanted her to or not.

"Nine months will be here before you know it, Sage. If you don't believe me, just ask any woman who's had a baby recently."

Sage knew to argue with her mother would be pointless. In the end she would get her way regardless. Besides being superwoman, she was also super stubborn. Her father had told her long ago he had learned to just let her mother have her way and be through with it. "All right, Mom, how does your schedule look on Friday?" she asked, knowing although that was her mother's day off from work, she probably had a zillion and one things lined up to do. "If you're free, we can do lunch."

"Friday is a good day for me, and lunch sounds like a wonderful idea. Maybe we can talk your father into joining us."

Sage chuckled. "I doubt Dad will want to sit through lunch while we make wedding plans, not even with the enticement of a free meal."

"Yes, but we should ask him anyway. I'm concerned about him, honey. He's been working a lot of late hours at the office. Inviting him to have lunch with us will be a way of getting him away from work for a while. And he'll do it if you were to ask him. That man will do anything for you, and you know it."

Sage smiled, knowing that was true. She was definitely her daddy's girl. Always had been and always would be. "Well, then I'll ask him, but he'll be bored silly. You know Dad. He'll prefer letting us plan things and just give him the bill. But I meant what I said, Mom. I don't want you and Dad paying for anything. I can afford to pay for my own wedding. And that's one of the main reasons I would appreciate it if you kept things within the budget I've established."

"We'll talk about that at lunch."

Moments later, Sage sighed as she hung up the phone after finalizing the lunch plans with her mother. She couldn't help but smile as she began taking off her clothes while walking toward the bedroom. When it came to her parents, she really felt blessed. They were the greatest. Being the only child had had its advantages . . . as well as its disadvantages. The advantage was that she was very close to her parents, especially her father. Her fondest memories while growing up were of the times she had spent with him. If Charles Dunbar had preferred a son rather than a daughter, he had never let on and didn't try making her into something she wasn't. He had not encouraged her to play sports like some fathers with only a daughter would have, especially a man who was as involved in sports as he was. He loved football, baseball and basketball. . . . If there was a ball involved, he was hooked. And although he had taken her to a lot of games while she was growing up, it had been because she had wanted to go and not because she felt she had to grab some of his time or attention. And he had spent just as much time at the dance studio, hair salon, and Girl Scout meetings with her as he had his other activities. He had done all of it while working his way up from a bank teller to branch manager and to his present position of bank executive. She was proud of him because she knew in his day that moving up the corporate ladder in the financial arena hadn't been easy for a black man.

Erol came home just as she was stepping out of the shower. Over dinner she told him about her trip to Alaska.

"How long do you think you'll be gone?" he asked as he dug into his meal. They had a rule that the first one home would start dinner. She had cooked a skillet of stir-fry vegetables with chopped chicken breast and white rice. She had also made a pitcher of iced tea and had stopped by the bakery on her way home and had purchased a couple of slices of carrot cake.

"Probably a week. Why?"

He looked up at her and smiled. "I was thinking that if I could get away, I'd love to join you. I've never been to Alaska, and I think it would be nice for us to spend some time together away from Charlotte. I can definitely use a break from work."

Sage nodded, again wondering if something was going on at work that Erol wasn't sharing with her. She decided not to say anything. She had to believe that if it was something she needed to know, he would tell her. "I think that would be a great idea. What are the chances of your being able to do that?"

His smile widened. "There's a pretty good chance if I can finalize the Rollins deal next week."

Sage nodded. "Well, I'm keeping my fingers crossed that everything will work out and you'll be able to join me."

Erol reached across the table and took her hand in his. "Thanks, babe, I need all the support I can get because I really do want that contract. This is a big job, and it will bring in a lot of money up front and in the long run since it includes continuous maintenance of the property. If Rollins is pleased with the way I do things, he might refer me to other companies. His contacts are enormous. I'm thinking about expanding the business on a regional or maybe even a national level if things work out. That's why I'm working my butt off to get this one. Competition is tight."

Sage smiled. "Yeah, but if they do their homework, they'll see that your company is the best."

That night while Erol held her in his arms, she closed her eyes and said a silent prayer that he would get the contract that he so desperately wanted. She had never known him to get this worked up over a business deal before. Even when they had made love tonight, although he had pleased her, she could tell his full concentration hadn't been into it as it usually was.

She snuggled closer to him, thinking that she and her mother were thinking on the same wave length because it seemed that their men were working too hard.

With an inward sigh, Sage decided that if Erol was not able to join her in Alaska, she would make plans for them to go away somewhere for a weekend when she got back, even if it was a short trip to New Orleans.

Sage looked over at her father the moment her mother left the table to go to the ladies' room. As always, she thought he looked extremely good for his age and appreciated that he cared enough to stay in shape. So had her mother. Delores Dunbar had also managed to stay healthy. Sage thought she had swell parents who still looked good together even after thirty years.

"You didn't really have to come, Dad, you know," she said after noticing the many times he kept looking at his watch.

Charles Dunbar smiled. "I didn't mind. Besides, listening to you and your mother make those plans really hit me that you're going to do it. Getting married is a big step, and I'm glad you decided it's what you want. I have to admit that for a while there I was beginning to wonder."

Sage couldn't help but return her father's smile. "Yes, and for a while I was beginning to wonder, too, but now I'm sure. Erol is good to me and he's good for me. I don't think I could ask for any more than that."

She studied her father for a while, then asked, "What about you, Dad? You don't seem relaxed today for some reason. You aren't letting work stress you out, are you?"

Charles Dunbar reached across the table and captured his daughter's hand in his. "No, sweetheart, work is fine. I've just had a lot on my mind lately, but things will be all right."

Sage nodded. "Mom's worried about you, you know. She thinks you're working too hard. I guess she's not used to you keeping such late hours at the office."

"No, I guess she's not." After a few brief moments, he opened his mouth to say something, then suddenly closed it.

Sage's dark brows furrowed. "Dad? What were you about to say?"

He tightened her hand in his. "Nothing that was important, sweetheart. I guess your old man is getting caught up in the fact that his little girl is not a little girl anymore." He smiled wryly. "Do you know the highlight of my day was coming home knowing you would meet me at the door every evening with a huge smile and a big hug?"

Sage chuckled, remembering those times. They had been the highlight of her day as well. "Yeah, and you always brought a gift home for me, even if it was something as simple as a rubber band." She lovingly met his gaze. "You spoiled me rotten, you know."

He laughed as he released her hand. "Yeah, I know, but I don't regret a day doing so. I think it was well worth it. I'm proud of what you've become."

Sage's eyes became misty. "Thanks, Dad, and I'm giving you and Mom all the credit. The two of you were and still are super. I love you."

He leaned over and reached across the table and tweaked her nose like he used to. "And I love you, too, sweetheart."

CHAPTER THREE

Gabe gave his construction foreman a serious yet teasing look. "I know you're miserable, but do you have to look it?"

"Sorry," Parnell Cabot said, grinning sheepishly, taking a leisurely sip of wine while glancing around the crowded room filled with immaculately dressed attendees. "It's just that I'm not comfortable being at these type of affairs."

Gabe nodded. He knew Parnell preferred being surrounded by steel beams, concrete and cement versus exquisite china, crystal-stemmed wine goblets and expensive-looking furnishings. Soft music was coming from a live band that was set up on the other side of the marble-floored ballroom. The crystal chandeliers that hung overhead illuminated the tables that were filled with appetizers and pastries while waiters were busy carrying trays of champagne around the room.

They were attending a party hosted by the mayor of Anchorage in honor of the city's newest employer, John Landmark. There wasn't any doubt with the extravagance laid out that the city's officials saw the wealthy tycoon's latest business venture as a definite boost to their economy. New jobs would be created as well as an increase in tourism once the resort was completed.

As Gabe continued to look at Parnell, he thought it wasn't every day that the man who headed his forty-man work team traded in his jeans and work shirt for a suit and tie. "Just relax, you're doing fine. All we need is to put in an appearance for Mr. Landmark's benefit, and then we can split. I don't know about you, but I'm still feeling the effects of jet lag."

Parnell's grin widened. "Same here, and besides that, I'd like to get back to the hotel to call and check on the girls."

Gabe nodded in understanding. Parnell's wife had been killed in a car accident three years ago, and he was raising their four-year-old twin daughters alone. As far as Gabe was concerned, he was doing a fantastic job of it, and Gabe couldn't help but admire and respect the man. He was a dedicated father as well as a hardworking foreman who was well thought of by the men who worked for him. He was an easy-going sort of guy, stern when he had to be but always fair.

At thirty-eight Parnell had been working for the company at least ten years, first starting out when Gabe's father was running things. He'd been promoted to head foreman two years ago, a position he had definitely earned. Because of his expertise, work ethics and attention to detail, there was no doubt that every building the Regency Corporation constructed was sturdy, safe and sound.

"Have you decided what you're going to do with the girls while you're working out here?" Gabe asked.

Parnell smiled and replied, "Yes. I'm moving them out here with me. There's no way I can be separated from them for that long period of time. Although I know my parents wouldn't have a problem keeping them while I'm here, they're my responsibility. They are my life."

Gabe knew the girls being Parnell's life was the truth. Other than work, everything else he did was centered on his daughters. And although he'd never mentioned it, Gabe had a strong feeling Parnell hadn't dated since his wife's death.

"Before I leave to return to Detroit, I plan to interview this older woman who is interested in a position as a live-in baby-sitter and housekeeper," Parnell said a few minutes later. "The manager at the hotel gave me her name, and she comes highly recommended. I also need to find us a place to stay."

Gabe nodded. He, too, had to check into temporary housing for his men as well as a place for himself. For lunch tomorrow, he and Parnell were scheduled to meet with John Landmark. Christopher would be flying in for that meeting but would immediately fly out afterward. He was heavily involved with working on a bid to present to the Marriott Corporation for another hotel they planned to build in West Palm Beach.

Gabe checked his watch. "Let's mingle for a few minutes longer; then we can leave."

"That sounds good to me."

A man who came up and introduced himself as a local Realtor who'd heard he was interested in leasing a home snagged Parnell's attention.

Suddenly finding himself alone, Gabe glanced around at the collection of people in attendance. He'd been introduced to several of them, all important people in the Anchorage community. Deciding to step out on the patio for a bit of fresh air, he moved toward the French doors. As he passed a hall, he couldn't help but notice a woman whose reflection was picked up on the wall mirror in front of him. He stopped, totally captured by what he saw.

He turned his head to see the actual woman, and the first word that came to his mind was magnificent. There was something about her, the way she was standing or perhaps the smile she had on her face—or perhaps the sparkle in her eyes while conversing with the man and woman beside her—that radiated confidence and self-assurance. A confident, self-assured woman outside of the bedroom meant a confident, self-assured woman inside the bedroom. He liked that. What man wouldn't? Confident women knew what they wanted, what they liked and what they needed. They weren't into playing games. They meant what they said and said what they meant. And they didn't do anything half-stepping, including blowing a man's mind while making love.

And more importantly, a confident, self-assured woman didn't carry around excess emotional baggage. She knew how to let go. She was secure enough in herself not to worry about things she would consider as trivial. She knew not to sweat the small stuff.

Gabe felt a tightness coil deep within his stomach as he continued to watch her. Something about her set her apart from the woman standing next to her who was also attractive. It could have been the striking combination of her dark almond skin, the medium brown coloring of her hair and the whiskey coloring of her eyes. Or it could just as well have been the outfit she had on, a stunning silk pantsuit whose teal color seemed to capture the essence of the light in the room and enhance everything about her. Whatever the reason, she looked absolutely sensuous, sexy and breathtaking.

As all those thoughts raced through his mind, he suddenly felt something that didn't make sense. He felt some sort of a connection to her, a link, which in itself was crazy since he didn't know the woman. And surprisingly, the connection wasn't sexual. If anything, it was protective, which really gave him pause. Why would he feel a protective instinct for a woman he had never seen before?

His heart stuttered slightly, and he shook his head, thinking for a quick, unexplainable moment that he'd lost it, and he could only assume the reason was that he'd been working a lot lately. But still he couldn't take his eyes off of her.

He inhaled deeply, disappointedly so, when his gaze captured her hand as she lifted a stemmed wine goblet to her lips. Not only was she confident and self-assured, but she was also taken. He knew an engagement ring when he saw one. He was not surprised and considered whoever had placed that ring on her finger a very lucky man as well as a very smart one. You didn't let a woman of this caliber stay single for long. Yet even realizing that she was spoken for couldn't stop the heat from shimmering in his gaze as he looked at her, glad she was unaware of him staring, and grateful for his unobstructed view.

"Have we mingled enough yet, Gabe?"

Gabe turned when Parnell walked up with an anxious look on his face. Giving the woman one final look, Gabe turned and smiled at Parnell and said, "Yes, we can leave now."

At sixty-two, John Landmark looked every bit the wealthy real estate tycoon that he was. An imposing figure with a larger-than-life height of six-five, he stood at the podium demanding attention as he spoke. And he was getting it from the group he had assembled, all key players in his next huge financial venture.

His dark black hair was thick and sprinkled with silver. The touch of gray added dimension to the man who had spent years increasing his vast holdings with the chain of department stores, hotels and shopping malls he owned around the country. The ski lodge outside Anchorage would be the first of its kind for his company. Anyone who'd ever spent any time with him knew he never did anything half measure. He always chose the best, and he felt the people sitting at the luncheon tables were that and more. Especially since their companies had been handpicked by him.

Any further words John Landmark was saying took a backseat in Gabe's mind as his gaze lit on the woman sitting a few tables over. She was the same woman from the party last night, and she looked just as good today as she had then. And for whatever it meant, that protective instinct he'd felt was still there, and he tried to immediately dismiss it.

She suddenly glanced his way and smiled briefly, a friendly gesture—not intended to be anything more—since her gaze and attention automatically returned to Mr. Landmark.

"Take your damn eyes off that woman and pay attention, Blackwell."

Christopher had leaned close to him and whispered the direct order for his ears only. Having been caught, he could only smile and nod.

At the end of the luncheon, Gabe felt compelled to walk over and hold a conversation with the woman who had stood and introduced herself to everyone as Sage Dunbar, promotional manager at the Denmark Groups' North Carolina office in Charlotte. Engaged or not, she had stirred his interest from the moment he had seen her last night. He'd been surprised as hell when she had walked into the room today. And he'd been given the chance to witness something he hadn't seen last night—her walk.

It had been sensuality in motion, a real sight to behold, as she'd made a graceful yet confident stride across the room to the table where other members of her company were sitting. That subtle movement of her body had revealed curves even the conservative navy blue business suit that she wore couldn't hide.

Her short laugh reeled his thoughts back in as it captured his attention, floating like whipped cream across the room, seemingly deliberately right to him. He saw the perfect opportunity to approach her when the same man and woman who'd been with her last night walked away, leaving her alone to gather her things off the table. After placing items in her briefcase, it was at that moment that she looked up and glanced his way and saw him staring at her.

Again her smile was one of friendliness, nothing more, nothing less. There was definitely nothing flirty about it. And then to his surprise, after closing her briefcase, she began walking toward him.

Just as earlier, her walk literally turned him on. Maybe it had to do with the confidence her walk alluded to. Or it might have been the air about her, one that indicated she didn't have a worry in the world, and that she liked who she was, what she was, and that whatever was going on in her life—her man, her family, her career—couldn't be better.

He remembered feeling that same way last year when everything in his life seemed to be going right for a change. The Regency Corporation had been awarded the Landmark deal, Christopher had fallen in love and gotten married, and it was last year that he'd met Debbie and their sex-only relationship had begun.

All thoughts of Debbie fled from his mind when Sage Dunbar came to a stop in front of him. Her name was as uncommon as the woman herself, and he was looking forward to hearing the history behind it.

"Mr. Blackwell," she said, holding her hand out to him. "It is indeed an honor to meet you, and I look forward to working with you and Mr. Chandler on the Landmark Project, even on a temporary basis." Her smile widened. "For which I have the big job of finding a suitable name to market."

The first thought that came to Gabe's mind was that her voice was just as sexy as her walk. He took the hand she offered, liking the feel of it in his, soft and tender. All too soon he had to release it. "And which I'm sure that you'll be able to do, Ms. Dunbar," he said, feeling completely comfortable in returning her smile.

She gestured in agreement as though it would be a sure thing. Again, he liked her confidence. After glancing around the room, she said, "I had wanted to meet Mr. Chandler before he left."

Gabe nodded. "Yes, well, unfortunately he had to leave immediately. There are business matters needing his attention back in Detroit."

Now it was Sage's turn to nod. "I wanted to take the opportunity to congratulate the both of you on your accomplishments and successes. I've read about them in *Black Enterprise, Essence* and a few other magazines and newspapers. I think it was special for Mr. Chandler to return to his hometown of Savannah and turn the low-income housing project where he once lived as a child into a brand-new affordable housing project. And for you to donate so much of what you made off the Landmark Project to the Tom Joyner Foundation to provide scholarships for the historically black colleges. As you can see I am definitely an admirer of you both."

Gabe chuckled. "And such a beautiful admirer."

"Thank you."

She had accepted his compliment easily, and he could tell it hadn't gone to her head. But then, he was certain that she probably received numerous such compliments.

"Since you work in Charlotte, can I assume you live there as well?"

"Yes, I've lived there all my life, at least since the age of two. I was born in Chantilly, Virginia. My parents moved to Charlotte when my father's company relocated."

"And what type of business is he in?"

"Banking. He worked his way up from a bank teller to his present position of bank executive. It took him almost twenty years to get to the top, but he did it."

Gabe nodded, hearing admiration in her voice for her father's accomplishment. Deciding to get to the meat of the meal, the one thing holding him back from pursuing her, he asked, "And your fiancé? What does he do?"

If she was surprised by his question, she didn't show it. "He's a landscape architect and owns a company. Right now he's operating on a regional level; but it's his dream to one day go national, and there's no doubt in my mind that he'll succeed. He's good at what he does."

Gabe could hear total admiration in her voice for her fiancé as well. "You sound like a woman who loves her man and believes in his abilities."

She met his gaze and without blinking an eye grinned and said, "I am and I do."

Gabe smiled. That one statement said it all. He had watched her facial features while she'd said it. She was a woman in love and didn't mind making it obvious. In his lifetime he'd met a number of women who, at certain times and in certain places, forgot they had a fiancé or even a husband. Sage Dunbar was not one of those women, and that thought gave him pause. He would love to meet the man that elicited such loyalty from her. His respect for her went up another notch, as well as his envy of the man who had undoubtedly stolen her heart.

"How long do you plan to be in Anchorage?" he asked. Although the thought of pursuing a relationship with her was out of the question, there was no reason why he couldn't enjoy her company since he knew where he stood.

"If everything goes as planned, I'll be able to leave tomorrow, which is earlier than I had expected. I had hoped my fiancé would be able to join me here and we could extend my time to take in some of the sights, but after talking with him last night, it seems that won't be the case. He's tied up with business negotiations on a particular deal he's trying to work."

A part of Gabe wondered if the man was smart after all. He doubted he would let anything, including business, keep him from spending time with this woman. "Then, how about joining me and my foreman, Parnell Cabot, for dinner. And if Rose Woods is free, I'd also like to invite her to join us as well."

Sage's smile widened. "Thank you, Mr. Blackwell, for the invitation. I'll check with Rose Woods to see if she's free tonight. As for myself, I'd love to join you and Mr. Cabot."

"Thank you, and please call me Gabe."

"All right, Gabe, and I'm Sage."

"Sage," he repeated, liking the way it sounded off his lips. "I'm sure there's a story behind your name."

She chuckled. "Yes, a rather short and simple one. My grandmother had three sons who each gave her a granddaughter in the same year. She was bestowed with the task of naming the three of us and decided to do so after her favorite spices. She claimed we would be the spice of her life. Ginger lives in Florida, and Cinnamon resides out west in California."

Gabe couldn't help but chuckle. "And of the three who's the oldest?" he asked, intrigued with the story.

Her eyes sparkled. "We're all twenty-six. Cinnamon's birthday is in March, mine is in August and Ginger's in October."

Gabe nodded as he continued smiling. "There's a story behind my name as well," he said as his smile widened into a grin. "My mother named me Gabriel thinking that if she did so, I would most certainly grow up to be an angel. Needless to say, by my first birthday she discovered just how wrong she was."

Later that evening, after coming out of one of the stalls in the women's bathroom, Rose glanced around, then stooped down to check to make sure she and Sage were alone before joining her at the sink to wash her hands. "Gabe Blackwell likes you, Sage."

Sage glanced over at Rose as she dried her hands. "And I like him."

Rose raised her eyes to the ceiling. "I don't think you fully understand what I mean, Sage. I mean he really *likes* you. He hasn't taken his eyes off you practically all evening."

Sage decided not to let Rose know that on several occasions she'd noticed him looking at her as well. "He knows I'm engaged to be married."

"That means nothing to some men."

Sage smiled. "I believe it means something to him. He doesn't appear to be the type of man who'd waste his time on a lost cause."

Rose wondered if it was truly a lost cause. For someone getting married, Sage wasn't showing the enthusiasm she would expect of a bride-to-be. "All I'm saying, my spice of a friend, is that I notice some interest on his part, although I agree, chances are since you're engaged he won't make a move to hit on you."

Sage adjusted her purse on her shoulder. "Well, my flower of a friend, you aren't the only one noticing things tonight. I happen to notice your gaze kept straying to Parnell Cabot more than once."

Rose snorted as she dried her hands. "Yeah, but that was before I found out it would be a waste of my time to get interested."

"Why? I think he's an extremely nice person and is pretty good-looking."

Rose stated, "Yes, being nice and good-looking has nothing to do with it."

"Is there a reason you feel that way?"

"Didn't you hear what he said? The man is a widower with children, four-year-old twin girls to be exact. And I make it a point not to become involved with men with small children."

Now it was Sage's time to raise a brow. "Why?"

Rose leaned against the Formica counter. "Because they're usually looking for a baby-sitter as well as a bed partner. And usually you find yourself being more of the first than the second."

"I can't see all men being that way."

"Yeah, but enough of them are. I can handle being a bed partner, but I prefer just not doing men with small kids."

Sage nodded and deep down felt there was more to it than that, something Rose wasn't telling her, but decided to leave it alone by changing the subject. "As much as I think Anchorage is a real pretty area, I'm looking forward to going home tomorrow, aren't you?"

"Yes, this place is way too cold for me. I bet these people wear overcoats year-round."

Sage smiled. "Personally, I like the weather here. It's the kind you can snuggle up under covers and stay warm with your man.

I hate that Erol wasn't able to join me here. I think he would have liked it, too."

"Are you going to let him know you're returning home early?"

"No, I think I'll surprise him."

Gabe took great pleasure in volunteering to escort Sage and Rose back to their rooms after dinner, which was easy enough since they were staying at the same hotel. Parnell had bid everyone good night, and Gabe knew he wanted to do the same to his daughters before it was past their bedtime. After seeing Rose to her room, he caught the elevator up to the sixth floor to see Sage to hers.

"You really didn't have to do this, you know," Sage said, smiling at him in the enclosed confines of the elevator.

"Yes, I did. One of Joella Blackwell's strictest rules was to always see a lady safely to her door."

"Joella Blackwell?"

"Yes, my mother."

The elevator door opened, and stepping out, they began walking toward Sage's room. "Is it true that your family adopted Christopher Chandler?"

Gabe laughed, remembering the article that had appeared in a certain newspaper last year. "I guess you can say that, although of course not legally. Chris was eighteen, and my parents decided they needed another son and I needed a brother. They thought since we were the same age it was perfect. However, at the time I didn't particularly like Chris and wasn't all that keen on the idea. But no one fights Joella Blackwell when she makes up her mind about something."

He grinned. "I think even Chris was overwhelmed by it all. He was a loner and had been all his life. He'd never had anyone to care for him before, except for his wife, Maxi, when they went to school together as kids, and one of his former teachers.

My parents proudly boast of him being their other son, and I'm proud to claim him as a brother."

Sage nodded. She had picked up on the special friendship the two of them shared when she'd seen them together earlier that day. "And what about Parnell? He's raising his daughters alone?"

Gabe answered, "Yes, his wife was killed in a car accident three years ago. The girls were barely a year old at the time. Parnell took her death extremely hard, and the only thing that held him to his sanity was those girls."

Sage shook her head sadly when she thought of the little girls who would grow up without a mother. "Who will take care of them while he's out here working?"

"He plans to move them out here with him. And whatever it takes, he's going to make it work. Chances are that he'll hire a live-in sitter to help out. Joya and LaToya are his whole world. He is the perfect father, and those girls are the apples of their father's eyes."

Sage thought about the special relationship she'd always shared with her father while growing up. When they finally came to her room, they stopped. "Thanks again, Gabe, for a nice evening. You certainly have your work cut out for you with the Landmark Project, and I do as well. But it's my belief that we'll both be successful."

Gabe nodded, hearing her confidence surface once again. "That's my belief as well. And congratulations on your upcoming wedding. Have you set a date?"

"Yes, June eighth of next year."

He smiled and said in all honesty, "I wish you and your fiancé all the best."

"Thanks, and if you're ever in the Charlotte area, let me know."

"I will, and I'd like you to do the same if you're ever in Detroit."

"Thanks. Well, I'd better go and start packing since I'm leaving tomorrow."

"I hope you have a safe trip back home."

She turned and inserted her key in the door, and it clicked open. Giving him a final smile, she said, "Good night," before slipping inside and closing it behind her.

Gabe walked away, and for the umpteenth time since first seeing Sage Dunbar, he thought that her fiancé was definitely a very lucky man.

CHAPTER FOUR

Sage waved goodbye to Rose and Mr. Poole as she walked out of the airport terminal tugging her luggage behind her. She was glad to be back home and couldn't wait to tell Erol how well things had gone in Alaska.

Five minutes later she was pulling her BMW out of the parking garage. She glanced at the time on her car's dashboard. Knowing Erol was probably at the office, she decided to surprise him and go there. But first she wanted to get him a gift for his office, so she pulled into a florist shop. After deciding on a small potted plant that sat in a beautiful ceramic bowl, she walked up to the counter to pay for her purchase, handing the lady her bankcard. She was admiring a beautiful arrangement of fresh-cut flowers when the sales person spoke.

"I'm sorry, but your card was declined."

Sage raised a brow. Her card being declined wasn't possible. She always kept a balance of at least a thousand dollars in her account, and since she hadn't used her card since the last time she had been paid, there was a lot more than that in her account. "There must be a mistake," she said, smiling to the older woman. "Could you try it again?"

The woman nodded and tried again. Moments later Sage

was given the same response—her card had been declined. Sage went into her purse to retrieve cash to make her purchase. This had never happened to her before, and she quickly assumed the mistake was due to a glitch in her bankcard. She was confident that once she contacted her bank, the matter would be straightened out. But still, she decided, she would stop at the first available ATM to verify her bank balance.

Ten minutes later she walked out of a grocery store upset. The ATM had indicated that she had a twenty-three-dollar balance in her account. Getting back into her car, she quickly strapped up and maneuvered her vehicle back into traffic, anxious to get to the bank before closing time. Someone at the bank had a lot of explaining to do.

In record time, Sage pulled her car into the parking garage that was connected to the bank as well as other office buildings. Taking the garage's elevator, she pushed the button for the floor where the bank was located. She wasn't surprised to find the bank busy, and instead of standing in line for a teller, she went immediately to a bank officer, someone she knew. Her father had worked at this particular branch for a few years before relocating in the bank's corporate office after he'd gotten a promotion. Adam Montgomery had been a bank teller when her father had been a loan officer.

"Miss Dunbar, it's good seeing you," Adam Montgomery said, taking the hand she offered him.

"Thanks, Mr. Montgomery, and it's been a while."

The older man smiled and took the chair behind his desk after offering Sage the chair in front of it. "Yes, it has. I ran into your father last month at a business meeting, and he mentioned you're getting married. Congratulations."

"Thanks."

Adam Montgomery leaned back in his chair. "Now, what brings you to me? Do you need a loan for that wedding you're planning?"

Sage shook her head, grinning. "No, sir, I'm trying to convince Mom to keep things simple." Sage then shifted in her chair as a concerned expression came onto her face when she remembered the reason for her visit. "Mr. Montgomery, the reason I'm here is because a short while ago I tried to make a purchase with my bankcard and was declined. I later stopped by a grocery store and checked my bank balance at an ATM, and it showed less than twenty-five dollars in my account. According to my records, I should have well over two thousand dollars in there."

Adam Montgomery frowned. "Then, there must be some mistake. What is your account number?"

Sage gave him the information he asked for and watched as he entered the information into his computer. She looked as his frown deepened.

"Umm, this is interesting," he said moments later. "Our records are showing that you withdrew two thousand and five hundred dollars out of your checking account two weeks ago."

Sage sat up straight in her chair. "Your records are incorrect. I haven't used my bankcard in three weeks, and I definitely didn't withdraw that much money at one time."

Mr. Montgomery looked at her and lifted a brow. "Then, we'll definitely get to the bottom of this," he said, standing. "I will have one of the tellers pull a copy of that transaction. Excuse me, I'll be right back."

Sage nodded as she watched him leave his office. She shook her head, wondering how the bank could have made such a horrendous mistake. It was a good thing she hadn't written any checks yet on her account. She made it a habit to pay all of her bills the first of the month. She stared through Mr. Montgomery's glass wall and watched him talking to another bank official before they walked to a computer that began printing documents.

Moments later, Mr. Montgomery returned with a document in his hand. "It seems our records are correct, Miss Dunbar, although you weren't the one who withdrew the money from your account. This shows the transaction was made by Erol Carlson, and he is named on your account as an authorized user."

Sage was momentarily taken aback by Mr. Montgomery's statement. Of course Erol's name was on her account; but he had never used it, and he definitely would not have withdrawn money without telling her. "That can't be possible, Mr. Montgomery. Although my fiancé's name is on my account, he would not have taken any money out of it without telling me first."

Adam Montgomery glanced down at the document in his hand before meeting Sage's gaze again. "Would you recognize your fiancé's signature if you saw it?"

"Yes, of course."

Mr. Montgomery handed the document to her. Sage recognized the signature immediately. It was Erol's. But how . . . Why? She held her breath while a million questions raced through her head. For the longest time she didn't say anything. She just continued to study Erol's signature in near shock. Her concentration was broken when she heard Mr. Montgomery clear his throat.

"Evidently your fiancé forgot to mention this to you, Miss Dunbar," the older man offered as way of an excuse.

Sage nodded, accepting his words but knowing that wasn't possible. No one could have that much of a memory lapse. What she was seeing didn't make sense. Erol had his own checking account, and her name was on his account as well; but neither of them used the other's checking account. And then there was the savings account they had together. Although both their names were on the account, it was mainly hers. She had made a pretty hefty deposit into it last year with the life insurance money her grandmother had willed to her.

Sage frowned as an unpleasant thought began forming in her mind. "Mr. Montgomery, would you check the balance of my savings account as well? In my estimation, I should have over fifty thousand dollars in it."

He nodded, then quickly left his office again.

Sage's hand trembled as she reached into her purse for her cell phone. She had to talk to Erol immediately. There had to be a reason he took the money out of her account without talking to her first, or even telling her about it. According to Mr. Montgomery, the money had been removed from her account over two weeks ago. As far as she was concerned, he'd had plenty of time to tell her about it.

She breathed in heavily when the phone to Erol's office was answered by his secretary. "Hi, Joan, this is Sage. Is Erol in?"

"No, Ms. Dunbar, he had a meeting with a client, but he should be on his way back to the office. He indicated he would be working late tonight. You may want to try him on his cell phone."

"Thanks, I'll do that." She then tried reaching Erol on his cell phone but got his recording instead. Deciding not to leave a message, she had disconnected the call and placed her mobile phone back into her purse when Adam Montgomery returned. She could tell by the look on his face that he was not about to deliver good news.

"It seems, Miss Dunbar, that all but one hundred dollars was taken out of that account as well, on the same day, and again by Mr. Carlson, who is listed on your account."

Sage's blood immediately went cold. She didn't want to believe what Adam Montgomery was saying. It couldn't be true. There was no way Erol would have touched her money without first discussing it with her. There was no way.

"Are you sure?" she asked, in a voice that trembled so bad she could hear it.

Sad, apologetic eyes met hers. "Yes, Miss Dunbar, I'm sure. Here is the document for that transaction if you would like to see it."

Sage took the second document he handed her. She had to see it for herself. When she did, a part of her wanted to believe it was all a mistake and this couldn't be happening. She tried to think of some explanation, some excuse, but couldn't come up with anything. She took a deep breath, forcing herself not to panic, not to jump to conclusions. There had to be a logical, acceptable reason why Erol had done this, and she intended to find out just what it was.

She stood on shaky legs. "May I keep these papers?"

"Certainly, and if there's anything further we can do, please call and let me know."

Sage nodded and turned and walked out of the man's office, literally fuming. When the elevator door opened she rushed inside, quickly pushing the button on the console that would take her to the parking garage. She had to see Erol. He had a lot of explaining to do.

By the time Sage walked into Erol's office less than fifteen minutes later, she was boiling mad. After leaving the bank, the more she had thought about what Erol had done, the angrier she had gotten. Since it was past closing time, she had met his secretary on her way out.

Without wasting any time, she walked down the hallway to his office and immediately opened the door. He glanced up, both startled and surprised to see her. He stood and came around his desk. "Sage? What are you doing here? When did you get back in town?"

She inhaled deeply, again trying to find a logical explanation for what he had done. "I returned earlier than planned," she said as calmly as she could. "Didn't your secretary tell you that I had called?"

"Yes, but I assumed you had called from Alaska."

She clutched the straps of her purse that hung on her shoulder as she struggled for control. Before her stood the man she loved, the man she was planning to marry. Suddenly she was seeing him as a man who had taken over fifty thousand dollars out of her bank accounts without telling her.

"No, Erol, in fact I was calling from the bank. I went there when my bankcard was declined for a purchase and I couldn't understand why." Her heart broke with the expression that suddenly appeared on his face—one of guilt.

"Sage, I can explain," he said, taking a step toward her.

She automatically took a step back. "Can you? How can you explain taking fifty-two thousand dollars from my account without mentioning a word of it to me, Erol?"

He breathed in and said, "I was trying to find the perfect time to tell you. In fact, I had planned on telling you everything when you got back."

Sage became livid. "When I got back! What was wrong with telling me before you did it!"

"I knew you wouldn't go along with the reason I needed the money."

"Which was?"

For a long moment he didn't say anything; then he said, "An investment deal. Edwardo told me about this hot investment tip on this invention that could be worth billions of dollars, but you had to have at least sixty thousand dollars to get in."

Sage inhaled deeply, trying to keep her anger in check, but was failing miserably. Edwardo Anders was one of Erol's frat brothers who was an investment broker. "So you took every penny we had and invested it without talking to me about it first?" she asked incredulously. She couldn't believe this. She didn't want to believe this.

"Like I said, Sage, I knew you would be against it, and all I could think about was getting in on such a great technological opportunity and being like one of those individuals who had the foresight to invest in Microsoft on the ground floor. I figured that in the long run, I would make back at least a hundred times the amount of my initial investment."

"So you took it upon yourself to make a decision such as that for the both of us, Erol?" she asked angrily. "You had no right to do that. At least you should have given me the opportunity of saying no, and you didn't do that. For all you knew I may have gone along with it, although I doubt it. I trusted you, Erol. How could you have taken advantage of me that way?"

"But don't you see, Sage? I thought I was doing something that would ultimately benefit the both of us. Even Edwardo didn't know the investment wasn't on the up-and-up and—"

"Whoa, back up," Sage said, suddenly becoming angrier. "What do you mean the investment wasn't on the up-and-up? Are you standing there telling me that you lost every single penny you invested?" Sage tightened her hand on her purse straps as she felt the floor beneath her feet begin to shift. She knew the answer to her question before Erol's lips formulated a response. The look on his face said it all. He had lost all of their money. Every single penny of it.

"I'm sorry, Sage."

Her heart felt heavy in her chest. The words he had just spoken had been the same ones he had whispered to her after they had made love over a week and a half ago. Now she had an idea why he had apologized, but she still needed for him to confirm it.

"That night we made love and you apologized afterward . . . You were apologizing for this, weren't you? You were apologizing for losing all that money."

He hesitated only briefly before answering. "Yes."

Sage fought back the tears she felt forming in her eyes. The next morning she had asked him about it, giving him the perfect opportunity to come clean and tell her what he'd done, but he had chosen not to, leading her to believe things were all right. Instead, she had to find out this way.

She had put Erol's name on her bank accounts not thinking she could not trust him to do the right thing. She suddenly felt like a fool. Pain, the likes of which she had never felt before, went through her when she thought of the money her grand-mother had left her. Paula Dunbar had left all three of her granddaughters fifty thousand dollars. And now Sage felt that because she had been stupid and naive, her grandmother's gift of love was lost to her forever. How could Erol have done this to her? To them? How could he have hurt her this way by taking away something so special? For that alone she doubted that she could forgive him.

Tears blinded her as she took off her engagement ring. Crossing the room, she walked over and offered it to him. "I can't marry a man I can't trust, Erol."

He refused to take the ring. "No, baby, you don't mean that. I know you're upset, but that's no reason to give up what we have. I'll make it up to you, Sage, I swear I will. If I have to work day and night, I'll replace the money, every penny of it, you got to believe that."

Sage blinked back more tears. "Money can be replaced, Erol, but trust can't. There can't be a relationship or a marriage without trust, and you destroyed whatever trust I had in you by doing what you did."

Since he wouldn't take the ring from her, she placed it on his desk, then turned and walked out of his office.

After driving around for nearly an hour with no specific des-tination in mind, Sage pulled into a Wal-Mart parking lot and brought her car to a stop. She couldn't do anything but rest her face against the steering wheel as the tears continued to flow, still not believing what Erol had done. It was bad enough he had used the money in her savings, but then he'd also used money in her checking account, money that should have been used to pay bills. If he had needed sixty thousand dollars, that meant he had used eight thousand of his own money. It was ob-vious he had gotten so caught up in that investment deal he hadn't thought rationally. How had he planned for them to pay the bills for this month? They both had large car payments, not to mention the rent on the apartment which was no small amount.

She jumped when her mobile phone rang. Knowing it was probably Erol, she refused to answer it. There was nothing he could say to her now.

Sage sighed deeply when the phone stopped ringing. She had to pull herself together. Going to their apartment was out of the question, since that would be the first place he would look for her and try to talk her out of breaking their engagement.

As much as she wanted to, she didn't want to go to her parents' home either, as least not yet. She wasn't ready to tell them what Erol had done.

When the phone began ringing again, she ignored it. She needed someone to talk to and immediately thought of Rose. Turning the car's ignition, she pulled away from the parking space after deciding to go to Rose's place. Even if Erol called Rose looking for her, there was no doubt in her mind that after telling Rose what he'd done, she wouldn't tell him a thing.

Rose opened the door, took one look at her and asked with concern, "Sage, are you all right?"

Sage tried holding on to her smile. "May I come in, Rose?"

"Sure," Rose responded, stepping aside. "Sage, please tell me what's wrong."

Sage nodded. As she turned toward Rose's living room, she heard a noise coming from Rose's bedroom. It was then that she noted Rose was wearing a robe, and it was obvious she didn't have on anything underneath.

"Oh, Rose, I'm sorry, I shouldn't have come. You have company," she said, moving toward the door to leave.

Rose reached out and grabbed her arm. "Whoa, slow down. You aren't going anywhere. Besides, he was just leaving."

No sooner had Rose spoken those words, than a man walked out of the bedroom, buttoning up his shirt. Sage blinked, and her mouth nearly dropped open. It was Mr. Poole. He glanced up, surprised to see her as much as she was to see him. He was wearing the same clothes that she had last seen him in earlier, which meant he had come home with Rose straight from the airport.

Sage racked her brain trying to remember if she had noticed something going on between them while they were in Anchorage or on the flight back home, and for the life of her, she hadn't detected a thing.

"Ms. Dunbar," he greeted, after clearing his throat.

"Mr. Poole." Goodness, she thought, the man was their boss, yet he stood in Rose's living room with obvious signs of what he and Rose had been doing. What on earth could Rose have been thinking to sleep with him? But then, Sage decided, she had problems of her own to deal with and couldn't get involved with anyone else's.

"Are you all right, Ms. Dunbar? You seem upset about something."

Sage felt her cheeks heat up. From the way both Rose and Mr. Poole were staring at her, it was obvious they could tell she'd been crying. "Yes, I'm fine, but a personal matter has come up. Will it be possible for me to have tomorrow off?"

He nodded as he continued to look at her. "Yes, sure. And if you need more time, let me know."

"Thank you." Sage nibbled on her lower lip, suddenly feeling awkward when he walked over to Rose and whispered something in her ear. Whatever he said made Rose smile.

"I'll see you when you return to the office, Ms. Dunbar," he said, holding her gaze.

Sage nodded as she watched him open the door and walk out, closing it behind him.

Rose didn't waste any time crossing the room, grabbing her

hand and pulling her toward the kitchen where she pulled out
a chair from the table. "Now sit and tell me what the hell is
going on, Sage," she ordered, taking a chair across from her.

At first Sage couldn't say anything, but her hesitation lasted
for only a moment. She could feel fresh tears spring into her
eyes when she met Rose's gaze and said, "Erol took nearly every
cent I have from my bank accounts without telling me."

"How could he do such a thing!" Sage didn't think she had
ever seen Rose so mad. After telling her friend the entire story,
she had watched Rose silently get out of her chair and walk
over to the sink to make coffee. She had said nothing during
the process, but after setting a cup on the table in front of her,
Rose evidently had gathered her wits and had quite a lot to say.

"I just can't believe he would do that to you, Sage. What on
earth could he possibly have been thinking about?"

Sage had the answer to that one. "Getting rich quick," she
answered bitterly.

"Yes, but he should have talked it over with you first," Rose
responded, shaking her head. She reached out and touched
Sage's arm. "Are you sure you want to go so far as to call off the
wedding, though?"

Sage nodded slowly, decisively. "Yes. Erol had the perfect opportunity to tell me about it that morning, and he chose not to.
And the thought that he let me go to Alaska without sufficient
funds in my checking account tees me off. What if I had
needed money due to some sort of an emergency? But the really
bad part about it is that he used the money my grandmother
gave me. He knew how I got that money and what it was for.
Part of it was to pay for our wedding and was to be used as a
down payment on our first home. The rest of it was to be put in
trust for our children."

For the longest time neither of them said anything; then
Rose asked softly, "When are you going to tell your parents?"

Sage inhaled deeply. More than likely Erol had phoned her

parents looking for her, although she doubted he would tell them why. "Tomorrow. I can't handle the thought of telling them today."

Rose nodded. "And you don't have to. You're welcome to stay here tonight and for as long as you need a place to stay. I have an extra bedroom."

After taking a sip of coffee, Sage said, "Thanks, but since my luggage is still in the car, I'm going to stay at a hotel tonight. I need time alone to think things through and make some concrete decisions. Besides, I wouldn't want to cramp your style with Mr. Poole."

Sage could tell by the sudden glare that appeared in Rose's eyes that what she'd said had offended her. "Look, Sage, what I do with Mr. Poole is my business."

Sage nodded. "I know that, Rose, and I'm sorry for what I said. I just don't want you to make a mistake. That man has slept with other women in the office. Doesn't that mean anything to you?"

"Not since I made damn sure he had on a condom."

Sage raised her eyes to the ceiling. "It's not just the issue of unprotected sex, Rose. He's using you. You're just another one on his list."

"Yeah, and the flip side to that is that he's just another one on mine. He got what he wanted from me, and I got just what I wanted from him, and I must say everything I heard about him is true. That man sure can—"

"Rose!"

Rose stood and crossed her arms over her chest and glared. "What's wrong, Sage? Does it bother you to discover I'm not a nice girl? Umm, what's the term they use for women like me? Oh. ,yeah . . . promiscuous?"

"Rose, I—"

"No, you're the one who's the nice girl, yet you're the one sitting at my kitchen table crying because her trustworthy boyfriend generously screwed her over. So pardon me for not wanting to get taken in by a man I thought I could trust. I've been there twice before. Remember, I'm the woman who walked in on her fiancé making out with another woman in a bed I was paying for. So forgive me for knowing just how they operate and deciding to enjoy them with the same attitude and detachment that they enjoy me, rather than fall head over heels in love with one and suffer the hurt and pain like you're suffering now. So the way I see it, after what Erol did to you, you're the last person who should be judging my lifestyle."

Rose saw Sage flinch at her words and immediately regretted saying them. She sat back at the table and reached over and touched Sage's hand. "I'm sorry, Sage, I shouldn't have gone off like that."

Sage tried smiling through the tears that clouded her vision. "No, you're right, I was being judgmental, and I'm the last person in a position to be that way. Hell, I'm the fool because I'm the one who's financially ruined because I trusted the wrong man. Maybe you have the right idea about love, trust and commitment after all, Rose. If you can't trust the man you're supposed to marry, then who can you trust?"

Rose scooted over closer to Sage and tightened her hand in hers. "You're not a fool, Sage, and you're wrong about me having the right idea. Maybe it's the right idea for me but not for you. Regardless of what Erol did, you're a one-man woman, and you can't help but believe in love, trust and commitment. It's part of your makeup. You're hurting now, but you'll get over it because you know that not every man is like Erol. You have your father and uncles to compare other men to. I didn't have that. My mother was a single mother, and all I ever saw was a string of boyfriends who only took advantage of her. For a while I let myself follow in her footsteps, but I'll never do that again. I will never love any man blindly. What I shared with Mr. Poole today was a sex-only encounter based on physical needs. The only thing I wanted from him was pleasure, and he gave me what I wanted. There was no love, expectations or commitment involved. And it had nothing to do with any curiosity on my part with him being white, because I've slept with white guys before in college."

Sage nodded as she wiped at her tears. Rose was right, a sex-only relationship worked for some people, but it wouldn't work for her. Even now with all the pain she was feeling because of Erol, she had to believe that some men could be trusted. "I need to go," she said, standing on somewhat shaky legs.

"What hotel are you going to?"

"I'm not sure yet."

Rose also stood. "But you'll call me as soon as you get there and let me know you're okay, right?"

"Yes, I'll call you, and if Erol calls here looking for me, just tell him you haven't seen me, okay?"

"Okay." Rose reached out and gave Sage a hug. "Do you need any money to hold you over for a while?"

Sage shook her head. "No. I have a credit card I can use, although it was nice having it paid off for a while."

Rose then gave Sage another hug. "You'll get through this, Sage. Trust me when I tell you it's not the end of the world."

Sage nodded, thinking maybe it wasn't, but for her it certainly felt that way.

CHAPTER FIVE

Sage checked into the Sheraton Hotel, the one that was located in Kannapolis. The short drive from Charlotte did her good, and she preferred spending the night at a hotel that was in another town, needing to put distance between her and Erol.

She called Rose to let her know where she was. Rose mentioned that Erol had come by looking for her, and with a straight face and without blinking an eye, she had told him she hadn't seen or heard from Sage since they had parted at the airport earlier that day. When she'd casually asked him if anything was wrong, he'd simply responded no, but asked her that if Sage did come by, to have her call him immediately. Rose also added that he looked rather pitiful.

As soon as Sage had taken a shower and changed clothes, she went downstairs to the hotel restaurant for dinner. She hadn't eaten a thing since leaving Anchorage, and her stomach was making hunger sounds. Twice she'd been tempted to call her parents but had decided against it. She sat in a booth, eating her dinner alone, trying not to dwell on her problems, when she happened to glance around the restaurant, noticing the other people and wondering what stories they had to tell.

Were most of them travelers passing through, lovers or married couples wanting a few days alone to enjoy the solitude of seclusion the small town of Kannapolis offered, or were some like her, people who needed to get away for a night to deal with things complicating their lives?

She had picked up her cup of coffee to take a sip when she recognized the couple who had just walked in. At least she recognized the man who was with the attractive woman. She smiled, wondering what sort of business dinner meeting had brought her father all the way from Charlotte. She was about to get his attention when something stopped her. Maybe it was the way his arm was placed around his dinner partner's waist, or the way the woman was smiling up at him, that made things look more like an intimate liaison than a business affair.

Sage inhaled sharply, forcing her mind and thoughts not to go there. She briefly closed her eyes and tried to convince herself that she was exaggerating; her mind was playing tricks. This mistrust thing with Erol had her on edge, suspicious of anything and everything, and now she was looking at a purely innocent situation through all-accusing eyes. Her father was an honorable man who loved her mother. Their thirty-year marriage was solid proof of that. There was no way he would be doing something sleazy and unfaithful by being involved with another woman, even one as young and pretty as the one he was with. The woman appeared to be in her midthirties, and although Sage would be the first to admit that at fifty-four her father was a very good-looking man, there had to be a reasonable explanation why he was here with that woman.

As a corporate business person, he often had dinner meetings with clients. . . . But while she continued to watch the couple, another deep, unnerving sensation settled in her stomach as it became obvious as time ticked by that the two were very familiar with each other.

Sage continued to sip her coffee and watched them. From where she sat, they could not see her, but she definitely could see them. When it was time for her to leave, she would have to pass their table, so she decided she would stay put for a while and be observant. She hated the fact, the very idea, that at that moment for the first time in her life, her trust in her father was wavering. She just hoped and prayed that she was misreading the entire thing.

She shook her head to clear her mind. *Stop being silly,* her mind admonished. *That man sitting over there is your father, for heaven's sake. He loves your mother and would be the last man on earth to be unfaithful. Get up and cross the room and speak to him. It will be perfectly all right for you to let him know you're here. But then you'll have to explain to him why you're spending the night here and not at home with Erol, and you aren't ready to do that; so chill and stay put. Enjoy some more coffee. And go ahead and order that slice of cheesecake you're dying to have. Then soon enough you'll see that Satan has been busy today, and now he's filling your mind with unrealistic thoughts because of what Erol did. You can't become distrustful of everyone because of him. Open your eyes and see that there is nothing going on between your father and that woman. Don't read anything into it that really isn't there.*

Satisfied she had gotten her mind straightened out, she caught the waiter's attention and asked for more coffee and that slice of cheesecake. She even became daring and requested that he squirt some whipped cream on top.

Sage forced her thoughts away from her father and his dinner companion to Rose and Mr. Poole. She wondered if things were really as Rose claimed—a sex-only thing—or would Rose become involved with their boss on a more emotional basis. From what Sage could see, his past history indicated he never stayed with the same woman for long. She wondered if that would be the case with Rose. It certainly didn't seem that Rose would lose any sleep over it if it was. She wished Rose would have shown interest in Parnell Cabot. He had seemed like such a nice person, a man who would treat a woman right.

As she took another sip of her coffee, her thoughts went to

Parnell Cabot's boss, Gabriel Blackwell. The man was as charming as he was handsome, but sometimes the charming, handsome men were the ones you had to watch out for. Hadn't Erol proven that?

Seeing that an attempt to get her mind off her father wasn't working, she glanced over in their direction and wished she hadn't. She took in a quick breath. Her father was holding the woman's hand.

Sage's nostrils flared in anger. She was seconds away from losing it, big time. She began shaking so badly, she had to set her coffee cup down. She watched as they stood to leave at the same time the waiter was returning with her cheesecake.

"I've changed my mind about the cheesecake, but charge it to my hotel bill anyway," she said to the waiter, who was looking at her in surprise as she stood. A part of her had to know that her father and the woman were leaving. Then maybe, no matter how damaging things had looked, the woman was a client who had tried coming on to him, and he had played along with her.

Deciding to keep a safe distance from the pair, Sage went into the gift shop that afforded a good view of the hotel's lobby. She watched, almost suspended in shock, as her father and the woman stepped into the elevator when it opened.

That doesn't mean a thing, her mind tried to tell her. *He's just being a gentleman and seeing the woman to her room. Didn't Gabe Blackwell do that very same thing with you in Anchorage? And it was all perfectly innocent with you and him, so why can't it be that way for your father and her?*

Sage paused, wanting to believe what her mind was saying. Leaving the gift shop, she walked to the lobby and sat on the leather sofa where she could see her father when he left the hotel.

Picking up a magazine, Sage began flipping through it. An hour had passed before she finally admitted to herself that her father wasn't coming back down any time soon.

*   *   *

With tears blinding her, Sage managed to make it back to her room with the realization that in the same day, the two men she had trusted most had let her down.

She had sat downstairs in the lobby on the sofa for three, close to four, solid hours, refusing to move. She had to be there when her father came down on the elevator; she had all intentions of confronting him. But when he did come down, and the woman was with him, Sage couldn't do anything but sit there and stare, her body numb and glued to the spot, as she watched them leave the hotel together, smiling at each other and holding hands, not even noticing her presence.

And that was when the tears she had fought so hard to hold back had come flooding down. How could he do this to her mother? Was he willing to throw away thirty years for a pretty face and a young body?

Moving in slow motion, a grief-stricken Sage put on her pajamas. She then sat on the edge of the bed and checked the calls she had missed on her cell phone, not surprised to see that all of them but one had been from Erol. She automatically deleted Erol's messages, not wanting to hear his voice, and retrieved her mother's message. The call had been made nearly two hours ago, during the same time Sage had been sitting in the lobby downstairs.

"Sage, I didn't know you had returned to town until Erol called earlier looking for you. He sounded worried. Is everything all right, sweetheart? Your father is working late again tonight, so I'll be visiting Mrs. Myers at the hospital. I'll have my mobile phone on if you need to reach me."

Sage swallowed the lump in her throat, thinking that no, everything was not all right with her, and she doubted things would ever be again. Not wanting to watch anything on television, she removed the remote from the bed and placed it on the nightstand. Something about her felt different, detached, lost.

The first thought that came to her mind was that her mother—her trusting and loving mother—had a right to know that her husband was not always working late as he claimed. She deserved to know that on some of those nights—this one in particular—he'd been laid up in a hotel room with a woman.

Sage blinked back more tears. Whoever said that when it rained it poured knew exactly what they were talking about. And for the first time her heart was beating so heavy in her chest she thought she would die. Betrayal from people you loved was nothing short of a deep, crushing blow, and tonight she was feeling the full effect. Erol and her father had definitely opened her eyes to things she had been blinded to for so long. Rose was right. A man could not be trusted, and Sage had learned that hard lesson all in one day.

CHAPTER SIX

The next morning when Sage stepped out of the elevator into the ornate lobby of the hotel, she felt that she had a somewhat better grip on things. She paused briefly, inhaling deeply, determined to face whatever problems she had head-on and deal with them as best she could.

There was nothing more she had to say to Erol, and since there was no way she could live with him any longer, she planned to move out. The big question was, where would she go? Under normal circumstances, to move back in with her parents for a while would be the most logical choice. But after what she had seen last night involving her father, being logical didn't play into anything anymore. The way she presently felt, the less time she spent around him, the better. She was too confused and hurt to think otherwise.

One thing was for certain, though: she intended to confront him about last night. There was no way she could not. She wanted him to tell her what he planned to do about her mother. She felt her mother had a right to know her husband was being unfaithful, and a sense of mother-daughter loyalty dictated that she be the one to tell her if her father did not. What woman wouldn't want to know that she was being made a fool of?

The first thing Sage wanted to do was to go to the apartment and pack her things, grateful that Mr. Poole had given her the day off. She had made a decision to remain at the hotel an additional night or two until she decided where she would go. She was tempted to take Rose up on her offer to stay with her until she got straight, although doing so would hurt her parents if she moved any other place than home. In her frame of mind, she really didn't care how her father felt about it. Her main concern was her mother's feelings.

A half hour later Sage frowned when she pulled into her apartment complex and noticed Erol's car, which meant that he had not left for work yet. Inhaling deeply, she brought her car to a stop. There was nothing she had to say to him. She wouldn't talk to him. She wouldn't even acknowledge his presence.

She had barely placed her key in the door when it was snatched open.

"Sage! Where the hell have you been! I've been worried sick!"

Sage's forehead wrinkled for a second, immediately recalling that she *had* broken up with Erol yesterday, so what was his problem? After what he'd done, she didn't owe him an explanation about anything, especially her whereabouts.

She met his gaze with a glare of her own, ignoring the fact that he looked as if he hadn't slept all night. As far as she was concerned, he had made his bed, so he could very well lie in it, even sleepless.

"I came to pick up some of my things," she said frostily, moving around him to enter the apartment. She passed through the living room and headed straight to their bedroom. He followed close behind, right on her heels.

"Sage, we need to talk about this."

"There's nothing to talk about, Erol," she threw over her shoulder and kept walking.

"Don't you think you're taking this to the extreme? I borrowed money from my folks to pay our bills for this month. And they said I didn't have to pay them back until we were back on our feet."

Sage turned so quickly she almost collided with him. "You wouldn't have to pay them at all if you hadn't done what you did," she said sharply. "You just don't get it, do you? It's trust you can't replace, Erol. I'd like to see you borrow that from your parents."

His lips tightened in a grim, straight line, and he folded his arms over his chest. "And you're willing to throw five years away just because I screwed up this one time?"

"Yes. All it takes is one big screwup. In this situation, it's not what you did, but it's how you did it. You knew how I would feel about it and did it anyway, without any consideration for my feelings. That tells me that you didn't give a damn about how I felt. You thought only about what you wanted, your own selfish greed."

His expression was regretful. "Okay, I was wrong, and I admit it. I should have told you when I had the chance."

"Yes, you should have." She then turned away and continued walking. When she got to the bedroom, she closed the door behind her.

She would be fine, Sage kept telling herself as she continued to pack, using the extra luggage she had. She was thankful that Erol hadn't come into the room and had left her alone. Like she had told him, there was nothing to discuss.

She had talked to Rose before she had begun packing. Rose had again assured her that she could stay with her for a while and that she would leave work and meet Sage at her apartment at lunch to help move her stuff in.

When Sage left the bedroom, pulling her luggage behind her, out of the corner of her eye she saw Erol sitting on the sofa in the living room as she passed through. She couldn't believe that he was glaring at her, actually pissed off that she had broken off their engagement and was moving out. When she reached the door to open it, she glanced over her shoulder at him. "I'll be back sometime later today with some boxes to get the rest of my things."

With nothing else to say, she left.

Sage had barely made it up the walkway to her parents' home when her mother opened the door with a worried look on her face.

"What's going on, Sage? Why didn't you sleep at your apartment last night?"

Sage lifted an arched brow. "And how did you know that I didn't?"

"Because Erol called again this morning looking for you. Your father and I have been worried sick. He was so worried he couldn't go into the office this morning."

Yeah, I bet that's the lie he told you as to why he couldn't go in, Sage thought, giving her mom a hug, while fuming on the inside at the thought of her father's duplicity. "I'm fine, Mom. Where's Dad?"

"He's upstairs taking a shower. He worked later than usual last night, and when I told him that you and Erol had had some sort of a tiff and you were missing, of course he became concerned."

"I wasn't missing, Mom. I merely spent the night at a hotel," she replied, following her mother into the house and closing the door behind them.

Her mother took her hand and met her gaze. "Are things that bad between you and Erol, Sage?"

Sage thought she may as well get it out. "Yes, Mom, in fact, I broke our engagement."

She wasn't surprised by her mother's sharp intake of breath. "What on earth did he do?"

Sage threw her purse down on the couch. "He took money out of my bank account without discussing it with me first."

Delores Dunbar shook her head, smiling warmly. "Sweetheart, your father takes money out of our account all the time. Just last week he took out a hundred dollars to buy something he saw advertised on television. A woman learns to grin and bear that sort of thing, and make sure extra money—namely his—is consistently put into the account."

Sage dropped down on the sofa. "We're not talking about a hundred dollars, Mom. We're talking about over fifty-two thousand dollars."

"Fifty-two thousand dollars!"

Sage glanced at the shocked look on her mother's face. "Yes, and that includes the money Gramma left for me," she said, fighting back tears. Each time she thought about it, she got upset.

Delores immediately joined her daughter on the sofa and hugged her. "Oh, honey, I'm sorry about that. What could Erol have been thinking?"

"Evidently not about me," Sage said angrily.

Her mother shook her head sadly. "Why would he need fifty-two thousand dollars?"

Sage wiped her eyes. "For what he thought was a sure-fire investment which turned out to be a hoax. He lost every penny he invested, of which almost ninety percent belonged to me. And what hurts so bad is the fact he didn't discuss it with me beforehand. He said he knew I would be against it and decided to go ahead and do it anyway."

Delores nodded. "I'm sure he thought he would get back more in return for his investment."

"Yeah, but that's not the point. The point is that I can't trust him anymore. He didn't consider my feelings. He knew how much I loved my grandmother and that the money in my savings account was her gift to me. How could he do such a thing?"

"Oh, honey. Sometimes men can be insensitive, but that doesn't make them totally awful people."

Sage leaned back and lifted a surprised brow. "And you think I should not have broken up with him?"

"I think the two of you should make an attempt to work things out, Sage. You both have too much time invested in your relationship not to."

Sage frowned. "There's nothing to work out, Mom. I trusted him, and he betrayed my trust. It's as simple as that."

Delores shook her head sadly. "Nothing about a relationship is simple, Sage. You have to be willing to work at it, iron out the kinks and flaws, and accept the fact that no one is perfect. Everyone makes mistakes."

Sage wondered if her mother would be singing that same song if she knew her husband had spent over three hours in a hotel room with some woman last night while she thought he was working late. "I never expected Erol to be perfect, Mom, but I did expect him to be trustworthy. Trust is important to me."

"And it should be. All I'm saying is that when two people love each other, and I mean really love each other, they need to try and work things out before calling it quits, which makes me wonder."

Sage arched a dark brow. "About what?"

"Just how much you *do* love Erol. Look how long it took you to agree to marry him. Even your father mentioned that you seemed to be dragging your feet in planning your wedding."

Sage's gaze locked with her mother's, not believing what she was hearing. "How could you wonder such a thing? Erol and I have been together a long time. I wouldn't have stayed with him if I didn't love him. And as far as me taking a long time to agree to marry him, I didn't see the need to rush into a marriage like he did."

"And you didn't think a long-term commitment, a marriage vow, was important?"

Sage sighed deeply. How could she tell her mother that she always had thought so . . . until last night? A marriage vow hadn't kept her father from sleeping with another woman. "Yes,

Mom, I think it's important. I just thought what Erol and I had didn't necessarily need a piece of paper to be solid."

"Long marriages run in our family, Sage."

"Yes, I know that. All I'm saying is that I agreed to marry Erol when I felt I was ready."

Her mother didn't say anything for the longest time, and then she asked, "And now, Sage?"

"And now the only thing I'm ready to do is to get on with my life—alone—without him." Sage heard movement behind her and knew her father was coming down the stairs.

"I'm sure your father has a lot to say to you, young lady."

Sage nodded and smiled tenderly at her mother, and tried to hide the hurt, anger and disappointment in her voice when she said, "Yes, I'm sure he does."

And I have a lot to say to him as well, she thought. She felt her throat close tight and could feel the stinging of tears in her eyes as she braced herself to come face-to-face with him.

CHAPTER SEVEN

At a time when she needed her parents more than any-thing, Sage didn't want to feel such animosity toward her father. But when she stood and met his gaze, she felt nothing but profound anger and disappointment.

Evidently, something in the way she was looking at him stopped him short when he descended the last stair. "Sage? Are you all right, sweetheart?" he asked slowly as his gaze raked over her.

"Yes, I'm fine." She knew her tone was just this side of curt, but that couldn't be helped. She'd already dealt with Erol, and now she had to deal with her father.

"Your mother and I have been worried," he said, coming into the room to stand in front of her and next to her mother.

Sage wanted so much to fling herself into his arms like she'd always done when she'd been hurt and upset about something, or just plain needed a hug. But not this time.

"Do you want to tell me and your mother what's going on with you and Erol?"

Sage sighed deeply. She didn't want to tell him anything, and at the moment she felt that given her present state of mind, being here wasn't helping at all.

"Sage?"

She sighed again, more irritably this time. "I've already told Mom, but just so you'll know, I discovered Erol is not as trustworthy as I thought," she said, letting her anger get the better of her. "I came back to town to discover he had cleaned out both my checking and my saving accounts of over fifty thousand dollars, and that amount included the money Gramma Dunbar left for me."

Charles Dunbar blinked as total disbelief covered his face. "Are you sure?"

Yes, I'm as sure of what he did as much as I'm sure of what you did, she wanted to scream, but instead she said, "Yes. I went to the bank yesterday and saw the documents he signed to get the money out. He even confessed to doing it."

"But for what reason?"

She was silent for a minute; then she answered, "For an investment scheme that went bad which means we lost every penny."

Her father shook his head sadly. "I admit Erol acted irresponsibly, but then, that's how it is with investments. You can make money and you can lose money."

Sage's heart pounded painfully in her chest. "Yes, but it wasn't his money to lose. He had no right investing my money into anything without talking to me about it first."

"Sage." She heard her father let out a deep sigh. "His name was on your bank account, wasn't it?"

Sage frowned, and her lips pursed. "Yes."

"Then, that means that technically, it was his money as well."

Sage felt stunned at the attitude her father was taking. "But it wasn't his to use without discussing things with me first, no matter what. If he does something like this now, I'd hate to think what he'd do once we're married. There is such a thing as trust in a relationship, Dad. One that's not only implied but also practiced. After being married over thirty years, I'd think you would know that."

"Sage!" her mother admonished. "No matter what's going on between you and Erol, you have no reason to speak to your father that way."

Sage closed her eyes, breathing deeply and thinking that she had plenty of reason. When she reopened her eyes, she met her father's gaze. He had tilted his head to one side and was studying her thoughtfully. She wondered briefly if her comment had him thinking as to why she would say such a thing to him.

Suddenly she felt mentally drained as well as emotionally abused, and she had no intention of apologizing. Deciding it was best if she left, she grabbed her purse off the sofa. When she met her parents' gaze, she tried smiling but knew she was failing miserably. "Look, I'm not in the best of moods right now, so I'll come back later."

"But where are you going?" her mother asked with deep concern etched on her face.

"Back to the hotel," she said, glancing at her watch and deciding not to tell them just yet of her decision to move in with Rose instead of moving back home.

"But why, Sage?" her mother asked softly. "Why sleep at a hotel tonight when you know you can move back here until you get things together?"

Sage sighed. She knew that to her mother "getting things together" was the same thing as her taking time to work out her problems with Erol. She shook her head. That would never happen, and in time her mother would realize that.

She reached out and lovingly touched her mother's arm. "The hotel is where I want to be for a while, Mom, to sort through some things, alone. Don't worry, I'll be fine."

"But—"

Sage reached out and hugged her mother fiercely. "I'll be fine, Mom," she repeated softly.

Quickly releasing her mother and refusing to meet her father's gaze, or even give him the hug that would have been so automatic, she headed for the door. She had made it down to the walkway and almost to her car when she heard her father calling after her, but she ignored him.

He caught up with her just when she was about to reach out and open her car door. Grabbing her upper arm, he turned her around to face him. A sheen of tears all but covered her vision, but she lifted her chin and met his gaze. His hold on her arm gentled when he saw she was crying.

"Oh, baby, don't cry. Everything is going to be all right."

When he tried pulling her into his arms, she abruptly pulled back, needing his affection and tenderness but refusing to take it. He was wrong; nothing would ever be all right again. "Save the loving kindness for your *woman*, Dad," she snapped.

She heard his sharp intake of breath and watched surprise flash in his eyes, something he quickly masked. "What are you saying?" he asked quietly, dropping his hands to his sides and taking a step back.

A pounding need to hurt him the way he had hurt her, the way he was hurting her mother, tore into Sage. "What I mean," she said, closing the space between them and speaking low just in case her mother was at the window looking and listening, "is that I know. I know about *her*. I saw the two of you together last night, Dad. You sought seclusion in Kannapolis, and so did I. Unfortunately, it was at the same hotel."

There was a long pause. Then he said, "Sage . . ."

"No," she said, holding up her hand and cutting off whatever he was about to say. "There's nothing you can say. What I saw last night pretty much said it all. Just like Erol, you're nothing but a fraud."

Charles Dunbar blanched, stiffened his spine and lifted his chin. "Need I remind you that I'm your father, young lady," he said in a stern voice.

Sage felt blood rush to her head and exhaled a deep, angry breath. "And need I remind you that you're also Delores Dunbar's husband, which is something you seem to have conveniently forgotten about last night."

Without giving him a chance to say anything else, Sage went to her car and got in and turned on the ignition. As she pulled out of the driveway, she struggled to get her breathing to normalize. Her gaze darted back to her father. He was standing in the same spot with a look of total shame on his face.

"And you're sure that I won't be putting you out?" Sage asked Rose as she followed her down the hallway carrying another box.

Rose looked over her shoulder at her and frowned. "Didn't we have this same conversation yesterday?"

Sage smiled weakly. "Yes, but I was making sure you hadn't changed your mind."

Rose grinned. "I haven't changed my mind, but I have ordered new springs for my bed so the next time Mr. Poole comes over the noise won't disturb you."

Sage raised her eyes to the ceiling and returned her friend's grin. "You aren't going to let me forget that, are you?"

Rose shook her head. "No time soon and it serves you right. But you don't have to worry about Mr. Poole anymore. He announced to everyone today that he's leaving."

Sage nearly dropped the box she was holding. "He's leaving?"

Rose laughed at her reaction. "Yes, he's leaving Charlotte but not the Denmark Group. He got this big promotion at the corporate office in California and will be leaving in a few weeks."

Sage nodded as she set the box down on the bed. Mr. Poole, even with his philandering ways, had been a good boss. Glancing over at Rose and seeing the satisfied smirk on her face, Sage could only assume that Rose felt the same way and probably had an entirely different definition of the word *good* when it came to Mr. Poole. "I hate to admit it, but I'm going to miss him."

"Umm, so am I," Rose said, smiling broadly and daring her to comment.

Sage had learned her lesson and had nothing to say on that subject, but did ask, "Was it also announced who would be taking his place?"

Rose shrugged. "No, but I figured it will be someone who can keep his pants zipped. Although Mr. Poole got a promotion out of this, I think transferring him to the corporate office was a way to keep him in line."

Sage thought what Rose said was probably true. "I'll be staying at the hotel again for the next two nights," she suddenly thought to remind Rose.

Rose nodded. "Did your parents lay a guilt trip on you for breaking your engagement to Erol?"

Sage shook her head. "No, not exactly, but although they admitted he acted irresponsibly, it's obvious that they feel it's something we can work out. However, I assured them it's not." She sighed, having no desire to go there with her parents, and Erol's parents had been just as bad. They had called her earlier at the apartment when she'd gone back to get some more of her things. She was glad Erol hadn't been there that time, but a part of her had resented him for getting his parents involved. And she knew they had spoken to her parents as well.

Sage couldn't understand why everyone felt she should forgive and forget. Evidently no one they'd ever trusted had wiped them clean of over fifty thousand dollars.

"So, what do you plan to do for dinner," Rose asked, breaking into her thoughts.

Sage remembered what she'd discovered yesterday while dining at the hotel restaurant and quickly decided she didn't want to eat there again tonight. "Why? What do you have in mind?"

Rose smiled. "I thought that maybe the two of us could go somewhere and enjoy a really nice meal."

Sage nodded and agreed. "That sounds nice, and I'd really like that."

"Sage?"

Sage turned before stepping onto the elevator that would take her up to her hotel room. She watched as her father crossed the lobby to her. She hadn't seen him when she had entered the hotel, and coincidentally, he had been sitting on the same sofa she had occupied for over three hours the night before.

"Dad, what are you doing here?" she asked when he came to stand in front of her. She tried not to notice just how tired and worn out he looked. She quickly dismissed the tired and worn look for one of profound guilt that was eating away at him.

"I think we need to talk."

Sage shook her head. If he really thought that, then he had another thought coming. There was nothing they had to say to each other, especially not now. Her pain was still too raw. "Dad, I don't want to talk to you right now. I—"

"Please, Sage, I need you to hear what I have to say."

She sighed. She didn't want to hear what he had to say. She knew he had cheated on her mother, and that said enough.

"Just a few minutes of your time, Sage. I do believe I deserve that," he added before she could say anything.

Sage swallowed and was reminded of the times he had been there for her, even when she had been wrong—like that night she had sneaked into the house way past midnight when she'd been sixteen years old. He had been the one who'd caught her climbing into her bedroom window. To this day her mother still didn't know about that incident. It had been Sage and her father's secret. But she quickly reminded herself that this was a totally different situation. A teenager sneaking into a house past midnight was nothing compared to a married man breaking his marriage vows and sneaking around and sleeping with a woman. Yet, for some reason, Sage couldn't trust her voice to speak, to turn down what he was requesting. So instead, she nodded. "All right. I was about to go up to my room."

They traveled in the elevator up to the eighth floor in silence. Sage figured they would save the talking until they were safely behind closed doors. When she reached her hotel room door and unlocked it, she pushed it open, resigning herself to whatever lay ahead. She wondered if any other woman in the world had ever gone through what she was experiencing simultaneously with her fiancé and her father. It was real tough when the two men you loved the most had fallen off that pedestal you had placed them on.

She tossed her purse on the bed when she heard him close the door behind them. She turned around. "I would offer you something to drink, but all I have right now is bottled water." She kicked off her shoes. "But please have a seat or you're more than welcome to look around and check out the place, although I'm sure it's probably similar to the room you and your lady friend enjoyed last night," she couldn't help but lash out.

Ignoring the hurt look on his face, she continued. "But then, I guess the hotel room's décor isn't what the two of you were really interested in, was it?"

Charles Dunbar's gaze dipped to the floor. Seconds later, he raised his head and met his daughter's eyes. "None of that is necessary, Sage. I already feel worse than you can ever imagine."

Sage pushed her hair back from her face. "Oh, I don't know, Dad, you've known me long enough to know my imagination can get pretty wild at times. That's why I'm in the business that I'm in. I just love coming up with creative ideas."

She sat on the bed. "And last night my mind was working overtime as I sat on that very same couch you were sitting on in the lobby tonight as I waited for you to come down so you could assure me what I thought I saw was all a misunderstanding. But after you were up there for over three hours, I figured that you and your companion had very little to say. In fact, I'm surprised the two of you could actually even walk straight."

Charles Dunbar took a sharp breath, then slowly walked across the room to stand in front of the only window in the room. He turned and faced his daughter's stormy expression. "I think you've said enough, Sage," he said tightly. After inhaling deeply, he then said, "Just so you'll know, that was our first time together," he said softly. "It was something that happened, but I assure you it won't happen again."

Sage blinked. Then the frown on her face deepened. "It won't happen again? It should never have happened in the first place."

"But it did, and I feel awful about it," he said in a voice that was even softer than before.

Sage actually flinched at his words. "Well, you should, since you broke your wedding vows to spend one night in a sleazy affair."

Charles Dunbar looked away for a few seconds, and when he looked back at Sage, the piece of her heart she had closed shut to him almost fell back open. She knew that this conversation, her hostile attitude, was defeating him, draining him of the dignity he always possessed, and was actually breaking him down. He had hurt her deeply and was no longer a hero in her eyes; he knew it and regretted it. And she could tell it was literally eating him up inside.

But at that very moment, she didn't care. A part of her refused to ease his pain and humiliation. There was another person she had to think about. "What about Mom?"

He snatched his head up and met her gaze. "What about your mother?"

"Are you going to tell her what you did?"

She watched her father sadly shake his head. "There's no need. During my thirty years of marriage, I was unfaithful to her only this one time. The woman and I had been working late." He met her gaze and implored her to believe him. "Neither of us meant for this to happen. It just did."

Sage held her breath as a dozen or so questions popped into her head, and she quickly asked the first one. "Is she married, too?"

"No, she's divorced."

"But she knew you were married?"

Her father hesitated briefly before answering. "Yes."

The slut, Sage immediately thought. That was what she thought of any woman who willingly became involved with a married man. For the life of her she couldn't understand why any woman would want to be the *other woman.*

"I disagree with you that there's no need for Mom to know. I think she has every right to know you've been unfaithful to her."

She watched her father release a long, slow breath before saying, "Not telling your mother is my decision to make, Sage, and not yours."

Sage pulled back. His words had been like a slap to her face. "It's not just your decision. I saw you. I know about it. Keeping it from Mom makes me feel disloyal."

"You shouldn't feel that way since it doesn't concern you. This is between me and your mother, and I should be the one to tell her about it."

"When will you tell her?" From across the room she could feel her father's tension.

"I'll tell her one day."

Sage shook her head angrily. "One day! When she's too old to care! There is something called AIDS, and I care about my mother's health if you don't."

She was taken aback by the furious expression that suddenly appeared on her father's face. "Do you think I'd place your mother at a risk such as that! I took the necessary precautions! I love your mother!"

Sage laughed. It was more in anger than humor. "You love

Mom? Then, it's a good thing I decided not to get married if committing adultery is the way a married man shows his love for his wife. Taking money out of my bank accounts without me knowing it was bad enough. I would hate to think that after we'd been married thirty years, the next best thing to expect was for Erol to engage in an affair . . . out of his love for me."

"Sage, you don't understand . . ."

"Yeah, Dad, you're right, I don't understand and doubt I ever will."

For the longest time there was total silence in the room. Then Charles Dunbar spoke. "Will you let me be the one to tell your mother at what I feel is an appropriate time?" His voice was so soft it was barely a whisper.

She sighed, not wanting to deal with anything any longer. A part of her wished she could leave Charlotte for a while. In fact, maybe it was a good idea if she did. The Denmark Corporation had several offices across the country, and maybe it wouldn't be a bad idea for her to check in to the possibility of transferring to one of them.

"Yes, Dad," she finally answered, in just as soft a voice as his. "I'll let you be the one to tell her . . . unless I witness something like it again. Then I'll be the one to tell her, no matter what."

Charles Dunbar nodded quietly before crossing the room. Before opening the door, he turned to his daughter. "I know I've hurt you deeply and have let you down, and for that I'm truly sorry," he said in a broken voice.

Tears slid down Sage's cheeks as she gazed into her father's crumpled and tormented face. "Yes, I'm sorry for that, too, Dad."

He shook his head. "I just hope and pray to God that one day you will find it in your heart to forgive me and let me redeem myself in your sight. You are my daughter, and I love you very much."

Without saying anything else, he stepped out into the hall-way and gently closed the door behind him.

* * *

The next day Sage returned to work. She was reviewing the document she had just completed, a *Request for Transfer* form. The three locations she had chosen were Florida, Texas and Alaska. Mr. Poole had informed her that morning that due to their exclusive contract with Landmark Industries and the future projects he had planned for Anchorage, a decision had been made to open an office in Anchorage. Although Sage much preferred relocating to Florida or Texas, at the moment she would be grateful for any of the three.

She looked up, surprised, when her secretary walked in carrying a huge vase containing a dozen red roses.

"These are for you, Ms. Dunbar," the older woman said, placing them on her desk.

Sage thanked her, knowing word would probably get around the office about the flowers. A number of people were curious as to why she was no longer wearing her engagement ring. She'd been surprised that anyone would even notice, which went to show just how observant some people were.

She took in a deep breath and let it out slowly. The flowers were from Erol, and the card read,

> *I hope you'll soon realize that you and I were meant to be together and find it in your heart to forgive me for what I did.*
> *Love Always,*
> *Erol*

Sage stood and walked over to the window, carrying the card with her. She reread it a second time, then closed her eyes, briefly wondering if she would ever be able to find it in her heart to forgive Erol. She also thought of her father. Would she ever find it in her heart to forgive him as well for what he'd done to her mother? For what he'd done to their special father-daughter relationship? And now what about her feelings toward men in general after the two most important men in her life had violated her trust this way? She would definitely find it difficult to let another man get close to her again.

Walking back to her desk, she glanced down at the transfer papers she had completed. She swallowed as she tried to calm her tormented heart. At the moment, she felt incapable of putting the past behind her and moving on . . . at least not here in Charlotte.

She had thought things through and had prayed about it. She needed to leave town, and whatever place Denmark sent her, she would make the best of it.

Having made her decision, she placed the card aside.

PART TWO

I am radiant in joy because of your mercy,
for you have listened to my troubles and
have seen the crisis in my soul.

—Psalms 31:7

CHAPTER EIGHT

Anchorage, Alaska
Four months later

The storm that had threatened to erupt all day finally broke, sending sheets of ice particles pounding down on everything in its path.

Gabe Blackwell stood by the window and watched the turbulent downpour, glad he had returned from his five-day fishing trip to the Kenai River before the torrential rain had broken free.

Moving away from the window, he crossed the room to the fireplace, thankful for the heat it generated. Sitting down on the sofa, he held a mug of the hot chocolate he had prepared earlier, laced with brandy to ward off the January chill. He took a sip and glanced around the house he had purchased a month earlier.

It had been a business decision for the company to buy the huge multilevel log cabin–style house instead of leasing it for the year he would be spending the majority of his time in Anchorage. He had fallen in love with the place as soon as the Realtor had shown him around. It was just what he'd wanted, something large, roomy and secluded. Another added plus was that it sat on fifteen acres of land, most of which was wooded, and had a panoramic view of several canyons and snow-capped mountains as well as a beautiful, huge stocked lake.

The inside of the house was an architect's dream, its unique design well worth the investment, although he had to admit that the forty-two-hundred-square-foot structure was more house than what he needed. During his first visit to Anchorage, he had made the decision not to live downtown in a condo but to escape civilization and enjoy the rustic beauty the rural area provided.

Setting his mug down on the table, he rubbed his chin that was covered with a day's growth of beard and couldn't help but smile. His mother would have a hissy fit to see him looking so unkempt. But he was enjoying the final week before construction of the ski resort began. A shave tomorrow would be soon enough.

The telephone rang, and he immediately decided to let the answering machine catch it. He wasn't ready to discuss business with anyone, and if it was a family member, he would immediately call them back. He just wanted to kick back and relax awhile and enjoy the peace and quiet.

He leaned back to rest his head against the back of the sofa when he heard the feminine voice that came across his answering machine:

"Mr. Blackwell, this is Sage Dunbar, marketing manager for the Denmark Group. We met four months ago while attending a Landmark Industries business meeting here in Anchorage. I don't know if you remember me. . . ."

Gabe lifted his head as immediate recognition hit. He definitely remembered the attractive, ultraconfident and very sexy woman. And one of the main things that stood out in his mind was the fact that she was engaged to be married . . . this coming June if he wasn't mistaken.

"As you are undoubtedly aware, the Denmark Group has opened an office here in Anchorage, and I'll be working as the manager of that of-

fice. I'm looking forward to getting with you to create the marketing scheme needed for the ski resort, which has officially been named Eden. Please give me a call so we can schedule a time the two of us can get together, hopefully this week. I can be reached at the Denmark office here in town. The number is . . ."

Gabe lifted a dark brow as he leaned forward. John Landmark had mentioned something to him about the marketing firm opening an office in Anchorage just to accommodate his needs. But at the time Gabe had thought it would be highly unlikely that Sage Dunbar would be involved in that venture since she was engaged to be married in a few months. She had mentioned that her fiancé owned a landscaping business in Charlotte, and Gabe couldn't see the man relocating that sort of business to Anchorage for Sage's career move. Did that mean she would be managing the office in Anchorage only on a temporary basis, and not for the full year that her services would be needed?

Gabe settled back in his seat as a number of questions went through his mind. All of them would be answered tomorrow when he returned Sage Dunbar's call.

Out of habit, Sage double checked the locks on all her doors before going into the bedroom to undress. She smiled. No matter how horrid the weather was outside, she intended to have a pamper-yourself night. She had already arranged the lit candles around the bathroom, and their flickering flames as well as their strong vanilla scent were transforming her condo into a working woman's haven. There was nothing like taking a hot bubble bath in a room illuminated with soft candlelight and drenched with the fragrance of her favorite flavor to ease her weary, torn mind and rest her tired, aching body.

Her first week at Denmark's Alaskan office had gone well. She had an excellent staff that was dedicated to Landmark Industries' needs. The first thing on her agenda had been to come up with a name for the resort, and earlier today John

Landmark had embraced the one her team submitted, Eden, with open arms. Everything about the resort, down to the very minute details, would be nothing short of paradise. The architectural design of the resort was breathtaking and would put any ski resort presently in operation to shame. Even the cable ski lifts were state-of-the-art. There would even be a few private rooms, larger than the normal size and equipped with an elegant king-size air mattress and a compact bathroom for those individuals whose romantic fantasy included being suspended high in the sky in a cozy setting with snow-capped mountains surrounding them.

Sage's smile widened. She was glad she had been the one selected to head up this office and appreciated Mr. Poole recommending her for the job before he'd left. If it had been left up to the man who the company had transferred in as Mr. Poole's replacement, she would never have gotten the recommendation. Larry Bakersfield had, in just the short time he had arrived at the Charlotte office, proved to be a male chauvinist of the worst kind. Sage hated that Rose was still in Charlotte working for the man and knew her friend was constantly completing transfer papers to be relocated elsewhere.

The four months Sage had remained in Charlotte after her breakup with Erol had been pure hell. She had caught it from both her family as well as his. Everyone thought she had taken things to the extreme by calling off their engagement. Only a few of her family members understood. Luckily for her, Cinnamon and Ginger had given their full support and understood her decision. Her parents, although they claimed they were remaining neutral, still let it be known that they thought her problem with Erol was something the two of them could work out.

The holidays had been the most difficult for her since her and her father's relationship was still strained, and more than once her mother had questioned her as to why. Then it had been hard not to be weakened by the flowers Erol would constantly send or by his invitations to join him for dinner. However, she had held to her resolve and consistently prayed to God that her relocation request with Denmark would come through.

For weeks after their breakup, she had felt totally alone and would be the first to admit she missed their friendship as well as the intimate part of their relationship. A soft sigh trembled from her as she was reminded that Erol was the first and only guy she had slept with.

As far as Sage was concerned, her move to Alaska had come at a good time, and since she had gotten a promotion out of it, that made things even better.

Neither of her parents had taken her decision to relocate to Alaska well, although she had assured them it would be a good career move. They, as did Erol, thought she was moving to get away from him, which was only partly true. She'd also needed to put distance between her and her father as well. He still had not told her mother about his affair, and each time the three of them were together, Sage found herself feeling like a willing party to his deceit.

In the bathroom, she began filling the tub with water while doing her daily stretch exercises. When she thought the amount of water in the huge bathtub was enough, she turned off the lights in her apartment with a special remote control she had purchased, stepped into the tub and sank down.

She closed her eyes as a picture of Eden came to mind, just how she pictured it would look when everything was completed. An hour or so later after toweling dry and slipping into her nightgown, she heard the phone ring. Thinking it was probably her mother or Rose, she quickly crossed her bedroom to pick up the phone on the nightstand next to her bed.

"Hello?"

"Sage Dunbar?"

Sage raised a brow, trying to place the deep, masculine voice and found that she couldn't. "Yes, this is Sage."

"This is Gabe Blackwell. I'm returning your call."

Gabe finished his drink and glanced around the bar. He had frequented the place several times with business associates from Landmark Industries and found the one thing he liked about the Garden Club was its classiness. On top of that, the restaurant served the best salmon dishes in the world, prepared by the finest chefs and served just about any way you liked. When Sage Dunbar had inquired about a place the two of them could meet and discuss business, this place had quickly come to mind.

He still wasn't sure what had driven him to call her at home last night. She had left only her business number on the answering machine, and even then he'd had no intention of contacting her before the next morning. But after hearing her voice, something had compelled him to call her. Instead of reaching her at the office, he had gotten her secretary, who had readily offered him her home number. After thinking about it, he'd decided since she had felt comfortable calling him at home, he would do likewise with her. Their conversation had been brief and very businesslike, with them ending the call less than five minutes after making dinner plans.

He glanced down at his watch. He'd arrived a good thirty minutes early, coming straight from the office. He and Parnell had met in an afternoon-long meeting to make sure they had all the necessary building permits in their possession. Eden would be the most beautiful ski resort to grace the face of the earth, and he was glad that the Regency Corporation had a major part in making it possible.

He was just about to raise his hand to the bartender for a refill when his attention, like every other man's sitting at the bar, was drawn to the woman entering the establishment. He felt a coiling heat, a deep burning sensation, flow from the base of his foot all the way to the crown of his head as his gaze took a leisurely sweep of her. Sage Dunbar was just as beautiful as he remembered. He hadn't realized until that very second that somehow he had committed to memory everything about her, and now it was all coming back to him, with vivid clarity.

He watched as she removed her overcoat and handed it to Rico, the maitre d'. She then whispered something to him, a question perhaps. Rico looked his way and pointed Gabe out to her. When she saw him she smiled—one as radiant and unpretentious as before—and began walking toward him. He stood, determined to meet her halfway while once again seeing the graceful sway of her hips which automatically worked in synergy with the supple movement of her body.

As she got closer, he almost missed a step when he noticed something about her, something he found different. Although she was smiling, and it was a smile that played at the corners of her mouth, emphasizing soft, full lips, the look in her eyes wasn't the same. That certain sparkle that had pulled him in, drawn him to her like a moth to a flame, was gone. And as she got closer, his gaze instinctively went to her hands.

Her engagement ring was also gone.

CHAPTER NINE

"So, Gabe, what do you think?"

Gabe studied Sage for a few moments. He doubted if she really wanted an answer to that question, although he knew she was asking what he thought of the marketing proposal she'd just presented for Eden and not what he thought of her.

"I think," he said, mesmerized by the dark whiskey coloring of her eyes that still captivated him even without their sparkle, "that Denmark knew just what they were doing by sending you here to handle things."

The radiant gleam in her expressive eyes told him that his comment had pleased her. But then there was another look in her eyes, one that disappeared as quickly as it had appeared. It was a look that had indicated she wasn't sure she could completely trust what he'd said.

"Thanks," she said softly. "But my job is easy since I'm selling Eden as nothing short of paradise, which I know it will be. You and your work crew are the ones putting everything together. Every time I take a look at that miniature model of Eden that I have on display in my office, I'm spellbound. I can't wait to see the finished product."

Gabe chuckled as he took another sip of his wine. "Just don't tell Parnell that. We're committed to finishing up in a year's time, weather permitting. Alaska isn't known for its kind weather, especially during the winter months, and January and February are the worst. But we're determined to put as many man-hours into the project as we have to, even twenty-four/ seven, in order to get the job done."

Sage nodded as she placed her fork on her plate and leaned back. The place Gabe had chosen for their dinner meeting was exquisite. Its décor was ornately elegant in a rustic sort of way, from the towering arched windows that displayed snow-capped mountains in the background, to the wrought-iron oil lanterns that hung on several of the walls. The furnishings came from a period in European history that was fit for a king, and a sheath of rich silk flowed from one corner of the room to the other, giving a startling effect to the fire that was blazing in the huge fireplace that sat in the center of the room.

"I met some of the members of your construction team this week and was surprised to discover some of them brought their families with them," Sage said, meeting Gabe's gaze.

He grinned. "Yes. Although it was their decision to make, Chris and I recommended that they do that."

Sage arched a brow. "Why?"

"Because the majority of the men are married and between the ages of twenty-five and forty. A year is a long time for them to be away from the women they love." Gabe's smile widened. "Statistics have shown that you can get more work out of a happy, satisfied man."

He gently rubbed his smooth-shaven chin as he gazed thoughtfully at her. "I guess the same would hold true for a woman."

She met his gaze before taking a sip of her wine. "I wouldn't know."

An invisible red flag suddenly went up in Gabe's mind when he saw the despairing look that appeared in her eyes. Although the subject hadn't come up, he had a feeling the reason she wasn't wearing her engagement ring had nothing to do with the size of it no longer being a fit. Evidently, there had been, or presently was, trouble in paradise. He decided not to play games and to just go ahead and cross the boundaries of what was considered proper by asking the question that had been on his mind all evening.

"And your fiancé?" he inquired quietly, watching the play of emotions that lit into her face—hurt and pain, another telltale sign which caused another red flag to go up.

Several long moments passed before she responded. "I'm no longer engaged."

"I'm sorry," he said, with all sincerity, thinking he was really damn sorry and was thinking that for whatever the reason, and without even knowing the details of what happened, her fiancé was a fool for losing her.

Sage shrugged lightly, remembering what Erol had done and how she was still trying to recover financially. "Don't be sorry."

He smiled. "All right. Then, I won't."

She smiled back and went one step further when her mouth tipped up into a dignified chuckle. "Are you always this agreeable?"

He raised his chin and looked at her, suddenly thinking that yes, with her he could always be this agreeable. Another red flag went up. "No, not always. I guess tonight it's the mood."

She tilted her head and raised a brow inquiringly. "And what mood is that?"

"The mood to not disagree."

Sage laughed then, actually laughed, and realized just how long it had been since she'd done that. "Thanks," she said, her amusement subsiding.

Gabe arched a brow, knowing what she meant but deciding to pretend not to. "For dinner?"

She smiled. "Yes, that, too. But mainly for making me laugh. I'm surprised that I still know how to."

He lifted a brow. "It's been that long?"

She took a slow sip of wine before saying, "Yes, nearly four months."

Gabe nodded. Whatever had happened between her and her fiancé had taken place not long after he'd last seen her. And whatever had happened had left a look of distrust and sadness in her eyes. "Well, I'm just going to have to make it my business to see that you have a reason to laugh more."

She looked away, and he could feel her backing off, slowly easing some distance between them. "Don't bother because it's easier said than done."

A part of Gabe began questioning his sanity. The signs were all there; the red flags had gone up, all three of them. For whatever reason, the confident, self-assured woman he'd met four months ago now had problems, issues, was on the rebound. She was the last type of woman he needed to be interested in.

At the first sign, the raising of the first red flag, he should have brought the evening to a close, an end, zilch. Yet he was still sitting at a table in an exclusive restaurant, across from a very beautiful woman who had excess baggage, namely an ex-fiancé who had probably done her wrong, and even worse, an ex-fiancé she probably still cared deeply for. Hell, he'd been there and done that and for the longest time had endured a broken heart as a reminder. A woman on the rebound was known to straddle the fence, not knowing which way her heart would go, and more times than not was nothing but trouble. He'd made a vow to steer clear of women whose hearts had been led astray and were having problems finding their way back. He didn't have time to play Dear Abby. So why in heaven's name was he still meekly sitting there? He should be halfway home by now. Good grief!

And on that thought he spoke up, surprising himself by meeting her gaze, giving her a quick grin and saying, "I'm Gabriel; an angel, remember. There's no job too difficult for an angel."

Before giving her time to respond, he stood. "I think we'd better leave before the weather gets worse. Come on, I'll walk you to your car."

An hour or so later Gabe entered his home. A long, deep breath rushed through his lungs from the intense cold weather outside. He'd endured cold days and nights in Detroit, but nothing compared to this.

He shifted his gaze around the room, appreciating the warmth and comfort it brought, and grateful still for the return of his sanity. Sage Dunbar was beautiful enough, alluring enough and way too desirable. She could make even the strongest man lose his resolve, forget any vows he'd made and even lose his common sense.

But he intended to hang on to his.

Quickly crossing the room, he picked up the phone and began dialing. If his problem was a result of the fact that he needed a woman, then he would offer a remedy to that, real quick like and in a hurry.

He smiled when he heard the sound of the soft, sleepy feminine voice. He'd forgotten about the four-hour time difference and had evidently awakened her. "Debbie? Hi, this is Gabe. I'm flying home this weekend and would very much like to see you."

CHAPTER TEN

Sage took a deep breath at the same time adrenaline pumped fast and furious through her veins. She studied the miniature layout of Eden that was displayed on the huge table in front of her. This was the part of her job that she enjoyed most, when everything started pulling together in anticipation of the final product. However, in this case, there would be no finality. Eden would grow and prosper for many years to come. John Landmark had ingeniously mastered not just a plan, but a concept that would rival even the likes of Vail, Colorado.

Over the past four weeks, she had visited a number of ski resorts including Vail, which was known as the largest one in America and was frequented by just as many Europeans as Americans. It would be Eden's strongest competitor. While there she had studied everything she could about it. To properly market Eden as the snow skier's paradise, she had to know just what it was about Vail that kept people coming back.

"So what do you think?" she finally asked Malcolm Grainger, the thirty-four-year-old man who was an instrumental part of her marketing team. Transferred in from Denmark's West Coast office in California, he had a strong background in marketing research and had accompanied her to Vail. Since returning, the two of them had worked diligently in putting together the first phase of Eden's marketing campaign.

A smile played around the corners of Malcolm's mouth. "I think you have the right idea, and John Landmark had it, too. It's evident by the way he has situated the buildings around the resort. Like Vail, he wants anyone coming to Eden to have all the shops, restaurants and nightlife they could possibly want within a short walking distance of their hotel or condo."

Sage nodded. That was the one thing she had liked most about Vail, its accessibility. Once they had parked and unloaded their rental car, they hadn't needed to use it again until it was time for them to leave. She wanted the same ease of convenience for Eden and intended to do whatever had to be done to bring in a number of upscale restaurants, lodgings and trendy shops. Already the likes of Armani Steak House, the Ritz Carlton Hotel and several well-known, upscale clothing stores had committed their presence. She was also working on a marketing plan to attract a number of nightclubs and casinos. People may like to ski in the daylight, but later they would want to enjoy the excitement of nightlife. "Can you imagine how much more marketable Eden would be if we included a state-of-the-art dinner theater, one that showed live plays as well as motion pictures?"

Malcolm pushed his glasses higher on the bridge of his nose. "Yes, I can actually visualize just what you have in mind, but to pull that off means restructuring this entire area and making it larger," he said, pointing to the scale model of Eden on the table. "We already have the space if we knock down this wall and combine these two buildings, which shouldn't be much of a problem due to their close proximity. An architect will have to redesign the interior to include a stage and vaulted ceiling."

Sage lifted an anxious brow. "But it can be done?"

Malcolm chuckled. "Yes, and I'm sure the architect would jump at the chance to do it since it would mean additional money in his pocket. But even if you convince John Landmark of the feasibility of your idea, you still have to tread lightly with the guy whose company is building the resort. His crew is working under tight time restraints, and he won't like it if he has to do anything major that will take more time. And what you're thinking about doing is pretty major."

Malcolm paused and lifted a glance at her. "But I can tell by that look in your eye that you feel it's worth a shot."

Sage nodded, smiling, as she picked up her clipboard. "Yes, I do, Malcolm. Not everyone who'll come to Eden will want to frequent the nightclubs or the casinos. I think that including the theater will add a touch of class and elegance."

"I won't present an argument there," Malcolm said, looking at his watch. "Sorry, but I got to run. I'm picking Leanne up from the airport."

A smile curved the corners of Sage's lips. Leanne was Malcolm's wife of ten years and was still living in California. She planned to join him in Anchorage at the beginning of the summer when the school year ended for their eight-year-old son.

Malcolm was a good-looking man, and it didn't go unnoticed that several women in surrounding offices intentionally flirted with him, some bolder than others. But Sage had never witnessed a time that he flirted back, or took the women up on their offers. It was good to know that some men still honored the wedding vows they made.

"Okay, but drive carefully, Malcolm. The snow is pretty deep on the roadways."

Malcolm nodded as he slipped into his coat. "Yeah, and you do likewise. And when you get home, you might want to think of how you'll get Gabe Blackwell to agree to go along with your idea to reconstruct that northwest building. It won't be easy."

Sage thought about the last time that she had seen Gabe, when they'd met at the Garden Club for a business dinner. That had been nearly a month ago. She knew he resided in Anchorage the majority of the time, but for some reason their paths had not crossed since that night. "I think that once I present my idea to him, he'll agree it would be worth the trouble. I really don't think I'll have any problem bringing him around to my way of thinking."

Malcolm nodded, then said with a jesting smile as he headed for the door, "I was in a business meeting with Blackwell one day when the firm that's handling the landscaping threw a few unexpected things his way, and I witnessed his reaction; so all I have to say to you is good luck."

Later that night after taking a shower and changing into her nightclothes, Sage stood in front of the fireplace and gazed thoughtfully into the roaring flames. It was snowing outside, and according to the weather reports it would snow all day tomorrow. She had a meeting with John Landmark first thing in the morning to present her most recent marketing idea to him, and come hail, high water or snow, she intended to make that meeting.

She was just about to reach for the poker to turn a burning log over in the fireplace when the telephone rang. Crossing the room, she quickly picked the receiver up. "Hello."

"Do you have any words of encouragement for a stressed-out friend?"

Sage arched her brow. Rose sounded so pitiful. "I told you last week if things continue to be uncomfortable at work, to file a complaint with the corporate office. Maybe then they will consider giving you a transfer, especially if they don't want to lose you. With your experience and excellent work record, you can get a job with just about any advertising firm in the nation, so don't let that jerk, Mr. Bakersfield, stress you out."

"I wasn't letting him stress me out, but today was a different story, Sage," Rose said softly. "Things really got to me today. I even went into the ladies' room and nearly cried my eyes out after the announcement was made that Mike Faraday would be getting promoted to advertising director, the job that I rightly deserve."

"What! Mike Faraday! Lazy Mike Faraday, who never lifts a finger to do anything? How could Bakersfield do such a thing!"

"Easily, since Faraday is a man. Although everyone is reluctant to breathe the words, we all know Mike's promotion is a clear case of sex discrimination. Mr. Poole had him on probation for his job performance just last year! Mike's promotion was the last straw."

Sage nodded. "What do you plan to do?"

Rose chuckled. "I've already done it. I turned in my resignation."

Sage blinked, surprised. Rose had worked for the company more than six years. "You did?"

"Yes, and I feel damn good about it. And before I could get home, the phone was ringing. Word had already reached the Martins Advertising Agency, and they were calling to offer me a job."

"Are you going to take it?"

"I'm not sure. It was just last year they were talking about layoffs. I told them I would get back in touch. I've decided not to rush into anything and to just take things easy for a while and not make any decisions about my future just yet. I have enough money saved to tide me over for a few months. I really would like to move to Florida, preferably Orlando or Miami. I'm sick and tired of cold weather."

Sage laughed. "Then, you'll never make it out here. It's been snowing for a week. And it doesn't just snow ice particles; it snows sheets of ice."

"You're kidding."

"No, I'm not. In fact, why not come and see for yourself. You'll have some free time on your hands since you're no longer with the elite employed," Sage said, smiling. "And you know you have a place to stay when you get here. So what's keeping you from catching a plane and coming here?"

"The cold."

"Hey, stop being a wimp and get your butt on a plane and fly on out."

"I'll think about it. And by the way, I saw your parents today."

Sage sat down in a wing chair. She usually talked to her mother at least twice a week but had spoken to her father only once or twice since she'd left Charlotte five months ago. He had called her a few days after she had gotten to Anchorage to make sure she was all right and had told her if she needed anything, to give him a call at any time, day or night. She had deliberately kept the conversation short and knew he had probably picked up on that fact. "Where were they?"

"Attending the annual jazz festival, and as usual they looked good together. Your parents are one of the few older couples I know who still seem to care so deeply for each other. They were even holding hands, which I found so touching. I always thought your mom was a special woman because it's clear to everyone how much your father loves and adores her."

Sage's mouth curved faintly as the image of her father and that other woman came into focus. If only Rose knew the real deal. Sage, too, had always thought her father simply loved and adored her mother. But that was before she'd found out about what he'd done behind her mother's back.

Deciding that she didn't want to talk about her parents anymore, Sage said, "So will you promise that you'll at least think about coming out for a visit?"

"Oh, all right. I promise that I'll at least think about it."

Not wanting to be too obvious, Sage watched through the window as Gabe Blackwell angled his way up the sidewalk toward the restaurant. She had to hand it to the man; he certainly looked good. In fact, he'd always been the epitome of male-model material each and every time she saw him. Because she'd been engaged to Erol when she and Gabe had first met, she hadn't allowed herself to think such thoughts, but now she did, even if it was with a "look but don't touch" policy. She couldn't imagine it being anything else beyond that.

He was tall and had broad shoulders and trim hips—a really nice physique. He was definitely the kind of guy single women would check out. His whole persona made a statement that he was a man who was successful in his own right. The expensive suit he was wearing definitely alluded to that fact, as well as the way he walked—as though he was sure of himself and his abilities.

Sage sighed when a depressing thought entered her mind. Erol had possessed that same air about him. But then, a part of her knew that in order to be a successful black businessman, you *had* to be sure of yourself if you wanted to hold your own and be competitive in a society that already had placed one strike against you.

A part of her couldn't help but wonder if Gabe Blackwell was the type of man who could be trusted. Not just in the business arena but on a more personal level. Could a woman place her trust in him and believe he would do the right thing by her in all areas of their relationship? Her nightly prayer to God continued to be to not let her view all men through distrustful eyes. She didn't want to become a person who was insecure and suspicious of any man who got close, business or otherwise. She still found it hard not to be that way.

Deciding to focus on business matters, Sage thought about her and Gabe's impromptu luncheon meeting and wondered how receptive he would be to her idea about adding the dinner theater. She was sure Mr. Landmark had already briefed him on it since the older man had been impressed with what she had presented. In fact, he had been so impressed that he had called one of his junior executives into his office to take a look at it.

The man had also thought her idea had merit. But he'd also been critical of the Denmark Group for not having thought of it *before* the architectural plans had been finalized. He didn't like the thought of having to make such a major change at this late stage of the game and felt that Gabe Blackwell would feel the same way. He did, however, go on to state that there was a provision in their contract with the Regency Corporation that allowed for building changes not resulting in undue hardship for the construction team. As CEO of the Regency Corporation, Blackwell would be the one to determine just what would be considered an undue hardship. So in essence, the decision rested with Gabe, although it would be in his company's best interest to be flexible to Mr. Landmark's wants if the Regency Corporation wanted to be considered for future projects.

A part of Sage regretted having to place Gabe in such a position—between a rock and a hard place—but her job as marketing manager was to do whatever she could to make Eden the number one ski resort in the country, and she felt that adding the theater would certainly help with her marketing strategy.

She met Gabe's gaze when he entered the restaurant, and by his frown she could tell John Lancaster had spoken with him and he wasn't a happy camper. But she was determined to be undaunted by his disposition. They were business associates whose only concern and whose sole connection was the success of Eden. She was sure she could convince him that her proposal was well worth the trouble.

Sage tried not to focus so directly on Gabe as he made his way to her table. But to avert her gaze and look either to the right or the left, or even out the window, would be useless. Whether she liked it or not, for some reason a part of her couldn't ignore Gabe Blackwell's presence even if she wanted to.

At that thought, she continued to hold his gaze, and for the first time in five years, she felt attracted to someone other than Erol. And as Gabe drew closer, she felt her heartbeat stutter slightly . . . no, more than slightly. She inhaled deeply when a warm feeling flooded her insides. And with that feeling came one of discomfort in the knowledge that she was attracted to another man less than six months after her breakup with Erol.

Okay, she admitted, there may be a driving force behind what she was feeling, considering the fact Gabe was good to look at, and she had already concluded that there was no harm in looking. She reached out for her glass of water when her throat suddenly felt dry, admitting that Gabe Blackwell had definitely grabbed her attention and she couldn't take it back.

Keep your mind on the issue at hand, Blackwell.

Gabe's mind was giving him that order over and over again. He had to remember why he was here and why he was not on his way to the job site as he'd originally planned. The phone call he'd received earlier from John Landmark had been more than enough to change his plans. It seemed that Sage Dunbar had come up with a marketing idea that had the older man excited. Gabe appreciated excitement like everyone else . . . until it involved doing something he saw no need to do. Of all the other things Eden had going for it, adding some expensive dinner theater wouldn't make or break the place. Besides, the people who would come to Eden would come first to ski and then to be entertained. So why not approach one of the restaurants about expanding their facilities to include such a theater. Instead of taking that approach, Sage Dunbar had come up with a proposal that called for actions that would require more time to complete and could delay the finished product by at least another four to six weeks. There were other projects lined up elsewhere for his men, although he admitted that none was as beneficial to the Regency Corporation's bankroll. John Landmark had put out a lot of money to be kept happy. So the way Gabe saw it, if Landmark wanted the damn theater, he would get it. But Gabe certainly wasn't happy about it and had a few choice words to say to the woman who had decided to suggest the changes in the first place. Her company had literally dropped the ball. What she was suggesting should have been part of the original marketing proposal presented in the very beginning before the architect had completed designing the resort.

Another issue he had with Ms. Dunbar was the fact that he found her so damn beautiful, even sitting at the table dressed in a conservative dark brown business suit. For the past four weeks he had tried getting her off his mind—even going to the extent of flying home to Detroit to bed another woman. But that hadn't worked. He had spent the weekend in bed with Debbie thinking about Sage, and that hadn't been good. Sleeping with one woman while his mind had been filled with fantasies of another was something that had never happened to him before. Unfortunately, Debbie had picked up on the fact that his concentration level wasn't where it should be. To be fair to Debbie, he had suggested that they stop seeing each other for a while since he would be spending the majority of his time in Anchorage anyway. Debbie had agreed since she was the type of woman who wanted all of a man's attention in bed and not just some of it.

So here he was, fighting an attraction for a woman that he didn't want to become involved with. He wouldn't balk at the opportunity to get to know her better if he was certain that she wasn't on the rebound.

Yet he couldn't stop the pounding in the center of his chest when he reached her table. He had thought of her often—although he hadn't wanted to. But she would not get next to him, he assured himself. They were associates who worked together and nothing more. The only time they had spent together had been for strictly business reasons. And no matter how much he wanted her, that would be the way things stayed.

"Sage."

"Gabe. How are you?"

He shrugged, taking the chair across from her. "That depends on you. I understand you met with John Landmark this morning and suggested an idea that may cause a delay in the completion of Eden."

Sage swallowed. Gabe hadn't wasted any time and had gone directly into the reason for their meeting. For that she should have been grateful and not feeling an unexplainable loss. "Yes," she said, trying to put a level of excitement into her voice, although she definitely sensed his displeasure. "Did he tell you about it?"

Gabe nodded, not taking his gaze off hers. "Yes, he told me about the dinner theater."

She smiled wryly, hoping some of her seemingly good mood would rub off on him. "So, what do you think?"

"I think your company dropped the ball, and now they've picked a hell of a fine time to decide that this is what Eden needs. Something like that should have been discussed in the planning stages and not after my men have laid the foundation to begin work."

Sage nodded, knowing he was partly right. The individuals who had been part of the Denmark marketing team to submit the original proposal hadn't necessarily dropped the ball by not coming up with the idea of the dinner theater, but they had lacked the vision she had for Eden. As a way to put her troubles behind her, she had immediately become enmeshed in the project as soon as she'd been selected to come to Anchorage. The key was to not make Eden comparable to the other resorts she had visited, but to make it better. There were many other ideas she and her team had come up with, but the one involving the theater was the only one that entailed major structural changes.

"Does it matter at this point, Gabe? I think the most important thing is to do whatever it will take to make Eden the ski resort all of us want it to be. I'm not willing to settle for second best. I want the best. And I think that you do, too. I've visited other ski resorts and seen some of the things they lack. Those are the things I want for Eden."

Sage stopped talking when a waiter came up to see if Gabe wanted something to drink. He declined anything. When the waiter walked off, Gabe leaned back in his chair. "That's all well and good, Sage, but did you give any consideration to my work crew?"

Sage lifted a brow bemusedly. "Your work crew?"

"Yes. What your company is proposing will result in my men staying in Anchorage longer than scheduled, possibly four to six weeks longer. Some, but not all, brought their families with them. What about those that didn't? They are as anxious to get back to their loved ones as the next person . . . except maybe for you."

Sage flinched. "What are you trying to say?" she asked in quiet anger, knowing she'd been a target and his words a direct hit.

Gabe leaned in close so only she could hear his words. "I don't know what happened between you and your fiancé, and frankly, I don't give a damn, since chances are the two of you will eventually kiss and make up. But I do care that you are using your move to Anchorage to give the guy a chance to miss you and straighten up and fly right. My men didn't come to Anchorage to escape their problems. They have a job to do, and they also have people they're eager to return home to. I personally don't appreciate you not considering them with your whim to make your fiancé suffer by deliberately finding ways to extend your stay in Anchorage."

Sage struggled to fight back the tears that weighed heavily in the back of her eyes. How dare he say such things to her. How dare he question her work ethics! "You think you have me and my situation all figured out, don't you? Well, you're so totally wrong about the situation involving my ex-fiancé and me, especially the notion of us getting back together, that it's pathetic.

It's also none of your business." She stood after throwing enough money on the table to cover the cost of the two cups of coffee she'd consumed.

"But then, I should have expected something like this from you. After all, you're a man. As far as I'm concerned this meeting is over." With that, she picked up her purse and walked out of the restaurant.

CHAPTER ELEVEN

Gabe rested his head against the seat of his car with his gaze fixed on the building across the street, the one the Denmark Group was leasing. For the first time in two weeks it had not snowed. There was a brisk coldness in the air, but the sky was clear.

He sighed deeply, knowing he owed Sage an apology. A big apology. He never should have said those things to her and had to make amends for his unprofessional behavior. His attitude had been the worst it had ever been, and he knew for him the issue wasn't just about the theater. The plain yet not so simple fact was that he was attracted to her—although he didn't want to be—and that had been one of the reasons for his grumpy mood. And to make matters worse, after he had thought more rationally about what she'd been proposing, he agreed that adding that dinner theater would be a good idea.

He'd also thought about the harsh words she had spoken about expecting a certain behavior from him because he was a man. Her fiancé must have really done a number on her for her to have such an attitude.

He was about to open the car door and walk across the street to her office when his cell phone rang. "Hello."

"Gabe, I got your message to call. What's up?"

Gabe's lips curled into a smile as he settled back into his seat upon hearing Christopher's voice. "Nothing much, but I just wanted to apprise you of a possible change in the layout of a few of the buildings for Eden."

"All right."

As briefly as he could, he told Christopher of the changes the Denmark Group suggested regarding the theater.

"Sounds like a good idea," Christopher said seriously. "I always thought the Landmark Project had more potential than what the original marketing team had come up with. Their ideas were good, but I had expected better, especially with all the money John Landmark is putting into the resort. He doesn't want it comparable to the other ski resorts; he wants it better. And as far as our work crew goes, they won't have to start the next project for thirty days after completing this one, so they'll be okay." A few moments later he asked, "Who is the person that came up with the idea for the dinner theater?"

Gabe heaved a gut-deep sigh. "Someone the Denmark Group sent as the marketing manager, a woman by the name of Sage Dunbar."

"Oh, yes, Sage Dunbar?"

Gabe raised a brow. "You remember her?"

Christopher chuckled. "Yes, from that meeting almost six months ago. And I also remember that you couldn't keep your eyes off of her. She was quite a looker."

Gabe frowned and blew out a frustrated stream of breath. He was actually feeling jealous. "Need I remind you that you're a married man?"

"No, and trust me, there's no way I'll forget my marital status. Maxi is all the woman I'll ever need and want." He chuckled. "And all the woman that I can possibly handle. I can't imagine my life without her. I was mainly asking about this Sage character for you."

"For me?"

"Yes. You may as well know that Ma Joella has elicited my help in finding you a wife."

Gabe's mouth twitched in amusement. "Thanks for the warning."

"You're welcome. And just so you'll know, she wants Maxi to introduce you to her cousin Fannie Mae from Blakely, Georgia. She's twenty-eight, been married twice and has four children."

Gabe cringed. "Tell Maxi not to bother."

Christopher's laughter echoed through the phone before he said, "I did."

"Can't say that I'm surprised by Blackwell's attitude," Malcolm said, tucking papers into his briefcase, ready to call it a day like the rest of the team had done earlier. Sage had just told him what he felt was an abbreviated version of what had happened at lunch. He knew she wasn't telling him everything that was said, but decided not to dwell on it since he was sure she had her reasons.

"Well, I can't accept it," Sage said in an irritated voice. "I would never do anything that would deliberately keep his men from returning to their families."

"Well, deliberate or not, you will be keeping them from going home when they anticipated, and I guess Blackwell, being the considerate, compassionate and trustworthy employer that he is, felt he had a right to speak out about it."

Sage lifted a brow. "And what makes you think he's a considerate, compassionate and trustworthy employer?"

Malcolm shrugged. "Just repeating what I've heard. His men like and respect him. They also trust that he and Chandler will make the right decisions about anything involving them."

"Well, I don't like being accused of being devious for my personal gain."

Malcolm nodded. "Don't lose any sleep over it. And with that last bit of advice, I'm out of here. Leanne and I have made plans to go out for dinner since the weather is nice for a change. There's no telling how it might be tomorrow. Don't hang around here too late. And try not to take Blackwell's attitude personally. It's all about business." He picked up his briefcase and said, "I'll see you in the morning."

"All right. I plan to leave as soon as I finish coming up with some more ideas for this brochure. Drive carefully."

After Malcolm had left, she thought about his suggestion of not taking Gabe's words personally. The thing about it was she had. She hadn't told Malcolm everything he'd said, especially his reference to Erol. It bothered her that Gabe would question her motives, and to tie Erol to it was unthinkable. He had crossed the boundaries of business etiquette when he'd attacked her personal life. In essence, he didn't trust her to be fair in her dealings with his company, and for a person who put a lot of stock in an individual's trustworthiness, the mere fact that he questioned hers didn't sit too well.

A few moments later Sage was studying the design of a brochure she was working on for Eden when she heard the door open and close. Thinking it was Malcolm returning, she didn't bother looking up. "Back already? Did you forget something?"

"No, I didn't forget to bring my manners this time."

Sage snatched her head up at the sound of the deep, masculine voice. Her eyes met those of Gabe Blackwell and visibly bristled when she remembered all the things he had said to her earlier that day. "What are you doing here, Gabe?"

"I came by to apologize for my behavior at lunch. I was completely out of line."

Sage was surprised by his apology. "You had no right to say those things," she said curtly, remembering his words.

"Yes, you're right. But when it comes to my men, I tend to get somewhat protective. I know the sacrifices a lot of them made coming here, and I want to make sure they spend as little time away from their families as possible. But I do think that what you're proposing is a good idea, and I would like to take a closer look at it to see how much time we'll have to extend our stay here if any."

Sage lifted a brow. Why was he being so cooperative all of a sudden? A part of her also wondered if she could trust his motives. What if he had gone to John Landmark asking that she be replaced? She sighed deeply, knowing that she had to stop questioning and dissecting everything. She was beginning to let her personal hang-ups flow into the business aspect of her life, and that wasn't healthy. Nor did it make good business sense to be one of those people who brought their personal problems to work. It was in her best interest to try and get along with Gabe Blackwell on a business level. She didn't have to deal with him at all on a personal one.

"Could you at least explain to me why you questioned my work ethics and my trustworthiness as one of your business associates?" she asked.

He met the glare in her eyes. "Maybe for the same reason that you distrusted me because I'm a man, Sage. I think the best thing for us to do is to put aside whatever hang-ups and differences we have. And the only excuse I can present for my earlier behavior is that I woke up on the wrong side of the bed this morning," he said as a wry smile touched his lips. *Especially when I opened my eyes and discovered it had all been a dream and you weren't in bed with me after all,* he thought further.

Deciding to accept his apology, Sage allowed the corners of her mouth to lift into a smile. "The wrong side of the bed, uh?"

Sage's smile actually made Gabe feel better, less the heel. A slow, reciprocating smile curved his lips. "Yes, the wrong side of the bed. Can you imagine such a thing?"

Sage grinned, remembering her mood swings a few months ago when any male had tried getting too close. She had been quick to lash out at them with her tongue, which had been so unlike her. "Yes, I can imagine it since I've awakened on that same side a few times myself." After a brief few moments, she said, "And I accept your apology."

Gabe's tensed body relaxed with her acceptance of his apology. "Thanks, I appreciate it. And while I'm here, I'd like to take a look at your proposal to see just how much work might have to go into it. I'll also need to make arrangements for you to speak with Parnell after the architect has revised his plans."

Sage relaxed, glad he was willing to work with her. "All right."

"Were you about to leave?" Gabe asked, noticing the blinds had been pulled down, and her coat and purse were placed across her desk.

"Yes, but that's okay. I'm eager to show you what I have. There's nothing waiting at home for me but a can of soup and a sandwich anyway."

Gabe chuckled. "Sounds like you have more waiting at home for you than I do for me. Trust me when I say that my cupboards are bare." He paused and leaned against the wall. "After we finish up here, how about having dinner with me?"

He held her stare, and Sage felt a torrent of warm sensations seeping through her limbs. To associate with him other than for business was not a good idea. She knew it, but a part of her felt some sort of pull toward him, and it didn't help matters that an irresistible smile creased the corners of his mouth.

"Dinner?" she asked, to make sure she'd heard him correctly.

"Yes, that thing we'll probably get deprived of if we go home, since our options don't seem too bright." His smile widened. "Besides, today should be one to celebrate."

Sage lifted a brow. "Celebrate what?"

"No snow."

Sage couldn't help but laugh, and then against her better judgment, she said, "All right, you've convinced me that there's a reason to celebrate. I'd love to have dinner with you after we finish up here."

Gabe thought of the last time that she had laughed with him, nearly a month ago over a business dinner. He had liked the sound then, and he liked it now. He felt a ripple of uneasiness at the thought. "Good, then let's begin."

Sage's stomach twisted, and she nervously twined her fingers together. She swallowed tightly when Gabe met her gaze across the table and decided that she couldn't take it anymore. He'd said he would give her his opinion of everything over dinner.

"Well, what did you think?" she asked anxiously, unable to hold back any longer. Not only had she given him her thoughts on the theater, but she'd also given him a rundown of her other ideas.

Gabe leaned back in his chair, smiling. "The theater will be the most costly, but depending on how the architect redesigns the interior, it's workable, and like I said earlier, I see a great benefit to what you have in mind. My only concern is the extra time needed to complete the job, and we won't know that until the architect draws up revised plans."

Sage nodded, was silent for a moment, then said softly, "About what you said today at lunch, about me deliberately prolonging time to stay here in Anchorage."

Gabe's breath snagged as he remembered what he'd said, what he had accused her of. "I was out of line," he said, regretting the words he had spoken earlier that day to her. Even if he had thought she had an ulterior motive for wanting to include the theater at this late date, he had no right to tell her that. "I had no right to say what I did," he added.

"Yes, but evidently you felt there was credence in what you thought or you would not have said it. What makes you think that I'm here pining away for my fiancé?"

As much as it bothered him to discuss this topic of conversation with her, he figured he had brought it on himself by accusing her of anything in the first place. He inhaled deeply as he met her inquisitive gaze. "I guess to me it made perfect sense.

When I met you a little less than six months ago, you were happy over the entire idea of getting married, and it was plain to see you really cared for the guy. Therefore, it stands to reason that whatever happened between the two of you is something that can possibly work out, and the cliché 'absence makes the heart grow fonder' may apply."

Sage shook her head to toss the memories of her breakup with Erol aside. She *had* been happy at the thought of getting married, and yes, she had cared for Erol deeply. But his actions had changed all that in a way she could not share with Gabe. "Trust me, it won't." She took a sip of her drink. "I'm sure there are a number of people hoping that Erol and I will work out our differences and get back together, including my parents and his. But I've told them it won't happen."

Gabe asked. "What about him? Your fiancé? Erol? What does he think?"

Sage didn't say anything for a moment, wondering why she was even telling Gabe as much as she was, and why it was important to her that he understood that she had no intentions of getting back with Erol. *It's because you don't want him to think you would deliberately use his men for your benefit,* she reminded herself. But deep down she felt there was another reason, one she wasn't quite ready to analyze.

"I'm not sure what Erol thinks, but I do know what thoughts I left him with. I was pretty straightforward in letting him know that we would not get back together."

Gabe nodded. He couldn't help but think of Lindsey, and what she had told him three years ago was pretty much the same thing that Sage was saying. Yet, within forty-eight hours of her ex-fiancé returning to town, they had miraculously worked out their differences. He would never forget the night she'd showed up at his house to let him know she and her ex-boyfriend were getting back together.

"Why don't you believe me?"

Gabe blinked when he realized Sage must have read his expression and had spoken to him. He decided to be honest with her. "It's not a case of me not believing you; it's a case of knowing how two people who love each other can put past differences aside and move forward regardless, no matter what the situation that caused the breakup, especially if the love they shared is strong."

He dropped his gaze from hers and picked up his drink. After swirling the contents around in the glass for a few moments, he said, "And like I said earlier, it was easy to see how much you cared for him."

Sage shrugged. "Yes, but all the things that a relationship is built on were there at the time. At least I thought they were. That's not the case now, so my feelings have changed. I loved him, yes, and I guess it would be immature to say I don't still care for him, but not to the point that I can forget what he did. I could never discount how he betrayed my trust."

He betrayed her trust. Gabe wondered what exactly her fiancé had done to make her sound so bitter, and so utterly convinced that she could not patch things up with him. Usually when there was a question of trust involved, it meant the involvement of a third party—possibly another woman. If that was the case, then she would definitely be hurt and distrustful. But would it be enough to keep a reconciliation from possibly taking place? It hadn't been for Lindsey, who ultimately forgave her ex for his infidelity. And even if there was no reconciliation, would Sage pigeonhole all men into the same category as her fiancé and become distrustful of the entire male population? He shook his head. Weren't there women without issues of some kind or another?

"What?"

He lifted his gaze to Sage. "What's what?"

"Why were you shaking your head?" Sage asked him.

He shrugged. "No reason," he said, deciding to drop the matter. It meant nothing to him whether or not she and her fiancé worked things out as long as his work crew wasn't caught in the middle.

Deciding to change the subject, he asked, "So how is Rose Woods? She came across as one sharp woman when we met."

Sage smiled, thankful for the switch to another topic now that they had cleared the air about a few things. "Rose is doing fine; however, she no longer works for Denmark. She's in between jobs right now until she decides what she wants to do. I've invited her to fly out and spend time with me, but she detests cold weather."

Gabe chuckled. "Yeah, it does take some getting used to. You seem to be doing okay with it."

She grinned. "I'm a person who can adjust to any given situation, or at least try. Coming here was a promotion, and I did say I was mobile when I was hired. Besides, I needed the change."

He nodded. "So did I. My mother was driving me bonkers."

Sage lifted a brow. "How so?"

Gabe leaned back in his chair. "Playing matchmaker. For the longest time she had given up on Chris and me and thought we would never settle down and marry. Then Chris got reunited with Maxi and—"

"Reunited? Were they married before?"

Gabe shook his head, grinning. "No, Maxi and Chris have known each other since elementary school, and believe it or not, he had a crush on her even then. He loved her all through school, for twelve long years. And because he thought he would never be worthy of her affections, he left town after graduating from high school without telling her how he felt. They met up again on a ten-year class reunion cruise and discovered they loved each other." He sighed. That tale was close enough, although things hadn't been that simple. But there was no need to go into any details about it with her.

"Anyway," he continued, "no sooner was the rice thrown over Chris's head, than my mother gazed at me with a look in her eye that said, 'You're next.' And since that time she hasn't given me a moment's rest from playing Cupid."

Sage laughed. She remembered her father telling her once that his mother had been just as bad. She sobered quickly when she thought of her father.

"Now it's my turn to ask what?"

Sage met Gabe's curious gaze. "What's what?"

"What made you stop laughing so abruptly."

Sage sighed. "Trust me, you don't want to know."

A part of Gabe wanted to agree with her that he really didn't want to know, but instead of saying that, he said, "I do trust you, Sage, since I have no reason not to, and you're wrong. I do want to know. All of us have secrets."

Gabe's voice held a bit of tenderness, and Sage couldn't help it when a feeling of deep appreciation washed over her. It had been so easy for him to say he trusted her. Would trusting someone, especially a man, ever come that easy to her again? "Do you, Gabe? Do you have secrets?"

A smile touched the corners of his mouth. "Yes, in fact I have a few. I've been waiting twenty years for my father to discover that I'm the one who at the age of twelve wasted two cans of his shaving cream on the dog next door. I thought the hairy mutt needed a shave. Unfortunately, he took a dip in another neighbor's pool before I could go after him with the shears."

Sage gasped, pretending she was shocked, absolutely mortified. A huge smile appeared on her face. "That's awful, simply shameful. You'll never get to heaven without first confessing that one to your father."

Gabe chuckled. "Yes, I'm still losing sleep over how to break the news to him."

Laughter flickered in Sage's eyes. She had to admit that Gabe had a knack for making her laugh. She really enjoyed his company. Possibly too much, she thought. That prompted her to glance down at her watch.

He took her cue and said, "I guess it's time for us to call it a night. Unless you think you can handle dessert."

She shook her head, smiling. "There's no way I can handle dessert. I'm stuffed. I never had a real taste for salmon until coming here. I didn't know it could be prepared in so many different ways. Everything was delicious, and I wish you would let me contribute toward the tab."

Gabe shook his head. "No, tonight was my treat." He met her gaze, wondering why he was a glutton for punishment, then thought what the hell and said, "If you're one of those die-hard women's libbers, then I'll reconsider the next time we go out."

Sage slowly lifted her brow and held his gaze as if she couldn't believe what he'd suggested. He had made the statement as if for them to have another date was a done deal. As far as he was concerned, it was. But he could tell by the way she was looking at him it wasn't.

"Do you think I assume too much, Sage?" He decided to beat her to the punch and ask.

For a long moment she stared at him. Finally, she broke eye contact and looked out the window.

"Sage?"

A frown had creased her brow when she met his gaze again. "Do you, Gabe? Do you think that you assume too much?"

He met her gaze with a level stare, wondering why it was important to him to take her out again, although every fiber of his being was screaming at him to back off. She had issues to deal with. He should patiently wait and let her work through them before making a move. But for some reason he didn't want to wait.

"The only thing I can assume with certainty is that you enjoy laughing, and I like seeing you laugh. And for some reason, I get the feeling that you don't trust me, and that bothers me since I make it a point to be the type of person anyone can trust in my line of business as well as the personal aspects of my life. So I'd like to give you the chance to get to know me. I'm not asking for anything hot and heavy, Sage, just friendship and a chance to see you again in a nice, comfortable setting like this. We do have to eat a decent meal every once in a while, so what's wrong with sharing it?"

"Just for friendship?"

"Yes." For some reason he was willing to break the rules for Sage Dunbar and hoped he wasn't making the mistake of his life. "So, are you willing to let there be a next time?"

Sighing, Sage leaned back in her chair. It was too soon to become involved with another man after Erol, especially when she had so many personal issues to deal with. But then, according to Gabe, they would be friends and nothing more. "Yes, Gabe. I'm willing to let there be a next time."

Later that night after getting ready for bed, Sage walked over to the bedroom window and looked out. It had started snowing again. Her lips twitched. If Rose was listening to the weather report, she might never decide to come out and pay her a visit. She also thought about the bet she'd made with Gabe.

She turned from the window when she heard the phone ring and quickly crossed the room and picked it up. "Yes?"

"You owe me five dollars."

Sage laughed. While walking her out to her car after dinner, Gabe had said he thought it would be snowing before midnight. She had told him she'd heard that it wouldn't snow again for at least a couple of days. He'd made a five-dollar bet with her that she was wrong and he was right. "Okay, so you win. Don't rub it in."

"I won't too much. But once you get to know me, you'll find out that I'm a person who likes being right."

Sage shook her head, chuckling. "It must be hard carrying around that big head of yours."

Now it was Gabe's turn to laugh. "Well, yeah, sometimes it is. Good night, Sage."

She grinned. "Good night, Gabe."

After hanging up the phone, Sage couldn't help but smile. He had a knack for making her laugh, and she really liked that. Gabe Blackwell was something else. She had to admit that he was definitely an all-right guy.

CHAPTER TWELVE

Without opening an eye, Sage reached across the bed to the nightstand to pick up the ringing telephone and drowsily said, "Hello."

"Sage, are you still in bed?"

Sage opened one eye slowly upon hearing the sound of her mother's voice. She then sleepily peered at the clock on her bedroom wall. "Yes, Mom, it's only six o'clock here. Did you forget about the four-hour time difference again?"

"Oh, sweetheart, I'm so sorry. I tend to forget about that. I'll just call you back later."

Sage slowly pulled herself up in the bed. "No, Mom, that's fine. I'm usually up by seven anyway." Now Sage's curiosity was piqued. Her mom rarely called in the morning. Usually they talked at night. "Are you all right? And how is Dad?"

"Your father and I are fine, but I'm sure that he would love to hear from you more often than he does. I wish that whatever it is that has you and him at odds would come to an end, Sage. You can't hold a grudge forever."

Sage swallowed. "What makes you think Dad and I are in a disagreement about something?"

Her mother chuckled. "Because I know you and I know your

father. And whatever it is I can tell it's bothering him. I also think I know what it's about."

Sage lifted a brow and pushed her hair away from her face. "Do you?"

"Yes. It has to be about what's going on with you and Erol. That's when this animosity toward your father started. You can't fault him for wanting to remain neutral in all of this, especially when we think that eventually you and Erol will get back together."

Sage shook her head. Her mother was wrong on two accounts. Her and her father's strained relationship had nothing to do with Erol, and the thought that she and Erol would get back together was far from the truth. Why was it so hard for everyone to see, including Gabe, that she and Erol would not be getting back together? Some things between couples couldn't be worked out, and this was one of those situations.

"He came by on Sunday for dinner."

Her mother's words pulled Sage back into the conversation. "Who came by for dinner on Sunday, Mom?"

"Erol. He looks so sad and lonesome without you."

Will he not give up? Sage thought as irritation flowed through her. Of course her parents felt a special closeness to Erol since he was the first guy she'd ever gotten serious about, and she could appreciate that even now they had retained that close relationship. But what bothered her more than anything was that it seemed Erol was trying to use that relationship in his favor and to his benefit.

"He should have thought about all of this before he took my money," Sage said through gritted teeth.

"Yes, and I'm sure he regrets what he did, Sage."

Sage blew out a frustrated stream of breath. "Fine, then I forgive him if that will make him feel better and get him off this guilt trip he deserves to be on. But forgiving him won't patch up things between us, Mom. I'm here in Alaska because I've moved on with my life, and I suggest that Erol do the same."

"He can't. He still loves you."

Sage inhaled deeply, and her lip curled sullenly. Erol must have really gotten next to her mother for her to take the role of becoming his messenger. "Then, I suggest he get over it, because I have."

For the longest time her mother didn't say anything; then she said, "You have, haven't you?"

Sage reached out with her free hand and began rubbing the back of her neck when she felt tension there. "Yes, Mom, I have, but it wasn't easy. No matter what you or anyone might think, I'm not going through a phase just to make Erol's life miserable. Nor am I doing the 'eye-for-an-eye' thing. It was Erol's decision, without any input from me, to do what he did. For me it's not about the money; it's about trust. I've told you that countless times, but you refuse to accept it. What Erol did hurt me deeply mainly because he didn't care enough to respect my feelings. I cannot marry a man like that. I don't want to spend the rest of my life living with a man I can't trust. There is no way I can ever get back with him."

There was silence on the other end of the phone, and Sage waited patiently for her mother to say something.

"I think I believe you, Sage."

Sage breathed in a deep-gutted sigh. *Thank you, Jesus! Finally!* "I'm glad, Mom," she said quietly, fighting back the tears. She knew both her and Erol's families were holding back, hoping and wishing that she would come to her senses. What they'd both failed to realize was that she had.

"The best thing that you can do for Erol, Mom, is to make sure he believes it as well. Feeding him false hope won't help the situation. I just hope that with the next woman he becomes serious about, he takes into consideration her feelings with any decisions he makes."

Sage heard her mother's long sigh before she said, "All right, Sage, you've set matters straight regarding your relationship with Erol; now what about your father?"

Sage frowned. "What about Dad?"

"Will you make an effort to resolve what's going on with the two of you as well? I've never seen him so down. You're his daughter, Sage, his only child. He loves you, and there has always been that special bond between the two of you. I don't want this thing with Erol to destroy that."

Sage inhaled deeply upon hearing the worry in her mother's voice. "Is Dad still working late?" she couldn't help but ask.

"No, he gets home on time like clockwork every day in time for the evening news. He even goes to prayer meeting with me on Wednesday nights. We're spending more time together than before. We're both missing you like crazy, Sage. Other than the time you left for college, this is the first time you've lived away from Charlotte. It's taking some getting used to."

Sage nodded. "I'm fine, Mom, and I'll call and talk to Dad real soon. I'm trying to accomplish some things here and move on with my life. It gets a little hectic at times, but I'm doing fine. I'm surviving this weather and doing what Denmark is paying me to do. The resort will be beautiful, and I'm happy about the part I'll be playing in its success."

"And we're happy for you as well. We're also proud of you. Both your dad and I are. Always remember that we love you, Sage."

Sage wiped a tear from her eye. "And I love you and Dad, too, Mom."

Malcolm looked up when a very bundled up Sage walked into the office. He smiled. "I thought you would probably work from home today. Anyone in his right mind definitely would have."

Sage chuckled as she pulled off her coat, mittens and knitted cap. "Then, why are you here?"

Malcolm grinned. "Because I'm not in my right mind. You don't know how hard it was to leave the warm coziness of my bed this morning, especially when Leanne was still sleeping in it."

Sage shook her head and laughed. "Yeah, I can see how that would be hard. After yesterday, I plan on this being a fairly light workday for me. I'm not doing anything but staying in my office and concentrating on that list of recommendations I plan to give to Mr. Landmark by the end of the week."

Malcolm tapped the pad he'd been writing on and gazed up at her thoughtfully before saying, "Leanne and I went to dinner last night. We saw you."

Sage paused at her office door and tilted her head and met Malcolm's gaze. Knowing more was coming, she said, "And?" She watched as a huge smile spread across his face.

"And it seems you were enjoying yourself. I had to rack my brain to remember that you were indeed dining with the same man you wanted to feed to the lions when I left you here yesterday afternoon."

Sage gave him a small smile. "Yes, well, he stopped by right after you left and apologized for his behavior at lunch. And he even admitted the dinner theater was a good idea. We discussed it more rationally this time, and I even shared with him some of my other ideas and thoughts about Eden. He was very receptive to them."

Malcolm mustered a huge smile. "So now he's on our side?"

Sage chewed her bottom lip in concentration. "I wasn't trying to win him over, since that's not how I like doing things. I just wanted to present my ideas to him."

"And did you?"

Sage blinked. "And did I what?"

"Did you present your ideas to him?"

"Yes." Sage met Malcolm's stare and noted his eyes shone with undisguised hope, not particularly for Eden but for her. The two of them had grown close since working together, and although she was his manager, she considered him as well as the other members of her staff as valued team players. But outside of work, she also considered Malcolm something of a big brother. She had confided in him about her breakup with Erol and the reason. She had needed another opinion, an unbiased one since both her and Erol's families thought she had been too hard on Erol by calling off their wedding. Malcolm had agreed with her that what Erol had done was thoughtless and inconsiderate and that trust, once violated, was hard to regain. He had fully understood her reason for deciding not to marry Erol. But she knew that as a friend, he was also concerned with her decision not to get serious about another man because of the trust factor. He thought the best and quickest way to get over Erol and to put the past behind her was to move ahead into another relationship with someone she felt she trusted. He thought she was the type of woman who believed in romance, love and happily-ever-after. She inwardly admitted that a part of her wanted to still believe in those things, but unknown to Malcolm, her father had done a pretty good job of corrupting those thoughts in her mind.

"Don't read anything more into my having dinner with Gabe than that, Malcolm," she said finally. "Gabe and I are nothing more than friends."

Malcolm lifted a brow. "Friends and no longer just business associates?"

Sage frowned. Her and Gabe's relationship had shifted from associates to friends, at least it was headed in that direction. But then, after talking with her mother on the phone that morning, she knew that unless she started getting out more, sharing her time with a man, even in just friendship, everyone would think that she was still carrying a torch for Erol. "Yes, Gabe and I decided to have dinner every once in a while as nothing more than friends."

"So the two of you will be dating?"

Sage drew in a long breath. "I don't exactly consider it dating since it's not with the intent of anything serious ever taking place. I'm not ready to get involved with another man again, and Gabe knows that. In fact, what I didn't tell you yesterday was that at lunch he'd even accused me of coming up with the idea of the theater just to extend my time here to make my ex-fiancé suffer before going back to him."

A small crinkle formed between Malcolm's brows. "He actually accused you of that?"

"Yes."

Malcolm smiled wryly. "No wonder you were fit to be tied yesterday and wanted to feed him to the lions. Even I know that's not the case."

Sage smiled softly. "Yes, but then, you know the full story. All Gabe knows is that when we first met nearly six months ago, I was a happily engaged woman who was looking forward to her wedding. Now that's not the case."

Malcolm shook his head. "But I still don't understand why he would think that although you called off your wedding, you and your ex-fiancé would get back together. Couples decide not to marry all the time—sometimes at the ninth hour—and go their separate ways, without looking back. Why would your case be any different?"

Sage shrugged as she remembered her conversation with Gabe over dinner and the reason he'd given her for thinking the way he did. "I think Gabe believes that two people who love each other can work through any problem." She chuckled. "He's right there in good company since my parents and Erol's seem to think that way, too. After talking with Mom this morning, she even alluded that Erol was still holding out hope that I would change my mind, return to Charlotte and marry him."

She crammed her hands into the pockets of her skirt. "Well, enough about that. I can't help what Erol or Gabe think. In time I will just prove them wrong, as well as everyone else. There is no way Erol and I will ever get back together."

A few hours later Sage leaned back in her office chair and listened to the slow ticking of the clock on the wall. It was the only sound around since Malcolm and the rest of her staff had left for lunch.

She glanced down at the legal pad on her desk that contained a lot of the notes she had made. She was just about finished and would have her secretary type up everything to have ready for her meeting with Mr. Landmark. Gabe would be at that meeting as well. She smiled when she remembered how he had sat in her office last night, on the other side of her desk, going over the papers she had given him to look at. She had been utterly quiet, and the only sound that had marred the tense silence was the same one that was marring it now, the ticking of the clock on the wall.

She could recall and would now admit that the woman side of her, the one that naturally appreciated the sight of a good-looking man, had studied him while he'd been unaware of it.

He'd been impeccably dressed in a tailored suit with the words *intelligent, competent* and *businessminded* written all over him. And then later, at the restaurant when he'd smoothly pushed all business aside, he had brought out the charm. Not in an overflowing way but in a way she wasn't used to. While talking business he had succeeded in keeping his expression impassive, the trait of a good businessperson. In his line of work it was good not to let a business opponent know what you were thinking. But when the business side of dinner had concluded, he had bestowed upon her a slow smile, one that had nearly turned her bones to mush before she had quickly pulled herself together, reminded that Erol was also a charmer—although in her opinion, not of the same caliber as Gabe. Gabe's charm seemed to come naturally, it seemed to be genuine, and if a woman wasn't careful, it could prove to be lethal.

Sage rose from her chair and walked over to the window. It was still snowing but not as heavily as earlier when she had arrived at work. Tonight was her pamper-yourself night, and she looked forward to lighting the candles in her bathroom and taking a well-deserved leisurely bath. Already in her mind she could smell the scent of vanilla. She smiled as she closed her eyes. She saw herself easing into the big tub filled with bubbles while the candlelight flickered across her naked skin with the soft sound of Kenny G and his saxophone playing in the background. And as the water and bubbles covered her body and she leaned back, she slowly glanced to the side. A man was standing in the shadows watching her. When he stepped forward, his image became vivid and crystal clear.

Gabe.

Sage snapped her eyes open and quickly turned away from the window. Sitting back down to her desk, she couldn't help but consider just where her mind had taken her a few moments ago.

She frowned. Although the path her thoughts had taken her down had been forbidden, challenging and . . . she had to admit . . . for a brief moment, an exhilarating experience, on a common sense level it really made no sense, at least not in any logical form.

There was no reason for her mind to have placed Gabe Blackwell in her bathroom watching her take a bath.

CHAPTER THIRTEEN

"**M**r. Blackwell?"

Gabe lifted his gaze from the documents he was reading upon hearing the sound of his secretary's voice over the intercom on his desk. "Yes, Caroline?"

"Mr. Cabot is here to see you."

Gabe smiled. "Please send him in." He stood for the man who as usual was doing a fantastic job in getting the construction of Eden under way. He gripped Parnell Cabot's hand in a firm handshake the moment he walked in. After Caroline left, closing the door behind her, he offered him a chair.

"I would offer you something to drink, but I know you're still on duty," Gabe said jokingly.

"Yeah, and after today I'd be tempted to take you up on that drink, even though I would know better."

Gabe lifted a brow, and a concerned expression immediately appeared on his face. "Any problems that I should know about?"

Parnell shook his head as he eased his frame into the chair across from Gabe's desk. "Nothing with Eden, so let me rest your mind about that. My live-in sitter, Mrs. Summers, informed me this morning that she might have to leave Anchorage for at least six weeks to care for her sister who'll be undergoing hip replacement surgery in Florida. That means that I'll have to try and find a new live-in sitter for the girls."

Gabe nodded. He knew that Parnell's four-year-old twin daughters had made the adjustment to Anchorage rather easily, thanks to Mrs. Summers. According to Parnell, it seemed the elderly woman had been a godsend. "Well, I hope things work out for you on that end, which I'm sure they will," he said, hoping to ease the man's worries somewhat. He knew how much it meant to Parnell to have his daughters properly taken care of.

"I'm sure they will, too."

Gabe smiled as he sat down behind his desk. "No matter who fills in for Mrs. Summers, once they meet your girls, they will be totally captivated. They're special."

Parnell beamed proudly. "Thanks, Gabe. I think that they're special, too, and they're pretty smart for their age; even Mrs. Summers said so."

Gabe grinned. Parnell's words had been spoken like the proud father that he was. Deciding to move on to the reason that he had summoned Parnell to his office, he said, "I hate to take you away from your busy schedule, but there's a new development that I need to cover with you."

Parnell nodded. "All right. Shoot."

For the next fifteen to twenty minutes, Gabe covered Denmark's marketing proposal regarding the dinner theater. Afterward, Parnell leaned back in his chair and asked, "How soon will the architect have plans for us to look at?"

"In a week. One good thing is that nothing with the foundation will change. Every modification is with the interior."

Parnell acknowledged what Gabe said. "Yes, but depending on what they want inside, we may have a long wait for building materials, so the sooner we can get those plans in our hands, the better off we'll be."

Gabe agreed. "That means that Landmark will need to get his interior designer working on this right away. I have a feeling he wants this as elegant as the dinner theater that's in the White House."

Parnell raised a brow. "There's a dinner theater in the White House?"

Gabe chuckled as he shrugged his shoulders. "Probably, since it has just about everything else. All I'm saying is that after talking with Landmark, no expense will be spared on this. He's very excited about it."

Parnell nodded. "I'm curious as to why those Denmark folks just thought of it."

Gabe replied, "Because at the time the original proposal was submitted they didn't have Sage Dunbar managing things. She's one sharp lady."

"Yeah, and a very good-looking one, too."

Gabe shot his eyes up from the papers on his desk, suddenly feeling ill at ease. Parnell's words had struck a chord within him, a very unexpected jealous chord. He met the man's gaze. "You think so?" he somehow managed to ask.

Parnell chuckled. "You'd have to be blind not to notice."

Gabe looked at Parnell for a long time. Suddenly, his mouth felt as dry as dust. Could Parnell be interested in Sage? "And you've noticed?" he asked quietly, curiously, cautiously.

Parnell's mouth tilted into a full grin. "Yeah, haven't you?"

Gabe's mind suddenly focused on all the things about Sage that he had noticed, although he hadn't wanted to. "Yes, I've noticed."

"That's good."

Gabe leaned back in his chair and lifted a brow. Parnell was smiling, and Gabe had a funny feeling that he was somehow the joke. "Is there something going on that I should know about?"

An innocent expression covered Parnell's face. "Something like what?"

Gabe frowned as he continued to stare at Parnell. Then a thought suddenly came to his mind. "My mother. Have you spoken to her lately?"

He watched as Parnell shifted uneasily in his chair. "What gives you that idea?"

"Just a hunch." When Parnell said nothing else, Gabe said, "Well, have you?"

Gabe lifted a brow when Parnell shrugged his shoulders. "Uh, I do seem to recall her calling a few nights ago to check on the girls. She does that sometimes, you know."

"Yes, I know." *And I'll bet every penny I own that the girls aren't the only person she's calling to check on.* He leaned forward in his chair and shook his head. *This is so typical of Joella Blackwell. First she enlists the help of Christopher and now Parnell.*

"The next time you talk to my mother, Parnell, assure her that I'm dating."

Parnell glanced at him dubiously. "Are you?"

"As much as I want."

Parnell shook his head. "But I'm not sure that will be enough to suit Ms. Joella. She's concerned with there not being enough women out here for you to properly choose from."

"And if there aren't? What does she plan to do? Ship a bunch over here for me?"

Parnell's smile spread slowly across his face. "Well, yeah, she had mentioned the possibility of doing that."

Gabe suddenly sat up straight in his chair. "She wouldn't."

Parnell shook his head as he grinned at Gabe's incredulous expression. "You ought to know your mother well enough to know that she would."

Gabe closed his eyes briefly. *Yes, she would.* He reopened them, knowing he had to have a very serious conversation with her. She was getting too out of hand. The next thing he knew he would be instructed to pick up a plane load of Bible-toting single women from the airport who'd been sent by his mother to provide him good food, the good gospel and a good reason why one of them should become Mrs. Gabriel Blackwell.

"I feel a headache coming on," he said miserably, placing a hand to his forehead.

"I'm glad it's you and not me, Gabe."

"Don't consider yourself immune to Joella Blackwell's shenanigans. Once she thinks I'm taken care of, she'll quickly switch her attention to you."

Parnell appeared taken aback. "To me?"

"Yes, to you. She won't rest until she's found a mother for your girls."

Parnell dropped his head into his hands. "Heaven help me."

Gabe started laughing. "Forget it. Heaven won't help you. If I didn't know better, I'd think my mother has special connections up there. You'll be on your own, buddy."

Later that night after talking to his mother on the phone, Gabe sat on the sofa in front of the fireplace and tried to relax. His conversation with Joella Blackwell had been taxing at best. He knew that everything he'd said to her had gone into one ear and out the other. According to her, there was no good reason a thirty-two-year-old man should still be single when there were so many good Christian women out there.

When he had pointed out that it seemed to him that it was the Christian women with all of the issues, she had calmly replied that there had to be a little rain in your life to appreciate the sunshine.

He rolled his eyes, looking at the ceiling. A little rain he could handle, but a full-blown storm he could not, nor did he want to. And when he had told her that he didn't appreciate her getting Christopher and Parnell involved in his love life, she had been quick to point out to him that as far as she was concerned, he didn't have one.

Gabe shook his head after taking a sip of the drink he held in his hand. Before hanging up, she had reminded him of his grandparents' sixtieth anniversary party that was only two months away, and nothing would make her happier than for him to show up with a woman by his side. And, if he couldn't find one on his own, she would be glad to help him out. He'd said, "Thanks, but no, thanks," and had quickly ended their conversation.

A few minutes later as Gabe continued to sit in the quiet room with the shifting of the fiery logs in the fireplace making the only sound, his thoughts went somewhere he'd tried avoiding all day.

Sage Dunbar.

His conversation with Parnell had brought her to the forefront of his mind, and there she had stayed for the rest of the day. More than once he'd been tempted to pick up the phone and invite her to dinner. But the more he'd thought about it, the more he'd decided that to do so wouldn't be such a good idea.

He leaned back to rest his head against the sofa as he pondered just what there was about Sage that caused him to continue breaking the rules. Rules he'd established after Lindsey, rules that had been fairly easy to follow until now.

What was there about her smile, and her laughter, that made him want to make sure one or the other became a permanent fixture on her face? What was there about her that had him not thinking straight?

After the ordeal he'd suffered through with Lindsey, the last thing he needed was to become involved with a woman on the rebound. Yet Sage was so deeply embedded in his thoughts that it wasn't funny. He was the last one who wanted to be amused, but he couldn't help the smile that appeared on his face anyway. Ahh . . . Sage was temptation at its finest. Just looking into her whiskey-colored eyes could make even the strongest man fall to his knees. Her fiancé had been a fool for whatever he did to make her call off their engagement. Had Gabe been blessed to find a woman like her, he would have done anything and everything in his power to make her happy.

He stood after making a quick decision. He walked over to the phone and began dialing the numbers he had memorized. He inhaled deeply when after a few rings a feminine voice came on the line.

"Hello."

After a brief pause, he cleared his throat. "Hello, Sage, this is Gabe."

A short silence stretched across the line as Sage's heart skipped a beat, caught off guard by the sexy sound of Gabe's voice.

She had just finished pampering herself and had slipped into her nightgown. "Yes, Gabe. How are you?" she asked as her heart continued to hammer in her chest. She closed her eyes, wondering what in the heck was wrong with her. She reopened them when she silently admitted that she knew. After spending nearly an entire hour leisurely soaking in a hot tub of bubble bath while fantasizing about him, she could no longer deny that she was attracted to Gabe.

"I'm fine. What about you?"

She pushed a lock of hair out of her flushed face. "Great. Did you meet with Parnell Cabot today?" She inhaled quickly.

There. She had immediately put his phone call on a business level.

"Yes, but that's not why I'm calling."

"Oh."

"I was calling to see if you would have dinner with me tomorrow night."

Sage swallowed the lump that formed deep inside her throat. "Dinner?"

"Yes, you know, that thing we agreed to do together on occasion as friends."

When she heard the teasing sound in his voice, she relaxed somewhat as a smile lit her face. "I do remember agreeing to something like that."

"Well, then, will you be available to have dinner with me tomorrow night?"

Sage nervously bit her lips as she tried thinking of a single reason she could not. "What time?"

"Umm, what about eight. Is that all right with you?"

"Yes, eight will be fine. Tell me the name of the place and I'll meet you there."

There was a slight pause. "I'd rather come by your place and pick you up. Would that be okay?"

Another moment of silence fell. The husky sound of Gabe's voice had actually sent shivers up her spine. "Yes, sure. That would be okay. At eight o'clock, right?"

"Right."

Sage swallowed hard again. "And the place where we're going, will the proper attire be dressy, business, casual . . . ?" she asked softly.

"Umm, let's try dressy but not overly so."

"All right."

He cleared his throat. "Well, I better let you get back to what you were doing before I called."

Sage blinked. She wondered what he would think if he knew that she'd just finished taking a leisurely soak in the tub while fantasizing about him. "Okay."

"Oops, I almost forgot. I'm going to need your address."

"Oh, yes, of course." She then gave it to him, and he repeated it for accuracy.

"I'll see you tomorrow. Good night, Sage."

"Good night, Gabe."

CHAPTER FOURTEEN

Sage stood in front of the full-length mirror in her bedroom and surveyed how she looked in the clingy black dress. Gabe had said "dressy but not overly so," and she hoped what she had on was appropriate. This was the second time she had worn it. The first time had been on her last night in Charlotte before moving to Anchorage. She and Rose had gone out on the town to celebrate.

She drew in a long breath as her gaze drifted over her curves. Because of the style of the dress, she wasn't wearing a bra and had decided on wearing a silky pair of thigh-high stockings. To solve the problem of her panties showing through the clingy material, she was wearing a black thong, and the thought of that piece of underwear underneath her dress made her feel sexy.

She turned around in the mirror as a heated sensation flowed through her. It had been almost six months since she had gotten all dolled up for a man, and it was the first time since her senior high school prom that the man had been anyone but Erol. Earlier that day when she'd thought about her date with Gabe, she'd felt strange. For so long Erol had been the only man in her life, the only man she cared about, the only one who mattered. Now all that had changed.

She turned away from the mirror and walked across the room to get her purse off the bed. Chances were that Gabe was used to more sophisticated women, but then she shrugged, reminding herself that the two of them were not actually going out on a real date. It was merely two friends sharing dinner. There was a difference. A big difference.

Then, why do I feel like butterflies are flying around in my stomach? she asked herself when she walked out of her bedroom. *And why does the thought that Gabe's coming to pick me up and may want to come inside for a short while after he brings me home bother me?*

She sighed deeply. *Mainly because this is all new to you,* her mind responded promptly. *You're embarking on a new phase in your life and trying to learn to trust again.*

"Yes, a new phase in my life," Sage said aloud to herself. "And remember that this is a friendship dinner and nothing more."

No sooner had she said the last word than the doorbell rang, and Sage suddenly forgot everything.

Taking a deep, calming breath, Sage slowly opened the door. Gabe stood just on the other side, looking so incredibly handsome that for a moment Sage felt her lips glue themselves together. She was totally speechless. She had seen him dressed in a suit many times, but never had she seen him wear a pair of tailored pleated slacks, a collarless shirt and sports coat. And everything was black. All black. She knew of no other brother who could wear the color better. She dragged her gaze up the full length of him, from the expensive-looking pair of shoes on his feet to the neatly trimmed hair on his head.

She then returned her gaze to his face and met his eyes. They were eyes that weren't staring at her but at her dress. She cleared her throat. "Hi, you're early."

His gaze met hers with a dark, piercing look, one that almost left her breathless. "Am I?"

She nodded slowly. "Yes, but since you're less than ten minutes early, you're forgiven."

He leaned against the doorjamb. A trace of humor shone in his eyes. "Thanks. I appreciate that."

She smiled. "You're welcome. Come on in while I get my coat."

She walked off, and Gabe stood unmoving for a moment when he saw how the back of her dress was designed. Her entire back was bare down to her waist. *Amazing,* he thought, entering the apartment and closing the door behind him. He quickly glanced around the living room, checking out the décor as he tried to get his mind off of her outfit, like that was actually possible.

Why are you here, Blackwell? a silent voice inside of him asked, not for the first time. His life had been going just like he wanted, so why was he allowing Sage Dunbar to become an addiction?

When she came out of a room with her coat thrown over her arm, he quickly cleared his mind and crossed the room to her. "Do you think this coat will be enough to keep you warm tonight?" he asked huskily as he helped her to slip her arms through the sleeves of the thick wool coat.

She looked up at him. "Yes, I think so. Besides, it's only cold outside, and we will be eating inside, won't we?" she asked, grinning.

Gabe took a deep breath and inhaled Sage's scent. It was a fragrance that he'd never smelled before but definitely liked. Being close to her was nearly driving him insane. "Yes, we will." He checked his watch. "I guess we'd better go."

Sage nodded as he led her to the door. "You haven't said where we're going."

He smiled down at her as they stepped into the hall, then closed and locked the door behind them. "It's a surprise."

* * *

And it was a surprise . . . in addition to being the most exquisite place Sage had ever had the privilege of dining. It was a quaint restaurant nestled in the mountains and adjacent to Chester Creek. A thirty-minute drive from her apartment, it had been a pleasant scenic route that bisected the city from east to west. Although the snow had stopped falling earlier, unmelted snow still covered the length of the creek.

"Tell me about Sage Dunbar."

Sage lifted her head from studying the intricate design of her tablecloth and met Gabe's gaze over the candlelight in the middle of their table. They had just completed their meal and were basking in just how delicious everything had been. "And what is it that you want to know?"

Gabe smiled as he met her gaze and took a slow sip of his wine. "Everything you haven't told me already."

Sage nodded, and a thoughtful expression appeared on her face. How much should she tell him? How far could she trust him? Then making a decision, she said, "My full name is Sage Simone Dunbar, and I attended public schools in Charlotte. When I decided on a college, I knew I wanted to attend Florida A and M University in Tallahassee, Florida."

Gabe lifted a brow. "That was a long way from home, wasn't it?"

Sage chuckled. "Yes, but that was the point. I was the only child and wanted freedom away from my parents' ever-watchful eyes. I thought Florida would be far enough to serve that purpose."

"Was it?"

Sage grinned as she took a sip of her own wine. "Yes. I did a lot of growing up while living away from home. I saw a lot and did a lot, and I always had fun. On the flip side of that, I never forgot why I was there and what was expected of me, so I ended up making decent grades and graduating with honors. So in essence, my parents had nothing to worry about and felt it had been money well invested."

"Did you return home to Charlotte after college?"

Sage nodded again. "Yes. I decided I'd been away from my family long enough and was ready to move back. The Denmark Group interviewed me in my last year of college, and I got the job. I've been working there ever since."

"And how did your fiancé fit into things?"

The unexpectedness of Gabe's question caught Sage completely off guard. She nervously licked her bottom lip as she glanced up at him. A deep heat settled in her stomach when instead of looking at her, his full attention was plastered to her mouth.

She inhaled deeply, deciding to be completely honest with him. He was an easy person to talk to, just like Malcolm, and for some reason, she felt comfortable trusting him to a certain degree. "I met Erol in college during my sophomore year. But we didn't start dating until my junior year. I wasn't ready to talk marriage after graduation, although he was. We compromised and agreed to live together until I felt I was ready to take the plunge." She smiled slowly. "It took almost three years for me to decide I was ready."

Gabe shifted his attention from her lips to meet her gaze. "And how long did it take you to decide to end your engagement?"

Sage gazed at him thoughtfully, remembering the day she had discovered all the money missing from her bank accounts. "Only a few seconds."

Gabe released a low whistle. "He must have done something pretty damn awful."

Sage swirled her wine around in her glass. "I think so. When I returned from my trip to Anchorage that time I met you, I found out he had taken all the money out of our bank accounts for some sort of an investment opportunity. Needless to say, he didn't discuss it with me beforehand, and to make matters worse, he lost every penny he invested."

"Had he done anything that impulsive before?"

Sage shook her head. "No. But I felt I couldn't trust him again."

Gabe nodded. "Yes, I can see why. Trust is an important thing between two people. Once it's been violated, it can never be restored."

She continued to hold his gaze and noted, "Sounds like you're talking from experience, Gabe."

He leaned back in his chair. "I am. I dated a woman for almost a year and had given her anything and everything I thought she could possibly want. The night before I was going to ask her to marry me, she came to me and told me that she wanted to end things because she was involved with someone else."

Sage breathed in sharply. "Just like that?"

Gabe nodded as he glanced down at the liquid in his wineglass. "Yes, just like that." He decided there was no need to tell Sage that the person Lindsey had gotten involved with was an ex-boyfriend who, although she had claimed otherwise numerous times, she had never completely gotten over, an exboyfriend she had ultimately dumped Gabe for, breaking his heart.

"Was it hard for you to trust again?"

He smiled at her. "Yes. After the breakup I poured myself into my work, becoming a workaholic, spending twelve hours or more at the office each day. Work literally became my life, and I refused to get involved with another woman for a full year or more. The only good thing that came of that time is that Chris thought he should be right there with me, working all those long hours."

Gabe's smile widened. "However, he didn't feel obligated to give up the women, which proved he had a hell of a lot more energy than I could imagine. He worked as many hours as I did, and pretty soon with the two of us at it, our company had more projects and more money than we knew what to do with. It was only when my mother stepped in and claimed we were working ourselves to death and began worrying about us did we slow down."

He took a sip of his coffee. "I think not wanting to trust again right after someone you care about has betrayed that trust is understandable. But at some point you have to let go and believe that there are people who *can* be trusted. Everyone isn't as untrustworthy as the individual who let you down."

A surge of sadness rose up inside of Sage, not only for herself, but for Gabe as well. What he'd shared with her had been both profound and deep. "So, what else is there I need to know about Gabe Blackwell other than the fact that he's no angel?" Sage asked, smiling, trying to bring back a lighter tone to their conversation.

Gabe returned her smile. "I went to the University of Michigan and earned a degree in structural engineering and then went after an MBA at the same school. You know the story of Christopher and how he got added to the family, and other than that there's not a whole lot to tell. I like working hard, yet I also enjoy having a good time."

She nodded slowly and smiled. "That sounds like a winner to me."

Moments later the waiter placed a huge slice of chocolate cake in front of them. It was so large they decided to share it.

"Umm," Gabe said after tasting his first bite. "I thought no one made chocolate cake as well as my mom. Now I'm going to rethink that idea, not that I'll ever tell her that. But then, she has my father singing her praises enough that she probably doesn't care what I think," he said, laughing.

Sage smiled. "Your parents have been married a long time?"

Gabe nodded after taking another bite of cake. "Yes, for thirty-four years. They had two years alone together before I came along. They tried to have another child, a couple more in fact, but from what I was told, she miscarried each time. I guess it was meant for me to be the only one. In a way, I wish there had been others. I had it rough as an only child with all the attention. It was a blessing when Chris came along and all my mother's attention was shifted to him."

Sage's smile widened as she rested her chin on her bent hands. "It sounds like your parents have had a long and wonderful marriage."

Gabe chuckled. "Yeah, they have." After taking another slice of cake, he glanced over at her. "But then, so have your parents, haven't they? Didn't you say they'd been married over thirty years?"

Sage frowned. "Yes, and I thought their marriage was happy, but I recently found out differently."

Hearing the hurt and anger in her voice, Gabe put his fork down. "You think they might be getting a divorce?"

Sage shook her head. "No. My mother loves my father. He's her whole life. They started dating back in their high school days. With my father it's a different story. He tried to convince me he loves my mother, but I don't believe him."

Gabe's eyebrows drew together. "And why don't you believe him?"

Sage met his curious and confused gaze. She hadn't told another soul about her father's indiscretion; but she felt she needed to tell someone, and for some unexplainable reason, she wanted to tell Gabe.

"Recently, a few months before I moved out here, I saw my father with another woman."

There was a pause at the table. "Are you sure you didn't misread things, Sage?"

She shook her head. "You don't know how much I wanted to believe that I did. But the evidence was all there. I confronted him about it the next day, and he admitted it. He said it had been a one-night stand and that he loved my mother. How can a man love one woman yet betray her trust that way? As far as I'm concerned, what he did was just as bad as what Erol did, even worse because Dad broke his marriage vows."

Pain filled her eyes when she added, "I found out about my

father the same day that I found out what Erol had done, so talk about getting hit with a double whammy in one day . . ."

Gabe reached out and gently took her hand in his. It felt soft and delicate. "I'm sorry."

Sage inhaled a deep, soothing breath. "So am I. My father and I were close, extremely close, and now we barely talk and in a way I prefer it that way. My mother doesn't know anything about it, and since I do, I feel like I'm a party to his deceit. I hate him for putting me in such a position. I feel so disloyal to my mother."

Gabe's hold on her hand tightened. No wonder he had sensed her mistrust of men in general. "Isn't your mother curious as to why you and your father's relationship is now strained?"

"Yes, but she thinks it's because I feel he's taking sides with what happened between me and Erol. My father considers Erol like a son, so of course he wants us to work out our problems and get back together. In fact, my family as well as Erol's feel what happened between us is something we can work out since we were together for so long. But like I told you earlier, that won't happen."

Gabe picked up his fork to eat another bite of cake as he pondered Sage's words. Moments later when the cake was all gone, he asked, "Did you enjoy yourself tonight?"

She smiled appreciatively at him. "Yes. Everything was simply wonderful, Gabe. Thanks for bringing me here."

"It was my pleasure."

Their gazes locked.

Held.

Sage inhaled slowly when she felt a shiver course through her. She couldn't recall ever feeling this way before. At least not of this magnitude, nothing ever this intense. A part of her wondered if perhaps the reason she felt this way was because she had not been intimate with a man for almost six months, and she and Erol had shared a pretty healthy sex life. But another part of her decided that wasn't the case at all. She could live the rest of her life celibate if she had to. She wasn't the type of woman who routinely engaged in toe-curling lust on a regular basis. Not even on an irregular one. As she mulled over that, Gabe broke into her thoughts.

"You're ready to leave?"

She released a long, slow breath. "Yes."

Before exiting the restaurant, he helped her into her coat then donned his own. And as if it was the most natural thing for him to do, he placed an arm around her waist as they walked through the parking lot to his car.

It was only after he had her seated inside the warm coziness of the vehicle, with her seat belt snapped firmly in place, did a question, a very important question, suddenly pop into her mind.

How would their evening end?

CHAPTER FIFTEEN

Sage felt tense and unraveled. Goose bumps were forming on her arm. She gave a sidelong glance to the man standing beside her in the elevator and wondered if he detected her nervousness. He had picked up on it in the car, she was sure of it, and she'd appreciated him keeping the conversation light and impersonal.

He had told her of his meeting the day before with Parnell Cabot, and already everything was being put in place to give Eden the dinner theater John Landmark wanted. Although her and Gabe's business discussion had been brief, it had afforded her time to collect herself, her thoughts and to relax.

But now she was nervous again. There was this shimmering heat flowing between her and Gabe. She felt it and knew that he felt it as well. He would have to be a dead man not to feel it, and she knew that he was very much alive.

How did a dinner date between two people who wanted to just be friends end? Did they kiss good night? And if so, what sort of kiss would it be? Would it be a chaste brush of his lips across her cheek, maybe even across her lips? Or would it be the kind that was a little more personal but not hot and heavy? Or would it be one drenched in sensuality that involved lips, tongues, teeth, gums—just about anything and everything. One that was incredibly erotic, hot enough to burn your toes, fill your senses and cause an ache between your legs.

Her fingers tightened on her purse. The latter type of kiss was reserved for lovers, a couple that had been intimate or was just about headed there. It was not one that would be appropriate for a first kiss and definitely not one shared by just friends.

The elevator doors swooshed open, and so did her breath. She sighed, tried to relax and decided to just follow Gabe's lead. She had a feeling he'd done this before. He did not come across as a man who would take advantage of any situation, and from their conversation at dinner, he knew that she hadn't dated a lot and that Erol had been the only guy she'd been seriously involved with.

As if he'd read her thoughts, he threaded his fingers through hers as they walked down the hall to her apartment door. She inhaled deeply. Maybe she was getting worked up for nothing. There was a possibility he might not want to come inside. There was an even greater possibility that he would give her a handshake instead of a kiss.

Fat chance.

He would kiss her. She felt it. She felt it in the warmth of his hand holding hers. She felt it in the quiet sound of his breathing as he walked beside her. She felt it in the occasional brush of his thigh against hers. She also felt it in her own labored breathing.

Okay, so we will kiss. One kiss. I can handle that, no big deal. But deep down she knew it was a big deal. The physical attraction between them was strong. Way too strong for friends who'd only shared dinner. For business associates. For mere acquaintances.

They came to a stop in front of her door. He untangled his fingers from hers and took a step back as if giving her space. She immediately felt the loss of his closeness. Glancing up, she met his gaze. His eyes grew dark under the scope of hers, and she suddenly sensed heat gathering first in the taut nipples of her breasts, then moving lower to that area between her legs.

She was utterly astonished at what she was experiencing. Undeniable need was rippling through her. Desire the likes of which she had never experienced before, not even with Erol.

"May I come in for a second?"

The sound of his voice, low and husky, nearly startled her out of her thoughts. The hall light illuminated his features. Somehow he suddenly appeared bigger than life, and the most sensuous looking man she'd ever laid eyes on.

Her thoughts went back to his question. He had asked to come inside, which meant that he hadn't assumed anything. If she said no, he would accept her answer and leave.

But if she said yes . . .

She finally nodded as he continued to hold her gaze. "Yes, you may come in."

Sage opened her purse and pulled out her key. Nervously, she inserted it into the lock. Her fingers were shaking, but the door eased open. She walked in with him following behind. She flipped a switch that brought a soft glow to her living room and took another step inside. She glanced over her shoulder as he closed the door behind them.

"Would you like something to drink?" she asked, turning to him and nervously licking her lips. She hadn't entertained a man in her own place in so long she wasn't sure what was proper anymore. She would give just about anything to get some advice from Rose about how to proceed. But then again, maybe Rose wasn't the one to get advice from. Her friend's definition of a good evening was ending it with sex, hot sex, even on the first date, especially if you really liked the person and thought he was safe.

Sage's hands tightened into fists at her sides. She really liked Gabe and thought he was safe.

"No, I don't want anything to drink, but I would like for you to come here for a second, Sage."

She blinked upon hearing Gabe's sexy voice, and without further thought, she took the few steps that covered the distance between them just as he'd asked. She felt every cell in her body vibrate with their closeness. "Yes?" She met his gaze. His eyes darkened a tad more, and he reached out and spread his fingers wide at her waist.

"I had a great time tonight," he said huskily, taking a step that brought them even closer.

"So did I," she responded softly.

He took another step, an even closer step, and she felt the hardness of his erection pressed against her midsection. He wanted her to know just how his body was responding to her nearness.

She blinked, then looked up and watched him lowering his head toward her. She began to tremble in anticipation. And as desire swirled through her, she felt her lashes flutter closed at the same time his mouth came down on hers.

The touch of his lips to hers sent powerful shivers of awareness through her. On instinct, she reached out and encircled her arms around his neck as he slicked his tongue gently across her lips, filling her senses. Of its own accord her mouth parted to take his tongue inside, and he began pleasuring her in ways she hadn't known existed. He gently nibbled, sucked and flitted and explored every recess of her mouth. His tongue stroked deeply, sensuously, coaxing her to share in the erotic kiss he was bestowing upon her with a hunger that took her breath away and made the warmth between her legs intensify.

She heard the guttural growl that emitted from deep within his throat that was purely primitive and purely male. And she couldn't do anything but follow his lead, devouring him as much as he seemed to be devouring her, drawing his tongue into her mouth and feasting on it, greedily, hungrily and without any sense of shame.

She felt his hand rub softly against her bare back the exact moment his fingers slipped beneath the back waistline of her dress and sensually caressed the soft flesh of her bare backside left exposed by her thong panties.

She knew without being told that they had already gone beyond what was proper for a first date. It wouldn't take much for her to begin inching down his zipper to release what she felt hot and heavy against her midsection.

Something, she didn't know what, sent out a warning to put an end to what they were doing. It could have been another apartment door closing in the background, or it could have been the fact that if they continued much longer, both their tongues would be sucked raw. Whatever it was, at long last, he lifted his head to end the kiss. But he let his hand stay just where he had it, cupping her bare bottom.

She breathed in deeply as a semblance of common sense returned. And with it came the realization of what type of kiss they had shared. It had definitely not been a kiss for a first date. Not even a kiss for a second one. And it sure as heck didn't seem quite proper that he was still standing close to her with his erection still cradled nicely between her thighs, jabbing her midsection while his hand was cupping the soft flesh of her bottom. But he didn't make a move to correct the situation. He evidently had her right where he wanted her—both in the front and in the back—and shamefully she admitted that at the moment, she was right where she wanted to be, too.

"Sexual chemistry is a powerful thing, isn't it?" Gabe finally said huskily, with his gaze glued to her wetted, swollen lips. He basked in the knowledge that he had made them that way.

"Is that what this is?" she asked, totally unsure of just what had them in such a state.

"Yes."

She nodded, willing to believe whatever he said. "Is it always this powerful?" she asked, wanting to know.

Gabe shook his head, totally blown away by her question. Did it mean that she'd never felt desire this intense before? Not even with her ex-fiancé whom she'd been with for five years?

"No, it's never been this way for me before, and I've probably been involved in a lot more relationships than you," he said in response to her question.

Knowing that was true, she said, "Well, we can't stand in this position all night, Gabe."

He chuckled. "Yeah, I guess we can't." He then released his fingers from the softness of her bare bottom and slipped his hand from beneath the back waist of her dress at the same time as he took a step back.

"I liked that," she said honestly, meeting his gaze.

He inhaled deeply and lifted a brow. "The kiss?"

"Everything. I liked the feel of your hand touching me back there and the feel of your body pressing against me," she replied huskily, truthfully.

"Damn."

Before Sage knew what he was about to do, Gabe pulled her back into his arms and kissed her again. This kiss wasn't as devouring as the other one had been, but still it sent blissful heat escalating through her entire body.

This time when he released her, she smiled. "I kind of like this sexual chemistry stuff." She refused to pretend that he didn't turn her on in a way that she liked. Over dinner they had pretty much set the ground rules that would dictate their friendship. Both of them had been open and had given each other a glimpse of what was underneath their businesslike exteriors.

Gabe couldn't stop the smile that spread across his lips. "Yeah, I like this sexual chemistry stuff, too."

She gazed up at him from underneath lowered lashes. "Do you think we let things move too fast tonight? Especially when we're just friends?"

Gabe chuckled. "There is such a thing as being intimate friends."

Sage frowned. She wondered if he was hinting at the same thing as a sex-only relationship and decided to ask him.

He thought about his past relationship with Debbie and shook his head. He didn't want to share anything like that with Sage. "No, I don't mean a sex-only relationship, Sage. What I'm saying is that we may have left your apartment this evening as friends, but I don't think friendship will work between us with all this chemistry we generate."

She lifted an arched brow. "Are you suggesting that we don't go out on any more dates?"

"No, that's not what I'm suggesting. In fact, I think just the opposite. We should continue to date with no restrictions, taking things at a pace that is comfortable for the two of us. I don't want you to do anything you aren't ready to do, and I'll know when you're ready."

She considered his words for a few seconds, then said, "And how will you know when I'm ready?"

He smiled. "I'll know." Then his gaze grew serious, and he reached out and threaded his fingers in her hair to hold her face in place. "But the one thing I won't tolerate, Sage, is playing substitute. Understood?"

Her eyes widened in startled shock. *Substitute? What is he talking about?* Then she remembered what he'd accused her of that day at lunch. How could he still think that she would use him as a substitute when Erol had been the furthest thing from her mind tonight?

Anger ripped through her, and she took a step back. "Maybe it's you who should understand something, Gabe. I don't play games. I've told you the real deal between me and Erol, and I don't know why you won't believe me and why you're so convinced that I'm still carrying a torch for him when I'm not. But since you seem to believe that, maybe it will be best if you and I don't go out again."

"Sage—"

"No, please just leave."

Gabe sighed. She was upset, and he knew it. He also knew that he had certainly made a mess of things. He wanted to stay and talk about it, but with the mutinous look on her face, he decided to do what she'd asked and leave, not wanting to upset her any further. He turned and headed for the door. He glanced back over his shoulder before opening it. "I'll call you."

She glared at him. "Don't bother."

He stopped and turned around. "Good night, Sage." He then walked out the door.

"Gabe Blackwell actually thinks that you're using him as a substitute for Erol?" Rose asked in astonishment over the phone line.

"Yes, can you believe such a thing?" Sage asked, still fuming. After Gabe had left, she had stripped off her clothes, taken a shower to cool her still-heated body, put on her pajamas and placed a call to Rose. She had totally forgotten about the time difference; however, Rose, who didn't have a job to go to the next day, was awake and eager to hear what she had to say.

"Yes, I can believe such a thing," Rose said softly.

Sage frowned. "And just what do you mean by that?"

"Hey, just hear me out before you get in a huff. First of all, although Erol has his strong points, too, in good looks and being a fine brother and all, I think Gabe is a man in a class by himself. Not only is he good-looking and fine as a dime, he's also pretty damn wealthy. However, on the other hand, you just got out of a relationship that you've been in for five long years with the same guy, and for that reason, I can see how Gabe might think you really aren't over Erol."

When Sage tried to interrupt, Rose said quickly, "Sage, think logically for a moment. Most people, especially an emotional woman as yourself, aren't able to wipe out five years of loving the same man within a six-month time period. I think it's unrealistic for you to even want anyone to believe that you still don't feel something for Erol."

Sage nervously bit her bottom lip. "Okay, so my love for Erol hasn't completely died, so what? That has nothing to do with

Gabe, especially when there's no way Erol and I will get back to-gether."

"And you're absolutely sure of that?"

Sage inhaled deeply, feeling angry and frustrated. "Why won't anyone believe me? I thought I had you in my corner, Rose."

"And you do, girlfriend. I'm just trying to make you see rea-son and for you to understand why Gabe would possibly feel threatened by Erol's memory."

Sage raised her eyes to the ceiling. "But that's just it. Erol doesn't occupy my memory. There are days I don't think of him at all."

"Have you heard from him since you've left?"

"Yes, in the beginning when I first got here, he used to call occasionally, but then I finally asked that he stop calling be-cause we had nothing to say to each other."

"Have you seen him?"

"No."

"And what if you were to see him, Sage? It's been six months since you broke off your engagement, and then you left Char-lotte for Anchorage. I want you to be honest with yourself as well as with me. What would be your reaction if you were to see him now? Can you honestly say without a doubt that you and Erol won't get back together? I know he hurt you by what he did, but when you think about it, the two of you had a pretty nice relationship before his screwup. He loved you, and I know for a fact that he still does. Whenever I see him he asks about you. And he looks so sad it's a shame. And to make matters worse, I hear he still isn't dating anyone. He actually believes that when you return to Charlotte, all will be forgiven."

Sage rolled her eyes. "Well, he's wrong."

"Then, you need to tell him."

Sage released a frustrated breath. "Don't you think that I have? I don't know what it would take for him to believe me other than for me to become seriously involved with someone else. But the craziness of it is that the one person I feel a desire to become serious about doesn't trust my feelings for Erol. I feel caught between a rock and a hard place."

Rose giggled. "Hey, that isn't a bad place to be, if you get my meaning."

Sage shook her head, grinning. "Is sex the only thing you can think about?"

"No, in fact, I haven't slept with a guy since you left Charlotte."

Sage lifted a brow. "Any reason for that?"

"No. I just want to make a few changes in my life, and before you ask, no, I'm not climbing the walls or anything. I've taken a pledge of celibacy for nine months."

"To who?"

"To myself. I just want to see how long I can hold out. I have three more months to go."

"And then?" Sage asked curiously.

"And then either of two things will happen. I'll either be so proud of my accomplishment that I'll try for another three months to make it a full year of celibacy, or I'll be so horny at the end of the nine months that I'll go out and make up for lost time."

Sage couldn't help but laugh, which was something she felt she needed to do tonight.

"But getting back to the subject of you and Erol," Rose said, breaking into Sage's laughter. "In this case I have to agree with Gabe Blackwell. Until you're absolutely sure this thing between you and Erol is over, and I mean really over, it won't be fair to get involved with Gabe. Sounds to me like he's probably been burned by some woman who used him as a substitute for someone."

Sage regarded what Rose said in silence for a while. Could that be the reason for Gabe's attitude? She remembered what he'd shared with her over dinner about the woman he had wanted to marry and how she had broken things off, *just like that,* because she'd become involved with someone else. Had that someone else been an ex-husband or an ex-lover?

Sage sighed deeply. "Maybe you're right, Rose. I'll call and talk with Erol tomorrow."

"Not good enough."

Sage frowned. "Excuse me?"

"I said a phone call isn't good enough. You should talk to him personally. The two of you should meet somewhere on neutral ground, without the interference of his family or yours, and get this matter cleared up once and for all. Think about it, Sage. Think about it real seriously if you want things between you and Gabe to ever go somewhere."

There was a long silence; then Rose said, "Oh, and before I forget, I've decided to come out and visit you after all. Lord knows after listening to your woes, someone ought to be there to help you straighten out the mess you seem to have gotten your life into without me."

CHAPTER SIXTEEN

Gabe glanced at the clock that sat on the nightstand next to his bed. It was four in the morning, and he was still wide awake. Getting up, he strode to the bedroom window and peered outside.

According to the weather reports, it was supposed to snow again today, which seemed to be an everyday occurrence for March. Except for that one day it hadn't snowed, the day he had gone to Sage's office to apologize. And from the way it looked, he owed her another apology. His mother had been right. He could not go around placing judgment on every woman who'd had a breakup with a former boyfriend by what Lindsey had done. Yet he had because he was afraid to take a chance on letting any woman get close to his heart again.

But tonight had shown him one thing with Sage. She had touched him deeper with a kiss than he'd ever been touched before. What he'd told her was true; sexual chemistry was a powerful thing. As much as he'd enjoyed sleeping with Lindsey, Debbie and a number of other women he'd dated over the years, none of them had elicited such intense and unabashed desire from him before. There was lust, and then there was lust.

What he felt with Sage was something he couldn't explain. He'd experienced sizzle with a woman before, and also skin-prickling heat. But with Sage, there was more, something different, something all-consuming. Without even trying, she was becoming elemental to his total well-being.

From the time he had arrived at her apartment to pick her up for dinner, there had been a frisson of immediate awareness flowing through every part of his body. But it hadn't just happened then. It had happened each and every time he'd come within feet of her, but before he'd been able to play if off. Not last night. Whether she realized it or not, she had displayed her growing trust in him. She had been open with her feelings while sharing information with him—unpretentious, honest— and at the end when he'd lit her fuse, she had become a spitfire.

His accusation had questioned her integrity, and she hadn't liked it one damn bit. It had made her furious, and in the heat of the battle she had gone from feminine to a confident hellion without missing a beat. Desire had sharpened her senses, armed her with more ammunition than he'd been prepared for. He thought she would accept what he'd said about not being a substitute without any fuss or argument. But that had not been the case. She had gotten madder than hell and had not backed down in her assertion that he was the one missing the point and not her. She'd been confident in her feelings and her belief in herself.

Why couldn't she understand that he couldn't be that all believing and trusting because it was his heart that was at risk and not hers?

My heart is at risk.

He turned and moved away from the window as a piercing pain shot through his chest. A reminder of what was at stake. An involvement with Sage could put him at risk of another heartbreak, and he couldn't survive that. His parents and Chris had been witnesses to the pain he'd suffered on the outside, but even they hadn't known the depth of pain that had ripped into his body and soul on the inside.

He went back to bed vowing that somehow and someway, he would do everything in his power to protect himself from the pain of being another fool in love.

Sage hung up the phone and nervously moistened her bottom lip with her tongue. She had just finished talking to Erol and hoped she wasn't making a mistake.

Their plans were set. Coincidentally, he had a business trip to Texas next week and was more than willing to prolong the trip a few days to meet with her. Although she had been careful not to say anything to give him false hope as to why the two of them were meeting, she could tell by the sound of his voice that he'd gotten it anyway.

She shoved away from her desk and walked over to the window. It was still snowing. She was grateful Malcolm had offered to be her chauffeur for their meeting at John Landmark's office. She hated driving around in this weather, especially when there was a lot of melted snow on the ground.

She inhaled deeply. Gabe would be attending the meeting, and she was trying to prepare herself to see him again. Sleep hadn't come easily for her last night. First her body had lain there practically throbbing all night, and if that wasn't bad enough, there was the fact that everything Rose had said about Erol had been in the forefront of her mind. Thoughts of both Gabe and Erol had made getting a good night's rest impossible. After today's meeting, she intended to have Malcolm drop her off at home. Her car could stay at the office all weekend for all she cared. She hadn't planned on going out anyway. Since the weekend weather called for snow, snow and more snow, she'd decided to stay inside where it was nice and warm and survive off soup and sandwiches.

She turned at the knock on her door. "Come in." She smiled when Malcolm entered.

"Are you ready to leave for the meeting?" he asked, going into her office.

"Yes, I just need to grab my briefcase. I doubt this will be a long meeting. All Mr. Landmark wants is for me to update everyone on the plans for the dinner theater as well as the other marketing ideas I have."

Malcolm nodded. He then quickly crossed the room to help her put on her coat. "Did I hear you say you'll be out of town a few days week after next?" he asked when they were walking out of her office.

"Yes. There's some personal business I need to take care of in Texas, so I'll be gone, but only for a day. I've checked and there are no meetings planned, and if anything comes up, I'm sure you'll be able to handle it in my absence."

He grinned. "Thanks for the vote of confidence."

She shook her head, smiling. "You've earned it."

"So as you can see, with all these marketing ideas we plan to have in place, Eden will become a household name." Sage finished her presentation. She glanced around the room. "Are there any questions you'd like answered?"

Gabe leaned back in his chair and watched his wonder woman in action. He was proud of the way she had conducted her part of the meeting. Even when Langley Mayhew, one of John Landmark's junior executives, had tried cornering her with relentless questions, she had not lost her cool but had answered intelligently, expertly and professionally.

The one thing he did notice was that she had not tried to avoid meeting his gaze. In fact, it seemed that she had deliberately made eye contact with him several times, and each time she had done so with total indifference. It was as if what they had shared last night never happened. If he didn't know for a fact that he hadn't dreamed the whole thing, he would think he hadn't actually taken such liberties with her like cupping her bare bottom in his hand or kissing her with such intensity her mouth had become swollen. Therefore, her indifference could mean only one thing.

She was still pretty damn mad at him.

He rubbed a hand along his jaw as he took a few seconds to continue to sit there and think about things, although the business meeting was now ending. Parnell lifted an inquiring brow at him, but otherwise said nothing as he packed up his belongings and left the room.

"You plan to spend the night, Blackwell?"

Gabe looked up into Langley Mayhew's grinning face. He had never cared much for the man, and after the way he'd badgered Sage during her presentation, Gabe liked him even less. In fact, he had a good mind to knock that silly grin off Mayhew's face, which surprised Gabe since he normally wasn't a violent person.

His gaze narrowed as he watched Mayhew cross the room to where Sage was standing packing her briefcase. Mayhew's voice, since the man didn't know how to speak softly, came across rather loudly in the room. Gabe decided to stay where he was and listen.

"That was a nice presentation you did, Ms. Dunbar. Perhaps we can go somewhere and have a few drinks and you can tell me more about it," Mayhew was saying.

Sage, in the most professional voice she had, said, "There's nothing else to tell, Mr. Mayhew. I covered everything in today's meeting."

Mayhew's smile widened, but didn't spread to his eyes, which were scanning Sage from head to toe. "Oh, but I'm sure there's something we can talk about over drinks."

Sage picked up her clipboard and pretended to study it. "No sir, I don't see anything listed that we need to discuss. But I do note another marketing meeting scheduled in two weeks; perhaps you'll have more questions for me then."

At that moment, Malcolm reentered the room, unaware of the conversation going on between Sage and Mayhew, and of the fact that the man was trying hard to hit on her. "Ready for me to drop you off at home, Sage?" he asked, smiling.

She quickly turned to Malcolm, returning his smile. Before she could open her mouth to say anything, Mayhew cut in.

"That's not necessary, Grainger. I'll drop her off at home," he said with authority, slanting Malcolm a look that reminded him of his position. Malcolm may work for the Denmark Group, but ultimately the Denmark Group was under Landmark Industries' employ, of which Mayhew was a top executive.

Malcolm met Sage's gaze. "Just say the word, Sage."

Sage knew that all she had to do was say that she would prefer Malcolm taking her home, and at the risk of incurring Mayhew's ire, Malcolm would. But she couldn't do that. There was no doubt in Sage's mind that Mayhew would deliberately try and make things difficult for Malcolm, and he had a wife and child to think about. This wasn't the first time Langley Mayhew had tried coming on to her, and she intended to talk to Mr. Landmark about it. There was such a thing as sexual harassment in the workplace.

"That's okay, Malcolm, I'll be fine."

Across the room, still sitting quietly and evidently forgotten, Gabe had heard enough. Mayhew might think of himself as Sage and Malcolm's boss, but he sure as hell wasn't his. And it would be a damn cold day in hell before he allowed the slimy man to be alone in the same car with Sage.

Gabe stood. "Ready to go, Sage?" he called out to her.

He saw her blink. He saw Malcolm's brow lift in amused comprehension and then saw Mayhew's jaw tighten in anger.

"I've offered Ms. Dunbar a ride home, Blackwell," Mayhew said through gritted teeth.

Gabe slowly strode over to the group of three. "Sage doesn't need a ride home since she's spending the weekend at my place."

His gaze slowly shifted from Mayhew's to meet Sage's. He saw the look of comprehension and appreciation in her eyes.

She followed his lead and said, "Oops, I'd forgotten about this weekend, Gabe. I'm sorry."

He smiled at her. "That's understandable. I'm sure you've had a lot on your mind in getting ready for today's meeting. We'll stop by your place to pack some things."

"All right."

She then turned her attention to Mr. Mayhew, seeing the angry look on his face. Not only had Gabe put a damper on whatever plans Mayhew had had for her, but he had also insinuated that the two of them were more than mere business associates and therefore she was off limits. "It seems that I don't need a ride after all, Mr. Mayhew, but thanks anyway."

Mayhew nodded, and without saying anything, he angrily walked out of the conference room.

"That man is a jerk," Malcolm said, watching the man's retreating back. He then turned back to Sage and Gabe. "I'm out of here, too. I hope the two of you have a good weekend."

Sage blinked as Malcolm walked away. "Malcolm, wait!"

Malcolm stopped walking and turned around. "Yes?"

Sage frowned at him. "I still need a ride home."

Malcolm smiled and pointed to Gabe. "I thought he was taking you."

Sage frowned. "No, he's not."

"Yes, I am," Gabe said, folding his arms across his chest.

Sage narrowed her eyes at him. "That little show was for Mayhew's benefit."

"No, it wasn't."

"Yes, it was."

Malcolm cleared his throat, interrupting Gabe and Sage's disagreement. "Sage, I'm going on home since it seems you're in good hands. Goodbye."

Before Sage could gather her wits and call after him, Malcolm was gone. She glared up at Gabe, who shrugged his shoulders as a smile tilted his lips.

"I guess you're stuck with me. We can leave now if you're ready," he said, reaching for her briefcase.

"I can carry it myself," she snapped, taking it out of his hands.

"Suit yourself."

Since it was the end of the day as well as the end of the week, most people at the Landmark office had left for the day, so when they got into the elevator and the doors slid shut, they found themselves alone. Sage pushed a button on the console that would take them to the bottom floor, and no sooner had the elevator begun to move, than Gabe reached out and pushed a button to stop it.

Sage glared at him. "What do you think you're doing?"

Gabe smiled as he leaned back against the panel wall. He really liked her when she got mad. She was fiery, bitchy and sexy. He met her stormy glare. "Ever had sex in an elevator?"

He saw that his question took her by surprise and almost knocked the wind out of her sails. Almost. He had to admire the way she quickly recouped and narrowed her eyes at him. "No, and this isn't going to be the day that I try it. Now, if you don't mind, can we go on down?"

He smiled at her. "No, not yet." Then a few moments later, he asked, "Have you ever been kissed in an elevator?"

Sage raised her eyes to the ceiling. *What is this? Sexual Harassment Day?* "No, I've never been kissed in an elevator," she snapped. "Now, will you start this thing moving again please?"

"No, I don't think that I will," he said huskily as he continued to stare long and hard at her. The dim lighting in the elevator made her features even more beautiful, he thought. There was just something about the right type of lighting reflecting off brown skin.

Gabe began wondering how in the world he had thought that he could walk away from her. Emotional baggage or not, he wanted her with every fiber in his body. All during today's meeting he had literally ached for her.

And he was still aching.

Sage narrowed her eyes at him. "Do you mind, Gabe? Like I told you last night, I don't like playing games."

He crossed his arms over his chest. "Then, what do you like doing, Sage? You don't make out in elevators, nor have you ever been kissed in one. So what do you do?"

She angrly closed the distance between them. "Oh, don't you know? I like using men as substitutes for my ex-fiancé, since stupid me doesn't know when to let go and move on with my life."

Before she had time to react, Gabe pulled on the lapels of her coat, bringing her face close to his. "Good, because today I feel like being used." He then lowered his mouth to hers.

The moment Gabe's mouth touched Sage, heat flooded her body, and any thought of resisting him faded into oblivion. She forgot all about the fact that she was supposed to be angry with him. Right now she had other things to think about—like the way he had deepened their kiss and how his tongue was doing crazy and wicked things to the inside of her mouth. His tongue was making love to it, stroking, thrusting and licking and literally staking a claim in a way he had not done last night, and she'd thought that had been the ultimate kiss. Boy, had she been wrong.

Sage heard herself moan . . . or was it Gabe. She didn't know, nor did she care. All that mattered was that he was kissing her, devouring her, and she was enjoying every tantalizing minute of it.

All too soon he ended the kiss, but not totally. He traced the outline of her lips and continued licking, nibbling and thoroughly tasting her lips as he intermittently whispered between each sensuous tongue attack, "You're not stupid. I'm the one who's stupid for saying what I did last night. I'm sorry, Sage."

Since Gabe had her lips engaged in something that had her bones turning to mush, she couldn't say anything. She could only nod her head. She was sorry, too. Sorry that some woman had hurt him so badly that he was distrustful to this degree.

Distrustful. She certainly knew how that felt.

There was so much she wanted to say to him. More than anything, she wanted to assure him that he was not Erol's substitute, but the sexual chemistry between them was in total control, making them use their lips and tongues for other things than talking.

He finally loosened his grip on her waist and rubbed his thumb against the smoothness of her cheek and the wetness of her mouth. "I guess we better get out of here before they call in the mechanics," he murmured, nearly breathless.

Still unable to speak, she nodded. He pulled her to his side after pushing the button that started the elevator moving again. When they reached the bottom floor and the elevator doors opened, Sage had to blink against the brightness of the daylight after having spent the past fifteen minutes in dim lighting.

Gabe grabbed hold of her hand, entwining his fingers in hers as he led her through the glass door. "I'm parked over here."

They said nothing as they walked together to his car, still holding hands. He opened the car door for her and then adjusted the seat belt around her, snapping it in place.

Sage watched as Gabe walked around to his side of the car to get in. Before starting the car, he leaned over and kissed her again. This one was a lot gentler than the one they'd shared in the elevator. Moments later, he pulled back. "We need to talk, Sage," he said huskily.

She let out a long, deep breath. "I know."

He then started the car. Sage remained silent, trying to gather her thoughts on what she would say to him. Should she tell him about her trip to Texas to meet with Erol? Would he see that as the inability to let go instead of seeing it as the ability to move on? She shook her head, not knowing what she should do.

"How long will it take you to pack?"

Sage, who had been looking out the window deep in thought, turned and gave Gabe a sidelong glance. "Excuse me?"

When he brought the car to a stop at a traffic light, he met her gaze. "I asked, how long will it take for you to pack?"

Sage raised a brow in confusion. "Pack for what?"

"The weekend. I was dead serious when I told Mayhew that you were spending the weekend with me at my place, Sage."

CHAPTER SEVENTEEN

Sage's eyebrows shot up. "Your place for the weekend?" At his nod, she said, "But, there's a lot we need to discuss."

With a slow smile, Gabe said, "And we can do it this weekend at my place, Sage. I'm not trying to rush you into anything; in fact, there're several guest rooms in my home. All I want is for us to be able to spend time together and talk. I've been to your place before; now you can come to mine."

"But for the entire weekend?" she asked with a frown, not sure this was the right route for them to take.

"Yes. After our talk there's a lot we can do this weekend, even though it's supposed to snow again. You mentioned over dinner the other night that you'd never gone fishing. That's something we can do since I have a stocked lake on my land. I also have a snowmobile we can use to go riding." He glanced over at her. "Besides, I'd really like to spend some time with you."

Sage considered his words for a moment. "And I will be using the guest room?"

He nodded. "If that's the way you want it."

"It is."

"Then, that's the way it will be."

* * *

A couple of hours later, Gabe stood in front of the huge window in his living room as his gaze took in the panoramic view of the canyons and snow-capped mountains. He leaned his head back and sniffed the air. There was the smell of the burning wood in the fireplace and an unmistakable scent of a woman. *The scent of Sage.*

The seductive fragrance of her perfume sent a powerful shudder through him when thoughts of the shower she was taking in the guest bathroom stood out in his mind. After taking her home, he had sat patiently in her living room while she had gone into her bedroom to pack. She'd reappeared less than twenty minutes later with an overnight bag.

During the forty-five-minute drive from her apartment to his home, they had talked about a number of things, making sure they kept the topic of their conversation off of them. She had told him of her indecisiveness about going home for Mother's Day because of the way she still felt about her father, and about Rose Wood's decision to come for a visit in a few weeks.

He, on the other hand, had told her how he had come to own the house and how Christopher's wife, Maxi, had done all of the decorating of the place. He'd also told her about Christopher and Maxi's son, Christopher Max, and how at eleven months old he had started walking last week.

As Gabe watched a family of squirrels dig their way through the snow in search of food, it suddenly occurred to him that other than Maxi, no woman had spent the night here. Then, brushing his fingers against the cold windowpane, he went still, stood almost frozen in place, as he stared at the feminine reflection that suddenly appeared in the glass. With the lights down he could see that Sage had entered the room behind him and was unaware that he knew she was there.

Gabe's heart began beating rapidly in his chest, and he decided not to turn around. When she was ready to let him know of her presence, she would.

In the meantime, he would enjoy her beautiful reflection since it hadn't dawned on her yet that she was being watched.

Sage had walked out of the bedroom with the intention of letting Gabe know she was there. But the sight of him had taken her breath away. He had changed clothes, and it was the first time she had seen him in anything other than business attire. It was hard not to appreciate the sight of a well-built man, especially from behind.

Even beneath his knitted sweater she could detect broad shoulders and a strong, muscular back. Then there was the firmness of his buttocks that looked pretty damn good in a pair of jeans. The way the denim material fitted over his backside left nothing to the imagination. Everything she saw was unmistakably actual visual perception and not something that was based on mere make-believe fantasy. This wasn't reality in motion but was reality standing still. To put it more bluntly, Gabe Blackwell definitely owned a great-looking tush. She'd never been one of those women who were attracted to a man's hind part before, but the way Gabe looked in jeans was enough to make her appreciate the fact that she was a woman with good vision.

And all of this was from the back. Heaven help her when he turned around and she saw the front.

Knowing that she couldn't stand there and secretly ogle him all night, Sage moved a few steps into the room. She wasn't sure if it was the heat being generated from the fireplace or if Gabe had turned the heating unit up a notch, but she suddenly felt hot. Hotter than she'd ever felt before.

She looked down and saw a half-filled glass of wine sitting on the coffee table next to her. Evidently, it was wine Gabe had started drinking but never finished. She picked up the wineglass and brought it to her lips.

Gabe watched Sage's every move. His heartbeat raced, and his chest tightened when he saw her place the wineglass to her lips. His breath caught when, with her tongue, she licked around the rim of the glass as if wanting to taste whatever spot his mouth had touched.

The thought of what she was doing made hot, rich desire flow through every pore in his body. He felt his body harden and his erection grew thick against his jeans.

He briefly closed his eyes, wondering how in hell he could have thought that he could bring her here and engage in any type of meaningful conversation with her without wanting to make love to her. He wanted to devour every inch of her in very delectable pieces, and that was only after making love to her all night long and all day through, in every position known to man and even a few that man didn't know about yet. He was feeling very creative.

Gabe didn't think he could last much longer when he watched as Sage tilted her head back, exposing a long, beautiful neck, and took a long swallow of what was left of his wine. And when she licked her lips afterward, he breathed in deeply and slowly turned around.

He met her gaze, and the look on her face was priceless, hot, aroused. Then he felt it again, that same powerful sexual chemistry that had the ability to render them defenseless. More than anything he wanted to touch her but knew that would defeat everything, especially her purpose for being there. They had to talk first.

"Do you like your room?" he forced himself to ask in a voice that didn't sound like his own.

She nervously licked her lips again, and seconds later a pleasing smile appeared on them. "Yes. It's simply beautiful and so wonderfully decorated. Christopher's wife did an excellent job. Everything is so color coordinated, so feminine and so perfect."

Gabe smiled. And just to think he had teased Maxi about over-doing it. "I'll tell her you said that." He moved away from the window and appreciated that since the lights in the room were turned down low, the dimness kept his erection from being so obvious.

He glanced down at the glass she held in her hand. "Would you like another drink?"

Sage also glanced down at the empty wineglass. A wave of amusement filled her, and she couldn't help but chuckle. "I was thirsty," she said, explaining why she had drunk his wine.

He nodded, smiling. "So I see." He then checked his watch. "Are you hungry?"

She shook her head. "No, I had a big lunch, but if you want to fix—"

"No," he quickly interrupted. "I'm fine."

Gabe's hands balled into fists at his sides. He wasn't fine. All he could think about was what had happened last night in her apartment with his mouth feeding, devouring, making love to hers.

He blinked when he realized she had said something. "I'm sorry, I missed that. What did you say?"

Sage smiled. "I asked if you wanted to start our talk now?"

He wanted to do more than talk but decided not to tell her that. "Do you?"

Sage shrugged. "We may as well. Then we can enjoy the rest of our weekend doing all those outside activities."

Gabe considered what she'd said for a moment. The activi-ties he wanted to do with her were definitely inside activities. "All right, we'll talk."

He motioned for her to sit on the sofa, and to be on the safe side, instead of sitting next to her, he took a chair across from her. He watched as she nervously tapped her hand on the table separating them.

She glanced up at him. "I need to know where you want our relationship to go, Gabe."

He slowly lifted a dark brow. "Where do you want it to go?"

Sage shrugged. "I'm not sure. We tried the friendship thing, and it didn't go over too well. There's a part of me that feels I should give myself more time before becoming seriously involved with someone. But then there's another part that feels I need to do whatever I have to to move on and put the past behind me. And before you ask, no, this isn't about Erol or any feelings I may still have for him. It's a decision about me and how I want to live my life."

She leaned back on the sofa before continuing. "Because I was involved in a relationship that lasted five years, I need time to enjoy being free for a while, without getting serious."

Gabe nodded. He clearly understood that. He hadn't gotten serious about anyone since Lindsey.

"And I want to get comfortable about trusting someone again."

Gabe met her gaze. "Do you feel you can trust me, Sage?"

She thought about his question. Deep down she felt that she could. If she didn't believe that, then she wouldn't be alone with him now, holding this conversation, exposing her pain and insecurities to him. "Yes, Gabe, I feel that I can," she finally answered.

Gabe smiled. "Thanks. Now, is there anything else you feel we need to discuss and get out in the open?"

"Yes, there's the issue of sex."

With that one single word spoken from her lips, Gabe's heart began beating rapidly in his chest. "Sex?" he asked huskily as thick desire flowed through his nerve endings.

"Yes, sex," Sage said, leaning forward. "I'm not comfortable with the idea of sleeping with a man just to have something to do. It's not in me to physically share myself with someone I don't care deeply about. Other women may not find it difficult, but I do."

Gabe nodded again. A part of him was glad that she did.

"So these sexual urges aren't helping matters," she said softly.

Gabe bit back a moan at what Sage had just said. He cleared his throat. "Sexual urges?" he rasped.

She nodded as she unconsciously skimmed the tips of her fingers over the smooth skin of her thigh that her skirt didn't cover. "Yes, or sexual chemistry if that's a better name for it. I felt it last night with you, and I hadn't counted on that happening," she said in a slightly irritated voice.

An amused smile curved his lips. "Neither had I. At least not to that extent." Then his expression turned serious as he watched the unconscious movement of her hand on her thigh. Seeing her bare skin reminded him of the soft feel of her flesh he had cupped in his hand last night. The memory made his front ache. Tilting his head, he met her gaze. "I wanted you bad last night."

A shiver of desire coursed slowly down Sage's spine with Gabe's words. She had wanted him badly last night, too. And it didn't help matters that with the way he was looking at her, his heated gaze was inflaming her entire body. "How bad?" she surprised herself by asking as a coiling tightness formed in her stomach and a torrential ache settled between her legs.

"Come here and I'll show you," he murmured huskily.

A shudder ran through Sage at Gabe's invitation. She exhaled a deep breath and gazed at him through heavy eyelids. "I'm not ready to have sex with anyone, Gabe," she said in a raspy voice. She crossed her legs when the ache between them intensified.

Gabe held up his hands. "No sex. Just foreplay."

Foreplay that doesn't end with sex? "How?" she asked, curious as well as aroused at the very thought.

Gabe leaned forward in his seat. "In a number of ways, but mainly doing what we did last night."

She raised a brow. "Kissing?".

He nodded slowly. "Yes, and touching."

Curiosity thrummed through Sage, and she wondered how they had gotten on the subject of kissing and touching. "No more than that?"

"No more than that."

"No sex?"

"No sex. I promise. Trust me," Gabe answered, his voice deep, husky, seductive. For the first time in his life, his restraint, his sense of honor and the ability to keep his word would be put to the test. He watched as Sage nervously nibbled on her bottom lip, contemplating his words, his request to prove her trust in him. Considering her disappointment with her ex-fiancé and her father, he knew that placing her trust in another man was not easy for her.

He sat back in the chair. The decision would be hers, and he would wait patiently for it, even if it took all night. And no matter what, he would abide by her decision.

His breath lodged in his throat when she slowly stood. He could actually feel the heat simmering in his gaze as he watched her walk around the table that separated them. And when she stood before him with as much desire in her eyes as he had in his, and at the same time openly proclaiming total trust in him for her well-being, a surge of tenderness and protectiveness welled up inside of him so profound, he almost couldn't bear it.

He stared up at her, and a sense of peace settled over him because at that moment, he knew why he had allowed Sage to weaken his defenses, soften his resolve and break his vow to never become involved with another woman on the rebound again.

Although they still had a lot of talking to do, a number of

things they had yet to work out, he still wanted her, because God help him, at some point since first meeting her six months ago, he had fallen in love with her. And he knew it was no use fighting it. However, he intended for both of their sakes not to leave anything to chance. He would not make the same mistakes with her that he'd made with Lindsey. He would not rush her or assume anything. They would not move from point A to point B until *he* thought she was ready . . . no matter what she thought.

"Gabe?"

His name, whispered so sweetly from her lips, reclaimed his attention. He swept his gaze over the outfit she had changed into after her shower, a blue pullover sweater and a black wool skirt that stopped midthigh. Her legs were bare, and her feet were encased in a pair of flat shoes.

Unable to resist touching her any longer, he said silkily, "Come closer and let me feel you."

Sage swallowed as Gabe's words filled her mind. He was close enough to touch her if he reached out his hand. But he didn't just want to touch her; he wanted to *feel* her, and he wanted her to come to him of her own free will.

She allowed her gaze to drift longingly over him as he reclined in the chair, looking more handsome, more desirable and sexier than any man had the right to look. He made a move to spread his legs apart, and she knew that he wanted her to come stand between them.

Inhaling deeply and tossing all doubts aside, she took a step toward him and stood just where he wanted her to, between his widened thighs. Their gazes held, and her body began heating with a need the likes of which she had never experienced before. Her breathing quickened when he reached out and touched the front hem of her skirt, then moments later, moved his hands to touch her thighs.

Sage sucked in a deep breath as Gabe slowly began trailing

his hands down her thighs, touching bare flesh. The feel of his hands on her was seductive, exquisite and decadent. She liked the way it felt.

His breathing became just as ragged as hers when his hand slowly moved from her thighs to her inner legs, gently nudging her knees apart to get his hands between them. Not going any higher than the hem of her skirt, he moved his hands gently up and down her legs as if just touching her brought him intense pleasure.

She closed her eyes, allowing herself to feel Gabe's touch deep in her mind, savoring every moment of what he was doing. She refused to open her eyes when she felt his hand slide higher, making its way underneath her skirt. And when he touched her intimately, his hand felt hot through the silky fabric of her panties.

"Open your eyes, Sage. Look at me."

Sage slowly did what he requested. Her skirt and slip were twisted around her waist, and she stood before him with her lacy black panties as the only thing covering her bottom.

She held his gaze as he continued to touch her, stroking her into a feverish pitch through the material of her panties. Then suddenly, she felt the urge to join her mouth to his.

He evidently had the same idea because he reached for her the same time she reached for him, pulling her into his lap and devouring her mouth with a degree of desperation and possessiveness that surprised her. But she didn't pause to think about it. The only thing she wanted to think about was what Gabe's mouth was doing to hers.

Pure, unadulterated desire touched every part of her body as his hand slipped beneath the waistband of her panties to touch her. His finger found that part of her it wanted. He used the same rhythm his tongue was using in her mouth to stroke her, spinning her out of control and taking her just where he wanted her to go.

Gabe broke off the kiss the exact moment her body began to shudder in his arms, and Sage screamed his name . . . *his name* . . . moments before collapsing against his chest.

Half an hour later Gabe was still holding Sage protectively against him in his lap while she slept. He had gotten great satisfaction bringing her pleasure, and just to think he had kept his promise to her.

Kissing, touching but no sex.

Inhaling deeply, he ignored the ache that still claimed his body. And it didn't help matters that his erection was still hard and was pressed intimately against her. Closing his eyes, he downplayed any need he had. Taking care of her needs had been more important to him than taking care of his own.

And bless her heart, she hadn't understood that she'd had those needs. He wondered if it had ever occurred to her that those "sexual urges" had been the result of her body going six months without something she'd grown accustomed to getting.

He shook his head. To Sage everything was supposed to be simple. But she had found out just how problematic life could be when her father and ex-fiancé had caused her grief, and although she hadn't yet admitted it to herself, her pain had not yet healed. She was in a state of denial if she thought that it had.

He also knew that in order for them to share a relationship that was strong, meaningful and absolute, it had to be based on love and not lust, trust and not mistrust, gain and not pain. And to make sure they moved in the right direction toward those goals, they would do things his way.

Leaning down, he kissed her damp forehead and then tightened his hold around her. Gabe knew at that moment, emotional baggage or not, Sage was the one person who could make him feel whole.

CHAPTER EIGHTEEN

Sage yawned and slowly stretched out on the bed when she came awake. Memories flooded her mind, and the last thing she remembered was . . .

"Oh, my."

She quickly sat up in bed and glanced around the bedroom. Someone had placed her atop the covers fully clothed. That someone had to have been Gabe. She glanced at the clock on the nightstand at the same time she picked up the aroma of food cooking. It was seven in the evening. Evidently, Gabe had decided to start dinner without her.

She drew a deep breath, wondering how she was going to face him after the way she'd acted, wanton and hot. No telling what he thought of her. Kissing him again hadn't been so bad, but she had actually let him touch her . . . there. Last night had been their first date, and already he'd made it to second base. She had dated Erol a full year and a half before she'd entertained the idea of sleeping with him, and before then all he'd gotten out of her was a kiss, a kiss that was nothing like the kiss Gabe had laid on her. Gabe had a way of turning a kiss into *foreplay*, just like he'd said. But she couldn't hold him responsible for what had happened. He had told her that he wanted to kiss and touch her. She just hadn't known to what extent he had wanted to touch.

She leaned against the bedpost, relieved that at least they had talked, although she had been the one doing most of the talking. She still wasn't sure what he wanted out of their relationship other than kissing and touching.

She reached up and let her fingers touch her lips. They felt sore. Rolling to the side, she grabbed her purse off the nightstand and fumbled through it in search of a mirror. She found one, and when she saw her reflection, she wasn't surprised that her mouth looked swollen and well kissed. Placing the mirror back in her purse, she flopped back on the bed, knowing she couldn't hide in this room forever.

Her heart began to race, her nipples felt tingly against her sweater and she felt hot between her legs when she remembered just what Gabe had done to her, just how he had touched her. She and Erol had always engaged in traditional lovemaking. Foreplay was something that happened before you did the real thing, to basically get you ready for that point. Foreplay had never been a stand-alone act, something in a league of its own.

Until Gabe.

The sound of a cabinet closing reminded her that he was busy in the kitchen and she needed to be in the kitchen helping him. It was not her intent for him to wait on her hand and foot this weekend. But then . . . it hadn't been her intent for him to seduce her either.

She shook her head upon silently admitting that as far as the seduction went, she'd been a willing participant. She had trusted him, and he *had* kept his word. There had not been sex, just kissing and touching. She glanced down at her outfit, knowing the best thing to do would be to change into something else, all the way down to her panties. She didn't want to wear anything that was a reminder of her and Gabe's earlier behavior.

She blew out a long breath as she pulled the sweater over her head, asking for strength to get through this.

She's going to have to wake up sometime. . . .

Gabe glanced in the direction of the guest bedroom. It had been over an hour, and Sage was still asleep. Placing the lid on the pot he had just finished stirring, he crossed the kitchen to get something out of the cabinet. Usually, he was a lot better organized when preparing dinner. But then, usually, he didn't have a feminine distraction asleep in one of his guest bedrooms.

He reached up for a small can of cayenne pepper and picked up another can instead. He breathed deeply when he read the label. *Sage.* He shook his head, smiling. One way or the other he intended to keep her in his hand. Placing the can of sage back on the shelf, he got the can of pepper he wanted and closed the cabinet door. He hoped she liked spicy foods. Everything was ready. All he had to do now was wait.

Then he heard the sound of her feet against the hardwood floor. He turned and stared at the entranceway to the kitchen, waiting, anticipating. He felt his heart trip into a higher gear. Had anyone told him a year ago that he would have been this excited, this mesmerized, this so much into a woman, he would not have believed them. It seemed Christopher falling hard for a woman wasn't the only miracle.

Gabe tapped his hand on the counter, impatient for Sage to appear. He wanted to see her. He needed to see her. Now.

No sooner had that thought formulated, than Sage walked into the kitchen. Their gazes met. His throat immediately went dry. He had to blink in order to focus. She looked so beautiful it was almost blinding. She had changed from her sweater and skirt and was wearing a large sweatshirt and a pair of well-worn jeans. If she thought that for one minute her outfit would be a total turn-off she had definitely miscalculated the effect anything that she put on her body had on him.

"Hi."

The soft sound of her voice brought him around. He smiled at her. "Hi. Did you enjoy your rest?"

Sage tried not to think about the fact that she had fallen asleep in his arms while sitting in his lap after . . . "Yes, thanks," she said in a rush. "And I want to apologize for falling asleep and not helping you cook dinner."

He leaned back against the counter. "No apology needed. You had a busy day, and I hope you're hungry."

An overwhelming day is more like it, she thought. "Yes, I'm starving," she said. "Is there anything I can do to help you?"

"You can set the table if you'd like. Everything you need is in the cabinet over the sink."

She nodded before quickly crossing the room. Gabe stayed right where he was and stared at her. He knew he was making her nervous and didn't want things to be that way. They would be spending the entire weekend together, and after what they had shared earlier, there was no need for them to start tiptoeing around each other. So he decided to make the first move. She had virtually told him what she wanted and didn't want out of a relationship, and later over dinner he would share with her his thoughts on the matter.

She was standing at the counter with her back to him, getting ready to open a cabinet to pull out the plates. He came up directly behind her and immediately felt her tense when she detected his presence. She quickly turned around.

He leaned closer, and without saying anything, he covered her mouth with his. His tongue was tamer, a lot gentler than it had been earlier, but he knew the passion was still there; there was no place else for it to be since he was kissing the woman his heart desired.

He hoped that kissing her that way was letting her know that what happened between them earlier hadn't been a mistake. There would be more kissing and touching, and when he thought their relationship was solid, strong and where it should be, there would definitely be sex.

He ended the kiss and took a step back, smiling at her faltering attempt to hide the gleam of desire in her eyes. "Thanks," he said, widening his smile at her.

She slowly raised an arched brow. "You're thanking me for the kiss?" she asked, as if such a thing surprised her.

His gaze caressed her face. "Yes, and for a lot of other things like being here with me, and for placing your trust in me the way you did."

Sage nodded. She *had* trusted him. "And could you also be thanking me for not helping you cook?" she asked, now feeling more relaxed as a teasing grin curved her lips.

Gabe chuckled. "Why is that? Can't you cook?"

She shrugged and decided to give him an honest answer. "No. Cooking was nothing I was ever interested in."

"Neither was I."

Sage tilted her head and glanced around the kitchen. "You seem to be running a tight ship to me. You actually look right at home in the kitchen."

A huge smile spread across Gabe's lips. "Only because of Christopher. He had to learn early to fend for himself, which also included cooking. When we shared an apartment together while away at college, he taught me everything I know."

Sage gave Gabe a curious look. "Everything?" she asked. Over dinner the other night, he'd told her more about his best friend, especially the fact that Christopher Chandler had been a womanizer to the third degree before settling down and marrying the woman of his dreams.

Gabe shook his head. "Okay, not everything."

"Thank goodness."

Gabe burst out laughing. He then took Sage's hand in his. "I'll help you set the table, and then we can talk some more."

* * *

"Umm, this is delicious, Gabe."

Gabe smiled, pleased that she liked the way he had cooked her pork chops. To him nothing tasted better than smothered pork chops over wild rice. Add fresh field peas to that along with a tossed salad and you had a pretty darn good meal.

During dinner they talked about a number of things, mostly Eden. They were now enjoying their second cup of coffee, and he knew it was time they continued their talk.

"Getting back to our earlier discussion, Sage."

He saw her ease back in her chair when she realized what they were about to discuss. "We did say we would talk everything through at the beginning so that we can enjoy the rest of the weekend," he reminded her.

"Yes, we did. But I thought we had talked already."

He leaned back in his chair. "No, you talked and I listened."

"Now is it time for you to talk and for me to listen?" she asked, already feeling nervous about what he would say.

"Yes."

Whatever he had to say, she owed him the courtesy of listening. After all, he *had* listened to her. "All right."

A few moments later, he began. "I just want you to know that I understand everything you said earlier about not knowing where you want our relationship to go. If you'd allow me to make a few suggestions, I think we can come to a reasonable solution about a few things."

Sage met his gaze. "Go on."

He then leaned closer. "It's not such a big a problem as it may seem, Sage. You just got out of one long-term relationship and are somewhat leery about getting right back into another. Top that with unresolved feelings you may or may not have for your ex-fiancé . . ." When she started to interrupt, he held his hand up. "Please hear me out before you say anything, all right?"

Sage reluctantly agreed.

"In no way am I saying that you still care deeply enough for the guy to ever get back with him. All I'm saying is that for you to still have feelings for him is understandable. After all, the two of you spent five years of your lives together as a couple."

He took a sip of his coffee, then said, "And then for me, there is the issue of Lindsey."

Sage raised a brow. "Lindsey?"

"Yes, the woman I had planned to marry. She's now happily married. My relationship ended with her three years ago. Yet, my past experience with her is the main reason I've avoided any serious entanglements since then. Therefore, since the both of us were previously involved with people we cared deeply about, I think the best thing we can do is to give each other time," Gabe finally concluded.

Sage's gaze became confused. "Time?" At his nod she asked, "Are you suggesting that we don't see each other?"

Gabe smiled. He liked hearing the disappointment in her voice. "No, quite the contrary. I think we should continue to see each other on a regular basis, but not get deeply involved until we're both sure that is what we want."

Sage released a long sigh, then asked, "Would you define *deeply involved*?"

"I'm talking about involved to the point where we would sleep together. You did say you weren't ready for anything like that yet anyway."

Sage nodded. She bit nervously on her bottom lip, thinking about all that Gabe had said. "Let me make sure I have this right. You're suggesting that we see each other on a regular basis in a no-sex relationship . . . until the two of us feel we would want to take our relationship to that level?"

"Yes."

Sage arched a brow. "Why? What would you be getting out of this?"

He smiled. "Precisely the same thing you'd be getting. A chance for us to continue to get to know each other and further our trust in each other in a developing relationship without the issue of sex clouding up anything."

"But what about those sexual urges men have?"

Gabe's smile widened. "Women have them, too."

Sage shrugged. "Yeah, but I've heard they're a lot harder on a man."

"And I'm sure there are women who'd have just as hard a time." Gabe didn't want to call names, but he'd bet that she was one of them. Whether Sage realized it or not, she was a highly sensually charged person. She had proved that by having an orgasm in his arms just from him touching her. They would both burn to cinders when the time came for him to be inside of her. He was getting extremely hard just thinking about it.

"Are you sure you're willing to try this?" Sage asked with uncertainty.

"Yes. I enjoy being with you, Sage. Besides, we proved this afternoon that there are other things we can do that are just as pleasurable as having sex."

Sage knew just what he was talking about but decided to ask anyway. "Kissing and touching?"

"Yes, and as we get more comfortable with each other and with our developing relationship, we can add one other thing."

Sage's curiosity was piqued. "One other thing like what?"

Gabe decided he hadn't wanted to shock her too soon, but she had asked. "Tasting."

Sage's hand trembled as she reached for her cup of coffee. She wouldn't ask Gabe for further clarification on that one. Too many racy, erotic images were already forming in her mind. Deciding to change the subject, she said, "I'll be glad to wash the dishes since you did all the cooking."

"There's no need since I have a dishwasher. But if you want, you can help me load it up. Then I suggest the two of us get to bed early since we have a busy day tomorrow."

Sage took a sip of coffee. "Doing what?"

"Going fishing, riding on the snowmobile, and getting some skiing in. I'm waking you up before the crack of dawn so the two of us can get an early start." His smile widened. "We'll have a lot of fun together."

Sage nodded. She didn't doubt his words since it seemed that they always had fun anytime they were together. The steamy, hot kind of fun.

While she watched him take a leisurely sip of his coffee, all she could think about was kissing, touching . . . and tasting.

Oh, my.

CHAPTER NINETEEN

On Monday morning Sage smiled as she sat in her office with an updated report on Eden in front of her. However, her smile didn't have anything to do with the report, although she was pleased with how things were progressing. Her smile was for Gabe and the wonderful weekend they had shared.

After dinner on Friday night, they had gone to their separate beds to get a good night's sleep. True to his word, he had awakened her the following morning before the crack of dawn to go fishing.

The lake on his land had been humongous, and just as he'd said, it had been stocked with all kinds of fish. After Gabe showed her how to use a fishing rod, they had spent that very cold morning drinking tons of coffee while catching fish for their dinner. Then later they had gone riding on his snowmobile and skiing.

During that time they spent together, they had shared a lot of conversation. He'd told her more about his family, and she had told him more about hers. She had also told him about her grandmother and how close they'd been.

He even told her of other projects his company had lined up

to do, and that one would take him to England for at least six months. He also mentioned that Christopher would be flying in next Monday morning and asked if the three of them could have dinner together the following Wednesday. He wanted her to meet his best friend, and she looked forward to it.

After enjoying a very delicious dinner of grilled fish, green beans and leftover wild rice—just as tasty as the night before—they had cleaned up the kitchen, and then later, since it had stopped snowing, they had gone walking.

Upon returning, she had taken a hot soak in the tub to warm her body. After changing into another pair of jeans and a pullover sweater, she had joined him in the living room. They had both agreed to always sit down and discuss things that were concerning them, keeping the lines of communication open between them as a way to continue to build trust. That was the main reason she had decided to tell him about her trip to Texas to meet with Erol.

At first he hadn't said anything. He'd sat next to her on the sofa in front of the fireplace, quiet, as if in deep thought. Then he had turned to her and pulled her closer to him and told her that he agreed with her decision to meet with Erol if that was what she felt she needed to do.

For the rest of the evening they had sat in front of the fireplace, drank wine and talked some more. She had totally enjoyed his company. It was only when it was time for them to turn in for the night that she had gone into his arms for the kiss she'd been starving for all day.

He had kissed her with a passion that overwhelmed her. And it had been her breasts that he had wanted to feel. The smile on Sage's mouth widened when she remembered that not only had he felt them, but he had tasted them as well. By the time he'd finished, she had become a wriggling mass of heated desire, and just like the night before, she had come apart in his arms.

That night while she'd slept alone, she had dreamed about him, and it wasn't helping matters that thoughts of him consumed her mind now. She was barely getting any work done.

She jumped when she heard the phone ring and quickly picked it up. "Hello?"

"Is it true, Sage? Is it true that you have agreed to meet and talk to Erol? To possibly work things out?"

Sage heard the happiness in her mother's voice and released a long, deep sigh, wondering how her mother had found out. "Mom, who told you that?"

"Ericka."

Ericka was Erol's mother. Sage frowned, wondering if Erol had shared the news with his parents after she'd asked him not to mention it to anyone. "Did Erol tell her that?"

"No, he didn't tell her anything, which Ericka isn't too happy about. She happened to overhear him talking on the phone. He was making dinner reservations for the two of you at some exclusive restaurant in Dallas. So tell me if it's true, sweetheart."

Sage refused to be pulled in by her mother's excitement at the prospect of her and Erol getting back together. "Yes, it's true, Mom, but not for the reason that you think," she said, deciding to put an end to any hope her mother was still holding on to. "I've met someone."

There was a long pause on the other end; then her mother finally said in a rather shocked voice, "You've met someone? Another man?"

Sage swallowed as she remembered her weekend with Gabe, the kissing, the touching, and the tasting. . . . "Yes. We've dated a few times and I really like him. At some point I may decide that I want a serious relationship with him, and if that's the case, I want to make sure Erol fully understands that what we shared is over. Completely. I'm hearing from too many people that he believes we'll eventually get back together, and that won't happen. He needs to get on with his life the way I'm getting on with mine."

There was another long pause. "The two of you really aren't going to get back together, are you?" her mother asked, as if finally realizing the truth.

Sage shook her head. She had thought that after her last conversation with her mother, she had gotten through to her. Evidently not. It had taken her mentioning another man to make her mother accept what she'd been trying to tell her all along. "No, Mom, we're not. Even if I hadn't met Gabe, there was no way for Erol and me to recapture what we once had. Everyone operates at different tolerance levels, certain limits to what they will put up with, and I place a lot of weight on trust in a relationship."

"This man you've met. His name is Gabe?"

"Yes, Gabe Blackwell."

"And he's from Alaska?"

Sage smiled. Now that the shock had worn off, the inquisitiveness had set in. "No, he's from Michigan. Gabe owns the construction company that's building the ski resort." Sage knew she was building up her relationship with Gabe to more than it was, but she was determined to make her mother realize things between her and Erol were completely over.

"Then, I'm sorry, Sage. I really thought things would work themselves out between you and Erol. I honestly had believed that; but I now see that you have made a decision that you feel is the best one for you, and I'm happy for you. In spite of how your father and I feel about Erol, we just want you to be happy. You're our daughter and we love you."

Sage didn't say anything for a long, quiet moment. She appreciated her mother's understanding words and knew what she'd just told her was difficult. Sage had known from the first time she had brought Erol home over Christmas break to meet her parents that they had approved of him and had immediately accepted him into the family and into their hearts. To them it would be like losing a son.

"Your father wants to talk to you, Sage."

Her mother's words recaptured Sage's attention. "All right." She braced herself for the sound of her father's voice. It was a voice that in the past she loved hearing and regretted their relationship wasn't what it used to be, especially now more so than ever.

"Sage?"

"Hello, Dad."

"You're all right?"

"Yes, Dad, I'm fine. What about you?"

"I'm okay." He momentarily got quiet and then said, "I heard bits and pieces of your and your mother's conversation but enough to know you've gotten on with your life and have met someone else."

"Yes. I'm really trying to move forward, and yes, I've met someone. His name is Gabe Blackwell. Right now it's nothing serious, we're just dating, getting to know each other, but I really do like him," she said honestly.

"I'm glad, and I just want you to know that your mom and I are supportive of whatever decisions you make."

Tears eased into Sage's eyes. There had never been a time her father had not been in her corner, and even now his approval of what she was doing meant a lot, although a part of her wanted to believe that it didn't. "Thanks, Dad. I appreciate that. Right now the main thing on my mind is meeting with Erol and making him see that there's no future for us."

"When will you see him?"

"A week from Thursday. I'm flying into Dallas that morning, and we're having dinner together that evening. Then I'm flying out first thing Friday morning to return here."

"Would it be possible for you to come home a few days for a visit?"

Sage's eyes squeezed shut. More than anything she wished

that were possible, but she wasn't ready yet. She needed more time before confronting the lies and deceit that awaited her there. God knew, her nightly prayer was to somehow find a way to forgive her father for what he'd done to her mother, and to her. His affair with that other woman had literally destroyed their bond. She opened her eyes. "No, Dad, not this time, but I am thinking of surprising Mom and coming home for the Fourth of July celebration."

That particular holiday was one the Dunbar family had set aside as an annual family reunion since it was also her grandmother's birthday. Sage had never missed the event since it had started when she was a child. She had always enjoyed going back to her grandmother's home in Tuskegee, Alabama. The hardest time for the family had been the year after her grandmother's death, but everyone decided to continue the tradition, no matter what.

"I really hope you do consider doing that," he said in a very hopeful tone of voice.

"I will."

"I'll let you talk to your mom, and I want you to take care of yourself. And no matter what, always remember that I love you," he said in a voice that was gruff but gentle as a whisper.

A rising wave of emotions, twenty-six years' worth of them, suddenly hit her with a burgeoning force. And then she knew that although what he'd done had hurt her, the man talking to her was her father and she still loved him. "And I love you, too, Dad," she said softly.

Moments later her mother returned to the phone, and Sage swiftly changed the subject to something else. They talked about Rose's planned trip to Anchorage and about her parents' neighbor, Mrs. Paul, who had won an award for community service. Half an hour later, they ended the call.

Standing, Sage walked over to the window and looked out. It would be another pretty day, without snow. She had successfully dealt with her parents regarding Erol; now she knew she had to be prepared to deal with Erol in Dallas. And a part of her was not looking forward to seeing him again.

The next week moved rather swiftly for Sage. She'd had a number of meetings to attend, proposals to send out and phone calls to make. A couple of days she had stayed at the office late, working on her agenda for the next day, grateful that they had gotten a week's reprieve from snow. But although her days and some of her evenings were busy, she still managed to spend time with Gabe. They went out to dinner twice and had lunch once, and each time they spent together, she found herself liking him more and more. Ever since that incident with Langley Mayhew, word had spread that she and Gabe were seeing each other; not that it bothered her that anyone knew. And Gabe didn't seem to mind anyone knowing either.

After what had happened between them with rising hormones that weekend at his place, they made an attempt to turn down the heat. Whenever he took her home, he would kiss her hungrily in front of her door, make sure she got inside safely and then leave. But Saturday night things had gotten a little hot when he had played another elevator trick after taking her out. This time when he had stopped the elevator, she had gone into his arms willingly, and by the time he had started it up again, she had been kissed senseless and robbed of her underwear, a wispy scrap of black lace he had put in his back pocket and hadn't returned to her yet. She was still shaking her head in amazement at exactly how he had done such a thing. And forcing her mind to remember what he'd done, detail by detail, only made her get all hot and bothered again, so she stopped trying.

Yet, they still hadn't made love. He somehow managed to be the naughtiest of naughty within the limitations she had set and still keep his word. Gabe Blackwell, she'd concluded, had a lot of smooth moves, expert hands and a willing tongue. He definitely liked to kiss, touch and taste. She couldn't imagine what he would come up with next.

Every night when she got in bed, she tried convincing herself that sexually, the two of them were moving too fast. They needed to slow down, especially when she thought about how slow her relationship with Erol had been in the beginning. When she and Erol had first started dating, she'd been young, barely twenty-one, with no sexual experience. Not that she considered herself overexperienced now, however. She had learned a few things, and she hated admitting it, but a lot of it had been during the last two weeks.

Gabe treated their attraction to each other, their strong sexual chemistry, as if there wasn't anything unusual about it. And because he seemed completely comfortable and at ease with it, she was beginning to feel that way as well. It no longer shocked her when their gazes met and held while heat flooded her insides or when his kiss would send tingling sensations through every part of her body.

Taking a deep sigh, Sage dragged her attention back to the document in front of her. Moments later, she checked her watch. It was almost noon. Gabe's partner, Christopher Chandler, was to have arrived in town that morning. She would meet him on Wednesday when she joined him and Gabe for dinner.

She smiled. She had heard a lot about Christopher and was looking forward to finally meeting him.

"Now that we have business out of the way," Christopher Chandler said, tossing the report he'd just read back on Gabe's desk, "I want to ask you something."

Gabe lifted a dark brow. He had picked up the man who was his best friend as well as his business partner from the airport that morning. After taking him home to drop off his luggage, they had gone to the job site and met with their work crew. Now he was sitting in Gabe's office, and from the look on Christopher's face, Gabe had a feeling he wouldn't like Christopher's question.

"What do you want to ask me?"

Christopher leaned back in his chair and met Gabe's gaze. "Why the guest bedroom I'm using is filled with the scent of a woman?"

Gabe couldn't help but laugh. The astonishment in his best friend's voice was priceless. It wasn't that Christopher was surprised that a woman had spent some time at his home, but it was the mere fact that she had slept in the guest bedroom and not his bed. Only someone with a sordid womanizing past as Christopher's could ask such a thing or have the astounding ability to pick up a woman's scent a whole week later.

"My relationship with Sage hasn't moved to that level yet," Gabe said, shaking his head.

"Losing your touch, Blackwell?"

"No, playing it safe and trying to protect my heart, although it may be too late."

Christopher eyed Gabe thoughtfully. "Are you saying what I think you're saying?"

Gabe leaned back in his chair. With a finger tucked under his chin, he met Christopher's gaze and responded, "I don't know. What do you think I'm saying?"

Christopher leaned forward, making sure he had Gabe's complete attention and to also make sure he picked up on every vibe Gabe emitted. "I think that this Sage woman has gotten to you."

Gabe nodded slowly. "And do you see that as a good thing or a bad thing?"

"It depends. That's why I'm dying to get to know her."

Gabe nodded again. Christopher was someone who could read a woman like a book. He had tried warning Gabe about Lindsey, but he hadn't listened.

"You may as well know she has issues," Gabe said quietly. "Pretty much the same ones Lindsey had."

Christopher's jaw tensed. "Then, why in the hell are you setting yourself up for punishment, Blackwell?"

Gabe sighed. "I'm hoping that's not what I'm doing, Chris. There's a part of me that wants to believe that Sage has her head on a lot straighter than Lindsey did, and that she's really let go and is ready to move on with her life." He wondered how he could even say that when in a few days Sage would be flying to Texas to meet with her ex-fiancé. The only reason he supported her going was because inside he knew that she would either return to Anchorage ready to continue what the two of them had started or to tell him that she and her ex had worked things out. It would be better for things between them to end now than later after she had wiggled her way into the pit of his heart.

But then, deep down he knew it didn't really matter; she was already there. After spending the last three years avoiding any type of a serious relationship with a woman, Gabe realized Sage had already wrapped herself around him pretty tight. He had never enjoyed being with a woman more than he had these past weeks. She had made him laugh and had filled an emptiness within him that had existed for so long. There were so many things about her that he wanted to explore, to get to know. And then there was the budding side of their relationship that definitely gave him something to look forward to, the intimate side. In a very short amount of time, Sage Dunbar had become his fantasy woman. There were sensuous bones in her body that hadn't yet been worked. Evidently, her ex-fiancé hadn't been one who was into exploring new and different things in the bedroom, and Gabe looked forward to teaching her everything he knew . . . and then some.

"Gabe?"

Christopher's voice pulled him back to the present. "What?" He stared at Christopher for a long, uncomfortable moment and wondered just how much he had figured out.

"A part of me doesn't want to see you get hurt again. Believe me when I say that I felt your pain, bro," Christopher said quietly. "But then there's another part of me that wants you to have just what I have, the very thing that I thought could never be possible for me. Maxi has done nothing but bring me immense happiness and pleasure, Gabe. And when I think of how I used to live my life, all the women I used to sleep around with and discard with no thoughts or feelings for them whatsoever, I feel blessed that God still felt I was worthy enough for Maxi to be mine. And then Christopher Max is the icing on the cake."

A lump formed in Gabe's throat that really didn't surprise him. He had known the old Christopher Chandler, the one who had been tormented by a past he couldn't forget. And Gabe was so very happy that he had finally found inner peace. And he hoped and prayed that God would find the same favor with him that he'd found with Christopher and grant him that same inner peace.

CHAPTER TWENTY

Christopher liked her.

That fact was so obvious Gabe couldn't help the smile that crinkled the corners of his mouth. Chris was so taken with Sage it wasn't funny.

Gabe had decided to prepare dinner at his home instead of taking them out to a restaurant. Leaving his office early, he had gone home to cook what he considered a feast, then left to pick Sage up from her home to bring her to his.

During dinner Christopher had been completely charmed by the likes of Sage Dunbar, and for any woman, other than Maxi and Joella Blackwell, to charm Christopher was not easy. Gabe had enjoyed taking a backseat while Chris and Sage got to know each other, first on a business level, then personally. She had engaged him in conversation about Maxi and Christopher Max, which were Chris's favorite topics of conversation. Gabe had actually seen his best friend blush profusely when after showing Sage a photograph of his son, she had gone on and on about how much Christopher Max looked like his father, a fact that Christopher was pretty damn proud of.

Later that night when he returned Sage to her apartment, Gabe couldn't help but grin.

"What are you smiling about?" she asked as they walked from the elevator toward her apartment door.

"Oh, I was just thinking about how taken Chris was with you tonight."

Sage smiled as she glanced up at him. "And I was just as taken with him. I can see how the two of you are such close friends. He's a pretty nice guy."

Gabe chuckled. He remembered a time a lot of women didn't think so. Christopher had been the type of man that women couldn't stand but couldn't resist either. Gabe knew that during that time his mother had constantly stayed on her knees praying for Chris's redemption. And like he'd told Parnell that day, he really believed his mother had connections up there.

"Would you like to come in, Gabe?"

Sage's question brought his thoughts back to the present. Oh, yeah, he definitely wanted to come inside. She would be leaving tomorrow morning to meet her ex-fiancé, and Gabe intended to leave her with something to think about. Before he left tonight, her mind would be so full of him she wouldn't be able to think straight. A couple of times during the course of the evening, he had wished that Christopher would get lost, just to have Sage all to himself. When he saw that wouldn't happen, then he had started counting the minutes, then the seconds, before he would take her home.

"Yes, I'd like to come in if you don't mind. I know you have a plane to catch in the morning, and I wouldn't want to keep you up late," he said, trying to keep the desire, the deep feeling of arousal, out of his voice.

"No, I don't mind," she said softly, opening the door.

As soon as Gabe stepped into her apartment, into the soft glow of lighting that filled her living room, he picked up her scent which was already embedded in his nostrils. Now inside her apartment, her scent was more prevalent. This was the place where she came home from work each day, to eat, to sleep, to bathe. This was her space, and he intended to invade it real good tonight.

"What would you like?"

Her question caught Gabe's attention, and he met her gaze. In all this thirty-two years, he was quite sure he had never wanted a woman as much as he wanted the one standing before him. But he knew that he had to stick to his goal. He didn't want a night with her; he wanted a whole lifetime. He blinked at the thought, taken aback by what he'd just decided. But then when a man loved a woman, he thought such things. The key with him would be to convince the woman that he was worth loving.

"Gabe?"

"Yes."

"I asked if there was something you wanted or did you want to talk?"

Gabe leaned against the closed door. He found himself smiling at her question. And since she'd asked . . .

"No, Sage, I don't want to talk, and yes, there is something I'd like, something that I want."

Sage swallowed, knowing the answer to her next question, but she found herself asking anyway. "What?"

"You."

For a full minute Sage didn't say anything. There was nothing she could say. He had every right to want her, especially after the past few weeks. Unselfishly, on five different occasions, he had brought her to the pinnacles of total fulfillment with orgasms so strong, so potent, so unlike anything she'd ever experienced that even now the thought of them was making her tremble inside. And each time that he had fulfilled her needs, his own had gone unsatisfied.

He'd been determined to keep his word to her, determined to prove he could be trusted. A part of her knew that trust was no longer an issue between them. In a way, it never had been. There had been something about Gabe that had let her know from the first that he was a man who wouldn't take advantage of her and her feelings. He was a man who proved to her that he would put her well-being before his own. He'd done exactly that over the past weeks.

She was woman enough to know that sexual pleasures should work both ways; yet for him they hadn't, and it was time to put his torment to an end. It was the first time she would try seducing a man, and Sage hoped she did it right.

"Tonight is usually my pamper-yourself night," she said softly, as a whirlpool of desire erupted in her stomach with the intensity of Gabe's gaze.

"A pamper-yourself night?" he asked huskily, pushing himself away from the door to come and stand within a few feet of her.

"Yes, it's a night that I pamper myself. I usually take a long, leisurely soak in the tub with lit vanilla candles all around and soft music playing in the background."

He nodded, then flicked a quick glance at the door that led to her bedroom and master bath. "Don't let me stop you. Go ahead and enjoy yourself. I'll sit and wait out here for you."

Sage took a step toward him. "Or you can join me."

Gabe considered it for a moment, the full extent of her invitation. He was a man who could take only so much, and would have to be made of stone to join her in a bath and not make love to her. Did she not know what she was asking of him? Did she not think there were limitations to their madness? Evidently, she didn't. He intended to push a lot of her buttons tonight, but they were buttons he knew he could push and still maintain control. She was asking for the impossible, and like he'd told her on several occasions, he was no angel.

"Thanks, but I'll wait for you."

She nodded. "If that's what you prefer."

He wanted to tell her it wasn't what he preferred but that he had no choice. The decision was the best one to make for the both of them.

"If you change your mind, I'll be right through that door," she said, pointing to her bedroom. "Make yourself at home. I'll be back later."

With a walk that had his full attention, astounded, he watched as Sage crossed the room to disappear into her bedroom. Rubbing a hand down his face, he wondered if he had literally lost his mind. She was getting naked in the other room, and here he was, standing in her living room with an erection the size of Texas.

Deciding to do something, anything, whatever he could, to pass the time away, he walked over to the television and turned it on. He tried to ignore the sound of her moving around her bedroom, the scent of vanilla candles being lit that filled the air and the soft sound of the music the television couldn't even drown out. Then when everything in the room suddenly went pitch black, except for the glow of candlelight that cast shadows of flickering light in the living room, Gabe knew he was in trouble.

Deep trouble.

Sage leaned against the back of the tub that was filled with bubble bath. She closed her eyes, not wanting to think about her trip to Dallas tomorrow. She wanted to concentrate only on the present, which included the man in her living room. If he was still in her living room.

She was hoping that he was following the candlelight to her bathroom. It would be just the way she had fantasized that day in her office when she'd thought of taking a bath with Gabe standing in the shadows watching her. She took a deep breath and forced herself to think positively. Gabe was a man, and men had certain needs. He couldn't last much longer.

Over the past two weeks she'd had to rethink her position about wanting to share a relationship without sex. Maybe for another couple sleeping together now was too soon, but for her and Gabe it made perfect sense. She smiled, not believing she felt that way. Never in a thousand years would she have thought she could feel comfortable sharing herself with a man she'd known only for a few months, although they had actually met seven months ago. But there was something about her and Gabe's relationship that wasn't normal. It seemed they weren't destined to take things at the pace most people took them. The sexual chemistry between them was too volatile, almost explosive, too plain old hot. And to top that off, she felt comfortable with him and the trust she had placed in him.

But then she had also discovered there was more to their relationship than just the sexual aspect of it. She enjoyed doing things with him, spending time with him, talking with him, working with him. It seemed that she and Gabe were a good combination, a solid match on all levels.

Sage slowly opened her eyes when she heard the sound of footsteps. She held her breath as she felt her body beginning to stir with anticipation, with wanting, with desire. She turned her head and locked her gaze on the doorway.

She stared for endless seconds before he finally appeared. The sight of him took her breath away. He had removed his suit jacket and had pulled his dress shirt from the waist of his pants. He didn't have any shoes on his feet, but he still had on silk socks. He looked sensuously comfortable, and at the same time laid-back. The multitude of emotions in his dark gaze said it all.

He still wanted her.

"I forgot to mention that I have a remote in here that controls all the lighting in the apartment," she said quietly, holding his gaze and explaining why the apartment had gone totally black. "On pamper-yourself night, the only light I want is candlelight."

He leaned in the doorway. "Evidently," he said slowly, not taking his eyes off of her.

Not wanting him to see too much too soon, Sage eased her body a little beneath the bubbles. Nervously, she darted her tongue out to moisten her lips. *Big mistake,* she thought, when Gabe's attention was drawn to her tongue.

She cleared her throat and placed her attention on his sexy-as-sin appearance. "Do you plan to take a bath with me?" she found the courage to ask, ready to take things to the next level. Especially with the ache between her legs intensifying in slow, tormenting degrees.

Still holding her gaze, he slowly walked into the room and rolled up his shirtsleeves to his elbows. "No, I'm not going to take a bath with you, but I intend to kiss you, touch you and taste you all over."

Sage watched his approach, and the only thing she could think of saying while her heart beat rapidly in her chest was, "Oh, my."

CHAPTER TWENTY-ONE

Gabe released a long, stirring breath as he glanced down. His gaze swept over the enticing womanly body submerged beneath a ton of bubbles. Sage wasn't letting him see anything just yet, which wasn't such a bad idea. If he was to see her now, naked and wet, he would lose control, and he couldn't do that.

He closed his eyes for a second, trying to get his bearings, maintain what little control he did have and remember his promise, his word, and he intended to keep it someway, somehow.

"Gabe, I'm ready to get out of the tub now."

Sage's words made him open his eyes. He met her gaze and immediately knew that for some reason, she wasn't going to make tonight easy for him. She would intentionally push him to the limit. Why? Was she counting on him not keeping his word so she could claim a reason not to trust him, which would make her walking away after tomorrow that much easier, that much more convenient?

He tightened his hands into fists at his sides. No, his thoughts couldn't go there. He refused to let them. He couldn't start doubting her or the ground they had covered over the past weeks. Her decision to become an enticing vamp tonight had nothing to do with seeing her ex-fiancé tomorrow. He had to believe in his mind as well as his heart that one didn't have anything to do with the other. So whatever plan she had in mind for them tonight, he had to keep his cool, let her take it to the heights *he* would allow it to go and make sure in the end, no matter what, they didn't make love . . . although, he thought, smiling, what he had in mind was penetration of a different kind.

"Gabe?"

His smile widened. She wouldn't have to call his name a third time. Grabbing a huge velour towel off the rack, he held her gaze as she slowly began standing.

He sucked in his breath, almost forgetting to breathe. She was a mind-blowing vision rising from the bubbles, with tiny rivulets of water coursing down her body. Standing tall, naked, wet and sudsy, she was the most beautiful and the most desirable woman he had ever seen.

He couldn't help but take a moment to appreciate what he saw. Everything. Every single curve, indention, hollow, body part. Nothing was missed during his scan of her body. Nothing.

Stifling a groan, his gaze lowered and made contact with that part of her he wanted desperately, but couldn't have yet. But boy, did he want it. When he saw her tremble, he reached out his hand to help her out of the tub. She was getting cold, and it was time to dry her off.

"I can do it," she said quietly, reaching for the towel when she stood on the floor mat in front of him.

"No, let me," he said softly. "I want to do it."

With trust in the depths of her eyes, she nodded and gave herself to his ministrations. Sucking in another deep breath, Gabe began drying off the water from her body, deliberately lingering in certain places, stroking her, patting her wet skin, flesh that felt hot to his fingers through the thickness of the towel. He moved the towel over her shoulders, past her breasts, down to her stomach, hips and thighs, deliberately saving the best spot for last.

He slowly began kneeling, patting her legs dry, parting her knees and drying between them, going lower and drying her ankles and liking the way the gold chain looked around her left ankle, and thinking her polished toes looked sexy, too.

Raising his head, he came eye level to that part of her he had to resist . . . up to a point. He lifted his gaze to hers, wanting to see her reaction to what he was about to do. Her eyes went wide, and her lips parted in surprise. He could tell by her expression this was completely new and an alien form of love-making for her. This would be her first time, but he had no intentions of making it her last.

But he wanted to handle it in the right way. He wanted her comfortable with it. Dropping the towel, he began using his hand and reached out and began stroking the soft skin of her stomach, and each time he stroked, his fingers slowly moved lower and lower at the same time he leaned closer. Then he began using the air from his lungs to blow her dry. Up close and definitely personal and with the same force one would use to blow out a hundred candles on a birthday cake, he watched, torturously so, as her body became dry in a very special spot with him as her personal blow-dryer. Her womanly scent surrounded him, filled his nostrils, his mind and his heart. She smelled of vanilla, a result of the candles and bubble bath she'd used.

He glanced up. Her eyes were closed and her breathing ragged, and she'd placed her hands on his shoulders for support. Inhaling deeply, he breathed in her scent and dipped his head for the exquisite taste he knew awaited him.

Sage came fully awake, rolled to her back and stared up at the ceiling. She clutched her pillow to a very naked body and released a deep moan as hot, tantalizing memories flooded her mind. Once again Gabe had pleasured her beyond belief, unselfishly and without reservations.

And while she had slept from sexual exhaustion, he had left and not received anything in return.

Nothing she had tried doing had pushed him beyond the limits of control. Instead, he'd concentrated on giving her intense pleasure. He had used his mouth to savor every part of her body, every texture. He'd taken the words *kiss, touch* and *taste* to entirely different levels than anyone she knew. Even now her body was tingling all over just thinking about all that he had done.

And still they hadn't made love.

Gritting her teeth, she smacked the pillows into the mattress. Gabe Blackwell had given her pleasure for the last time without letting her reciprocate. When she saw him again, he'd better be ready, because she had a thing or two to show him, and the next time she would be the one in charge.

Cold water cascaded down Gabe's body as he stood in the shower and wondered how many of these he could take. Tonight it had been hard to leave Sage, after tasting her from head to toe.

He closed his eyes and rested his head against the back of the shower wall. The scent of her would be forever embedded in his nostrils, and the taste of her would always be implanted on his tongue. Everything, every part of her, had been exquisite.

The woman was made for him. He knew it, and he believed that she was beginning to realize it as well. A part of him tried not to think about what she would be doing in Dallas. He had to believe that Friday evening when he called her, she would be back in Anchorage and would want to see him.

Deciding it was time to get out of the shower before he caught pneumonia, he stepped out and began drying himself off. If anyone had told him he would have endured all of this torture in the name of love and trust, he would not have believed them.

He heard the sound of Christopher moving around in the kitchen. His best friend had one more day to spend in Anchorage before leaving to return to Detroit and to his wife and child.

Wife and child.

Gabe shook his head and groaned. He couldn't even begin to think of a future with Sage until he first let her confront her past.

Sage stood at the hotel's reception counter and glanced around the lobby of the place where she would be staying for the night. The weather in Texas was hot, definitely a lot different from Anchorage. She checked her watch. She had agreed to meet Erol at four. That would be just enough time for her to get to her room, unpack, shower and change into something else.

"Here you are, Ms. Dunbar," the hotel receptionist said, reclaiming Sage's attention as she slid a door key-card to her across the counter. "Your room has been ready since noon."

Sage nodded. "My plane was delayed. They had to de-ice the runway."

The pretty young woman, who appeared to be in her early twenties, gave Sage a warm chuckle. "Boy, I can't imagine something like that while suffering from this Texas heat. Where're you from?"

"I flew in from Anchorage," Sage responded, smiling, glancing down at her key-card to see what floor she was staying on.

"Well, welcome to Texas."

"Thanks." Moments later Sage stepped into the elevator. Her thoughts shifted to Erol. She knew he was staying somewhere in this same hotel, attending a business meeting that ended today. She hoped the two of them would be able to sit down and discuss the past, clear things up for the final time and walk away friends.

More than anything, she wanted to get back to Anchorage and be with Gabe.

After a quick shower, Sage slipped into a mint green dress. She applied her makeup, combed her hair, and picked up her purse to leave the room. She glanced at the huge arrangement of flowers that had been delivered an hour ago, a gift from Erol. She didn't want to remember what the card said. She knew from his words that he was thinking that by the end of the night the two of them would have patched things up.

Upon reaching the lobby, she noted a number of people were checking in. According to someone who'd ridden down with her in the elevator, there was a big rodeo in town, and a number of the riders were staying at the hotel.

"Sage?"

Sage turned to the sound of her name being called and drew in a long breath. There was nothing about Erol that had changed except it appeared that he had lost a few pounds. He was still nicely built and good-looking.

A keen feeling of finality passed through her upon remembering what they once had and what they would never have again. He stopped in front of her and took her hands in his, leaned down and kissed her cheek. "You look good, Sage," he complimented, looking her up and down.

She smiled wryly. "So do you." She glanced around. "Do you want to stay here and eat or do—"

"I've made reservations elsewhere. My rental car is outside."

She nodded. She remembered her mother mentioning that was how Erol's mother had learned the two of them would be meeting in Dallas, because she'd overheard him making dinner reservations. "That's fine."

"How was your flight into Texas?" he asked as they began walking toward the glass doors that led outside.

"It was fine, but I'm missing Anchorage already."

He raised a dark brow. "You're missing all that snow?" he asked, as though the very thought of it was pure crazy.

She decided not to tell him that snow had nothing to do with it. She was missing a certain individual.

"The weather reports say snow has been coming down practically every day there," Erol added when she didn't say anything.

Sage shrugged. "You get used to it."

"I doubt if I could."

Then, it's a good thing you don't have to, she thought as they waited for the valet attendant to bring Erol's car.

During the drive over, he had done most of the talking, telling her about their friends and what they were doing.

"Patty is upset that you don't call her anymore, Sage," Erol said, breaking into her thoughts. She glanced over at him. She was sure he knew why she had stopped calling his cousin.

"I'm sure you know why I thought it was best if Patty and I cool things for a while, Erol. She's your cousin and she loves you. She couldn't understand why I did what I did." Sage knew that deep down neither did he.

"Yeah, but still, she was your friend," he said, as if it shouldn't matter that Patty had started getting on her last nerve. And as far as them being friends, Erol's cousin had been her friend whenever it was convenient for her, like whenever she got behind in a bill and wanted to borrow money.

"You could have moved in with her instead of Rose Woods while we tried to work things out."

Sage shook her head. She almost reminded him there was never a time when they tried to work things out. That hadn't been an option she'd given him and, as far as she was concerned, with good reason.

She glanced at her watch, wondering how much longer it

would take to reach the restaurant. Already she felt a headache coming on.

The restaurant was exquisite and overlooked a beautiful park in downtown Dallas. After they had eaten dinner and were drinking cups of coffee, Erol leaned back in his chair and looked at her. "I really like the way your hair is styled. I can't get over how good you look, Sage."

"Thanks." She knew it was time for them to talk about why she had come to Dallas. Over dinner they had talked about a lot of things, basically keeping the conversation light. She opened her mouth to speak, but before she could get out a single word, Erol started talking again.

"I have something for you," he said, smiling, reaching into his jacket pocket.

She lifted a brow. "What?"

"This," he said, handing her a white envelope. His face was actually beaming as though he had some sort of a secret. "Go ahead and open it," he said, leaning toward her.

Sage peered up at him from beneath lowered lashes as she began opening the envelope. Inside was a cashier's check for the fifty-two thousand dollars he had taken from her accounts. She looked up at him. He was still smiling.

"That business deal with Herb Rollins went through, and that's from my first earnings. Already I've been awarded contracts for his other locations, so money will be rolling in real good this year I'm thinking about expanding my work force."

"That's good news, Erol, congratulations," she said, folding up the check and placing it in her purse. "And thanks for returning my money."

"I guess that means we're all right."

She glanced up at him. "All right?"

"Yes, I took the money out of your account, and I just gave it back. All of it." His smile widened. "That should wipe the slate clean, and we can move on."

Sage lifted a brow. "Wipe the slate clean? Move on?"

"Yes, reset a date for our wedding."

"Reset a date for our wedding?" She hated sounding like a broken record, but she was so astounded at what he was saying she couldn't help repeating it.

"Yes," he said, grinning proudly. "We can call Reverend Jones from my room later." After taking a sip of coffee, he added, "And you can believe me when I say that I'll never do anything like that again."

Sage shook her head. She wondered if it had even occurred to him that he was doing the same thing now. Without discussing anything with her, he had not only made assumptions, but had also started making plans, plans he didn't know if she would or would not be okay with. He'd even suggested they call Reverend Jones from his room later.

She leaned back in her chair. "We can't reset a wedding date, Erol."

He glanced up at her as if the thought of it were news to him. "Why can't we?"

"Because nothing has changed between us."

Surprise filled his face. "Yes, it has. I paid you all your money back."

"But I told you in the beginning that you can replace money but not trust. I can't trust you anymore."

Erol inhaled with frustration. "What you're saying doesn't make sense, Sage. The reason you got upset in the first place was about the money."

Sage shook her head. "Yes, the money was part of it, but the reason I got upset was because you discounted my feelings and did just what you wanted to do, without caring about how I felt or without first discussing it with me. And if you did it once, you'll do it again."

"I said I wouldn't do it again."

"But that's just it, Erol. I can't trust you to believe that you won't," she implored, trying to make him understand. "The reason I wanted to meet with you was to make sure that you understood that there could and would never be anything between us again. We're over, Erol. Finished."

He looked absolutely stunned. "No, it can't be finished. I love you, Sage."

"Yes," she said tenderly, as tears moistened her eyes, hoping in her heart that Erol would be able to let things go like she had. "And there was a time that I loved you."

He met her gaze. "But not anymore?"

"No, not anymore, Erol. At least not the way it should be. I love the memory of what we had together those five years, but that's it."

He still looked confused. "But I don't understand. You're willing to throw away everything we shared over money?"

She shook her head. He still didn't get it. "It wasn't over money, Erol. It was over the issue of trust. There has to be trust between two people in a relationship."

He reached across the table and captured her hand in his. "Then, we'll get it back."

"No, we can't," she said, pulling her hand from his.

Erol said nothing for the longest moment; he just stared at her. Then he said quietly, defeatedly, "There's someone else, isn't there?"

Sage let out a careful breath. She knew it was a question that she didn't have to answer but decided to do so anyway. They needed to leave Dallas with a solid understanding that things between them were over. "Yes, I've met someone. Only recently have I been able to feel that I can trust someone again."

For the longest time Erol didn't say anything, and Sage knew he was trying to deal with everything she had said to him. "Are you happy, Sage?" he finally asked in an emotional voice.

Sage closed her eyes briefly against a wave of regret. "Yes, I'm happy. I love my job, my health is good and I'm happy to know that you're doing well in your business. But more than that, I'm happy for the five years you and I shared, and when I look back,

Erol, I'll see them as good years. They were years that were meant to be. But now we have to move on in different directions. There will always be a special place in my heart for you, and I hope the same holds true with you for me."

Sage saw the mistiness in his eyes and said, "There is someone out there, someone who is meant to be Mrs. Erol Carlson, and when you find her, I hope for you the very best."

From the way he was looking at her, Sage knew at that very moment that Erol had finally accepted that things between them were over.

"If you ever need me, Sage, all you'd ever have to do is call, any time, any day. You know that, don't you?"

She wiped a falling tear from her eyes. "Yes, Erol, I know and thank you."

CHAPTER TWENTY-TWO

A cold, hard breeze made Gabe wrap his jacket tightly around him as he walked his property. He paused when he reached the lake. The memory of Sage and that Saturday morning that he had taught her to fish stood out in his mind. He smiled. She had looked so beautiful all bundled up from head to toe, and the first time she'd made a catch, she had danced around as though it had been one of the happiest moments of her life.

He glanced at his watch. Her plane should have arrived over three hours ago, but according to Malcolm, her flight had been delayed due to bad weather flying into Anchorage. He was missing her like crazy and had thought about her all day yesterday and today. Now it was almost late evening, and he still hadn't heard anything from her.

He had called and left a message on her answering machine asking her to contact him when she got in. He had hoped to hear from her last night and had wanted his voice to be the last one she heard before going to sleep. But she hadn't called, and his mind had begun imagining some of everything, of what she was doing and whom she was with. He'd finally reached the conclusion there was nothing he could do. It was her life as well as her decision as to what man she wanted in it.

He started walking again, this time back toward the house where a cup of warm brandy awaited him. He would take a shower and sit in front of the fireplace and wait for the call he was anxious to get. He had almost reached the back entrance to his home when he picked up a stick that had been buried in the snow to throw it.

"Gabe?"

He held his hand frozen in midair as his heart began beating wildly in his chest. He was really losing it. He'd actually thought he heard Sage call his name.

"Gabe?"

Finally accepting that the sound wasn't a trick of his imagination, he quickly turned around. Sage was standing a few feet away from him all bundled up in a coat and snow boots, with a scarf around her neck and a fuzzy-looking hat on her head. Even with all of that, she still looked adorable.

"Sage? When did you get here?" he asked, overwhelmed at seeing her. It was as if his very thoughts had made her appear.

"I came straight from the airport over thirty minutes ago. I saw your car and figured you had to be here. When you didn't answer the door, I went back and sat in my car awhile. But when it started getting late, I decided to check out back. You mentioned that you occasionally go walking in the evenings."

He nodded and watched as she folded her arms nervously across her chest. His brow rose with a question that he didn't really want to ask. The mere fact that she had come to see him straight from the airport after spending time with her ex-fiancé didn't bode well. Had she come to tell him that she and Erol had worked things out? A feeling of déjà vu shifted over him. He would never forget that similar time with Lindsey. He cleared his throat. "Is there a reason why you're here, Sage?"

Forcing a smile, Sage nodded, thinking Gabe didn't particularly act as though he wanted to see her. And all this time she couldn't wait to leave Dallas to get back to him. She wrapped her arms tighter around herself. Maybe she had made a mistake in coming.

"Sage?"

She met his gaze and knew that whether he still wanted her or not, she had to say what she came to say. "Yes, I was hoping that we could talk."

Gabe sighed, feeling a sense of doom coming on. "All right, let's go inside."

"Boy, it feels nice and warm in here," Sage said as she began removing her coat, scarf and hat.

Gabe shrugged as he removed his jacket and then nodded toward the fireplace. "You may want to go stand in front of that to warm up some more."

Sage nodded. When she'd first arrived, she'd had other plans on how she wanted to warm up, mainly in his arms, more specifically in his bed, but now with the way Gabe was acting, she wasn't sure it would be appropriate to harbor any such ideas. "Thanks. I think I'll do that." She quickly crossed the room to the huge brick fireplace that was emitting a massive amount of heat.

"Would you like anything to drink?" Gabe asked, leaning against a bookcase as he watched her. The dress she wore looked good on her and was shorter in length than the ones she normally wore, and thick black tights covered her legs. But that didn't matter. He didn't have to see her legs to know how gorgeous they were. Hell, he even knew how they tasted since he had done a good job licking them all over the last time they were together.

"Yes, I'd like something to drink."

Sage's soft voice brought him back around. "You want brandy?" he asked.

"Is that what you're drinking?"

"Yes."

"Then, that's what I'll have."

Nodding, he went to the corner of the room where the bar was located. He decided to ask the question that would open up his world or effectively close it. "So, how was your trip?"

Out of the corner of his eye, he saw her shrug. "It was all right. In fact, I believe it was rather productive."

He shook his head, not having a damn clue what that meant. So he decided to come at it from a different angle. "Did you and your ex get to spend time together?"

Now feeling warm enough, Sage crossed the room to sit down on the sofa. She felt tired. She had left Dallas early only to have to sit and wait all day at the airport for her flight to leave. "Yes, we had dinner last night, and he even took me to a rodeo afterward."

Gabe turned so his back was completely to her as he drew in a long, silent breath. *She and her ex had had dinner and had gone to a rodeo afterward?* His heart sank. He began feeling angry, frustrated and disappointed. He turned around, deciding they may as well have their talk and get things over with.

He walked over to the sofa with Sage's brandy in his hand. "Here you—"

He stopped in midsentence. Sage had curled up on his sofa and had gone to sleep.

Without giving it a second thought, he placed the glass of brandy on the table, then swung Sage up into his arms, cradling her against his chest, and made his way toward the guest room. He gently placed her on the bed, then stood back and studied her sleeping form for several long moments.

He loved her. There was no use asking for the thousandth time how he had let such a thing happen, because it *had* happened, and it was too late to question it. He swallowed against the tightness he felt clogging his throat.

He loved her and didn't know how he was going to give her up.

* * *

Sage yawned and slowly stretched out on the bed when she came awake. She glanced around the room. Déjà vu. She had awakened in this same room before with the aroma of Gabe preparing food in the kitchen.

Her gaze locked on her luggage that he'd brought in from her car. Why? It wasn't as if he'd been glad to see her, so why would he assume she would be spending the night? Swinging her legs off the bed, she reached for her purse, deciding to use her cell phone to call Malcolm to let him know she was back.

"Hello."

"Malcolm, this is Sage. I just wanted to let you know I'm back."

"Sage, where are you? I just tried calling you at home and didn't get an answer. Are you in a safe place?"

Sage lifted her brow. "A safe place?"

"Yes, a torrential blizzard is headed for the city. They predict several feet of snow in the morning and suggested that everyone just stay inside and keep off the roads." He chuckled. "In other words, we're snowed in for a day or so."

Sage nodded. No wonder Gabe had brought her bags in. "Yes, I'm in a safe place. I'm at Gabe's. I came straight here from the airport."

"Good. He called the office a few times today for you. He seemed kind of anxious to see you."

He could have fooled me, she thought, recalling Gabe's reaction when he'd first seen her earlier. "Well, I'm here, and this is where I'll be if you need to reach me."

"All right and you stay put."

She smiled. "Oh, I will unless Gabe kicks me out."

Malcolm's laugh came in loud over the phone. "Don't hold your breath for that to happen. He likes you a lot. That was obvious when he went up against Langley Mayhew that day. Blackwell was territorial at its best."

Not wanting to discuss what Malcolm assumed was Gabe's feelings toward her, she said, "Look, I need to call home and check my messages. You can reach me on my cell phone if you need me."

"Okay and you take care."

"You, too, Malcolm."

Sage then called her home number to retrieve her messages. Not surprisingly, her mother had called to see how things had gone with her meeting with Erol. Rose had called wanting to know that very same thing.

The sound of Gabe's deep, husky voice gave her a start. Her pulse quickened as she listened to his message:

"Sage, this is Gabe. Call me as soon as you get in. I need to know what it's going to be, or should I say who it's going to be. I'm staying up late to hear from you."

Sage lifted a dark brow, pondering the contents of his message. After a few moments, understanding dawned on her, and she shook her head. Did he actually think that after seeing Erol she would decide the two of them should get back together? She sighed deeply, knowing that was exactly what Gabe thought . . . or at least what he couldn't rule out as a possibility.

A part of her suddenly became angry that he had no more faith in her than that. His assumptions only proved that he still didn't trust her emotions. He still wasn't sure of her.

But then, how sure was she of him?

After what her father and Erol had done, she had wondered if she would ever put her faith and trust in another man again. And although Gabe had never done anything for her to question his integrity, a part of her had held back, though she wanted to believe otherwise. But things had been no different for Gabe. Because of what his former girlfriend had done, he was leery of the same thing happening. Yet, he had set himself up for that possibility, willing to take a chance that this time things would work in his favor.

And they had.

She had no intentions of getting back with Erol, and seeing him again only confirmed that. But Gabe had no way of knowing that until she told him.

And she intended to do just that.

Gabe walked over to the kitchen cabinets and took down a bowl for the soup he'd made. At times he found it hard to believe that he was running two households. Although he spent most of his time in Anchorage, his house in Detroit was just as equipped as this one, even more so because he still considered it his primary residence. His time in Anchorage was temporary, and once Eden was well under way, he would spend less and less time here, returning only when needed. He was beginning to like the town, even with all the snow.

He turned when he heard the sound behind him. Sage was standing in the doorway. He hadn't expected her to be up so soon. The last time she had slept for over an hour.

He stared at her a few moments before saying, "You fell asleep."

She looked chagrined. "I know. Sorry."

Gabe shrugged. "You don't have to be. It's understandable that you'd be tired.' *After dinner and a rodeo,* he thought, then despised himself for the bout of jealousy he felt. He cleared his throat and focused on the window and what was going on outside of it. "A blizzard is headed our way, and they suggested that everyone stay inside. I took the liberty of bringing your bags in since it wouldn't be safe for you to drive home tonight in this weather."

Sage nodded. "No sweat, as long as you don't mind company."

Gabe returned his attention to her. "I don't mind. In fact, I was about to have a bowl of soup and eat a sandwich. Would you like to join me?"

She smiled. "I'd like that. And we need to talk."

A lump formed in Gabe's throat, and his heart slammed against his chest. "Can we wait until after we eat?"

Sage lifted a brow. "If that's what you prefer."

"It is."

"All right. I don't see a problem to wait until then." She glanced around. "Is there anything I can do to help?"

"Yes, you can set the table, please."

Set the table for soup and sandwiches? . . . Instead of asking why such formality, Sage merely nodded and crossed the room to do as he'd requested.

Sage looked across the table at Gabe. He'd been extremely quiet, thoughtful, as if his mind was on something that was important to him.

After taking a bite of her sandwich, she decided to start off the conversation by asking him something that had her curious.

"Do you set the table for every meal, no matter what it is?"

He glanced up from studying his soup. He smiled, and it appeared that his features lit up from fond memories. "Yes, and it's Christopher's fault. Since he didn't have a background that had taught him the proper way to do certain things, he decided to teach himself. He didn't know anything about proper etiquette, so he bought a book and put everything he read into practice. Since we lived together, I thought it would help in his learning process if I participated, and after a while it became a habit."

Sage nodded, remembering reading an article in *Ebony* magazine how, considering his less than desirable childhood, Christopher was now a successful businessman who participated in numerous charities involving children. Her respect for the man went up another full notch.

She met Gabe's gaze. "He was lucky to have you for a friend."

Finished with his soup and sandwich, Gabe leaned back in his chair. "I think we're lucky to have each other, and my mother would be quick to tell you that luck had nothing to do with it. She sees our relationship as Divine intervention and says we are *blessed* to have each other. And I have to agree with her."

While his response had been simply stated, Sage knew that a large degree of emotions had gone into it. After seeing him and Christopher together, it was easy to see that they not only considered themselves business partners and best friends, but also brothers. The fact that they didn't share the same blood had nothing to do with it.

She was also astonished by the type of person Gabe was. His loyalty to Christopher, even to the point of being willing to share his parents, was astonishing. She recalled as a younger child wanting another sibling, and when she saw that wasn't going to happen, she had resolved that she would be the only one. And as such, her parents became hers, exclusively and without any competition from another child.

She placed her spoon down after finishing her soup. "That was delicious, Gabe. Thanks."

"You're welcome."

His response of only two words was stated in a low, deep voice and sent every nerve ending in her body tingling with sexual awareness, and it didn't help matters that he was looking at her through those gorgeous dark eyes of his, or the fact that his gaze had suddenly dropped to her mouth.

There it was again, that none-too-subtle change in the air surrounding them, the emergence of that strong sexual chemistry. She had felt it since the moment she'd stepped into the kitchen, but now it was getting stronger.

She cleared her throat. "Do you need help cleaning up the kitchen?"

He blinked, and his gaze moved from her mouth and refocused on her eyes. "No, in fact, I plan to load up the dishwasher. You can go and get comfortable by the fire, and I'll be in shortly."

"All right. I think it's time we talk."

He pushed his chair back and stood. "Yes, I think it's time that we talk, too."

Moments later while standing in front of the fire, Sage couldn't help the wry smile that touched her lips. She and Gabe did a lot of talking. She'd never had this many talk sessions with Erol. But she felt the open communication between her and Gabe was good. There was nothing wrong with getting their feelings out in the open.

She wondered what had been going on in his mind the entire time they'd been eating. Did he actually think there was any way for her to walk away from him? But then, he probably didn't know what he had come to mean to her. She hadn't known herself until she'd seen Erol face-to-face.

Everything she'd done in the past had been to please her parents and make them happy, including bringing home the type of man she knew they would approve of. But what she hadn't accepted until yesterday was that although Erol had been her parents' choice, he might not particularly have been hers. She had remained in a relationship with him for five long years after having convinced herself he was the one she wanted. Yet, she had dragged her feet each and every time he'd mentioned marriage. Her inner self knew what her mind had refused to accept. Erol had not been the man for her. But like she'd told him, she didn't regret any of it. Being with him had given her a chance to get to know herself and to be herself. And just like it had been meant for them to spend those five years together, it had been meant for it to come to an end.

Then into her life walked a man by the name of Gabriel Blackwell. He hadn't come in like a whirlwind, or with the force of a locomotive. As smooth and calm as the waters on his lake, he had entered her life as first a business associate, then as someone she wanted to become friends with, and now a man she wanted as a lover.

She still didn't know where she wanted their relationship to go, but she did know she wanted it to go somewhere. From the time they had acknowledged this thing between them, this strong sexual chemistry, he had tried doing the right thing, whatever she'd asked, fighting beyond unreasonable temptation to stay in control and keep his word, to prove that he was a man she could trust.

She quickly pushed aside her emotional fears of putting her trust in another man and knew that she did trust Gabe, and it was time for him to know it.

"Sage?"

Gabe's deep voice startled her. She'd been so caught up in her thoughts that she hadn't heard him enter the room. She met his gaze and knew without a doubt that he was the man she wanted. "Yes?"

"Do you want anything to drink before we get started?"

She smiled at him. "No, I don't need anything. I'm fine." And for the first time in seven months, she truly felt that way.

She walked over to the sofa and sat down, ready to let Gabe know just what he meant to her.

CHAPTER TWENTY-THREE

For all of her outward display of confidence, Sage felt nervous and sensed the need for a drink after all. "I've changed my mind, Gabe, and would like something to drink."

He nodded, then walked away toward the bar.

Suddenly, the whole idea of telling Gabe how she felt was causing a certain amount of uneasiness to coil up inside of her. Did she really want to get right back into a committed relationship after having recently gotten out of one? And if she wasn't ready for a committed relationship, would a noncommitted one work just as well for them? And what would happen after Eden was completed and they went their separate ways?

She sighed. She could never settle for an uncommitted relationship with Gabe. The thought of him with someone else didn't sit too well with her.

"Here's your drink."

Sage glanced up when Gabe's low, sexy voice intruded on her reverie. He was handing her a glass of brandy.

"You fell asleep before you could drink it," he said as he sat down on the sofa beside her. "I kept it warm for you."

She accepted the glass. "Thanks. I'm not as cold as I was before, but I could still use this." She didn't add that it could possibly calm her nerves. It didn't help the situation when Gabe stretched his arm across the back of the sofa, making her heart skip a beat and making her want to slide closer to him.

But they needed to talk. And then . . .

"So, how was your trip?"

Sage lifted a brow. He'd already asked her that earlier, before she fell asleep, which could only mean he wanted more details than she had given him. "Erol and I had dinner and talked. I told him that things were over between us," she said quietly.

"And?"

She met Gabe's dark stare as she took a slow sip of her drink. "And we agreed that they were."

Gabe shook his head as if he thought something was missing. "Just like that?"

She shrugged. "No, not exactly. He paid back the money he had taken and thought that doing so would patch up things."

"But it didn't?"

"No, it didn't. I told Erol that I didn't love him anymore."

Warm relief spread through Gabe with Sage's words. He began to feel relaxed, grateful, thankful and happy. "So things are really over between you?"

Sage turned around in her seat to face him, feeling both angry and frustrated that he still doubted her. Tilting her chin up, she met his gaze. "Things were over between me and Erol over seven months ago, Gabe, and I've known that. The only reason I met with Erol in Dallas was to make sure he knew that as well. Our families have been trying to keep his hope alive, which was unfortunate as well as unfair to the both of us, but especially to him. They meant well, but it didn't help the situation, and he had refused to get on with his life, thinking we would one day get back together. I felt he needed to hear it directly from me . . . again."

She turned her head and looked at the fire blazing in the fireplace and remembered Erol's expression when she'd mentioned her involvement with another man.

"Sage?" Gabe reached out, and with the tip of his finger, he guided her chin back to face him. Their gazes met and held. "What aren't you telling me? There *is* more, isn't there?"

His touch felt warm, tender and gentle, and she gave him a small smile, suddenly feeling oddly self-conscious, which when added to her nervousness made her stomach flutter. "I told him about us, about you. I didn't give him your name, but I did tell him there was another man in my life."

Sage's breathing deepened when Gabe's gaze darkened. "Am I, Sage? Am I the man in your life?"

Sage exhaled a deep, unraveling breath. She'd asked herself that same question several times since last night. Deep down she wanted him to be but . . . There was something he hadn't told her, something she needed to know. "That depends, Gabe."

At his inquiring gaze, she said softly, "All this time you've doubted me and my true feelings for anyone after my breakup with Erol. Why shouldn't I doubt you and your feelings after your breakup with her? The woman who caused you so much pain? How do I know you're over her and that she's not a threat?"

Gabe leaned forward with his arms resting on his thighs. His gaze moved away from Sage and went to the roaring flame in the fireplace. For the longest time he didn't say anything, but sat still and concentrated on the blaze. Then he spoke, his voice filled with the pain he appeared to be feeling.

"Because Lindsey successfully destroyed all the love I had for her," he said, his voice filled with a bitterness that Sage had never heard in it before.

"Why? Because she left you for her former lover?"

"No, I would have gotten over that eventually. It was for another reason."

Sage wondered if he would tell her the other reason and felt her stomach constrict with disappointment that he was willing to hold something back after they had agreed to always talk things through to build up the trust factor in their relationship.

She began chewing on her bottom lip, waiting patiently to see if he would say anything else. When she thought he would not, he shifted his gaze from the fire to her.

"I was never supposed to know, and even now she doesn't know that I do know." He sighed deeply, and continued, "And the only other person who knows, other than the person who told me, is Christopher."

Sage sat still, seeing a rise of fury surge through Gabe and watching his shudder of pain. "Know what?" she asked softly, wanting to share in whatever anger and pain he was enduring.

He started to speak, then hesitated, as if saying the words was a pain he couldn't bear. Finally, he met her gaze and held it. "She aborted my child."

A shocked look etched itself in Sage's expression. She didn't try to hide it. She couldn't have even if she had wanted to. "Are you sure?"

Gabe leaned back against the sofa, his arm finding its place across the back of it again. "Yes, and I had no idea she was pregnant. I guess she and her fiancé didn't want a reminder of the time she'd spent with another man, and my child became the sacrifice."

Sage shook her head. "But . . . how did you find out?"

"Carol, a woman who used to date my cousin years before he was killed in a boating accident, but with whom I've remained good friends over the years, worked as a nurse at the same clinic that Lindsey went to have the procedure done. Carol remembered Lindsey, but Lindsey didn't remember her. She said that Lindsey and a man, who I assume was her boyfriend, came to the clinic. She overheard them talking in the waiting area. He was assuring Lindsey that she'd made the right decision, and that having an abortion was the only way they could move forward and not be reminded of her time with another man. Carol became suspicious and against the clinic's policy and also invading Lindsey's right of confidentiality and privacy, she read Lindsey's medical records and figured that due to the timing of everything, the child was mine."

He inhaled deeply. "Because of the way I obtained the information, there was nothing I could say or do to Lindsey without putting Carol's job in jeopardy."

Sage reached out and took Gabe's hand in hers. No wonder he had trouble dealing with women on the rebound. "Oh, Gabe, I'm so sorry."

A severely pained look covered his expression. "Yeah, so am I. After I found out, I went through a period where I didn't want to have contact with another woman. I wanted to find Lindsey and make her tell me why she'd done it. I wanted her to explain how she could destroy another life, a life that was partly mine, just because her boyfriend didn't want a reminder of what we'd shared. I hated myself for being so blinded by love that I couldn't see that she never really loved me but was still carrying a torch for him."

He looked back at the blaze again. "And I made a vow that I would never, ever get involved with a woman on the rebound, a woman with emotional baggage, a woman who couldn't let go of her past and move on with her life. I had done so before, and what it cost me was something I could never recover."

Sage's heart reached out to Gabe, his pain and to what he'd lost. Some men would not have cared that their ex-girlfriend had aborted their baby. Some would have even offered it as a suggestion when discovering their girlfriend was pregnant. But not Gabe. He was an honorable man who did honorable things, and he believed in doing what was right. He was a man any woman would want to love and to trust.

For a long moment, she stared at him as an indescribable ache settled in her heart. His gaze was still focused on the blazing fire, but her gaze was focused on him.

"If I were to get pregnant from you, I would never get rid of your baby, Gabe," she whispered softly, knowing she meant every single word.

He turned and looked at her, saw the mistiness in her eyes that she couldn't hide even if she'd wanted to. He stared at her as if weighing in his mind what she'd said. "You wouldn't?" he asked quietly, reaching out and tucking a wisp of hair behind her ear.

"No, I wouldn't."

Silence fell around them, and for the longest moment, neither said anything. Finally, Gabe broke the silence. "Thank you."

Then, automatically, without even thinking twice about it, Sage went into his arms, and he held her. He held her tight for the longest time, and she wondered if he was finally letting go. She wondered if he was now realizing that he had been no different from the women he had vowed not to date. He had not let go of the past and moved on. He'd been a man on the rebound, a man with excess baggage, a man who also needed to learn how to trust again.

She suddenly realized just how similar she and Gabe were, and just how much they needed each other.

And just how much she wanted him.

He pulled back just long enough to rest his forehead against hers and said, "So am I, Sage? Am I the man in your life?"

She nodded. "Yes, if that's what you want to be."

"It is." He leaned away from her and gave her a warm smile. "Now that we have that part cleared up, do we continue talking or do we make decisions?"

She heard the huskiness in his voice. She also heard the thick desire in it. He brushed her lips with his, making talking impossible anyway, but she was determined to try and said, "We make a decision as to where we want our relationship to go now."

The first thought that came to Gabe's mind was that at that very moment, the only place he wanted it to go was the bedroom so he could do to her all those things he'd been dreaming about doing. But he couldn't rush her into anything. "I'm letting you call the shots, Sage. I'm ready to take it to the next level if you are."

Tingles of excitement raced through Sage at the thought of what that level entailed. "I'm ready," she said softly, not knowing how much longer she would be able to hold on to her sanity if he continued to nibble at her lips the way he was doing.

"You sure?"

"Yes, I'm ready for everything you're ready for, Gabe."

"Everything?"

"Yes, everything."

Gabe wondered if she knew what she was saying. Maybe she didn't have a clue what his "everything" encompassed. He stood and slowly pulled her up with him and slid his hands down her back to pull her closer to him. He wanted her to feel just what she was doing to him.

He knew the moment she did, and instead of pulling back, she moved closer into the cradle of his hips, as if the front of her was drawn like a magnet to his erection. The feel of her so close to him, so connected, even through the material of their clothing, made his body throb unmercifully. He knew his "everything" included making love to her and needed to know if she fully understood that.

He stared down at her, held her gaze, wanting her to see the deep desire driving him that had his entire body in turmoil. But just to make certain there wouldn't be any doubt, he leaned down and captured her mouth in his, determined to make love to it, to feast on it, to absorb her into himself and to make her want him as much as he wanted her.

They had kissed hot and heavy numerous times, had taken their kisses to several heights and then some, but like their relationship, he was determined to take their kisses to another level. He wanted his brand all over her. He reacquainted his tongue with every taste and every texture of her mouth. And her tiny moans of pleasure went straight to his groin and only intensified his determination to make her his. He continued to kiss her hard and thoroughly.

"It's getting hot in here," Sage managed to whisper when Gabe released her mouth, but only long enough to lick away at her lips.

"You have too many clothes on," he responded, nibbling at each corner of her mouth and using his tongue to repeatedly trace around it.

"Umm, that can be fixed." In a move that she knew he would find brazen, she pulled out of his arms, and her hands went to the buttons at the front of her dress. She began undoing them one by one. She watched him through lowered lashes and couldn't help noticing he was having difficulty breathing and even a hard time standing still as he watched her every move. When the front of her dress hung open and showed a black lace slip, she heard him groan.

Pushing the dress down past her shoulders, she stepped out of it and kicked it aside, and stood before him in her bra, slip, panties, and tights and snow boots. "Will you help me take my shoes off, Gabe?"

He nodded as he sat down. Standing before him, she lifted her leg onto his lap. He removed both of her shoes, and then stepping away from him, she reached under her slip for the waistband of her tights and began tugging them down. When she had taken them completely off and had also removed her slip, he barely found his voice upon seeing the wispy scrap of black lace covering her femininity. "I thought I had taken those."

She smiled, remembering what had happened in the elevator the week before. "This is a matching pair." Slowly easing down onto the sofa in front of him, she placed her knees between his widened muscular thighs and brought her breasts eye level with his gaze. The tips of her breasts strained against the lace material of her bra, and then he began using his tongue to lick through the thick fabric while stroking the soft skin of her lower belly. The world seemed to spin around her. His touch was making desire race through every, over every, nerve in her body.

And when his fingers gently skimmed her inner thighs, she couldn't take any more and lowered her lips to his and whispered, "Make love to me, Gabe."

CHAPTER TWENTY-FOUR

Sage opened her eyes the moment Gabe placed her in the middle of his bed. She'd always wondered how it would feel to be swept off her feet, and now she knew. He had gently scooped her up into his arms and strode up the stairs to his bedroom.

She watched as he took a step back and kicked off his shoes, and when a chill touched her body, she moved to pull back his thick quilt.

"Going someplace?" he asked, smiling, as he pulled the belt from his pants.

"I'm a little cold and thought I'd get under the covers."

He nodded as he continued to watch while she snuggled beneath the covers. His bed would be filled with her scent, and he intended to become entrenched in her feminine aroma. "I'm going to warm you."

"Are you?" A bewitching smile curved her lips.

"You can count on it," he said, chuckling softly as he removed his shirt.

He watched her watch him as he unzipped his pants and slowly took them off, leaving him clad only in his briefs. Her gaze ran the full length of him from head to toe but seemed to concentrate on his center that was bulging, solid and hard as a rock through his underwear. He had no shame with her seeing just what she did to him and just how much he wanted her.

"I want our first time to go slow, Sage."

"Slow," she repeated, not taking her eyes off him when he tugged at the elastic waistband of his briefs. He saw her gaze fixed on that very spot as if it was glued to it. And when he completely uncovered himself, the expression on her face was priceless.

"Oh, my."

A smile tilted his lips as her words whispered through sultry lips. "Is that a good thing?"

She met his gaze and smiled. "Yeah, looks pretty good to me." Her attention returned to his erection. "As good as it gets." She then scanned his well-toned, athletically fit body, admiring all of him. "And then some."

Gabe's smile widened as he moved to the bed and dropped to one knee. Wanting to finish undressing her and see all of her, he pushed back the covers and began removing her panties and bra. Her body felt warm, hot and fiery all over.

He had seen her naked before, that time he had dried her after her bath, up close and personal. Now he was seeing her again, and as before, he was amazed by her body's beauty, every intimate detail. A shaft of heat began spreading fast and furiously through his body. He wanted her and had wanted her from the first time he had seen her, but giving respect to the fact she was an engaged woman at the time, he had not done anything about his interest. But now she was no longer engaged and was presently in his bed, and he planned to do a lot about it.

He pulled her naked body to him and kissed her. Trying to keep the kiss as light as he could, he couldn't hide the hunger he felt when he moved his mouth over hers, tasting and claiming, and the kiss became deep, intense, riveting, as he mated with her mouth in a French kiss that was more French than anything he'd ever shared with a woman, while his questing fingers reached out and touched her breasts, liking the way they fit in his hands.

Slowly lightening the pressure of his mouth on hers, she released a moan and arched her body closer to his. A moan escaped him as well, as he eased her back onto the bed.

Kiss, touch and taste.

Placing her arms above her head, his hand began a total exploration of her body, and his mouth followed as his tongue ravished her all over, making her shudder, moan and thrash about in the bed.

"Gabe." She called his name on a low, urgent plea as heat flared through her. Her body quivered under the assault of his mouth, and she clenched the bedcovers in her fist.

Gently, Gabe released her hand, ready to join them in a way that he had dreamed so much about over the last few months. He wanted Sage more than he'd ever wanted another woman. He took several deep breaths to calm his racing pulse, determined to take things slow. He reached over in his nightstand drawer for the pack of condoms he had placed there when he'd first arrived but had never used.

"Let me," Sage requested softly, raising up, grabbing his hand and eagerly taking the condom from his fingers.

He watched through desire-intense eyes as she opened the packet. And when she touched him with trembling fingers, teasing him with languid caresses of her thumb to his swollen erection before sheathing him in latex, he squeezed his eyes shut and groaned. She was driving him insane, and he was too far gone to care. He opened his eyes and met the heat shimmering in her gaze.

"I have to mate with you," he whispered hoarsely, desperately, needing to be inside her so badly that he ached all over, especially in his loins. When she eased back against the pillows, his inflamed body moved into place over hers.

He gazed down at her, feeling total want and need for her. "Slow," he reminded her in a voice that was low and seductive.

"You think so?" she asked coyly, returning his smile while skimming the tips of her fingers over the surface of his hairy chest.

"I was hoping so," he murmured huskily, leaning down, not being able to resist flicking his tongue across the swollen tip of her breast.

Biting back a moan, she breathed in deeply. "You may be asking the impossible."

He shifted to meet her gaze. "Nothing is impossible with us, Sage. We're a perfect fit."

Gathering her close and still holding her gaze, he lifted her hips to him and slowly entered her, stretching her, filling her completely, burying himself inside her to the hilt.

"Aaah, baby." He released a long, deep, guttural moan when her womb clenched him snugly. She couldn't move and neither could he. It was as though they were glued together in that position. Moments later, he reached up and weaved their fingers together, then entangled her legs with his, wanting to be joined with her in every way. She tried to move, but he held her down tight; and when he felt her womb clench him again then quiver with him in its clutches, he sucked in a deep breath.

"Don't," he said softly.

"I can't help it," she said breathlessly upon realizing he was holding still to make sure her body adjusted to his. With trembling fingers she reached up and traced the line of his jaw, tight from restraint as he tried maintaining control. She didn't want him to be in control. She wanted him to be out of control like she was. "You feel good inside me, and I want you, Gabe. Now." She arched her body to take him deeper.

Not able to take any more, he eased his hips back, for just an inch, then forward, beginning a rhythm of thrusting in and out of her over and over, increasing the rhythm, expanding his strokes, engaging in the most powerful and the most soul-stirring lovemaking of his life. The pleasure of being inside of her, mating with her, was so intense, he began growling in sensuous pleasure as a sharp, spiraling need consumed him, making him want her even more and throwing the notion of going *slow* right out the window.

He began pumping frantically into her, strong, powerful thrusts. She managed to keep in tune with him, feeding and abating with the fluid movement of her body. She raked her nails down the length of his back and moaned deep in her chest as she rocked against him in the fast-paced rhythm he set, urging him deeper and deeper.

The turbulence of their lovemaking consumed them, and when Gabe felt Sage's body shudder uncontrollably beneath him, he closed his eyes and tossed his head back, giving in to his own earth-shattering release. Every part of his body felt connected to her in an intimacy so profound it took his breath away.

He lowered his head and kissed her as slow shudders shook him, taking him into a world where only the two of them existed. And the only thing he could think of when he gathered her up into his arms, their bodies damp from the whirlwind of passion they had shared, was that the next time they *would* take it slow.

Or at least they would try.

They tried several times that night and still didn't take things slow. Each time they came together seemed more passionate than before. After a while they stopped trying and resigned themselves to the fact that whenever they made love, although there would be plenty of foreplay, there would be no time devoted to teasing preliminaries. The sexual chemistry between them was too strong, and the two of them were too greedy. They wanted it all.

Sage couldn't believe just how her body responded to Gabe. It was as if his touch was what it needed and most desired. Why?

She ignored the question, thinking there had to be a logical explanation. And she refused to believe that she would be responding that way to any man, after five years with the same man. A part of her believed she could only respond this way with Gabe.

A knot formed in her stomach when she thought of all the things that had happened since moving to Anchorage and the part Gabe had played in it. After what had happened with Erol, she had wondered if she would ever let another man get that close to her again, and then to top it off, her father's unfaithfulness had convinced her that there was no such thing as total love and commitment between two individuals. But being with Gabe had helped her to see the world in a new light. She had dealt with Erol, and now she knew she would have to find a way to deal with the issue of her father and the hurt he had caused her. She could not continue living each day with one part wanting to despise him and the other wanting to love him the way she always had.

Sage knew the moment Gabe had awakened when he reached out and pulled her closer into his arms, and she went into them willingly as anticipation rose inside of her.

"I can't get enough of you, baby," he said huskily, letting his fingers stray down to cup her bottom before slowly caressing their way to her front. As soon as he touched her in that place that seemed to have throbbed for him all night, she sucked in a deep breath.

"Too tender?" he asked with deep concern in his voice.

"No, too greedy. It wants more." She stroked her hand down his hairy chest past his tight stomach to that part of him her body wanted. It felt hard, rigid to her fingers. "I need you inside of me, Gabe."

After putting on another condom, without wasting any time, he leaned down and kissed her deeply while he placed his body directly over hers. She felt the blunt tip of him probing her entry, and shifting slightly to raise her body to meet him, she felt him enter, stretching her, filling her, pleasing her and loving her.

She heard his sharp intake of breath and knew his thoughts were the same as hers. Tonight they had proved just how good they were together.

When he began moving in the rhythm and pace he wanted them to go, sounds of ecstasy she couldn't hold poured forth from her throat, making him intensify their kiss that much more. A delicious hot sensation poured through her. She didn't want to think of the future that was not promised to them. She only wanted to think of now. And then later when it was time to let go and walk away, she would have no regrets.

Gabe woke the next morning with a long, satisfying stretch and a contented smile on his lips. Flipping onto his back, he gazed up at the ceiling as memories, stark, potent, clear, flooded his mind, making his body get hard all over again. In all his thirty-two years, he had never experienced anything like he had last night with Sage. And that included his lovemaking sessions with Lindsey and Debbie. Something was different. Nothing was the same. The kiss, the touch, the taste was uniquely Sage. Last night she had definitely become the spice of his life.

He smiled. He hadn't known he had so much stamina. Each time they had made love, he'd been left feeling drained and depleted. And all it had taken was her touch, her smile, that desirous look in her eye, to make him suddenly feel renewed, reinvigorated, revived.

He rolled to his side when he realized Sage had not gone to the bathroom as he'd assumed. He inhaled sharply when his nostrils picked up the scent of bacon. Pushing back the covers, he knew his huge bed would never be the same again without her in it. For that matter, no bed he slept in without her would ever be the same.

As he stood and headed for the shower, he knew that he wanted Sage Dunbar in his life forever.

When he entered the kitchen fifteen minutes or so later, he stopped short at what he saw. Sage was standing at the refrigerator, bent and looking into it. What made the scene so heartstopping arousing was the fact that she was wearing one of his chambray shirts that hit her midthigh, and from her position it was plain to see she had not put on her panties. He leaned against the doorjamb, wanting to get an eyeful of that part of her rounded bare bottom he liked so much. It looked too damn tempting.

He couldn't help but recall that his hands had touched every part of that bottom and wanted to do so again. But first they needed to eat, and it seemed she had decided to do the cooking. He cleared this throat. "Good morning."

Sage quickly turned around, almost dropping the orange juice she held in her hands. She smiled, thinking there was just something special about a good-looking man early in the morning, especially one who looked like Gabe. He was wearing a pair of faded jeans and a shirt similar to the one she had on. His hung open, exposing his hairy chest, a chest she loved kissing, touching and tasting. The thought of all they had done the night before caused a flutter to pass through her midsection. "Good morning. I didn't know you were awake. Do you want a cup of coffee?"

Straightening, he slowly crossed the room to her. Taking the carton out of her hand, he pulled her gently to him as a warm smile curved his lips. "This is what I want, Sage," he said moments before leaning down and joining his mouth to hers.

Just that quickly, the fires of desire roared to life between them; sexual chemistry was at its best and all thoughts of the breakfast she was making were put aside when Gabe decided he wanted to be fed another type of meal altogether.

Breaking off the kiss, he scooped her into his arms and turned to leave the kitchen.

"Wait, I need to turn off the stove."

With her cradled tenderly in his arms, he walked across the room to the stove and turned it off. They would worry about breakfast later. "It's done."

A quick look out of a window they passed indicated it was still snowing heavily. Neither minded since they had plenty of things to do on the inside to occupy their time, and not a one of them was worrying about what was happening with the weather on the outside.

PART THREE

I can do all things through Christ who strengthens me.

—Philippians 4:13

CHAPTER TWENTY-FIVE

The following weeks flew by in a furor of activity for both Sage and Gabe. The snowstorm had held everyone hostage inside of their homes for two full days. Then afterward, they were faced with the chore of playing catch-up with those things they had put off during the time they were snowed in.

Gabe immediately met with Parnell to make sure the construction of Eden would resume as soon as possible. Initially, they had considered the effects of the weather and had made allowances for it. Parnell had found another woman to watch the girls but wasn't completely satisfied with her. She was good at keeping an eye on his daughters but was a disaster everywhere else. She did not keep the house tidy the way the former live-in housekeeper had done, and he'd found himself picking up after the older woman more than he was picking up after his girls. She was notorious for keeping a messy kitchen, which was one of Parnell's pet peeves. He found himself coming in from a hard day's work only to tackle another hard day of work cleaning his house.

"You're okay?" Gabe asked his foreman when the two of them had finished going over some items that had cropped up.

Parnell rubbed his hand over his face. "Yes, but I don't know how much longer I can last, Gabe. Mrs. Miller is getting worse every day, and all those good housekeeping habits I've instilled in my girls are being thrown out the window. I had to explain to them last night why they can't eat in their bedroom when Mrs. Miller eats in hers."

Gabe leaned back in his chair and nodded. "Sounds to me like you and the woman need to have a long talk."

Parnell's face took on a look of frustration. "That's just it. We've had a long talk, and it got us nowhere. She thinks she can do just what she pleases because she knows I need someone to care for the girls." He shook his head, clearly upset. "If this keeps up, I may have to send them back to Mom until this job is over, and I really don't want that."

Gabe nodded again. He knew how much having his daughters with him meant to Parnell. He checked his watch. He was meeting Sage for lunch. "Well, I'm sure something will work out. What about Bill Phelps's wife? Hasn't she kept them before?"

Parnell shook his head as he folded up the blueprints he and Gabe had gone over. Bill Phelps was one of their electricians whose wife had come to Anchorage with him. She had volunteered to watch the girls during the day. "Yeah, but she's too easy. The girls run all over her, and she lets them. Besides, Marcy Phelps can curse like a sailor when her soaps aren't going the way she wants them to go. You wouldn't believe what the twins have repeated after visiting with her."

Gabe chuckled as he stood and put on his coat. "Well, like I said, I'm sure something will work out."

Parnell looked at Gabe expectantly. "You seem happy, Gabe."

Gabe raised his brow, wondering when he'd ever not been in a good mood. Even when he'd gone through that episode with Lindsey, he had kept his pain from showing. "I'm always happy, Parnell."

"Then, you seem *happier.*"

Gabe smiled, knowing where the man's thoughts were going. "Yeah, I am happier."

"Would it have anything to do with a certain woman by the name of Sage Dunbar?"

Gabe snapped shut his briefcase as his smile widened. "It might."

Moments later while riding in his car on the way to the restaurant to meet Sage for lunch, he reflected on his conversation with Parnell. Although he hadn't admitted it, he knew his happiness had *a lot* to do with Sage. His thoughts drifted to the time they had spent at his place during the snowstorm. That morning after waking up and finding her preparing breakfast in the kitchen and taking her upstairs to make love to her, they had returned downstairs again around noon. The breakfast she had been preparing had become lunch. Then later, after playing a game of strip poker, they had made love again on a quilt in front of the fireplace.

But they had done more than make love for those two days. They had also talked. She'd shared with him fond memories of things she and her grandmother had done together and how hard she had taken her grandmother's unexpected death from a heart attack. She'd also talked about her strained relationship with her father. Just from listening to her, Gabe knew that her father's infidelity had hurt her deeply and had disillusioned her thoughts on the whole aspect of love being true and pure.

They had talked about it, and although she had listened to his take on things—that she should not let that one episode cloud her mind and heart to true love—he had a feeling she already had. She had also told him the decision she had to make regarding whether she would go home for the Fourth of July. Gabe had tried convincing her that the thing to do was to resolve the issue between her and her father and move on to rebuild their father-daughter relationship. But she felt that as long as her mother did not know about what had happened, she was caught in the middle.

As Gabe turned into the restaurant's parking lot, he thought about the weeks that lay ahead. Sage had spent a few nights with him, and he'd even stayed overnight a couple of times at her place. But since her friend Rose Wood would be arriving tomorrow, Sage felt she should spend the night at her own place a lot more since she would have a guest.

He understood that but didn't too much like it. He had grown accustomed to those mornings he would wake up and find her in his bed. She gave all new meaning to the phrase, *morning delight.*

Gabe saw her the moment he walked into the restaurant. She was sitting waiting for him in the lobby. Her face lit into a smile when she saw him and immediately crossed the room. "Hi."

Not being able to help himself, he leaned down and brushed his lips across hers. "Hi. Have you been waiting long?"

She shook her head. "No, I just got here. I had a meeting with Langley Mayhew." At Gabe's arched brows, she laughed and said, "And no, he didn't get out of hand. I think you effectively put an end to any ideas he had regarding me when you insinuated we were lovers."

Gabe's lips tilted into a smile. "We are lovers."

Sage nodded, unable to argue that point, especially considering all the things they did while alone in the bedroom. "Yeah, but we weren't at the time," she reminded him. "But trust me, Mayhew was a perfect gentleman today."

"And if he ever stops being a perfect gentleman, you'll let me know, right?"

Sage looked up at Gabe when she heard the seriousness in his tone. She held his gaze and saw something that suddenly took her breath away. In his eyes as well as his mind, she belonged to him. The night she had declared that he was the man in her life had pretty much established that fact. It wasn't that he was insanely jealous or anything of that sort, but he was a man who believed in taking care of and protecting what was his.

And she was his.

She had to acknowledge that she was his in a way she had never belonged to Erol, even after being with him for five years. Erol had been traditional, but there was nothing traditional about Gabe, especially in his lovemaking techniques. There was no limit to what he would do. In the bedroom there was no taboo on anything just as long as they both were comfortable with it.

"Are you hungry?"

His words invaded her thoughts. "Yes, I missed breakfast this morning," she said, smiling, knowing he knew the reason why. She had spent the night with him, and when she'd tried slipping out of bed to fix breakfast, he had pulled her back into his arms and had made love to her again.

"Then, I'm going to feed you." He motioned for the waiter to get them a table. "What are your plans for this evening?"

She shrugged. "I don't know. What are yours?"

He met her gaze. "I know what I'd like to do."

She raised an arched brow. "What?"

He leaned down and whispered in her ear. Her face turned crimson. She grinned up at him and said, "Oh, I think that can be arranged."

And it was arranged.

Sage's heart rate increased, and she took a long, deep breath, hoping to steady her voice when she removed the last stitch of her clothing later that evening in Gabe's bedroom. He lay naked in bed, propped against a pillow, and watched her strip through desire-filled eyes.

"Just remember I'm still a novice at this," she said breathlessly. She felt electricity flow between them from across the room and wondered what there was about him that made every nerve in her body come alive with need.

"No other woman can or has pleased me more, Sage."

She met his gaze, thinking that was an odd statement to

make considering the number of women he probably had been involved with since puberty. For him to claim that she pleased him more than any in the past was hard to believe. "Why?"

He raised a brow. "Why what?"

"Why are you saying that to me? You don't have to, you know."

Gabe continued to hold her gaze. To him, every moment he spent with her including this one was important, and he wanted her to know it. He also wanted her to know how he felt but knew that because of her disillusionment with love, he had to tread lightly.

"I know I don't have to say it, but I want to always be honest with you, like I want you to always be honest about things with me. And what I told you is true, Sage. No matter how many women have been in my past—and there aren't as many as you may think—I've never enjoyed making love to them like I have to you."

Naked, she came and sat on the edge of the bed. "But I still don't understand why. I'm not all that experienced, at least with all the things you like doing."

He smiled. "Yeah, and in a way that's what makes it so special, like that night in your bathroom, after your bath. It was something you'd never done before, but you trusted me enough to try it and discovered it was something you enjoyed as well."

She nodded. *Yeah, I enjoyed it all right.* With Gabe she'd discovered another side of her sexuality. In bed with him she felt sensuous, feminine and passionate. And at times, she also felt wanton and burning with a heat that only he could quench, which baffled her even more because Erol had not been an inconsiderate lover. And each time she and Erol had made love, they had shared passion. But it wasn't of the magnitude of what she shared with Gabe. Gabe could make her wet and achy between her legs just by looking at her. He could make her nipples feel sensitive just by being in the same room with her.

Making love with Erol had been good, but with Gabe it was overpowering, magnificent. It was like an adventure.

He knew how to explore new heights and take her there with him, all the way to the top. And he cherished her entire body. There was no part of it he didn't want to kiss, touch or taste. Then there was his craving to try new and different positions, some she hadn't thought possible, and he'd always made sure it was something she was ready to try. And so far she'd been game to anything he had introduced her to with no regrets.

Like now.

What he'd suggested at lunch was simple enough, and when she'd thought about it, she was surprised they hadn't tried it before now. But Gabe had always taken the lead in their lovemaking, and she'd followed. But now he was giving her the chance to be the one in control, and she liked the idea.

"But why would I be able to please you that much, Gabe?" she asked, still wanting to know, needing to know.

Gabe inwardly sighed. She would not let up on her inquiries until he told her something that made perfect sense. It would be so easy to end her questions by just telling her the truth, that he had fallen in love with her so deeply that he couldn't think straight or about any other woman in his past, but he doubted that would be enough of an explanation since he had told her he'd loved Lindsey, too. But the difference was that since loving Sage, he'd discovered there were contrasting phases of love, and then there were things that were meant to be. Fate. The only reason he could come up with as to why the love he felt for her was deeper, stronger and more monumental than any he'd shared before was because he felt she was his soul mate, his other half, his perfect fit. He hadn't felt this attuned to Lindsey. He had thought that many times since he and Sage had become lovers, and now he knew it was true, more so than ever. He was just giving her time to realize it, too.

He sat up in bed. "You please me that much because you do. It's as simple to me as that, Sage. And what's so unique and awe-inspiring is that you can do so without much effort. You have the ability to be a ray of sunshine in a part of the country that is usually covered by snow."

He drew in a deep breath, exhaled slowly and continued. "And when we make love, when I'm inside of you, a part of me wants to stay there forever. When I'm locked into that part of you, it's like that's where I belong, and there's no other place I'd rather be, feeling you surround me, clench me and pull everything I have from me."

He watched her eyes darken and added, "But although I feel all those things, there is still more between us than just sex, Sage. I like the way we sit down and talk about things, how we confide in each other and discuss things the way we do. And I believe you have an inner strength that you don't even realize that you have. It's a strength that I admire and one that will see you through to the light even when your way is dark. You proved that when you had to face up to both Erol and your father falling off the pedestals you had placed them on."

She tucked a strand of hair behind her ear and met his gaze beseechingly. "But I was hurt and had a hard time with the trust factor, and I didn't want to believe in true love anymore. Even now I don't know if I can or ever will again."

He smiled at her understandingly. "In time you will. One day someone will enter your life who will heal all your hurts and will show you that there is such a thing as love in its purest form. And by that time, you'll come to realize that none of us are perfect; we're all humans and make mistakes. All of us are tempted by things we shouldn't be, whether it's the need to increase our assets like Erol or the need to stray away from home like your father."

She nibbled nervously on her bottom lip. "Do you think you would ever be unfaithful to your wife if you had one?"

"I intend to be faithful to any woman I marry, Sage. I don't know why men cheat or why women cheat for that matter. All I know is what my intentions are."

Sage lifted her chin defiantly. "I bet my father intended to do the same thing."

Gabe refused to let her compare him to her father. He leaned toward her. "I'm not your father, Sage. You have a beef with him and not with me, and I've told you my thoughts on the matter. You should hear his side of things."

Her gaze darkened at the memory. "I already did. He said it was something that 'just happened.' He could give me no other explanation than that."

"Then, maybe it's one you should accept."

She lowered her head, and when she lifted it moments later, tears filled her eyes. "But I can't. He took a vow to love my mother, forsaking all others. But he didn't do that, Gabe."

Gabe reached out and pulled her across the bed and into his arms. He kissed her eyes before moving his mouth down to kiss her lips. His mouth feasted on hers in a way that made Sage forget everything, including her father. The only person she wanted to concentrate on was Gabe and how he was making her feel.

Remembering what she'd promised to do—what she wanted to do—she pulled back from his kiss and straddled his body, pushing him back down in the bed. She needed to be a part of him this way, now, to forget. She wanted to concentrate only on him. She met his hot gaze as her thighs parted. She eased her body down onto him, taking him inside of her. She bit down on her bottom lip at the feel of her vaginal muscles clamping down around him as he continued to enlarge inside of her.

He'd told her to pretend she was riding a horse. She had never ridden a horse before, but had seen enough westerns on television to know how it was done. So she caged his thighs between hers as she created a rhythm. She refused to close her eyes for wanting to watch him. She wanted to see his eyes darken with need, glisten with greed and flare with the passion she was stirring.

His hand held her hips as she rode him to her heart's content, and each time she went down to him, met his strokes, she felt the contractions that shook his body. Then moments later it came . . . the same time as his. She cried out his name when the first tremors slammed through her, catching her in a stampede of sensations she had never felt before. And when she bore her hips down on him for deeper penetration, he tightened his hold on her, thrusting upward, his body bucking uncontrollably.

It was during that precise moment that they both found the peace as well as the pleasure they needed.

CHAPTER TWENTY-SIX

"So, have you made out with Gabe Blackwell yet?"

Sage met Rose's inquisitive smile from across the breakfast table. Rose shot straight from the hip and didn't believe in wasting time finding out anything that she wanted to know. As soon as Sage had picked her up from the airport, she had been a bundle of questions, first about the weather and then about work. Now that the preliminaries were out of the way, it seemed Rose planned to zero in on her love life.

Sage's body became hot when she remembered just how many times she had "made out" with Gabe. "Yes," she admitted, smiling. She leaned back in her chair, knowing her friend probably wanted the nitty-gritty details, but she wasn't planning on giving her any. What she shared with Gabe was too special and not open for discussion.

Rose smiled excitedly. "I'm happy for you, Sage. I had worried about you after that Erol episode."

Sage lifted a brow. "Worried about me in what way?"

"I was worried that you would never find another man to trust as well as to love."

Sage frowned. *Love? Who said anything about love?* Her heart began racing at what Rose was insinuating. She cared for Gabe deeply. She respected him, enjoyed being with him and definitely enjoyed making love with him. . . . But love had nothing to do with it. With love came total and complete trust, and she'd been there before with a man. She trusted Gabe in a way she hadn't thought she could another person this soon, but trusting him with her heart was too much to consider doing. Love involved too many emotions, and they were emotions she didn't want to encounter just yet. She liked the level to which they had taken their relationship, without the issue of love being involved. Jeez! She had just worked through the trust factor with him.

Sage met Rose's gaze. "I don't love Gabe, Rose."

Rose lifted a surprised brow. "Sure you do. What other reason would you have for sleeping with him?"

Sage shrugged. "For a number of reasons. I like him and he's good in bed."

Rose shook her head, frowning. "No, Sage, that's my line, not yours. For you there has to be more, and deep down I had to finally admit that's what I envied about you. You've never sold yourself short and settled for less than what you wanted or deserved. All women need a man to love and who will love them in return. You had that with Erol, and I believe you can have that with Gabe. You've never settled for a loveless relationship, so why do you want me to believe that you're doing so now?"

For the longest time Sage couldn't answer her. It was not surprising that she didn't have anything to say, especially when she had to admit that she'd told herself many times that the emotions Gabe stirred up within her were more turbulent than those she'd shared with Erol.

"Don't let what Erol did darken your chance for happiness, Sage."

She took a sip of her coffee as she met Rose's gaze. "But isn't that what you did? You let what your ex-boyfriend did turn you against the thought of ever falling in love."

"Yes, and I admit I was wrong."

"And what changed your mind?" She wondered if Rose had met someone and just hadn't told her yet.

Rose smiled wryly. "I finally went to church a few times with Mrs. Childers."

Sage nodded. Evelyn Childers was an elderly lady who lived in Rose's apartment building. She had been trying to get Rose to go to church with her for the longest time.

"I did it just to get her off my back," Rose continued saying. "But then I really liked the service. It seemed like the minister was speaking directly to me. It was as if he had somehow singled me out and knew my life's story."

Rose took a sip of coffee, then said, "Anyway, after that, I decided to go with her another time and even went to Bible study with her. At first I felt out of place, but everyone made me feel right at home. I've been going a lot, getting spoon-fed a little at a time, trying to find myself and decide what I really want and who I want and not to settle for second best. I want a man who will treat me thirty or forty years from now the same way your father treats your mother."

A lump formed deep in Sage's throat. She forced a smile and reached out and touched Rose's hand, grateful that she had never shared with Rose what her father had done. That would have really made Rose think that all men were shallow, no good and couldn't be trusted.

"I'm glad you're finding inner spiritual peace, Rose."

Rose shrugged. "Well, I'm a long way from being completely there, Sage. I still fall short at times, but at least I'm trying."

Sage nodded. "None of us are perfect. We're all human and make mistakes." She realized after she'd spoken that what she'd just said to Rose were the same words Gabe had said to her just last night.

"It was a tough lesson, but I'm learning."

"And that's a start. I'd like for you to go to church with me on Sunday I enjoy the services and think you will, too."

"I'd like that," Rose said with enthusiasm ringing in her voice. "Has Gabe ever gone to church with you?"

Sage lifted a brow upon realizing that he never had, probably because she'd never asked him. "No. I've never asked him."

Later that day while sitting in her office, Sage thought about her conversation with Rose. Her stomach felt funny at the sudden realization that she was beginning to like Gabe more than she should. Things weren't supposed to be that way since the two of them didn't have a future together. When Eden was over, they would go their separate ways. She had known that and was fairly convinced that he knew it as well.

Then, why was she dreading when that time would come? And why was she suddenly feeling such a sense of loss? She inhaled deeply when the sudden need to see Gabe became so fierce she could barely breathe, think or see reason.

She glanced at her watch. It was past five already. She and Gabe had made no plans for tonight. She had told him that weather permitting, she would be going shopping with Rose. And he'd indicated that he would be spending most of the day at the job site, and then later he planned to work late at the office.

After trying a few times to read the documents in front of her, she finally gave up. She stood. Retrieving her purse from her desk drawer, she walked out of her office, and less than fifteen minutes later, she was pulling into the parking lot of the building where Gabe's office was located.

Gabe lifted his head at the first whiff of Sage's scent. His breath stopped, and he glanced up. She was standing there, in the doorway to his office. He breathed again.

He tossed the papers aside on his desk. His secretary and office staff had left over an hour ago, and he wondered how Sage had gotten in since they had locked up, although it didn't matter to him how she'd gotten there, only the fact that she was.

God, he thought, she was beautiful, sexy as hell, standing there wearing a plaid wool skirt and navy blue blazer. And there was something about the look in her eyes that had never been there before, but he would recognize it anywhere.

Hunger of the sexual kind in a woman who intends to take matters into her own hands and do something about it.

That realization made his pulse pound. It also made his body react in the most reflexive way. He wondered how long she'd been standing there, watching him work.

She must have read the questions because she cast him a somewhat nervous smile and said, "I've been here for a few minutes. The security guard let me in after I convinced him I had a surprise for you."

Gabe nodded as he watched her wet her lower lip with the tip of her tongue. "And do you?" he asked softly, feeling his gut clench and his lower body get harder by the second. Boy, was he aroused.

She looked at him, bemused. "And do I what?"

He smiled. "Have a surprise for me?"

She thought about the reason she was there, her urgent need to see him, but inwardly admitted that it went a bit farther than that. She had felt a compelling need to be with him, lie with him, make love with him—on the desk, on the floor—she didn't care. She'd never felt this intense before, this naughty. Nor had she ever had the urge to be reckless or spontaneous. But then, wasn't it Gabe who'd told her last month, after robbing her of her panties in the elevator, that there was nothing wrong with recklessness and spontaneity every once in a while?

"I don't know about a surprise, but I desperately wanted to see you," she finally said, openly and honestly.

"For you to admit something like that *is* a surprise, Sage," he responded, standing up from his desk and coming around to sit on the edge of it.

Sage was first drawn to his attire, a pair of jeans and a sweat-

shirt. She remembered he had been at the job site a great por-
tion of the day. She was then drawn to his midsection. He
wanted her. His erection was plenty proof enough.

"I'm glad you came. I've been thinking about you," he said
hoarsely.

His words pulled her out of her reverie, and she met his
gaze. "You have?"

"Yes. In fact, I've been thinking about you all day."

She nodded, pleased by that. "I've been thinking about you,
too." She swallowed. "I hope I didn't interrupt anything."

"No, like I said, I've been thinking about you all day. Besides,
I'm due for a break." He crossed the room and taking her hand
in his said softly, "Come with me."

Together they walked through the reception area of his office and to the elevator that was across the hall. All was quiet. It
was obvious that everyone had gone home. The entire building
was technically closed and empty except for the security guard
on the first floor. She wondered where Gabe was taking her
when the elevator arrived and they stepped in.

His hand went to the panel, and he pressed the button.
When the elevator began moving, she asked, "Where are we
going?"

He reached out and pressed a button on the panel that suddenly made the moving elevator come to a stop. He then leaned
back against the elevator wall and met her gaze. "Nowhere."

She blinked, at first not understanding until she saw his
hand lower to the zipper of his jeans.

"I once asked you if you'd ever made love in an elevator,
Sage, and you said you hadn't. I want to change that today. Is
that all right with you?"

Sage blinked again and inwardly admitted that she had come
to his office to make love but had figured they would do it in
his office, not in an elevator. The thought of making out in his
office was bad enough—but an elevator. . . . What if someone
caught them?

Evidently Gabe read her mind and said, "Everyone in their right mind has gone home for the day. But we aren't in our right minds, are we Sage?"

Sage shook her head. She couldn't speak for him, but she certainly felt crazy with desire. "No."

He smiled. "And I agree. So this is what we're going to do to cure this insanity of ours. I'm going to make love to you here, right now, hard and fast. All right?"

Sage nodded. The visual picture that formed in her mind from Gabe's words made the area between her legs feel hot and achy, more so than it had been feeling when she'd left her office to seek him out.

"All right?" he repeated. He wanted her to answer him, to confirm she was with him all the way.

"All right."

"That's good. Now lift up your skirt."

Without thinking twice, she began inching up her skirt, and when it reached her waist, she saw his eyes widen in total surprise, or maybe shock was more like it. She cleared her throat, thinking she should explain.

"I stopped by the ladies' room," she said softly. "You seem to have a problem returning every pair of underwear you take off me, so I thought I'd play it safe this time and be prepared since I'm running low on stock at my place."

The heat in his gaze flared as he looked at her, completely naked below the waist, and remembered the number of times he had confiscated her panties without returning them. He smiled, and without further thought he began easing down his zipper. "Smart thinking about the underwear, but I'm not sure you've played it safe, Sage."

Thinking he meant protection, she touched the pocket of her jacket. "I brought condoms with me."

He moved toward her as he began releasing himself from his jeans. His eyes stayed glued to that part of her that he wanted to be joined with. When he stood directly in front of her, he pushed her jacket from her shoulders before reaching down and touching her intimately. "You're wet and ready."

She nodded, knowing she couldn't do anything but agree with him. But then that wasn't all she was. She was hot to the core, and his touch was making things worse.

Before she could respond, his mouth came down on hers and swiped whatever words she was about to say from her lips. He kissed her with an urgency that stole her breath as he made every bone in her body melt. Then she felt him lift her, widen her legs apart to fit them around his waist. She felt the tip of him pressed against the entry to her, and when he suddenly increased the pressure of their kiss, she felt him ease inside.

He took a few steps forward and pressed her against the wall of the elevator as he began pumping into her. It was then that she remembered they were making love without using the condoms. She decided not to worry about it since she'd been on the pill since college, although she'd never told Gabe that.

She moaned deep within her throat at the thought that nothing, not even latex, separated them, and that he was inside of her and would hold nothing back when he came. Suddenly, she was filled with desperation to feel him release inside of her. She wanted the experience of having his hot semen bathe her insides.

Her muscles surrounding him tightened, and she began doing something he had taught her to do. She began milking him, clenching him, pulling everything out of him each time he pumped into her.

She heard the growling sound that he released from deep within his throat when he realized just what she was doing. His rhythm increased, and his hold on her hips tightened. He drew his mouth back, breaking their kiss as he continued to thrust frantically into her.

"Do you know what you're doing?" The eyes staring into hers had taken on a darker shade than any she'd seen before.

"Yes," she said, arching and moaning when he widened her legs to go inside her deeper.

His breathing escalated. "But we didn't . . ."

She knew what he was about to say. "It's all right. I've been on the pill since college, and even if there's a slipup, Gabe, I'll be fine. I would want your baby."

Her words were like a catalyst that broke his control, as if the thought of her having his child was more than he could handle. He proved her right when he looked deep into her eyes and then totally lost it. His words become Swahili, French, German, all rolled into one, just moments before she heard his shout of pleasure from deep within his throat at the same time she felt a flood of warm liquid shoot into her body. His release triggered hers, and she continued to milk him, refusing to let up or let go. She wanted every drop of what he had to give her and then some.

It seemed that they came forever, neither wanting to stop the tremors that racked their bodies or the gasping breaths that made breathing difficult. He trailed kisses down to the base of her throat as he groaned relentlessly and continued to pour himself into her shuddering body.

Together they were swept up in a wave of intense pleasure that knew no limit to its endurance.

Reality slowly descended upon Gabe, and it was moments later before he found the strength to pull out of Sage's body and ease her legs to the floor. He pulled her gently and protectively to him, kissing the dampness on her forehead and helping her to ease her skirt down.

"Are you all right?" he asked, thinking that he'd never done anything so intense before in his life. Even now his body felt sensitized.

"Yes, I'm all right," she whispered, still in awe as to what they had done. "Do you think the security guard is curious as to why this elevator is stuck in midair?"

Gabe shook his head, smiling. "No. He probably hasn't even noticed. I understand he usually takes a nap around now." He pushed the button to start the elevator moving again after picking up her jacket and handing it to her.

"I didn't think I would see you today," he said softly, looking at her while zipping up his pants. "But I'm glad I did."

Sage smiled, wondering what there was about Gabriel Blackwell that made her go ditzy. "I'm glad I did, too. That was really an exhilarating experience."

Chuckling, he nodded. "Yeah, I think so myself."

Sage smiled. "One thing is for certain."

Gabe lifted a brow. "And what's that?"

"I'm sleeping good tonight."

Gabe couldn't help but laugh. When the elevator came to a stop, he pulled her into his arms. "So am I, baby, so am I."

CHAPTER TWENTY-SEVEN

"I really enjoyed church service," Rose said, kicking off her high-heel shoes. "And it was nice seeing Gabe Blackwell again."

Sage crossed the room to hang up her jacket in the closet. "Yes, and I think he enjoyed the services, too. I should have invited him long before now but never thought to do so. I liked him being there." She thought there had been something special about standing next to him sharing a hymnbook and sitting next to him in church holding hands while the pastor had delivered the message.

"I can't believe how fast Eden is getting built," Rose said, interrupting her thoughts. "They'll be finished with it in no time."

Sage's heart sank at that thought. The beginning of Eden meant the end of her relationship with Gabe. She would remain in Anchorage for three to four months after that, but she knew that he would be moving on. There were other projects his company had lined up, including that job in England. "Yes, it seems that way, doesn't it?" She had taken Rose to the job site directly after church. "It will be a beautiful resort once it's completed."

Rose nodded as she flopped down on the sofa. "And what's with Parnell Cabot? He seemed a lot friendlier when we first met over eight months ago."

Remembering what Gabe had shared with her about the man, Sage said, "It seems that things aren't working out with the lady who's keeping his kids, and he's going to have to let her go. And since he hasn't come up with another sitter, there's a chance that he's going to have to take the girls back to Detroit to his mother." Sage sighed. "According to Gabe, he really wanted the girls here with him."

"Did he try putting an ad in the papers?"

"Yes, that's how he got this woman, so he's skeptical about doing it again. His first sitter came highly recommended, but this one has issues with keeping his house clean," Sage said as she grabbed a magazine off the table.

Rose shook her head. "That's a shame. I'm sure he has enough on his mind without having to worry about his girls. And they're cute as buttons." She had seen them with their father at church. They had looked pretty, dressed in identical dresses with little matching bonnets on their heads.

Sage looked curiously at Rose. "You know, you've been complaining about being bored around here every day."

Rose raised a brow as Sage sat in the chair across from her. "So, what of it?"

"I was just thinking that it would give you something to do every day."

Rose eyed Sage warily. "What will give me something to do?"

"If you were to watch the girls for Parnell." Sage smiled. "You certainly seem to get a kick out of watching their father."

Rose shrugged. "Well, that can't be helped since he's so darn good-looking. But like I've told you, I don't do men with kids."

Sage chuckled. "Yeah, and like you've told me lately, you aren't doing men period, so what's the problem? What are you afraid of?"

It was a long time before Rose spoke. "Attachment. I never told you this, but I once dated a divorced guy who had a two-year-old son. While Mark and I dated, Little Mark became the world to me, and I think a part of me always figured that one day I'd be his stepmother. It was only later that I found out that while I was at Mark's house taking care of his son, he was seeing other women. When I confronted him about it, he told me I was getting too possessive and broke things off. Ending things with him wasn't so bad, but losing Little Mark is what really tore me apart," she said sadly. "I often wonder if he remembers me. He'd be around twelve years old now."

Sage crossed the room and sat down next to Rose on the sofa. "Hey, I'm sorry. Had I known, I would not have suggested it."

Rose shook her head. "No, that's okay, and like you said, you didn't know." Moments later, she stood, sighing deeply. "What time is Gabe coming to take us to his place for dinner?"

Sage glanced down at her watch. "He said he'd be here around four."

Rose nodded, smiling. "That gives me at least an hour to take a nap. I'll see you later, girl."

Sage watched as Rose quickly left and headed toward the guest room. She was sorry that Rose had had a past filled with men who just hadn't wanted to do right. She hoped that Rose's future was a lot better.

She then thought about her own future. She would continue to take one day at a time with Gabe, enjoying everything he offered. And when the time came for them to go their separate ways, she would learn how to deal with it and have no regrets.

Gabe raised his eyes to the ceiling. "Yes, Mom, everything is fine. And yes, I'll be coming home for Grandma and Grandpa's anniversary party. And no, I don't need you to find me a girl to take. All right, Mom, I love you, too. Now may I please talk to Chris?"

Gabe ran a hand down his face when Christopher got back on the line. "Hey, man, I thought you agreed to keep Mama busy so she could stay out of my business."

After a few moments, he said, "Well, maybe you and Maxi should adopt a baby or something." He knew that due to a medical condition, Maxi couldn't have any more kids, and they had talked about adopting. "Christopher Max needs a sister."

Gabe smiled. "I don't care if he's a handful; that's beside the point. Joella Blackwell needs something to do. If she wouldn't drive me batty, I'd send for her to come and watch Parnell's girls, but I'm not a glutton for that much punishment."

Gabe chuckled at Chris's reply. "Well, do something about her. I'm counting on you. Goodbye," he said, quickly ending the conversation before his best friend could back down.

He stood and walked across the room and looked out of the window. His mother was determined that he not come to his grandparents' anniversary party alone, and he didn't plan to. He intended to ask Sage to go to Detroit with him, and he hoped she'd agree to do so.

"I talked to Parnell Cabot today," Rose said as she dried the last dish Sage had washed.

Sage raised a brow and turned around at the sink. "Really? When?"

"Around lunchtime. I went out to the job site to see how things were coming along."

Sage nodded and wondered if that was the only reason Rose had gone out to the job site, but decided to just listen and let her do all the talking. "And?"

"And he was there," Rose said, placing the dish in the cabinet. She turned back around to Sage. "I told him that I had decided to hang around longer than I originally planned, and since I wasn't doing anything during the day, I could watch the girls for him."

Sage raised arched brows, surprised. "What made you decide to do that?"

Rose shrugged. "I just couldn't see him sending his girls away. He loves them so much, and he'd be miserable the entire time without them."

Sage nodded, knowing that was true, but still, that didn't explain why Rose had offered her services, especially after what she'd shared with Sage a week ago.

"And besides, like you said the other day, it's not like I have a lot to do around here every day while you're at work. I may as well put my time to good use."

Sage smiled. "I'm glad you're doing it, and it will work out perfectly."

"I think so, too, although he did tick me off today and almost made me withdraw my offer."

Sage lifted a brow. "Really? What did he do?"

Rose's face took on an irritated expression. "He asked me for references, which made me feel like he thought I had a criminal record or something."

Sage laughed. "Oh, Rose, he didn't mean it that way, and you know it. You can't blame parents for being cautious these days, you know. And he probably wanted to make sure you were up for the job. I can imagine that two four-year-olds can be a handful."

"Well, I'll be able to handle them. I used to earn money baby-sitting as a teenager."

Sage smiled. "Then, I'm sure you'll have everything under control."

Rose placed the dish towel on the rack. "I'm going to start in a few days. I'll go to his house every morning before he leaves for work at six and stay until he gets home which is usually around five. Since it seems the snow days are officially over—thank goodness—I won't have to worry about that."

Sage shook her head, smiling. "Seems like you and Parnell have come up with a workable plan."

"Yes, but it'll only be for three weeks until that lady comes back."

Sage studied Rose intently for a moment. "Why are you so uptight about it?"

Rose shrugged. "I'm not. I'll do fine, but I plan to stay detached."

Sage wondered how Rose would manage to remain detached from a good-looking, single man who had beautiful twin daughters. But she decided not to ask Rose that. "Do whatever you think you have to do, Rose."

The house was completely dark, and the candles were lit. The scent of vanilla filled the room. It was pamper-yourself night, and everything was the same except the place. Gabe had convinced Sage to hold her weekly ritual at his place instead of hers, and she had readily agreed.

He lay propped up against the pillows in his bedroom with his gaze occasionally straying to the connecting bathroom door. Sage had been in there for almost an hour already. Soft music, the sound of Miles Davis, floated through the room, and he thought a few times he actually heard her humming.

He smiled. Just like his body was humming in anticipation of tonight. It had been almost two weeks since they had made love. That quickie in the elevator a week ago didn't count. It had been that long since they had shared a bed, and he was antsy, hot with readiness. He had missed her and was glad she had agreed to spend the night.

"Gabe?"

He glanced up, and she was there in the doorway, a beautiful vision dressed in the sexiest nightgown he had ever seen. His breath caught. His pulse rate increased. The candlelight hit her at an angle that made her seem too stunning to be real. But he knew that she was real. She had planted herself so deeply in his heart, there was no way he would ever be able to get her out of there, even if he tried.

He sat up in bed. "Come here, baby."

She seemed to float over to him and crawled into bed next to him. Her scent of vanilla made his nostrils flare with desire. She eased under the covers and snuggled close to the warmth of his body.

"I missed this," she said softly. "This closeness, the need for you to hold me in your arms while I sleep."

Gabe glanced down at her, smiling. "You don't have sleep on your mind, do you?"

She shook her head, grinning. "No, sleep is the furthest thing from my mind."

"It's the furthest thing from my mind, too," he said huskily, lifting her atop him and wrapping his arms around her tightly. "Do you feel like riding?"

She leaned down and met his lips, licking them from corner to corner. "I was hoping you'd ask."

Later that night the ringing of the telephone woke them up. Although Sage was fully aware of it, she remained nestled in Gabe's arms while he shifted his body to reach over and answer it.

"Yes?"

After a long pause he said, "Okay, I'll tell her."

Sage sat up in bed after hearing the conversation. "You'll tell me what?"

Gabe ran a hand down his face to wipe the sleep from his eyes. He then reached over and turned on the lamp, bringing brightness to the room, trying not to concentrate on Sage's naked body.

"That was Rose. Your father just called, upset. He's at the hospital. Your mother became ill during the night, and he had to rush her to the emergency room."

Sage was out of bed in a flash. "Did Rose leave a number where I can reach him?"

Gabe nodded as he also got out of bed. "Yes. She said for you to call him on his cell phone."

She nodded and immediately rushed to the phone and began dialing. Gabe went into the bathroom, and when he returned moments later, he could tell by the redness of Sage's eyes that she'd been crying. He quickly crossed the room and pulled her into his arms. "What is it, baby? What's wrong with your mother?"

Sage wiped tears from her eyes. "I don't know, and Dad says the people at the hospital aren't telling him anything. I can't get much out of him, Gabe. He's literally falling to pieces. I need to be there."

He nodded in agreement. "Do you want me to make flight arrangements?"

She smiled her appreciation, glad he was here with her. "Oh, would you? I can't seem to think straight right now."

He nodded as he began putting on his pants. "Get your things together and I'll take you home."

"That's not necessary, Gabe. I have my car here, remember?"

He smiled as he zipped up his pants and watched her slip into her bra and panties. "You won't be able to drive all the way to North Carolina, Sage."

At her bemused look, he said, "When I said that I'd take you home, I was talking about taking you home to Charlotte. I have my pilot's license, and it shouldn't be a problem to get a plane tonight and fly you home."

Sage stopped what she was doing. "You'd actually take time off work to fly me home?"

He reached for his sweater and pulled it over his head, then said, "Of course I would."

She turned to face him. "Why? Why would you go to all that trouble for me?"

Gabe shook his head. He didn't want to believe she could ask that after what they'd shared over the past months. And he'd felt the same uncertainty coming from her when he'd asked her about accompanying him to Detroit for his grandparents' anniversary party next week. She never had said one way or the other if she would attend with him.

Deciding it was time to get a few things straight, he crossed the room to her. "Do you really want to know the real reason that I would go to all that trouble for you, Sage?"

She nodded. "Yes."

He reached out and touched her shoulders, to make sure he had her full attention. "Because you mean a lot to me, Sage. In fact, you mean everything to me. I love you."

He watched her blink. Then, when she had fully comprehended what he'd said, she turned around and continued dressing. "No, you don't."

"Excuse me?"

She turned around to face him. "I said that you don't love me. You love what we share, but that doesn't connect to me as an individual."

Gabe crossed his arms over his chest. "So you think I made love to a nameless, faceless body all those times?"

"No, of course not, Gabe. It's just that you can't love me."

"Can I ask why?"

Sage sighed, as though the question was too annoying to answer. "Because you can't We haven't reached that level yet, and I never intended for us to. I've loved one man in my lifetime and look what happened. And then, after what my father did, how do you expect me to believe in love?"

Gabe was beginning to feel frustrated and angry. "I expected you to believe in it because I've not given you a reason not to during the time we've been together. Do you think I was making love to you for the fun of it? Each time we made love, Sage, for me it was for love. The only reason I hadn't told you how I felt before now was because I wanted to give you time to get yourself together after Erol."

She whirled on him then, giving him a sharp look. "To get myself together?"

"Yes."

She exhaled angrily. "Why is it that everyone thinks I didn't have myself together after I broke up with Erol? I didn't need any pining time. He betrayed my trust, and that was reason enough to walk away and not moan over it. So you've wasted your time with me if it was intended to get the heartbroken Sage through a difficult time."

"I didn't say that, and please don't put words in my mouth, Sage."

"Well, I don't want to have this conversation, Gabe. I just got out of an involved relationship and don't want to get into another one. I figured when your company was through here that that would be the end of it."

"Of us?"

"Yes."

"Well, you were wrong; we belong together."

"No, Gabe, you're wrong; we don't belong together. You were also wrong for putting more stock into our relationship than what was there. We should have talked about it. I would have saved you the trouble. I don't want or need love in my life."

After saying those words, she grabbed her overnight bag off the bed and left, slamming the door behind her.

CHAPTER TWENTY-EIGHT

"Let me make sure I got this right. Gabe told you that he was in love with you, so you gave him hell?" Rose asked as she assisted Sage with her packing.

Sage raised her eyes to the ceiling as she folded a nightgown to put inside the luggage that was spread open on her bed. "I did not give him hell, Rose. I merely tried explaining why I thought he was wrong."

"For loving you?"

Sage frowned. "No, for thinking he loves me."

Rose strolled over to the bed and sat down. "Oh, so now he's not old enough to know his own heart, is that it? Just how old is he anyway? Thirty? Thirty-one?"

"He's thirty-two."

Rose nodded and laughed lightly. "Oh, then that explains things. Everyone knows that a thirty-two-year-old man, a very successful one at that, would be confused about something as complicated as love."

Sage stopped packing and drew in a long, deep breath, then exhaled slowly. "You don't understand, Rose."

Rose stood and glared at her. "You're right, Sage, I don't understand. A good man, and I mean a really good one, is hard to find, so the way I see it, when you find one, you latch on to him and keep him forever. You certainly don't throw the love he expresses to you back in his face."

Sage's heart thumped wildly in her chest. "I didn't do that."

"Yes, you did if you said to him all those things that you told me you said. Think about it, Sage."

Sage placed her hand on her hips, angry and frustrated. "But I don't want him to love me, Rose. Can't you see that? And I don't want to love him. I should never have let things go this far between us. I should have put an end to things when I saw how my need for him was becoming overwhelming, and when the thought of Eden being completed made me have stomach cramps because I knew everything between us would have to end then."

Rose reached across the bed and grabbed Sage's trembling hand. "Hey, nothing has to end, Sage," she said softly. "People conduct long-distance relationships all the time. Just look at Malcolm and his wife. They didn't break up because of the time and distance separating them." She studied Sage intently. "There's another reason for you not wanting Gabe to love you, and you know it."

Sage pulled her hand free to wipe the tears from her eyes and to continue packing. "What other reason could there be?"

Rose crossed her arms over her chest. "One that's connected to Erol. You don't want Gabe to love you because the one man who you thought loved you the most let you down, so it stands to reason . . . in your mind . . . that Gabe will eventually do likewise."

Sage closed her luggage. Rose didn't know the half of it. Actually, the *two* men she had loved the most had let her down. But in her mind that had nothing to do with Gabe. She just wasn't ready to take their relationship to the level that he wanted to take it. "That's not true."

"Isn't it? You need to think real hard on what you're doing, Sage. You're throwing away the love of a good man, a man who loves you to distraction; even I can see that. That night we had dinner at his place was definitely an eye-opener. He couldn't look at you without wanting you with pure love shining in his eyes. Hell, even someone distrustful of love like me could see it."

Rose sighed deeply before continuing. "And I would give anything to have a man love and want me that much, Sage. Your relationship with Erol sheltered you from what's out there, sweetheart, what most women have to choose from. There's a pool of die-hard players, baby-daddies and just plain old no-good jokers who want to spend their money, and yours, too, with the gall to think that it's all right to have a different woman every damn day of the week. I know, Sage, because I've had to deal with them and you haven't."

Without saying anything else, Rose turned and walked out of the room.

When Sage arrived at the airport, a uniformed man who looked like a security guard met her. Then she recognized him as the security person for Landmark Industries.

"Ms. Dunbar?"

"Yes?"

"I'll be glad to escort you to gate seven."

Sage lifted a brow, not understanding. "Gate seven?"

"Yes. The plane has been fueled and is ready to go."

Sage didn't want to sound dense, but there was no help for it. "The plane?"

The man's patience had to be admired. "Yes, the private plane that is scheduled to fly you to Charlotte, North Carolina. Mr. Blackwell made arrangements with Mr. Landmark to use the company's jet for your trip. I understand an emergency has come up in your family."

"Yes, my mother has taken ill." She shifted her carry-on to another hand. "Is Mr. Blackwell the person who will be piloting the plane?"

"No. He's made arrangements with Mr. Landmark for his personal pilot to take you home," the man responded.

Sage nodded. After all the things she had said to Gabe, she could understand why he wouldn't fly her home personally. But she couldn't understand why he had gone out of his way to help her after everything she'd said to him. She would have thought he would not want to have anything to do with her.

"Ms. Dunbar?" The uniformed man's voice forced her attention back to him.

"Yes?"

"Are you ready?"

She glanced around the airport terminal, wondering if Gabe was around anywhere. When she didn't see him, she returned her attention to the man. "Yes, I'm ready." She then followed him to their destination.

Gabe tossed the money for his coffee on the counter when he saw Sage walk off with the uniformed guard. He had to come to see her one last time before she left, just to make sure she was all right, even if it was from a distance. He had wanted to go to her, and talk to her, and assure her that everything would be all right with her mother. And he wanted to tell her again that he loved her.

A piercing pain shot through his chest upon remembering all she had said, and then how she had walked away from him and his love. A part of him had wanted to go after her and make her see reason, to make her realize that she was making the wrong decision regarding them. But he couldn't.

He had taken Sage on with emotional baggage and all. He'd known the risk, but still his heart had fallen deep. It had fallen deeper than any heart should fall, and her words of rejection had cut him to the core. They had made it difficult to draw breath into his lungs.

And yet he still loved her.

For the second time in his life, a woman who couldn't let go of the past had kicked him to the curb. A part of him wondered why he was torturing himself. A heart could only break so many times.

Gabe walked over to the window as the private jet carrying Sage home prepared for takeoff. He suddenly felt the most devastating loss of his life because that plane was carrying away the woman he loved, and he knew his world wouldn't be back to normal until she told him that she loved him, too.

As Gabe walked out of the airport terminal, he thought he would be most happy when Sage could walk into a room, any room, filled with people and know that she was the most loved person there, and openly, honestly and sincerely feel it and accept that love from him.

Sage settled back in her seat as everything became tiny objects out of the plane's window.

Gabe had come.

She had seen him standing at the terminal window while the plane sat on the runway preparing to take off. Even after everything she'd said to him, he had come to see her off anyway.

A lump settled deep in her throat as emptiness consumed her. She suddenly felt alone as the finality of what she had done hit her hard. Rose had been right. Gabe had told her he loved her, and she had given him hell.

Sage closed her eyes. She had a lot to deal with: her mother's illness, losing Gabe and seeing her father again. She wrapped her arms around her middle, not wanting to think about anything right now. She needed peace for just a little while.

As her eyes remained closed and her body began to relax, it was Gabe's face she saw in the deep recesses of her mind. It was Gabe who was smiling at her, just moments before he leaned down to kiss her. Her mind filled with happy thoughts, and Gabe was a part of all of them.

CHAPTER TWENTY-NINE

After renting a car at the airport, Sage drove directly to the hospital. Once she had checked in with Patient Services, she caught an elevator that would carry her up to the fifth floor, the intensive care unit.

She saw her father sitting in the waiting room as soon as she stepped off the elevator. She stopped suddenly. His face looked haggard, worn and torn. He resembled a man who had gone through pure hell over the past ten hours or so. She had never seen him so downtrodden, unkempt. Being in the business arena, he'd always taken pride in his dress; but at that moment, it was evident that he didn't give a damn, that he was worried about something more important to him than his appearance.

Her throat felt too tight even for a word to slip through to let him know of her presence, so she just stood quietly, not letting him know she was there. He was staring into space as if he wasn't even aware of his surroundings, a man battered, terrified and grasping on to the last ray of sanity and prayer. He resembled a man who looked as though he felt totally useless as well as fearful of losing the most important thing in his life.

Sage wrapped her arms around her middle when it hit her then, just that quick, and just that hard, that her father *did* love her mother.

"Dad?"

He turned quickly upon hearing the sound of her voice. Her stomach dropped suddenly, and she shivered and gulped in a sharp breath when she saw tears in his eyes. The only other time she'd ever recalled seeing him cry was at her grandmother's funeral.

He stood and walked over to her, and automatically, without words being exchanged, they embraced. When she felt him shudder, she tightened her hold around him. "It's okay, Dad. Mom's going to be all right. Come on, let's sit over here and you can tell me just what the doctors said."

One arm remained steady around his waist as she guided him over to a group of chairs. It took him a while to get his breath. Then he spoke. "The doctors still don't know anything definite and are still running tests. For a while they thought it was some type of viral infection, possibly meningitis, but the results came back negative, thank God."

Sage nodded. She thanked God for that, too. "When was the last time you spoke with a doctor?"

"Not since this morning. I was in your mother's room when a nurse asked me to step out while they ran more tests." His voice broke when he said, "I can't stand seeing her lying there like that, Sage. If anything were to happen to her, I don't know what I'd do."

Sage swallowed. "Dad, Mom is going to be all right; we have to believe that. I don't think I ever remember her being sick, so that means she's a fairly healthy person; and she's under the best of care. We have to believe she will be all right."

Sage knew she was convincing herself of that as well as him.

"Mr. Dunbar?"

Both Sage and her father turned at the sound of the masculine voice. It was the doctor. Both of them were on their feet in no time.

"How is she?" Sage asked before her father could form the words.

The tall, gray-hired man looked at Sage from under thick, bushy brows. "You're Mrs. Dunbar's daughter?" he asked, his expression friendly.

"Yes. I'm Sage Dunbar."

He reached out his hand. "And I'm Doctor Connelly." He then turned to address both her and her father. "We think we've located the root of Mrs. Dunbar's problem. It seems that her appendix is about to burst and has begun leaking fluid into her system. We're taking her to surgery immediately to remove it."

"Her appendix?" Sage asked.

"Yes. Now that we know what's causing the problem, it's a fairly routine surgical procedure that shouldn't take but a couple of hours. However, I need to be honest with you and let you know that due to her high blood pressure, it may complicate things."

Sage frowned. She hadn't known that her mother had high blood pressure. Not knowing that information made her realize that she had never really inquired about the true nature of her mother's health. Like most young people, she thought her parents were in good health and would be around forever.

"I'll be back out as soon as the surgery is over."

"Can I see her?" Sage asked.

"Sorry, but we've already started prepping her for surgery. We want to get started right away before the fluid gets into her bloodstream. I'll be back out as soon as the surgery is over, and then I'll let you see her."

"Thank you, Doctor," Sage said as everything he'd said weighed heavily on her mind. After he left, she turned to her father. "Do you want to walk with me to the café to get a cup of coffee?"

"No, I'd rather sit and wait right here, just in case the doctor comes back out."

Sage knew there was no sense in telling him that they wouldn't be seeing the doctor again until after the surgery. "Do you want me to bring you anything?"

"No, I'm fine."

She nodded. "Just try to relax, Dad, and I'll be right back." She had started to walk off when her father called after her. "Sage?"

She turned back. "Yes?"

"Thanks for coming."

Sage looked at him. Had he thought that she wouldn't come because of the differences between them? Had that special relationship they'd always shared eroded to this?

Knowing she needed to be by herself for a while and think things through, she nodded and quickly walked toward the elevator.

A couple of hours later, Sage and her father sat across from each other in the waiting room. Other people were in the room, but conversations were muted as everyone waited for word of their loved ones from various doctors.

Sage shifted her gaze to her father, and again she thought of how battered he looked. Although he'd said he hadn't wanted anything, she had brought him a cup of coffee anyway. He drank half of it, and now the rest was sitting on the table in front of him, cold.

There hadn't been much conversation between them. She had tried talking about Eden and the progress that had been made, but he hadn't taken the bait. His mind was still concentrated on the surgery being performed on his wife.

"Has anyone called Reverend and Sister Jones?" she asked, breaking into the silence.

He glanced up at her and nodded. "Yes. They came earlier today and indicated they'd be coming back later."

Sage nodded. Her mother was close to the elderly couple. "What about Uncle Jess and Aunt Mable?"

"Your aunt left a few days ago to fly out to California to see Ginger. Jess stopped by a little before you got here. He said he would be coming back when he got off work."

Sage was about to say something when she saw Dr. Connelly coming toward them. Her father saw him at the same time and quickly stood and asked, "How is she, Doctor?"

He smiled. "She's doing fine. We managed to keep her blood pressure stabilized during the surgery. We have her on strong antibiotics to fight off any possible infections."

"Can we see her?" Sage asked eagerly. From the look on her father's face, she knew a great weight had been lifted from his shoulders.

"Right now she's in recovery. We have her pretty sedated, so she won't even know you're there. I'm hoping that we'll be able to have her in a room in a few hours. The two of you may want to go home and get some rest and come back later."

Charles Dunbar shook his head. "No, I'm staying."

"So am I," Sage chimed in.

Seeing their resolve, Dr. Connelly said, "All right. After she comes out of recovery and gets settled in ICU, you can both visit with her, but only for a short while."

After the doctor left, Charles Dunbar looked at his daughter. Tears of happiness and relief shone unabashedly in his eyes. "I think I'm going to go downstairs to the café and get something to eat."

Sage nodded and then realized that this was the first time he'd eaten since she had arrived at the hospital. She decided to go with him to the café to make sure he ordered something more nourishing than a sandwich. "If you don't mind, I think I'll go with you, Dad."

He shook his head and wiped the tears from his eyes. "No, I don't mind. In fact, I'd like that."

* * *

Sage and her father were able to see her mother a few hours later when she'd been placed in a room in ICU. At first Sage's knees almost buckled under her when she saw her mother's still body lying in the hospital bed hooked up to a number of machines.

Now it was her father who gave her support when she closed her eyes to block out the sight before her. Placing a firm arm around her, he said, "Remember what Doctor Connelly said, Sage. She came through, and everything is going to be all right."

Sage nodded and opened her eyes as he released his hold on her. She then watched, in silence, as he crossed the room to the bed where her mother lay and lovingly trailed his fingertips down the side of her cheek before leaning down and kissing it. He then pulled a chair closer to the bed to sit down, taking her mother's hand in his and gently caressing it.

Again Sage thought that this was a man who truly loved his wife, and she suddenly became overwhelmed with confused thoughts as to what could make a man who loved his wife fall into the arms of another woman.

She shifted her gaze to the other side of the room where a number of floral arrangements sat on the table. One particular arrangement caught her attention since it was so much larger than the others.

Crossing the room, she went to see who had sent them. Opening the card, her stomach pitched suddenly. She sucked in a breath.

The flowers were from Gabe, and the card simply said, *Wishing you a speedy recovery, Gabriel Blackwell.*

"Who sent those, Sage? They weren't in here before."

Sage turned upon hearing her father's question. She met his gaze. "They're from Gabe Blackwell."

From the way her father nodded, she knew that he remembered the name from that time she had mentioned Gabe to him.

"That was thoughtful of him to send them."

She nodded, thinking of other thoughtful things Gabe had done. "Yes, it was, wasn't it?"

It was over an hour later before her mother came awake, slowly raising her eyelids. Without saying anything, she acknowledged their presence by gazing at them and nodding before closing her eyes again.

"With the medication the doctor has given her, she'll probably sleep through the night," the nurse said to them. "This may be a good time for the two of you to go home and get some rest."

Sage nodded, agreeing with the nurse. After a long flight, she needed to at least shower and change. But she could tell by the defiant look in her father's eyes that getting him to leave would definitely be a problem.

She looked down at her mother sleeping peacefully. "She's right, Dad. We both need to get some rest and be ready to come back first thing in the morning." When he started to protest, she said, "Neither of us will do Mom any good being tired and worn out."

For the longest time he didn't say anything, and then he asked quietly, "Will you be coming to the house?"

A knot formed in Sage's throat. She hadn't really thought about where she would be staying, although staying at her parents' place was the logical choice. "Yes, if it's all right with you."

Charles Dunbar crossed the room and placed his hands on his daughter's shoulders. "Of course it's all right with me, Sage. It's your home and will always be your home."

Sage nodded and reached up and covered one of his hands with hers. "Then, let's go home, Dad, and make plans to return early in the morning."

Reluctantly, he agreed. She then leaned down and kissed her mother's cheek and whispered, "Dad and I are going home, Mom, and we'll be back in the morning." Sage wasn't sure if her mother heard her or not but wanted to let her know in case she woke up again and they were not there.

She saw her father hesitate, then quickly concluded that he wanted to spend some private moments with his wife. "I'll be right outside the door, Dad."

"Thanks, Sage."

They were back at the hospital before the first sign of dawn broke in the morning sky. The nurse from the night before met them after they had gotten off the elevator. "Mrs. Dunbar had a very peaceful night," she said, smiling. "If she continues doing well, the doctor may remove the feeding tube to see if she can take solid foods."

Sage smiled widely at her father. That was good news to hear. Seeing one less IV line hooked to her mother would mean all the difference in the world to her, and she knew her father felt the same way.

As soon as they had arrived home last night, she had showered and changed clothes while he had answered the many phone messages that had been left on the answering machine. And then while he had showered, she had done likewise, making sure her family, both near and far, got an update on her mother's condition. Then she and her father had gone to bed. Knowing her mother's condition was good, sleep had come fairly easy for her, but she'd wakened a number of times upon hearing her father move about, restless and unable to sleep.

The devil had been busy, and evil thoughts had consumed her mind while she'd lain in bed listening to him. She'd almost been convinced that guilt and not love was eating away at him, but then after saying a prayer, asking God to rid her mind of such corrupt thoughts, she'd held on to the belief that it was love.

She stopped short when they entered her mother's room. Delores Dunbar sat propped against the pillow, awake, and she was no longer using the respirator. Knowing she could not give her mother the hug that she wanted to give her, Sage quickly crossed the room, but her father had reached her mother before her.

"Baby, you scared twenty years off my life," he said, leaning down and gently framing her face in his hands, before placing a kiss on her lips.

Sage stood back and watched them, suddenly feeling like an outsider in her parents' world. Evidently, during the time she'd been in Anchorage, their relationship had grown closer. A part of her wondered if her father had told her mother about his affair yet, and she decided she didn't want to think about it. Making sure her mother was happy while her condition improved was the most important thing.

"Sage?"

She got pulled out of her thoughts at the quiet whisper of her mother's voice. She walked over to the bed. She met her mother's gaze and smiled, fighting back the tears she felt behind her lids. "You gave me a scare, too, Delores Dunbar."

Her mother slowly nodded while keeping her eyes on her daughter. "I didn't mean to."

Sage took her mother's hand in hers. "How do you feel?"

Delores smiled. "Sore."

Sage chuckled. "Yeah, I can believe that."

Since her mother was still in ICU, the time to visit was limited. The only good thing they had to look forward to was the fact that if her condition continued to improve, she would be sent to a private room on another floor where visiting restrictions would be lifted.

Relief rushed through Sage, knowing that her mother was healing. On the plane flight from Anchorage, she had been plagued with the fear of losing her, but now seeing her on the mend made her feel extremely better.

At least, a part of her felt better. There was still that small part lodged within her chest that ached—her heart. Although she didn't want to think about it or, even worse, admit it, she missed Gabe.

She missed him a lot.

Two days later, Sage's gaze settled on her mother's smile. It had always been a generous smile that Delores Dunbar had reserved for everyone she knew, and Sage didn't want to think about how close she had come to losing that smile, to losing her mother.

"Whatever you're thinking about must be serious."

Sage blinked, realizing that her mother had spoken and had caught her staring. Sitting up in the hospital bed, Delores was eating solid foods, something she had begun doing yesterday for the first time since being admitted.

"No, it isn't too serious," she said, crossing the room from where she'd been standing at the window for the past fifteen minutes. At first she'd been thinking just how vastly different Charlotte was from Anchorage, and that was based on more than just the weather. Even the shape of the skyscrapers was different, and there were no snow-covered mountains in the background, no wilderness trails and . . . no Gabe Blackwell.

"That serious look just got more serious."

Her mother's words startled Sage from her thoughts. She smiled and took the chair across from the bed. "Just thinking about some things."

"Some things like your father?"

Sage lifted a brow. Her father had left half an hour earlier to drop off a package at the office. They expected him to return at any time. He spent most of his days as well as his nights at the hospital. "Why would I be thinking about Dad?"

Delores Dunbar wiped her mouth with a napkin and pushed her tray aside. "Mainly because I couldn't help but notice that your relationship seems to have improved, and I'm glad. The two of you had me concerned for a while."

Sage nodded, not wanting to discuss this with her mother when she knew she was wrong as to the reason why her and her father's relationship had gotten strained.

"He was right, you know, Sage. It didn't really concern you. It was about me and him."

Sage blinked. She wondered what her mother was talking about. Did she have an idea what was going on between her and her father and why? Sage met her mother's gaze, and as if she was blessed with the ability to read her daughter's mind, Delores said, "Yes, I know what happened, Sage, with your father and that other woman. He told me."

"He did?" Sage whispered in shock, not so much that her father had finally admitted the truth to his wife, but that her mother was calmly sitting in bed as if it was no big deal to discuss the fact that her husband had committed adultery.

"Yes, he did. I've known now for a while, but I didn't bring it up to you whenever we talked on the phone because I felt when the time was right for us to discuss it, then we would."

Sage leaned back in the chair. "How can you sit there and be so calm about it?"

Delores chuckled. "Oh, trust me, I had my moments when he told me. For the first time during the thirty-one years of our marriage, I made him sleep in another room. That was all the time it took for me to analyze the situation."

"And apparently forgive him," Sage said brusquely, not sure she liked how accepting her mother seemed to be about everything.

Delores shook her head, smiling. "No, the forgiving part came over time with prayer. A lot of prayer and an assessment of what I had and what I'd be throwing away, as well as what I could have done to prevent what happened."

Sage frowned. "Surely you're not blaming yourself for what he did?"

Delores smiled. Her daughter had a lot to learn which she knew she would if she kept right on living. "The woman in me couldn't help but do that at first. No woman wants to know that her husband could not resist temptation. But then I had to realize that there is no perfect human being other than the Father. Man is weak, he is likely to sin many times over and if we love that person, we have to find it in our heart to forgive. As an individual, you have to let go of what that person may have done to you. You have to be responsible as well as accountable for that. Then that person who caused you harm and pain has to atone for his own transgressions."

"So as far as you're concerned, it never happened?" Sage asked. Her mother was too forgiving, too tolerant and way too nice, she thought.

"No, Sage, it happened; both your father and I know that. We just chose to move on in spite of it. We love each other deeply and wanted nothing or no one to destroy our marriage. The flesh is weak. As sinners we fall down, but then we get up. A person who is truly the child of God would not kick that person back down while he's struggling to get up."

Sage stood and walked over to the window and looked out. Sunlight was streaming through. It had rained earlier, and she could see a rainbow in the sky, a beautiful rainbow with a multitude of colors.

She turned back around to face her mother. "So you think I *should* have been as all-forgiving to Erol as you apparently are to Dad?" she asked in a voice more resentful than she intended it to be, but that couldn't be helped.

"I'm not saying that, Sage. All I'm saying is that you should forgive Erol, but forgiving someone doesn't automatically mean reconciliation with that person. It means reparation with that person, making amends, repairing. Although in a committed relationship, a marriage sanctioned by God, it's not an option to walk away and not try to make things work. There was something in our vows that said 'for better or for worse.' You and

Erol were not married, just engaged. You hadn't exchanged any vows before God yet. So if you felt you were not suited for whatever reason, it was best that the two of you parted ways when you did."

"We weren't a good match," Sage said softly.

"Evidently not. If you had been, you would have found it in your heart to not only forgive him, but to put it behind you and move on in spite of it. The love you had for him would have overlooked what he had done once you had forgiven him."

Sage didn't say anything for the longest time, deciding she'd rather concentrate on her parents than her and Erol. "So you've put what Dad did behind you and moved on?"

"Yes, but that doesn't mean we didn't cry together, pray together and seek private counseling with Reverend Jones. But we had to take stock in what we had. We had a beautiful daughter we both loved, a lifetime of good memories and a future of just as many more. But what really convinced me was in knowing your father truly loved me, and in me accepting that the flesh is weak. That's called loving in spite of—which is the same philosophy God uses on us. He loves us in spite of our wrongdoings, our transgressions, and He's accepting that we're weak and will make mistakes, a lot of them."

Sage nodded and turned back to the window. Moments later she turned and met her mother's gaze. "I wanted to hate him for what he did to you. He disappointed me, and I felt he let me down."

"That's why we can't elevate men, Sage. Men are subject to fail and to sin. Your father has always been superhuman in your eyes. He walked on water as far as you were concerned, and I'm sure it hurt you to find out he can fall to the bottom like anyone else. So can I. What if it had been me that you saw that night instead of your father?"

Sage raised a brow, clearly unable to consider such a thing, and said as much.

"Well, it could have been. During my marriage, several men

have approached me, and if I had been under the same type of stress your father had been under . . . Who knows? I may have yielded to temptation, too."

"And just what type of stress was he under?"

Delores leaned back against the pillows. "He was going through a lot at work. You know how it is, some companies wanting to push out their older employees for a much younger staff. So your father had to work harder, longer hours to prove he still had what it took. I wasn't as supportive as I could have been—and I can see that now. While he didn't tell me everything that was going on with him at work, I felt something was bothering him, and I became concerned. But not concerned enough to start spending more time with him to get to the root of the problem. Instead, I became more and more absorbed in what I was doing—my church work, my charities, my frustrations with you for not wanting to move forward and make wedding plans, and my own job. I wasn't there for him. Unfortunately, someone else was."

Sage tipped her head back and smiled at her mother. Only a strong woman, a very strong woman, could admit as well as accept something like that. "You're something else, you know that?"

Delores chuckled. "Oh, I don't know about that. Right now I feel that you're something else, too. It seems you've successfully moved beyond Erol just like you said you had."

Sage nodded. "Yes, I have but decided that I'm not ready to get that involved with anyone again right now."

Delores chuckled. "Well, it looks to me like you already have."

Sage lifted a brow. "What do you mean?"

"It means that I can't help noticing the number of times you've looked at those flowers that Mr. Blackwell sent, and the expression on your face when you look at them."

Sage briefly closed her eyes. In addition to being all-forgiving, her mother was also all-observing. "Well, yes, I happen to think they are beautiful."

"And what about the man who sent them?"

A visual of Gabe flashed into Sage's mind. She couldn't help but smile. "I happen to think that he's beautiful, too."

"But?"

Sage inhaled deeply. "But I'm not ready to fall in love again."

Delores nodded. She couldn't help wondering when Sage would realize that she had already taken the fall.

Later that evening Sage glanced around the room that had always been hers while growing up. Because her parents had been hard-working people, they had always provided her with nice things. She could certainly stand in the middle of her room and say that she had been truly blessed to have Charles and Delores Dunbar for parents.

She thought about the conversation she'd had with her mother earlier at the hospital, and again thought of how strong and courageous she was, as well as forgiving. Sage knew she had to find it in her heart and be just as forgiving. As her mother said, God loves us in spite of our wrongdoings, regardless of the countless mistakes we make. He also holds us accountable to find it in our hearts to forgive someone who has hurt us; and in turn, that person has to be the one accountable for his own transgressions.

Turning, she walked out of the bedroom to look for her father. She found him in the kitchen, standing at the window, quietly looking out at the backyard.

He evidently heard her approach, and without turning around he said, "I was just looking at that big oak tree and remembering the time I built you a tree house up there, although by the time your mother added those silly-looking lacy curtains and painted the walls pink, it became an elevated doll house."

He chuckled. "She wasn't too happy that I had built it in that tree and not on the ground. She just knew one day you would fall and break your arm or something. But I knew better. I knew just what sturdy stuff you were made of. . . . After all, you were a Dunbar."

He slowly turned around. "But that tree house, or that doll house if you want to call it that, became our special place. I remember climbing up there with you and reading Bible stories to you. And the one you liked the best was the story of how little David, with God's help, slew the big and mighty Goliath. David became your hero."

He inhaled deeply and looked down as if studying the tiles on the floor. "In recent months David has become my hero, too, because when faced with his wrongdoings, he asked God's forgiveness. And when forgiven, he went on to be one of the greatest kings that ever lived. God showed him just how much he meant to Him, in spite of the wrong he'd done, by having one of David's heirs deliver His son into the world. That was a prime example of God's mercy and forgiveness, and for David that was an awesome blessing."

He lifted his gaze and met his daughter's. "I'm not David, but I feel blessed to have a woman like your mother love me in spite of what I've done. She still believes in me in spite of the fact that I've hurt her and have caused her pain. I don't know if you will believe this, but I intend to spend the remainder of my days loving her, appreciating her and knowing when things get rough for me again not to yield to temptation but to stay strong and depend on God to get me through any difficult time I encounter."

He wiped his hand across his face, removing the traces of tears that were beginning to form there. "I know it will take time for you, but I'm hoping and praying that one day you will find it in your heart to forgive me, Sage. I never meant to hurt you, and you'll never know just how much pain I've endured knowing that I lost your love and respect. My prayer each and every night is for God to make me a stronger person than before, a better person, and to never let me hurt the people that I love again."

Sage inhaled sharply as she blinked back the tears gathering in her eyes. Her father had spoken from deep in his heart, a heart filled with regret for what he'd lost. Suddenly, her own heart began overflowing with love and tenderness for him, more than she thought possible. And she could no longer cling to the "wrongs" he had done when she could remember so many "rights." He'd always been a good father, a supportive father, a kind and loving man.

He still was.

That was evident by the love and dedication he'd given her mother, especially during her illness. But she also knew that for her mother to be basking in so much love, affection and confidence, her father was living each day to reassure his wife that she was deeply loved and appreciated.

"I'd like to have my daughter back."

Her father's words, spoken in a husky, deep, emotional voice, cut into Sage's thoughts, and without hesitation, she quickly crossed the room to him and wrapped her arms around him, holding him tight. She cried for the both of them, for all they had endured over the past eight months and, more recently, the past four days with her mother's illness.

"I love you, Dad," she said between sobs. "I love you and I forgive you. And most important, I will always be your daughter. No matter what."

And Sage intended to make good on that promise.

CHAPTER THIRTY

A week later, Sage was returning to Anchorage filled with happiness that she and her father had resolved their differences and that her mother was at home resting, with her condition improving daily. Aunt Mable had returned and had taken over her mother's care while her father returned to work.

As Sage tightened her seat belt in preparation for landing, her thoughts shifted to Gabe. She had tried calling him a few times and had left messages, but he hadn't returned her calls. After talking with Malcolm, she knew that he was still in Anchorage because her coworker had seen him at a few meetings. A part of her didn't want to believe that not responding to her calls was Gabe's way of letting her know that he had severed the ties between them.

She wrapped her arms around her stomach, remembering the exact time and moment she'd finally accepted that she was in love with Gabe Blackwell. It was when Ginger and Cinnamon flew in to see her mother and they had spent time catching up on things that were going on in their lives. Her two cousins had excitedly told her about the men they had met and fallen in love with. Seeing them glowing, happy and looking very much in love made Sage realize that she felt the same way about Gabe. There had been a reason she was missing him the way she was, why she constantly had him on her mind.

She loved him.

She had tried fighting it, tried convincing herself that it wasn't possible, but deep down in her heart she knew that it was true. And after what she'd said to him, she knew her biggest challenge was in convincing Gabe that it was true.

She inhaled deeply, wondering if perhaps another reason he hadn't returned her calls was because he had already started seeing someone else. She didn't want to think it, but that was possible. Maybe he thought, considering everything, that she was more trouble than what she was really worth, and that since one woman had already broken his heart, he didn't intend to get hurt a second time. And if he still cared deeply for her, how could she convince him that she'd made a mistake and she was willing to make a relationship between them work?

As soon as the plane landed, she gathered her luggage and caught a cab straight to Gabe's office, knowing chances were she would find him there. Riding up to his office in the elevator reminded her of the time they had made love in it. Her mind became filled with other pleasant memories of the intimate times they had shared.

His secretary smiled upon seeing her.

"Ms. Dunbar, welcome back."

Sage smiled. "Thanks. Is Mr. Blackwell in?"

His secretary shook her head. "No, I'm sorry. He flew out yesterday morning for Detroit to attend his grandparents' anniversary party."

Sage nodded. She remembered he'd mentioned that to her. In fact, the last time they'd spent together, he had asked her to fly to his home with him and be his date that night. Fearing things were moving too fast between them if he wanted her to go home with him to meet his family, she hadn't answered one way or the other if she would go. In fact, she had jumped to another subject.

"When will he be returning?" she asked the woman.

"Not for another week."

Disappointed that it would be another week before she saw Gabe again, Sage's stomach dropped. "All right. Thanks for the info."

Feeling totally defeated, she turned and left Gabe's office.

"The way I see it," Rose was saying as she stood in front of the mirror blow-drying her hair, "if your man isn't here, then you should go to him."

Sage leaned against the bathroom door, shaking her head. "Rose, I can't do that, especially since I don't know how Gabe feels about me."

Rose turned and looked at her, clearly annoyed. "He told you that he loved you."

"Yeah, but that was almost a week and a half ago."

Rose leaned against the bathroom sink and shook her head. "That's right, I almost forgot that Gabe is a man who, according to you, doesn't know his own heart."

Sage glared. "That's not funny."

"You're right, it's not funny; it's pathetic. Will you give Gabe credit for at least having the intelligence we both know he has, Sage. The man loves you. If he didn't love you, he would not have called me every day to find out how your mother was doing, as well as to see how you were, since he knew we kept in touch."

Sage lifted a curious brow. "Why would he call you and not me? I left a couple of messages for him."

"Because, in his own words and not mine, he wanted to give you space and time to think."

"Well, he certainly did that," Sage said, drawing in a shaky breath.

"In that case, you should tell him. But I wouldn't wait until he returns. It's time you take matters into your hands like I'm doing."

Sage looked at Rose curiously. "What kind of matters are you taking into your own hands?"

Rose grinned as if she had a secret that she wasn't sharing. "You'll find out soon enough. All I can say right now is that I plan to offer Parnell a business deal that he can't refuse."

She then waved off any further inquiries from Sage. "No more questions about it since we're not talking about me. We're talking about you and Gabe and how you can fix your screwup. I have plenty of suggestions if you care to listen."

Sage tucked a loose strand behind her ear as she went into the bathroom and sat down on the edge of the bathtub, feeling desperate. "Okay, let's hear your ideas."

The following morning, Sage was on a plane again, en route to Detroit. She inhaled deeply to calm the butterflies floating around in her stomach. She had gone over and over in her mind all the words she planned to say to Gabe when she saw him. But deep down she knew the final words would be spoken from her heart.

CHAPTER THIRTY-ONE

Sage tried to relax as she stood in front of the door after ringing the doorbell. From the sound of music and voices she heard on the other side, she knew the anniversary party had begun.

It hadn't taken much probing to find out everything she'd needed to know from Gabe's secretary, including where his grandparents' anniversary would be held and the proper attire. She'd barely had enough time after her plane landed to check into a hotel and quickly change. She glanced down at herself. Since she would be meeting his family for the first time, she didn't want to wear anything brow-raising, yet on the other hand, she wanted to wear something that would definitely capture Gabe's attention. She felt the dress she was wearing, one she had purchased at a dress shop in Anchorage, was perfect.

The door opened, and an older woman with beautiful silver gray hair and a smile that reminded her so much of her mother's stood in the doorway looking radiant.

"Yes?"

Sage swallowed and hoped what she was about to say sounded convincing. Automatically, she reached out her hand. "Hello,

I'm Sage Dunbar, a friend of Gabe's. He invited me here tonight, but I had to leave Anchorage when my mother became
ill before letting him know whether I would attend."

The woman accepted her hand without hesitation, and although Sage was sure they had never met before, she saw the
woman's eyes light up when she'd said her name.

"Hello, Sage, and I'm Joella Blackwell, Gabe's mother. Is
your mother all right?"

Sage blinked, upon realizing the stunning woman was Gabe's
mother. "Yes, she's doing fine, so I thought I would take Gabe
up on his invitation; but he doesn't know that. I tried calling him
earlier on his cell phone when I arrived and couldn't reach him."

The older woman chuckled. "That doesn't surprise me.
He's been doing errands for me, lots of them, and probably
deliberately cut his cell phone off thinking I would be calling
with additional things for him to do." She stepped back. "Please
come in."

"Thanks," Sage said nervously. As soon as she entered, she
swept her gaze around the room. There were a lot of people in
attendance, but there was no sign of Gabe anywhere.

"Don't worry," Joella Blackwell said, chuckling again. "He's
around here somewhere, and I bet he's hiding out so I won't
find something else for him to do. And wherever he is, there's
no doubt in my mind that Christopher is with him. They're like
two peas in a pod, those two."

Joella Blackwell was beaming from ear to ear, and Sage wondered why. She then remembered what Gabe had once shared
with her about his mother's chronic matchmaking antics.

"If you'd like, I can help you look for him in this crowd,"
Joella Blackwell offered, still looking pretty pleased with herself.

Sage shook her head. Just in case Gabe would not be happy
to see her, she didn't want to have an audience when he asked
her to leave. "If you don't mind, I'll just look for him myself."

The woman smiled, and for some reason, Sage had a feeling that just like her mother, this woman could read her mind.

"Yes, that's fine. And after you find him, make sure he returns you to me so that I can introduce you to everyone."

Sage couldn't help but return the older woman's cheerful smile. "All right." She then walked off in search of Gabe, hoping that when she saw him, he would be willing to hear her out.

Christopher took a slow sip of his punch while he studied Gabe. They were standing outside on the lit patio, taking a breather from the multitude of well-wishers who'd come to congratulate the elder Blackwells on their sixtieth wedding anniversary.

Gabe and Chris hadn't had a chance to talk, at least not privately, since Gabe had arrived two days ago. Ma Joella had kept them both busy doing various chores in preparation for the anniversary party.

"You okay, bro?" he finally asked.

Gabe met his gaze. "Yeah, man, I'm okay."

Christopher nodded. He was hearing one thing but seeing another. Instead of ignoring it, he decided to push forward. "I thought Sage would be coming with you tonight."

Gabe took a sip of his punch, then responded, "She left to return home on an emergency. Her mother took ill and had to be hospitalized a week and a half ago." There was no reason to bore Chris with the details that even if there had not been an emergency, chances were Sage would not have come.

"And how's her mother doing?"

"From what I understand she's recuperating nicely."

Christopher nodded and took another slow sip of punch. "So the only reason for your long face is because you miss her."

If only you knew, Gabe thought. Yes, he was missing Sage like crazy. And the way they'd last spent their time together didn't help matters. "Yeah, I miss Sage, man. I miss her a lot."

"If that's true, it will make what I have to say a lot easier."

Gabe whirled around at the sound of the familiar feminine voice. His pulse quickened when he saw Sage, and he drew in a shaky breath. "Sage, what are you doing here?"

Sage struggled to pull air into her lungs. "You invited me."

"Yeah, but you never indicated you would come, and that was before you said all those things that night."

Sage's mouth went dry under the intensity of Gabe's gaze. "I shouldn't have come?" she asked, needing to know if she'd made a mistake in coming, and if he wanted her to leave.

Christopher cleared this throat, deciding to intervene. "I think the two of you need privacy, so I'm going back inside." He walked over to Sage and leaned down and kissed her cheek. "It's good seeing you again, Sage, and I'm looking forward to introducing you to Maxi and my son."

"Thanks. I'd like that." She watched Christopher leave, then turned her attention back to Gabe. If there was any doubt in her mind that she loved him, that doubt was erased as she met his gaze. She loved this man with all her heart.

"I'm glad you came," he finally said, answering her question.

That made hope rise up in Sage. "Are you?"

"Yes."

"I'm glad I came, too."

Gabe nodded. "How's your mother?"

"Her condition has improved. She's home and recuperating nicely. I arrived back in Anchorage early yesterday and went by your office. Your secretary told me you'd be gone for a week, and I couldn't wait that long to see you again."

Gabe lifted a brow. "Why?"

"To say some things to you?"

Gabe laughed and shook his head. "Haven't you already said enough?"

Sage knew she deserved that, and it made her more determined to set things right between them. She inhaled deeply, working up her courage. His expression was unreadable, and she was unsure what his feelings were. She had overheard him telling Christopher that he had missed her, and that meant something. At least she hoped so. "I had a chance to think about things while I was away, Gabe."

He leaned against the patio rail, shoving his hands in his pockets. "Did you?"

"Yes."

"And what things did you think about, Sage?"

"I thought about how much I cherish our friendship, our unique closeness and just how lonely my life would be without you in it." She paused to steady her voice before she continued. "And I thought about what you mean to me."

Gabe continued to look at her, and Sage knew he wasn't giving her an inch. She had botched things up between them, and he intended for her to make things right on her own without any help from him.

"And just what do I mean to you, Sage?" he asked slowly. The gaze that held hers never wavered.

She swallowed deeply because what she was about to say was coming straight from her heart. "You mean everything to me, Gabe, and I'm sorry I only recently figured that out."

"Define what you mean by everything," he said throatily, with emotions deepening his voice.

She knew what he was asking, what he wanted her to admit. She took a step forward and stood directly in front of him. "I love you, Gabe, with all my heart. I'm sorry for not realizing it before and for walking away. But I was afraid and allowed my insecurities to take control of my mind. Being away from you gave me time to think, and I'm willing to take things to the next level."

He shook his head. "That's not good enough for me anymore, Sage."

Sage felt as if the patio floor had dropped from beneath her with his words. "Oh." She blinked back tears. Was he telling her that he no longer wanted her?

Gabe took a step closer and reached out and touched her wet cheek. He immediately knew she had misunderstood what he'd said. "The reason it's not good enough anymore, Sage," he decided to clarify, "is because I think we would be short-changing ourselves if the next level is all we're aiming for. If you love me the way I love you, then you would agree."

Tears ran down Sage's cheeks. "Agree to what?"

"Agree that there won't be any levels between us. I want a solid relationship, one built solely on love and trust and not levels. You are the woman I want in my life forever, till death do us part and all that good stuff."

Sage smiled through her tears. "And I want you in my life forever, that till death do us part and all that good stuff, too," she said softly. "You were right, Gabe. We do belong together. I don't want to belong to any other man but you. I love you so much."

Gabe took another step forward, bringing her thigh to thigh with him. "And I love you so much, too." He placed his finger under her chin and lifted it to meet his lips. Sage melted into him, needing his touch as much as she needed to breathe.

She mated her tongue with his hungrily, realizing that eleven days apart had caused a wave of desire to consume her as well as him. His mouth was hot, his body aroused, and he was sending signals to her that she interpreted. He needed to make love to her just as much as she needed him to make love to her.

When she heard the clearing of someone's throat, she pulled away and blushed, wondering who had caught them in such an overindulgent situation. She almost dropped when she turned and saw it was Gabe's mother.

"I see you found him," Joella Blackwell said, smiling brilliantly at Sage.

Sage nodded, clearly embarrassed that the woman had come upon her and Gabe literally kissing their mouths off. Before Sage could think of anything to say, Gabe pulled her closer into his arms, wrapped his hands firmly around her waist and answered in a voice that was filled with deep emotion, "No, Mom, I found *her*. I found the woman I've been waiting my whole life for, and she's my perfect fit."

EPILOGUE

One year later

"Welcome to Eden, Mr. and Mrs. Blackwell."

"Thanks, and we're glad to be back," Gabe said to the smiling hotel receptionist.

Sage glanced around the immaculate hotel, completely in awe. Everything was beautiful, pristine, impeccable and elegant, from the rich-looking carpeting on the floor to the expensive curtains adorning each window. She glanced up at her husband and smiled, proud of both of their contributions in making Eden a reality.

They had married two weeks ago in Charlotte and had immediately left to get lost at sea when they took an Alaskan cruise where they had watched from their private balcony as eagles dived for fish in Alaska's Inside Passage and marveled at the Alaskan glaciers they passed. Seeing a glimpse of Glacier Bay and the orcas at play in the icy waters had been breathtaking. But nothing, Sage thought, was more breathtaking and beautiful than the man she was now married to.

And now they were in Eden and would be staying a week preparing for the grand opening celebration. John Landmark had spared no expense for the huge gala affair. Then a week after the official opening, her resignation from the Denmark Corporation would go into effect, leaving a capable Malcolm in charge. She would be spending time traveling with Gabe and acting as marketing manager for the Regency Corporation, a position she looked forward to.

But no position, she thought, was more important than being Gabe's wife. The wedding had been an extravagant affair, which had made her mother, as well as Gabe's mother, extremely happy. It seemed that Joella Blackwell had been looking forward to the day her son married just as much as Delores had been looking forward to hers. The two women had become good friends over long distance and even visited each other during the year Sage and Gabe had given them to plan the event.

Sage had had eight bridesmaids which included her cousins, Ginger and Cinnamon, as well as Rose and Christopher's wife, Maxi, whom Sage thought was simply a wonderful person, the most kindhearted, genuine individual she had ever met. She could understand how Christopher could love his wife the way he did. Maxi Chandler was truly a class act, and the two of them had immediately become good friends.

Gabe smiled down at Sage, and as always, the sexual chemistry between them flared to life. And from the way he was looking at her, Sage knew that he couldn't wait to get her alone again.

"We have a few days of privacy left before everyone starts arriving for the grand opening."

She nodded. She knew by everyone he meant her parents and his, as well as Christopher, Maxi and their son, and Parnell Cabot and his daughters, along with Rose. Sage shook her head when she thought of Rose and Parnell's marriage six months ago.

It seemed that the two of them had made some sort of a business arrangement when they'd decided on a marriage of convenience—just to make sure that no matter where Parnell had to travel to work, his girls would be there with Rose as his wife looking after them. But Sage knew that all it took when she saw Parnell and Rose together was to look at them to see that their marriage was getting more convenient in a number of ways, and what had started out as a business affair was no longer the case. It was definitely a love affair, and they were now a family. Rose simply adored the twins and considered them as hers.

Sage chuckled. Rose considered Parnell as hers, too, and the man who everyone thought would never fall in love again was finding true happiness for a second time.

Gabe and Sage hadn't been in their hotel room ten minutes before they began removing their clothes, deciding to unpack later. They had booked the honeymoon suite, and everything about the room breathed elegance and romance; but the room's décor was the last thing on their minds. They needed to be in each other's arms, and to reaffirm their love in a very intimate way.

When she lay naked in the middle of the bed, Gabe took a step back and picked up the phone. "Yes, this is Gabe Blackwell. Please hold all my calls. Mrs. Blackwell and I don't want to be disturbed."

"Umm, Mrs. Blackwell, I can't get over just how much I love the sound of that," Sage whispered as she straightened the pillow behind her back and watched her husband step out of the last of his clothing. Every time they came together like this, they strove to make it beautiful and wonderful for each other, and always succeeded.

Her breath caught as Gabe's gaze scanned her naked body from head to toe. "You are the most beautiful creature I've ever seen, both in and out of clothes, although I like you out of clothes the best."

Sage smiled when she saw the hot look in his eyes and knew that tonight he would be very creative. Her body trembled, and she licked her lips when she thought of all the possibilities.

Making love with Gabe continued to be an awe-inspiring adventure and the most exciting experience she'd ever encountered.

"Don't do that," he said huskily, looking at her mouth.

"Do what?"

"Lick your lips like that. It makes me want to eat them right off your mouth." Easing into bed beside her, he immediately began kissing her throat, right below her left ear. He'd learned fairly early that kissing that particular spot could make her come apart in no time at all. And he definitely wanted her to come apart.

Shifting his body, he lowered himself to his knees in front of her and reached across the bed for the additional pillow. Gently lifting her lower body, he tucked the pillow under it. This position tilted her body at a very special angle for him.

He leaned forward, needing to taste her mouth, savor everything special about her, and by the time he had tasted her entire body, her sighs and moans had sent an electrical charge through him so strong he had to connect with her immediately.

He placed his body over hers and slipped inside of her. She knew they would find heaven like always, which seemed to fit since they were already in Eden. Everything they did seemed to fit.

In the long, slow moments that followed their joining, Gabe remained still for a second, savoring the feel of being inside of her, the feel of her feminine muscles clamping down on him, holding him, milking him, nearly driving him insane. And then he began to move, in a slow, precise rhythm; one she picked up on automatically as she spread her thighs wider for him and wrapped her legs around his back.

The pillow her backside rested on made him go that much deeper, touch areas within her that he normally didn't touch, and she purred relentlessly at the feel of him moving on top of her, hip to hip, thigh to thigh, inside and out.

And when he felt her body beginning to shudder, his automatically did likewise, and they came together, crying out each other's name, needing to be one this way as husband and wife, as lovers, as friends, as two people who were a perfect fit in every way.

In the long moments that followed, Gabe removed the pillow from under her and pulled her into his arms, holding her tightly to him, right next to his heart. "I love you," he whispered, kissing the dampness from her forehead.

She smiled, nearly gasping for breath after such a beautiful, intimate encounter with her husband. The flush of her orgasm had not yet faded, and her body was still trembling. This was how it was supposed to be, she thought, as she snuggled closer to his side. Whenever two people who had committed their lives together united as one, all the pleasures God intended for them to have, to share, were theirs. There was a reason He had given certain body parts to them for them to feel this way, and she knew her husband had every intention of exploring every aspect of "hidden pleasures" during their lifetime.

"And I love you," she finally was able to dredge up enough strength to whisper. Moments later, she said, "You were wrong, Gabe."

He lifted a brow and gazed lovingly down at his wife. "I was wrong about what, sweetheart?"

Her smile widened. "Your mother didn't make a mistake in naming you Gabriel, because you are truly an angel. My angel."

PERFECT TIMING

New York Times bestselling romance powerhouse Brenda Jackson's classic novel takes two friends on a sexy, emotional journey . . .

Maxine Chandler and Mya Rivers were once the best of friends, sisters by choice. Now, a ten-year class reunion cruise to the Caribbean could renew their powerful bond—just when they need it most . . .

After heartbreak and tragedy, Maxi doesn't expect her shipboard romance with a former high school rebel to be more than a sizzling distraction, but then he offers her a gift so profound she can't refuse—even when it could mean a crushing loss. Mya, on the other hand, seems blessed with a perfect marriage and family. But her work is taking over her life and another woman might be taking her husband . . .

As they struggle with the limits of love, loyalty, and trust, Mya and Maxi reclaim a deep and abiding friendship—one that will inspire them to face the future, whatever it may bring . . .

Prologue

"Why are you so sad?" Seven-year-old Maxine Chandler pushed the long braids covering her head away from her eyes to get a better look at the girl sitting alone watching the other kids play. Just that morning the teacher had introduced her as Mya and said she was new at school and had moved to town from someplace where it snowed all the time. Maxine wondered if the reason she looked sad was because she was missing the snow.

"I want my mommy and daddy," the little girl answered in a voice that sounded like she was about to cry.

"Where are they?" Maxine asked curiously, feeling herself about to cry too, although she didn't know why.

"They went to heaven and left me behind. Now I have to stay with my granny," the little girl answered.

Maxine nodded as she looked down at the girl thoughtfully. She shoved her hands into the deep pockets on her dress and asked, "Don't you like your granny? I like mine."

The question made the little girl lift her head up and push her chin out. "I like my granny just fine, but sometimes I miss my mommy and daddy awfully bad. I get lonely."

Maxine nodded knowing that if her parents went away she

would miss them too. She suddenly felt really bad inside. "Do you want me to sit with you for a while so you won't be lonely?"

Mya looked up at Maxine and then, after a short while, she scooted over. "If you want to."

Maxine sat down on the bench next to Mya. Silently they watched the other kids in the schoolyard who were running around having fun. After a while Maxine said, "I'll share my parents with you. My momma said my daddy always wanted another child."

"You're the only one?"

"Yes."

"So was I," Mya said softly.

Neither said another word for the longest time. Then Maxine asked, "Well, do you want to be my parents' other child or not?"

Mya thought about Maxine's offer. "Does that mean I'll have to leave my granny and come live with you?"

Maxine pondered Mya's question then answered. "Yes, more than likely you'll have to live at my house. My daddy says he only feeds what's living under his roof, so you'll have to come live with us if you want to eat."

Mya tossed Maxine's words around in her mind. Blinking away more tears she looked at her. "But I don't want to leave my granny. She needs me now that my mommy and daddy are gone."

Maxine nodded. "All right, but if you change your mind let me know. But we can be friends can't we?"

Mya wiped away her tears and smiled. She was glad she didn't have to leave her granny and go live with someone else for now. "Yes, we can be friends."

"Best friends?"

Mya's smile widened. "Yes, the very best. For the rest of our lives."

Maxine scrambled to her feet and reached out her hand to her new best friend. "Come on, let's go play."

Evelyn Jerott, the girls' teacher, watched as they rushed off with their long braids flying in the wind behind them. Standing not far away while watching the other kids in her care, she had overheard the two little girls' conversation. She smiled. Maxine Chandler's approach to Mya Ross had been perfect timing. Evelyn had been concerned whether Mya would sit by herself all day or whether she would eventually mingle with the other kids. Mya's grandmother had explained the situation to her that morning regarding Mya's parents' death in a car accident. Her heart had gone out to the little girl but now she had a feeling she would be okay. Mya was laughing and running around with a new friend.

Evelyn sighed. She had a feeling that the friendship that had just been made between Maxine and Mya would be a special bond that would last a long time.

A very long time.

PART ONE

When the clouds are heavy, the rains come down; when a tree falls, whether south or north, the die is cast, for there it lies.

—Ecclesiastes 11:3

CHAPTER ONE

Maxi
Twenty-one years later

Maxine "Maxi" Chandler hated the smell of a doctor's office. It was the same scent one found in a hospital—a medicinal, antiseptic, and sterile odor.

Since she was Dr. Frazier's last patient for that day, the waiting room was empty. She'd had consultations scheduled earlier with four of her students and had appreciated the late appointment time. The side door opened and Pauline Warren, a lady in her early sixties, appeared. It seemed Mrs. Warren had been Dr. Frazier's nurse for years.

Maxi took a deep breath. Pauline had called her yesterday to let her know that the results of her tests had come back. In a few minutes she would know if the medication the doctor had prescribed for her a few months ago had improved her medical condition, or if the worst-case scenario was what she was now up against.

"The doctor is ready to see you, Maxi," Mrs. Warren said, smiling.

Maxi stood, returning Pauline's smile. That same smile had had a calming effect on her frazzled nerves when she had

undergone her first GYN exam before leaving home for college
at eighteen, almost ten years ago. Also, that same smile had offered sympathy to her four years ago when Jason had gotten
killed.

"And how is your mom?" Pauline asked as she led Maxi to
one of the empty examination rooms.

"Mom is fine and wanted me to tell you hello."

Pauline nodded, closing the door behind them. "I take it
that she and Mr. Hudson still haven't made any wedding
plans?"

Maxi laughed. "No, they haven't." Her mother, a widow for
nearly ten years, and Walter Hudson, a widower for probably
just as long, had been seeing each other for years. "Do I need
to undress?"

"No. The doctor just wants to talk with you and go over the
results of your tests."

Maxi nodded. She'd had a queasy feeling in her stomach
ever since receiving Pauline's call.

"Dr. Frazier will be with you in a minute" were Pauline's last
words before turning and exiting the room.

Maxi sat down in one of the chairs. No matter what Dr. Frazier had to tell her, she had to believe that she could handle the
news. How many times had her mother told her that the Lord
never put more on you than you could bear and trouble didn't
last always? Taking a deep breath she glanced around the
room. For the second time that week she thought about Jason
and how his death, which had occurred a week before their
wedding day, had nearly destroyed her. He had been on his way
to pick her up for dinner when a drunk driver crossed the me-
dian and hit him head-on, killing him instantly at the age of
twenty-six. He had moved to Savannah seven years before from
Ohio to open an insurance agency.

Maxi's thoughts came to an end when the door opened and
Dr. Frazier entered. Although she studied his features for any
tell-tale signs, there weren't any. There was nothing about him

that gave anything away. Not even a small hint. He appeared jovial as usual.

"How are you, Maxi?"

"I'm fine, Dr. Frazier, and you?"

He chuckled. "I have one year, three months, and twenty-four days before retirement, so I'm doing pretty good. I talked to Sonja last night and she's making plans to go on your class reunion cruise. What about you?"

Maxi inhaled deeply. Dr. Frazier's daughter Sonja, now a gynecologist herself in Atlanta, had graduated from high school with her. To celebrate their ten-year class reunion, a seven-day cruise to the western Caribbean had been planned. "I've decided not to go. This summer will be much too busy for me." As a college professor teaching African-American studies at Savannah State University, she had agreed to instruct several classes during the summer term.

"Everyone can use some R and R every now and then, Maxi. Always remember that. There's nothing worse than working yourself to death. Vacations are things people should strive to have at least once a year. Besides, I'd think you'd want to go to the reunion. According to Sonja you were the most popular and most well-liked girl at Beaches High, and were friends with just about everyone."

Maxi nodded. And that was one of the main reasons she didn't want to go. Five years ago she had attended her five-year reunion with Jason, as an engaged couple. Although she had gotten over losing him, she didn't want people who didn't know about his death to open old wounds by asking her about him. "I'll keep that in mind, but I know you didn't summon me here to talk about my high school class reunion."

"No, I didn't." Dr. Frazier took a seat across from her. "The results of your tests came back." He opened the chart he held in his hand. "I'm sorry to inform you that the medication I placed you on isn't working like I had hoped, and there's no other alternative now but surgery."

Maxi took in a deep breath. "Which means if I want a child I need to get pregnant before the surgery." It was a statement and not a question. She bowed her head. It had always been her dream to have children. But then she'd always wanted a husband too. Now it seemed that both were lost to her forever. "Is there any chance the test results are incorrect?" she asked, knowing she was pulling at straws but pulled at them anyway.

"No, Maxi, I'm sorry, but then deep down I think you knew surgery would have to be the answer, didn't you?"

"Yes." She tried smiling. "But a girl can have hope, can't she?"

"Yes, she can." For the longest time he didn't say anything else but continued to look at her with concern on his face. "I still think you should consider going on that cruise. Being around old friends will do you good."

Not if I have to put up with them pulling pictures out of their purses and wallets, displaying their perfect families, she thought. After ten years most were heavily involved in careers and families. More than likely they would want to talk about both. Although she had the career she'd always wanted, she didn't have the family she'd always dreamed about having.

She stood. "I'll think about it," she said, knowing deep down that she probably wouldn't. She checked her watch. "I'd better go. I'm sure it's been a long day for you. Thanks for everything, Dr. Frazier. You will be the one doing the surgery, won't you?"

"Yes, if you decide to do it."

"Do I have a choice?"

"Not if you want to be completely well."

"Then I guess that's that. But I want to put off the surgery for as long as I can."

"All right, but if you begin having problems I want you to re-think that decision. Your monthly cramps will only continue to get worse until the matter is taken care of."

Maxi nodded. "I'll be in touch, Dr. Frazier." She walked out of his office thinking that somehow she would deal with what lay ahead. Somehow she would find the strength to do so.

* * *

Later that evening after enjoying a quiet dinner alone, Maxi went through her closets in search of her high school yearbook. Her conversation with Dr. Frazier had made her think about her former classmates. Many of them had moved away after graduation to attend college, never returning except for occasional visits. Out of a class of over two hundred students, only half of them still made Savannah their home. Although she had left to attend Howard University in Washington, she had returned to the historic coastal town that she loved.

She flipped a few pages of the yearbook, most of them now yellow with age, and checked the section where all the seniors' pictures were. She studied the pictures. The class of 1992 had graduated students who were now doctors, lawyers, federal judges . . . there was even a movie star or two in the group, as well as a few living the life of crime. She knew for a fact that George Buford was in jail for armed robbery. At one time he had made the FBI's most wanted list for robbing more than fifteen banks.

Maxi turned to her senior picture and smiled, grateful the hairstyle she had worn back then was no longer stylish. Her gaze then moved to the photo of the young man next to her— Christopher Chandler. She'd had a big-time crush on him during their entire senior year. Because they'd had the same last name it seemed they had always been in some of the same classes throughout their entire twelve years of school. He had come from an area of town that some considered ghettoville and was always known for getting into trouble. Rebellious, wild, and filled with anger and bitterness because of how society had treated him, Christopher had taken pleasure in being the town's bad boy. Raised by a mother with a reputation of sleeping around, who had enrolled him in school two years later than she should have and only after the school officials had threatened her with legal actions, he had barely made the grades to graduate. She couldn't help but recall the scandal that swept through Savannah during their senior year of school involving Christopher's mother and the city's mayor. To this day Maxi believed the reason their science teacher, Mr. Thompson, who'd for some reason had taken a liking to the rebellious Chandler, had teamed him up with her for their science project was because he had known Christopher's hidden potential. And giving him something to do that required a lot of concentration would take his mind off what was being exposed in the newspaper about the high profile affair. The project had taken first place at the Science Fair. Christopher had surprised even her with his hard work and dedication to the project. And she had found out something about him during the six weeks they had worked closely together on the project. It had been something the other students and some of the teachers had not known, and probably never discovered. Underneath his undisciplined bad boy exterior, Christopher had a brilliant mind. It wouldn't surprise her if the boy who'd been voted "least likely to succeed" had become a success. It would serve them all right, those who had snubbed him and had considered him nothing more than a thug. Although his name had come up at the last class reunion, no one had heard anything about him since the day he left town after graduation. His mother had committed suicide a week before graduation and he claimed when he left that he would never return to Savannah.

Maxi then turned the page and glanced at a picture of the guy who had been captain of the football team and the girl who had been captain of the cheerleading squad. Childhood sweethearts, their love had been the ultimate storybook romance. Both had left to attend college in Texas. After college they had married, and he had begun playing professional football. Mya and Garrett Rivers were still happily married and living in Dallas. She and Mya had been the best of friends all through school, each other's confidantes. But due to a misunderstanding they rarely stayed in touch. The last time she had seen Mya had been two years ago when Mya's grandmother had died and Mya had returned to Savannah for the services. Before then the last time she had heard from her had been when Mya had called offering condolences after hearing about Jason's death.

Jason.

Maxi closed the book and a feeling of loneliness washed over her when she thought about him. They had met at the birthday party of one of her co-workers, Sandra Miller. He had been a neighbor Sandra had invited. Maxi had liked him from the very beginning. He'd been a dynamic conversationalist. And he'd been pretty pleasing on the eyes as well, with his handsome features. He had asked her out and from that night on they'd become almost inseparable. They had enjoyed each other's company just that much They'd been dating a little more than a year when he had asked her to marry him. Everyone thought they were the perfect match. And they had wanted the same things out of life—marriage and a big family.

Maxi sighed deeply. The sudden loss of Jason had been a brutal blow. So was the thought that after her surgery, she would never be able to give birth to a child. She shook aside the brief moment of depression, not wanting to bring back into focus her conversation with Dr. Frazier. The last thing she needed was to feel sorry for herself. Seeing those red check marks under some of her classmates' names, indicating those who were now deceased, had reminded her that at least she was still alive. Five people in her class had died since their last reunion five years ago. So no matter how big you think your problems are, someone else's problems could always be bigger, which makes yours relatively small.

Dr. Frazier had been right. Maybe she should consider going on her high school class reunion cruise. She had always enjoyed the friendships of former classmates and, maybe at this time in her life when all seemed bleak, being surrounded by friends was what she needed. Besides, there was a good chance

Mya would be going and maybe they would be able to spend some time together, renewing their deep friendship that had somehow fallen by the wayside.

Before she had a chance to change her mind, Maxi picked up the phone to call the travel agency that was handling all the arrangements. Since the trip was only six weeks away, she hoped it wasn't too late.